MAGIC'S LIVING INFERNO

Superman slowed his approach, hovering just beyond the fire's reach. He could feel the heat. He smelled burning wood and the ozone stench of electrical wires burning. But if it was real, he would hear screams. He combed the other apartments, and in none of them did he see anyone who appeared panicked, or who even seemed to notice the blaze. Cars drove down the street, pedestrians passed unconcerned right through the walls of fire.

Which means it's for my benefit, Superman thought. *The fire's not really there—it's some kind of trap.*

The fire had been created, and was being controlled, magically. As soon as Superman got close, the fire coalesced into a solid arm, which darted toward him slamming into him like a giant fist. The force of the blow—hot, amazingly powerful—sent Superman spinning three blocks from the building . . .

Novels from the DC Universe

Last Sons

Inheritance

Helltown

Trail of Time

DC UNIVERSE

Trail of Time

Jeff Mariotte

WARNER BOOKS

NEW YORK   BOSTON

Copyright © 2007 by DC Comics
All rights reserved. No part of this book may be reproduced in any form or by any electronic or mechanical means, including information storage and retrieval systems, without permission in writing from the publisher, except by a reviewer who may quote brief passages in a review.

Cover design by Don Puckey
Cover illustration by James Jean
Book design and text composition by Stratford Publishing Services

Warner Books and the Warner Books logo are trademarks of Time Warner or an affiliated company. Used under license by Hachette Book Group, which is not affiliated with Time Warner Inc.

Warner Books
Hachette Book Group USA
1271 Avenue of the Americas
New York, NY 10020
Visit our Web site at www.HachetteBookGroupUSA.com

Printed in the United States of America

First Printing: March 2007

10   9   8   7   6   5   4   3   2   1

DRAMATIS PERSONAE: DC UNIVERSE

BAT LASH: To observe smooth talking ladies' man Bartholomew Aloysius Lash, one would never suspect the multiple tragedies in his past. His parents were murdered, their farm stolen by swindlers, and Bat himself became a wanted man after killing a crooked sheriff's deputy in self-defense. He set his sights on finding the man who killed his family, and having done so he roamed the West, playing cards and seeking adventure.

Dark Lord Mordru: Stories claim that Mordru was never born, and will never die. No one knows if the first part is true, but he has lived since Earth's beginning and has proven his immortality many times over. Mordru is a formidable sorcerer who will stop at nothing to amass power in the service of evil.

The Demon/Jason Blood: Etrigan, a demon, was summoned from Hell by Merlin (Etrigan's half brother) to help save King Arthur's Camelot from the forces of Morgaine Le Fey. When Camelot fell despite their efforts, Merlin bound the demon Etrigan to peasant Jason Blood, who would henceforth be two beings, able to switch back and forth between them through the use of a simple spell. Immortal, Blood has become a professional demonologist living in Gotham City—but few know of his personal connection to the subject of his expertise.

Dr. Occult: Two infants intended to be sacrificed to Satan were rescued by a group of mystics called The Seven, and raised under their tutelage. Their original names unknown, The Seven named the infants Richard Occult and Rose Psychic. As adults, Richard (now Dr. Occult) and Rose opened a detective agency specializing in supernatural crimes. During one adventure they were fused into one body (but able to appear at will in either the male or female form).

El Diablo: Trying to stop outlaws who had robbed his bank, Lazarus Lane was left comatose by a bolt of lightning. Although Lane's body is immobile, with the help of an Apache shaman friend named Wise Owl, his spirit emerges as masked avenger El Diablo to fight evil wherever it may be.

Felix Faust: Felix Faust's precise origins are lost in the mists of time, but he lived in ancient times, suffered defeat, and was then resurrected in the twentieth century body of sorcerer Dekan Drache. Making up for lost time, Faust has devoted his magical abilities and knowledge to the study and practice of evil.

Johnny Thunder: To avenge the humiliation of his lawman father, mild Mesa City schoolmaster John Tane put together a colorful costume with a mask and dyed his hair black. As Johnny Thunder, he could do things that John Tane never could—teaching the next generation of Westerners by day and battling crime at night.

Jonah Hex: Born to a mother who abandoned the family during his childhood and a drunken father who sold his son to Apaches, Jonah Woodson Hex overcame these early obstacles to become a respected officer in the Confederate Army. After he lost faith in the rebel cause and was accused of leading his men to slaughter, he returned to the Apache tribe, only to kill a chief's son in battle. He was punished by being horribly scarred and banished, after which he became a celebrated bounty hunter and a feared gunman.

Lois Lane: This ambitious reporter works for editor-in-chief Perry White at the *Daily Planet*, Metropolis's pre-eminent newspaper (along with Jimmy Olsen and others). As one of the first people to encounter Superman when he appeared in Metropolis, she gave him his name and eventually fell in love with the new guy in town. After working together for several years, she married Clark Kent (after he had revealed to her that he was also Superman).

Phantom Stranger: With his origins shrouded in mystery, no one knows just who he is or where he came from, but he has walked the Earth since time immemorial, helping those in need and using his mystical knowledge and powers to fight the constant advance of Chaos.

Scalphunter: Kiowa warriors abducted young Brian Savage from his family in the 1840s, and raising the boy among them, called him Ke-Woh-No-Tay, or "He Who Is Less Than Human." Savage grew up believing himself Kiowa, and in accordance with their traditions felt that taking the scalps of enemies transferred great power to him. Whites who knew of him called him Scalphunter. He was later revealed as the son of trail boss Matt Savage, and finally met his father at the end of the old man's life, although he would not renounce the only identity he knew.

Superman/Clark Kent: With his home planet of Krypton facing imminent destruction, infant Kal-El was sent to Earth, where the baby was found and adopted by Martha and Jonathan Kent of Smallville, Kansas and named Clark Kent. Exposure to Earth's yellow sun gave Clark incredible powers, and as an adult the Man of Steel puts those powers to use as Earth's champion, Superman.

Vandal Savage: Vandar Adg was a chieftain of a tribe of Cro-Magnons in Europe until radiation from a fallen meteor gave him an incredibly advanced intellect and immortality. Over the centuries he has used both to advance his knowledge of the dark arts, and has been known by a variety of names, including Genghis Khan and Jack the Ripper.

ACKNOWLEDGMENTS

Superman and the other characters who appear in this novel have been formed by many, many hands. So many people have brought tales of these characters to the world—writers, pencilers, inkers, colorists, letterers, production artists, editors and publishers—since the day Siegel and Shuster first brought Superman into existence, that to begin to name them would take almost as many pages as the story. Besides, many of them worked, and work, in virtual anonymity, behind the scenes, and yet they are every bit as important to the final product. Those people, the artists and the craftspeople and the office staff and the executives alike, are the ones who inspired this work, and it is to all of them that I dedicate this book.

Also, to David, who provided invaluable assistance.

—JJM

DC UNIVERSE

Trail of Time

CHAPTER ONE

Clark Kent dreamed of flying.

He swept and sailed, stooping like a hunting hawk, then soaring into clear blue skies, turning, twisting, looping around on his own trail like Ouroboros himself. He laughed as he flew, his mouth open, and he could taste the air rushing in, cool and sweet with a flavor almost like fresh spearmint. Below him, the upreared spires and wide avenues and arching highways of Metropolis glittered in the morning sun.

The sensation was liberating, thrilling. To be weightless, unbound by gravity. To have the wind buffet his face, whip his hair, press his clothing tight against his skin. To know true, limitless power.

He had dreamed the same thing often these last several nights. But it always came to an end, as it did on this morning. Clark awoke in his bed, his body feeling heavy, weighted down by gravity and responsibility. With a groan, he reached for Lois. Her side of the bed was empty and cool. She had been up for some time, then. He groaned again and rubbed his eyes, then pawed the nightstand beside the bed for his glasses. Fitting them into place brought the room into focus. Turning as he rose, Clark put his feet on the floor and walked to the curtained window. Sweeping aside the curtain to gaze at the sky, he wished he could recapture, even for a moment, the thrill of free flight.

Instead of the crystalline blue he remembered from the dream, the sky was its usual leaden gray, with darker clouds, almost black, roiling inside. From the high-rise apartment, the view swept over rooftops and towers of concrete and glass jutting toward the charcoal clouds. Bright points of flame jetted from tall chimneys. Others issued smoke that merged with the cloudscape. Metropolis, industrial center of the Eastern Seaboard.

Through the thick haze, Clark could barely make out the fiery orb of the red sun, rising in the east.

Pulling on a robe against the morning's chill, Clark padded into the living room, and through that to Lois's office. She sat at her desk, fingers flying across her computer's keyboard, her dark hair pulled back off her face and tied in a ponytail. Clark waited until she paused before interrupting.

"Morning, Lois."

She swiveled to face him. When she did, and he saw her intent brown eyes, her sculpted cheekbones, the wry half smile curling her generous lips, he wondered if it was really possible to fall in love with someone over and over and over, or if it was just one continuous arc of emotion interrupted by peaks that cropped up every time his gaze found her again. Whenever he remembered that they were married, he couldn't believe his luck.

"Morning? I guess it still is. Not for much longer, though—I thought you'd sleep till noon."

Clark glanced at the digital clock on her desk. "It's just after seven."

"In your world, maybe," she said. "But not everyone on Earth functions on Metropolis time, Clark. I've already been on the phone with half a dozen people in Europe, running down that lead I got yesterday from Farris."

Clark suppressed a groan. Henry Farris, king of conspiracy theorists. Lois knew better than to encourage him, but this time, Farris insisted, he really *had* something, and whatever he'd told her at their secret meeting had convinced her that he was right.

Running down leads wasn't their job, though. Reporting the news was. *I wish you'd leave that stuff alone,* he might say, to which she would reply something like, *You just tell your stories, Clark, and leave the real news to me.* They'd had the conversation so many times he didn't even need her participation anymore.

"Well," he said, knowing it would do no good to lecture, "seven is still seven as far as I'm concerned, and I've got to get in the shower if I'm going to be at the Planet by eight-thirty."

She let the smile take over the rest of her face. "Shower?" she asked. "As in, naked?"

"Generally, that's how it works."

Lois turned back to the computer, saved whatever it was she'd been working on, then spun around again. "Maybe if I help, we'll both get to the Planet by nine."

"But that's . . ." Clark caught himself in time, returned her grin. "Sure, nine's good."

*   *   *

He was at his desk by ten after, half-expecting to see Perry White breathing fire for his lateness. The *Daily Planet*'s editor-in-chief had other worries, though. He apparently hadn't noticed Clark's tardiness. Clark had to log in when he sat down at his workstation, however, and Perry's bosses were never as distracted as Perry. Certainly Barton, the uniformed guard at the newsroom's door, had caught it as well—Barton's gaze flicked toward his wristwatch when Clark stepped from the elevator in his blue suit, white shirt, and red-and-white-striped tie. The rules governing Clark's employment mandated that he begin work at nine, and the fact that he frequently started earlier didn't compensate for late days. He swallowed nervously as he logged in, then tried to put it behind him so he could reach the day's required word count.

Clark's current beat was Metro, although he helped out with other sections as need be. He opened the file that had arrived on his desktop that morning and began the first story. "Metropolis Mayor Graces City with Gifts of Insight, Intelligence and Kindness," the headline read. Below that, in smaller type: "Mayor James Armstrong, sensing a need in the citizens of Metropolis before it was even expressed, has decided to increase the number of Public Safety officers in popular shopping and dining areas at times of peak traffic. Additionally, Public Safety patrols will be increased at other times, with the officers frequently dressed in civilian clothing instead of uniforms, the mayor explained, in order to better fit in among their fellow residents."

In other words, he's beefing up uniformed and plain-

clothes law enforcement presence, the better to spy on the citizens of Metropolis. The story's meaning was clear enough. Clark drummed his fingers on the desktop for a moment, looking for a way to obscure the truth a bit more artfully than the release had.

A minute passed. Clark knew he had to speed things up—to make his word quota for the day, with his late start, he'd have to work even faster than usual. Failing to meet the quota wasn't an option he liked to think about.

He positioned his fingers on the keyboard, started typing. "Putting into action the next step in a program that has already made Metropolis the safest major city in the nation, Mayor James Armstrong today announced additional measures that will guarantee the long-term reduction, if not outright elimination, of any criminal activity in the city." He read over the sentence. Clunky, but it got the point across. He'd wanted to begin with the measure's intent—cutting crime. The details would come later in the story. Most people didn't read that far down.

Never mind that, as it was, one couldn't walk three blocks in the city without seeing a squad of Public Safety officers. Forget the fact that any minor deviation from the law would result in half a dozen witnesses calling in reports, hoping to add points to their own Meritorious Citizenship rolls. Clark couldn't argue with the results—crime in Metropolis was at historic lows.

As is freedom. The voice inside Clark's head sounded disturbingly like Lois's. She was always going on about freedom, individual liberty, social justice, that sort of thing. The truth was, the *Planet*'s readers didn't care about abstract concepts like that. They wanted to know they'd be safe out shopping or walking home after a late supper.

They wanted reassurance that no threats from foreign shores could reach them here at home. Their concerns were concrete—family, home, job, food on the table and roof over the head stuff, not the vapor that Lois obsessed about.

Clark loved Lois Lane more than life itself. Didn't mean he understood her.

Complete understanding, he had learned, was not a prerequisite for love.

Nor, it seemed, for anything else. Clark didn't understand the world he lived in, though he had grown up here like anyone else. Despite all the efforts made by Mayor Armstrong, President Daniels, the military, and Public Safety officers, Metropolis felt like a city under siege. Everywhere he went he saw uniforms and weapons. The city's factories burned day and night, belching fire and smoke into the air, turning out more arms and armaments every day. It stood to reason that there should be an end point, a stage at which reasonable safety was assured, and the nation could afford to slow down its output.

Somehow that never happened. The threat was always imminent, according to officials. The state of alert could never be drawn down, the factories never allowed to still. Everyone needed to be monitored; anyone could be an enemy of the state. Two weeks ago, Rob Courtland, the reporter in the cubicle next to Clark's, had disappeared after writing a piece that didn't precisely conform to its original intent. Clark had always hated the man's over-powering cologne, but without him there the office smelled sterile, empty. He understood the rationale behind Courtland's apprehension, although it frightened him. What if something *he* wrote was misinterpreted? Could the same thing happen to him?

If his response to such incidents was fear, Lois's was outrage. She saw secret machinations behind the events of everyday life. Somebody else, she insisted, controlled both Armstrong and Daniels. Some puppet master tugged their strings, making them front men who carried out their unseen lord's agenda.

Clark rose from his desk, risking a few seconds away from the keyboard to see if anyone watched him. Even thinking about such things unnerved him. He didn't believe the Daily Planet employed clairvoyants, but it didn't pay to take unnecessary chances. Lois took enough chances for both of them. He respected her ideals, sometimes wishing that he shared them. When he rose from bed at three in the morning and held dead-of-night conversations with his own soul, he had to admit that recasting official news releases as real news stories felt wrong.

Lois spent her workday doing the same, though. She used her private time away from the Daily Planet offices for what she considered her real calling. That was why she got up early and stayed out late, risking arrest or worse.

Frightening Clark half to death.

Someday, he thought, *maybe she will have a breakthrough and be able to prove one of her theories. But where will she run the story? Perry would kill it in a heartbeat. It'd never see print in the* Planet.

He sat back down, hands on the keyboard. Two more quick stories, and he'd have caught up, reached his word count. He'd made good time today. Perry would be pleased, as would those to whom Perry reported.

Whoever they are.

CHAPTER TWO

Clark would just absolutely freak *if he knew I was here,*
Lois Lane thought. *It's a good thing he doesn't get out
much.*

Her day at the Planet had been frustrating, as usual. Almost unbearable. She ran the International Desk, which
meant transcribing releases about how President Daniels
worked tirelessly to woo trading partners, or worse, stories about the shadowy, sinister efforts of groups around
the world whose singular goal was the destruction of the
United States and all of its people.

There was plenty of sinister around, Lois knew, and no
shortage of shadowy. But she believed both stemmed
from the people who wrote the "news" releases in the first
place, not the unlikely underground cells of fanatics and
mad bombers about which she had to write.

She made it through the day just the same. Clark had
gone home to start dinner, while she followed up on a
bit of information she had squeezed from a contact in

Germany early that morning. Which had led her to the office of a warehouse abandoned months before by its tenants. In the office, her source had claimed, records had been kept—true records, not the kind that were always ginned up for public consumption. These records would enable her to trace munitions purchases, backward and forward. The German refused to name the person at the end of the trail, the one who ultimately made the decisions about who would receive what weaponry, but it wasn't President Daniels.

It was, her source had claimed, someone before whom Daniels knelt in absolute obeisance.

Lois had tried to press, hoping to learn why records would still be here if the warehouse had been abandoned, but the German wouldn't say. All will be revealed, he had promised, when you get into that office.

No easy task. Street patrols had to be avoided, and the streets of Metropolis were thick with surveillance cameras. Mayor Armstrong swore that nothing happened in the city without his Public Safety officers being aware. Lois knew that wasn't true, but it was a definite challenge to get around unnoticed. Wearing a black sweater and jeans with black leather boots, carrying only her purse with a flashlight, notebook, and small digital camera inside, she stayed to the shadows as much as possible, dodged the patrols, and made her way to the abandoned steel structure.

She had heard about the occasional incident of graffiti or window-breaking at empty structures in Gotham City—although those reports had never been never officially confirmed, and Lois had not seen any of it firsthand. Here in Metropolis, she noted, the vacant warehouse was as clean and freshly painted—at least on the outside—as any occupied structure.

A side door to the warehouse had been left unlocked, and Lois waited in a dark doorway until she was certain no one watched the place. Satisfied, she slipped inside.

The door opened into a vast space. Steel shelving units, covered in dust, divided the room into smaller segments, but the ceiling was invisible in the darkness overhead, and although the shelves were empty, she couldn't see the back wall through them. She took the flashlight from her purse and played the light's beam across the concrete floor, revealing scuff marks in the dust. The place had a mildewy smell, as if rain had leaked in since the warehouse had been deserted.

Lois realized she was breathing through her mouth in sharp, shallow bursts. Noisy. She closed her mouth, swallowed back her anxiety. *Nothing to worry about, Lois,* she told herself. *Place is empty.*

Still, the fine hairs at the back of her neck twitched as if she'd been given an electric charge.

A large glass window toward the rear wall threw Lois's light's beam back at her, startling her. The warehouse office, she guessed. The glass was dark, smudged, and she couldn't see anything behind it, even when she came right up to it and tried to shine her light through. Painted black on the inside, maybe, or just a very dark tint to the glass. A door to one side was closed but not locked.

Lois turned the knob and pushed the door open, hinges squealing. She let her light precede her into the room. It caught the edge of a wooden desk, and she raised the beam. The desk's top was scarred, burned, filmed with dust. Empty. Moving the light around, she spotted a second desk, gunmetal gray, and an old-fashioned steel filing cabinet. Maybe that's where the information she had been promised would be found. A light switch by the door proved useless. Quickly dismissing the rest of the office, she crossed to the cabinet and tugged at the top drawer.

It stuck. Locked? Lois cursed silently, playing the light around looking for the lock. Not seeing one, she returned to the handle and yanked as hard as she could.

This time, it gave way and rolled toward her on its tracks so fast that she had to hold it back.

Inside she found file folders containing purchase orders, inventory reports, bills of lading. It would take hours to comb through all this paperwork, she knew. Maybe days. And would it be worth the effort? So far, everything looked perfectly innocent. Flipping through the files she hadn't seen any reference to any kind of weaponry or other military goods.

She brushed a stray lock of hair away from her eyes. Her German source had been right about the location of the warehouse, right about its being empty, even right about there being paperwork inside, which was unexpected, to say the least.

Given all those things, she had to keep trying.

Pulling a stack of files from the drawer, she carried them to the desk and spread them out. An old wheeled chair sat in one corner. She blew dust off it, then wheeled it, squeaking up a storm, to the desk. Returning to the cabinet for another armload, she reflected that Clark would start to worry about her pretty soon. Worrying about her was what he did best. She'd never trade him for anything, but sometimes she wished he was a tiny bit more . . . what? Self-sufficient? Gutsy? Sometimes he acted like he was too weak to survive without her, and she had to remind him that he had done fine before they met.

Well, I'll be late tonight. He'll just have to make do.

She sat down with a sigh, placed her flashlight on its side to illuminate the desk's surface, and started into the files. She'd been working through them for ten minutes before she saw something that made her fish out her notebook.

An invoice from VSS, a company name she had seen a few times in the past. Her investigations had turned up evidence—not proof positive, but convincing to her—that VSS was a front company for Vandal Savage.

Which tied into her theory. She believed that President Daniels owed his job to a man named Vandal Savage. And more—his fealty, as well. Savage called the tune, Daniels danced.

She didn't know much about Vandal Savage. No one did. His was a name that was whispered in the streets, denied in the corridors of power. Superhumanly powerful. Possibly a magician, a wizard of some kind, if one went in for that sort of talk. A force behind the force. Maybe he was an incredibly wealthy arms magnate or something like that—stories differed on the source of his wealth and his uses of it. At any rate, Lois figured, the more the politicians disputed his influence, the more convinced she was that he was the one who truly held power.

That's what Lois believed. Could something in here provide the link she needed?

She was so immersed in the files that she didn't hear anyone coming until the door squeaked open.

Three men crowded the doorway, their flashlights

nearly blinding her. But not so blind that she couldn't see their guns.

"Ms. Lane," the man in front said. "We were told we'd find you here."

"If you came to kill me," she replied, releasing a piece of paper and moving her hands up to massage her temples, "couldn't you have done it before I gave myself this massive headache?"

"Did anyone mention killing?" the same man asked. She couldn't get much of a sense of any of them, couldn't make out details past the circles of their bright flashlights. They were big, broad-shouldered. The one voice she had heard was gravelly and low-pitched, with an eastside Metropolis accent. "We've only been asked to make sure you don't go anywhere for a while."

"Why not? Someone coming to see me? A fan?"

"What we weren't instructed to do was answer questions," the man said. "So if I were you, I'd save them."

"How long is this going to take?" Lois asked. She put her hands down on the desktop, close to her flashlight. It wasn't much of a weapon, but it was all she had. "If it's going to be hours, we might as well get acquainted, right?"

"I was told you'd be a chatty type," the man said. "But I'll tell you what, Ms. Lane. I have no interest in being buddies with you." He snickered. "It'd most likely be one of my shortest friendships, anyhow."

He touched one of the other men on the arm. "You stay with her," he instructed. "We'll look around, make sure she didn't bring any friends. Keep her here, and don't let her pull anything smart. Kill her if she tries."

"Don't worry," the other man said. His voice was softer, almost feminine, with just a hint of a nervous quake. Lois tried not to smile. If he was scared of her, she'd be able to manipulate him in no time.

The first man and his partner left. The one remaining behind leaned against the doorjamb. Casual, or trying to appear so. He folded his arms over his chest, flashlight illuminating Lois and the desk, gun pointed almost jauntily toward the floor.

"So, think we'll be here a while?"

The man didn't answer.

"I'm Lois. If we're going to be stuck here, we might as well be friendly, right?"

"I was told not to talk to you," the man said. He still sounded nervous. Lois was plenty nervous herself, but determined not to show it.

"I know that," Lois said, keeping her tone light. She didn't want him to think she had an agenda. "But I just thought it'd make the time go faster, you know? I mean, you're the one with the gun. I don't know why you're here, or really why any of us are here. But here we are, right?"

"Here we are," the man echoed.

"Can you at least tell me your first name? Or any name, just so I can call you something. Seeing as you have a gun and everything, I don't expect you to tell me your real name."

"I don't think so."

"It's not like Vandal Savage is ever going to find out," Lois prodded.

The circle of light twitched, taking on an oblong shape on the desk's legs and the floor. Lois didn't allow a smile to cross her face, even though the beam wasn't on her. That comment had reached him.

"What the hell," he said, regaining control of his light.

It hadn't been off her for long enough for her to reach the cell phone in her purse. "Not like you'll live to do anything with it."

"That's right," Lois said confidently. The ease with which he revealed her probable fate concerned her, but she couldn't show it. "What the hell?"

The man shifted his position again. Lois considered offering him her chair, but then decided not to. Keeping him uncomfortable would likely pay off more than a bit of momentary courtesy, in the long run.

"You can call me Joe," he said.

"Okay, Joe, I will. Do you have any sense of how long we'll be here? Are we waiting for someone?"

"I'm not supposed to answer questions," Joe said.

"Of course you're not. I know that." *You weren't supposed to tell me your name, either.* "I just thought maybe you could speculate, since I'm obviously in the dark. Literally, as well as figuratively."

"I don't know how long," he said, voice taking on an angry tone. Was she pushing too hard, too fast? "We're waiting for someone, but I don't know when he'll get here."

"Not Savage?" she asked. "That would be something, wouldn't it?"

"Of course not Savage. I've never even seen him in person. Why would he come here?"

"What," Lois pressed. "You don't think I'm that important?"

"Lady, I have no idea how important you are. I just know how important I am, and I'm just important enough to stand here with a gun to keep you still and quiet. While we wait."

"For someone who's not Vandal Savage."

"I've heard the name, that's all. Never met the man, like I said. But I'm sure he's not coming here."

"But you do work for him."

"If you think I'm telling you who I work for, you're nuts."

"That's been suggested before," Lois said. "But I'll take it from your answer that you don't work for Savage."

"Of course not," Joe insisted. "You seem to have a real problem understanding who you're talking to. I'm low level. Muscle and a gun, that's all."

"Oh, come on, Joe," Lois said. Asking questions, squeezing the reluctant for information, these were critical job skills as far as she was concerned. A little psychology, a little flirting, and lots of trial and error. "I think it's you who are underestimating yourself. I'm no small prize, you know. They wouldn't have a peon guarding me."

"Sorry, lady, but I don't even know who you are."

Ouch. Joe's words stung. Lois was no global celebrity, but she liked to think everyone in Metropolis had at least heard of her. "You don't read the *Daily Planet*?"

"I watch TV," Joe said. As if that covered things.

Clark insisted that it did. The news offered on TV, he claimed, was every bit as valuable as what the *Planet* provided. Regurgitated pap, he said sometimes. Where was the societal value in that?

Which was why Lois insisted in putting more effort into her stories. More than Perry expected, or even wanted. She spent most of her time regurgitating the same sort of thing that Clark did, but the difference was that she believed when she brought Perry the right story, he would run with it. To believe otherwise—to accept that Perry was just as much an owned man as Armstrong, Daniels, and virtually everyone else in powerful positions—would cripple her, make her unable to go on doing what she had to do.

"I've been on TV, too," Lois said. "But I'm in the paper more. I'm one of their writers."

"That why you're snooping around here?"

"Yes," Lois said. Her eyes were growing accustomed to the dark, and she could see more of Joe. Not in any detail, but at least she had a sense of him. Smaller than the first guy, lean, with sloping shoulders and narrow hips. She couldn't tell what he was wearing, but his head was uncovered, hair short and spiked. "I was snooping, and I got caught. It happens. Usually I agree not to do the story, or even better I talk to whoever's involved, let them tell their side of things."

"I don't have a side," Joe said. "I do what I'm told, that's my side."

"Still, you have a point of view. You're not a blank slate, Joe. Savage wouldn't want anyone working for him who couldn't think on his feet. I know, I know, you've never met Savage, but if we follow the path to the top, right? Of course it's him calling the shots."

"I don't know that."

"Maybe not for a positive fact, but you know in your heart, right?"

"I don't hear names like that," Joe said flatly.

"Oh, you're good, Joe. You really are. You're the kind a reporter hates because you just won't give anything away. If Savage does know about you, he must love that."

"Haven't had any complaints," Joe said.

"I'm sure not. Do you know anything about why we're

here? Was this all a setup from the beginning?" She had trusted her German source, but maybe that trust had been misplaced. Savage, or someone else, could have reached out, and Lois had been betrayed.

"Above my pay grade," Joe replied.

"Again, I'm just asking for your speculation. You don't have to tell me anything definite. And if I won't be living through this, then what's the difference, right?"

"And like I said, I'm just muscle, I'm not part of the whos and whys and whatnots."

"What's he after?" Lois asked. "Savage, I mean. And I know you don't know, I'm just guessing you have a different perspective than I do. Being on the inside and all."

"I just hear what everybody else hears," Joe answered. "Savage is some kind of super billionaire. He's got his hands in everything—drugs, arms, gambling, women, legitimate businesses, politics. I don't know what he'd want with me or with a newspaper reporter."

"You've got me there, Joe," Lois said. "I don't either. I'm just trying to make some sense of whatever this is that I walked into while I still can."

"I mean," Joe went on, "sometimes you hear the name around, you know? But guys say a lot of stuff when they're just shooting the breeze, throwing back some drinks. Doesn't mean anything."

"They talk about him, though? Savage?"

"Sure. A few like to think we're part of some big scheme, something important."

"Do they say what they think it is?"

"Oh, all kinds of stuff. Some say that Savage runs the world. Others say just part of the world. We're just helping him keep things in order, they say."

"And what do you think, Joe? You're a smart guy."

"Joe was so smart, he'd keep his yap shut," another voice boomed from the darkness. It was the first man again, the one who had ordered Joe to watch her. He sounded angry. "And if you were as smart as you think, Ms. Lane, you wouldn't be asking a guy who doesn't know jack a lot of stupid questions."

"I've never been as smart as I think I am," Lois said, trying to be disarming. Once again, she wished she could see the faces of the men she was talking to. It was hard to know how to play them when she couldn't gauge their reactions. "I'm just trying to—"

"Never mind what you're trying," the man said. "It won't work, and I've already been instructed how to deal with you anyway."

"Instructed by whom?" Lois asked. She didn't like the sound of that at all. It had a certain finality to it that disturbed her, and she wished she'd been able to reach her phone, get a message to Clark. Not that he could have done much, but maybe he'd have been able to send some Public Safety officers.

The man didn't answer, so she tried another approach. "So what's the plan, then?"

"The plan, Ms. Lane, is that you're going to die." The man said it with a casualness that made the cold words even colder. "You've been asking too many questions, flipping over too many stones, and there doesn't seem to be a better way to make you stop."

"I can stop," Lois said, unable to keep the desperation from her voice. "I'm good at stopping, you have no idea. Listen, we can talk about this."

"Don't bother, Ms. Lane. The decision's been made."

"But I thought we were waiting for someone."

"Change of plans." Lois heard a metallic click, and then a bright flash blinded her. *Muzzle flash,* she thought. At the same moment, a booming noise, deafening in the small office, assaulted her ears and pain lanced into her like a hot poker above the ribs.

Shot, she realized. *I've been shot.*

Lois should have been upset, but before that occurred to her, there was another blast, and she was no longer aware of anything at all.

CHAPTER THREE

February 560

Tapestries lining the castle walls did little to cut the chill that seeped in from outside. The floors and walls seemed to hold in the cold, releasing it little by little, just enough to keep a man from ever feeling truly comfortable unless standing beside one of the massive fireplaces. Torches held by iron sconces on the walls offered some light but little warmth.

But at least inside Arthur's fortress, one was safe—for the moment—from the attacking forces of Morgaine Le Fey. Vandal Savage knew that beyond Arthur's walls, Hell had been unleashed. Savage had no particular problem with the concept, but *this* Hell was not one of his making, and he had no interest in someone else's version.

He sipped from a mug of hot mead and looked across the table at his two companions. Felix Faust, in his ridiculous dark blue sorcerer's robes and peaked helm. Faust's dark eyes were deeply recessed in his head, almost buried by knobby cheekbones and a protruding brow. His nose hooked over thin lips, turned perpetually down except when—as now—he chewed nervously on them.

Beside Faust sat Mordru, who liked to be called the Dark Lord Mordru, a habit Savage refused to indulge. His hair was long and dark, flowing over his shoulders. Like Faust, he favored dark blue, although his garb tended more toward the practical. There was a maniacal aspect to his gaze that Savage found disturbing, if potentially useful. A trimmed mustache and beard surrounded his cruel mouth.

The table at which they rested was no Round Table, but a rough-hewn piece put together from local ash by one of Camelot's less-skilled artisans. The chairs likewise—every time Vandal Savage shifted his weight, he feared his would split beneath him.

"Camelot is lost," he said by way of opening. He picked a morsel of game from a platter in the center of the table, bit it in half. It had a spoiled taste, but he didn't care. Beside the platter, a thick candle hissed and spat as its flame burned, as if in miniature imitation of the flames that razed the villages beyond the castle walls. "Nothing anyone can do will save it now."

"Why should this concern us?" Faust asked. "What is Camelot to me?"

"You must needs answer that for yourself," Savage replied. "Both of you. For the nonce, it offers us secure refuge, where we might come together on this occasion. What other place would be so hospitable?"

"How hospitable, if Arthur knew we were here?" Mordru wanted to know. He reached for a piece of meat, too.

"Arthur knows not, 'tis true," Savage said. "Such is the beauty of Camelot, is it not? There are enough people here, with enough competing loyalties, that even such as we could find someone willing to allow us entry." He put the other half of the spoiled bite in his mouth and spoke while clenching it in his teeth. "And to provide us with this fine repast."

"The meat's no good," Mordru pointed out.

"And were I not immortal, that might disturb me," Savage answered.

Mordru scowled. "Never have I thought of you as one who spoke in riddles, Savage," he said. "Tell us why you summoned us to this desperate place. I have business to attend elsewhere, as I'm sure Faust does."

"Unless there is some profit to be had from Camelot's destruction," Faust added.

"Morgaine attacks with dark magics, in league with demonic armies," Savage said. "Men of sorcery can always profit when raw magical power is in play, especially when used in the service of death. But that is not the specific reason for my summons."

"What, then?" Faust demanded. He reached for a hunk of the bad meat, as if not wanting to be left out.

"Camelot is lost," Vandal Savage said again. "And so are we."

Mordru came out of his chair, mouth open, bits of the meat he had been chewing spraying onto the table. "What say you?"

Savage waved his palms toward the table, trying to calm the excitable Mordru. The other sorcerer whipped long hair from his eyes and sat, gripping his own edge of the table tightly. "Explain yourself, Savage," he muttered.

"I have been scrying and reading portents for some time," Savage told them. "Led to this pursuit, I might add, by my own future self, sending me messages to prepare me for what is to come. And what I have learned troubles me greatly."

"Tell us what it is," Faust urged. "What troubles you so?"

"When Camelot falls, a light shall be extinguished from the Earth," Savage explained. "Reason, justice, decency, all shall vanish."

"Then all's well," Faust said, with a dry chuckle. His laugh sounded to Savage like the ropes and gears of the rack, drawing ever tighter.

"A dark age shall descend over Europe," Savage continued, ignoring the other man. "Over England and all else. While it all sounds magnificent, for such as we, there is a worry in the offing."

"What could it be?" Faust asked. "The world you describe would appear to me ideal."

"The problem," Savage replied, "is that it shall not last. Hundreds of years will pass in this way—the blink of an eye for us—then the light will grow again, brighter than ever. Reason will return. Science will rule the day. Civilization, with all its attendant 'virtues,' will flourish across the Earth. When that day comes, sorcery will no longer rule. We shall be a forgotten part of history, no longer in the seats of power. Indeed, we shall be hunted down like vermin, hiding in the shadows, afraid for our very lives."

"Knowing this now," Mordru suggested, "is there not some way we might avoid this fate?"

Savage smiled. Mordru had chanced upon the truth. "This is why I summoned you both," he said. "For I believe that there are yet actions we can take to alter the future I have seen in the stars and signs."

"Actions?" Mordru echoed. "Then what, man? Tell us what we must do to avoid this fate."

Savage took another chunk of meat, popped it into his mouth. Not because he was hungry, but because he wanted to delay the moment, to savor it a while longer. He had no doubt that his own powers exceeded those of Felix Faust and Mordru. Singly, if not together. At this moment both waited for his wisdom, his insights.

Together, the three of them could be an unbeatable force.

But if there were to be a "together," an alliance of any kind, Vandal Savage wanted to be at its head.

When the attention of both sorcerers was riveted upon him, he began to outline his plan.

CHAPTER **FOUR**

May 1872

A drop of sweat ran from the spot where the rider's hat met his forehead and splatted into the dust on his saddle fork, just beside the horn. Sweating was good, though—it meant he had not completely dehydrated, even though the day was as hot and dry as Satan's own fire pit.

The rider was tall and lean. From a distance he appeared to slump forward a bit, but he was reading sign, not slipping from his saddle. He wore a Confederate Army jacket with the insignias torn off, belted at the waist by a pistol rig, holster hanging against his left hip. A second six-shooter was tucked into the front of the gun belt for a quick right-handed draw. On his head sat an officer's hat of the same rebel gray. Blue jeans covered his legs, and the boots in his stirrups were dust-caked and worn.

He had tracked five owlhoots and their captive from San Angelo, Texas, all the way across New Mexico and well into Arizona Territory. They had passed through the mountains and high valleys of the southeastern part of the territory and entered its low, scorching deserts. A long, hot ride. From time to time he had been able to see their dust ahead of him, or the smoke from their cookfire lingering in the morning sky, but he had never been able to catch up to them.

He had closed the gap, though. After nine days on the trail, he would catch them today.

Jonah Hex didn't think of himself as the most patient man on Earth, but when something was worth doing he could bide his time until it was done.

In this case, the rascals he tracked had attacked a ranch belonging to a man named Fred Bates. They'd killed Bates and all his hands, cut loose his remuda, ridden down the barbed-wire fences that penned in his cattle, burned his ranch house and his bunkhouse, and stolen his payroll, which he had just brought back from the bank. Jonah figured it was the payroll they were after all along, and the rest of it was just men out for some misguided fun.

Before they left, they snatched up Bates's nineteen-year-old daughter Josie.

With two pack animals and Josie's mount, that made eight horses Jonah was tracking. More than enough to leave a clear trail, except where the ground got especially rocky and bare or when they cut through water. He had lost the trail a couple of times, but never for very long. If the men hadn't had a five-day head start, he'd have been on them before they reached the Texas border.

Jonah Hex wasn't particularly partial to Fred Bates or any of his ranch hands, or Josie, for that matter, even though she was young and curvy, with hair as yellow as autumn grass and eyes of cornflower blue.

But Fred Bates owed Jonah two hundred dollars, on

account of Jonah had helped the rancher out with a little rustling problem he'd been having. Bates was supposed to have taken Jonah's money out of the bank the same time he got the payroll money, and when Jonah came back to San Angelo after a little side trip collecting the bounty on an *hombre* named Ernesto Gilligan, he meant to pick it up at the ranch.

When he got there, all he found was burned-out rubble. A neighbor told Jonah what he knew—staring at Jonah's horse, rather than Jonah's scarred face, the whole time—and Jonah lit a shuck out of there, figuring that when the men had taken the F Bar B payroll they had taken his two hundred dollars as well.

A man had to make a living. Jonah didn't choose to make his stealing and murdering, as these men did. He earned his way just the same, and when someone took his money, it was his duty to get it back.

General, Jonah's chestnut mustang, picked his way between thorny mesquite, pointy-leafed yuccas, and barbed chollas. *Everything in this damn place has something sharp on it,* Jonah thought. *It's like the planet don't want anyone to cross through here without it leaves its mark on 'em.*

No one lived out here but a few half-crazy ranchers, Apache Indians, and the soldiers assigned to the Territory to fight them. Jonah couldn't believe the goal of the men he followed was anywhere around here—they were just passing through, maybe to California, or Mexico.

If they weren't careful, the Apache would get them before he could. Trying to collect his money from an Apache war party could be a mite tricky, so he hoped it didn't come to that. "Come on, General," he said aloud. "Let's pick it up a little."

If he were being followed, Jonah Hex would have done without a fire at all. In Apache country he would never dare to light a fire. This late in the spring, the nights still got cool, but they'd be a durn sight colder without a scalp to keep some of your body heat in. That was supposing the Apache let you live at all, which was no certainty. These men were either unaware that someone had tracked them from the Bates place, ignorant of their own where-abouts, or unconcerned about being found.

He didn't much care which it was. After spotting the glow of their fire, he left General tied to the trunk of a scrub oak about two miles back and closed the distance on foot. His twin ivory-stocked Colt .44 Dragoons were holstered, and he carried his Winchester Model 1866 lever-action rifle. A half-moon floated low in the sky, sil-vering the desert shrubbery and the outspread arms of the tall saguaros. Jonah circled the fire, smelling the mesquite branches they burned, and came toward it from the north, so his shadow wouldn't precede him into the camp.

The men had stopped for the night on the side of a slope that would offer them a little protection against a wind that was picking up out of the west. The hillside was rocky, dotted with cactus and mesquite and a few tall yucca stalks.

Jonah could hear conversation and laughter when he was still some distance off. That would cover any inad-vertent noise he might make. More confident than ever, he covered the rest of the distance and stopped just beyond the glow of the fire. He stood as still as a shadow, and if any of the men in the circle of light looked his way, they didn't see anything. Not even the horses, picketed on the far side of the camp, seemed aware of the bounty hunter's presence.

Five men, as he had been told. One squatted on his haunches by the fire, hat tipped back on his head, poking at the coals with a stick. Two leaned back against saddles, one smoking and the other drinking coffee from a tin cup. These were the ones laughing and telling jokes. A fourth sat in the dirt, off by himself with a Sharps rifle across his bony knees, looking toward a still bundle that Jonah figured was Josie. The fifth had already gone to sleep in his bedroll.

Guy with the Sharps was the first priority, then. Putting him down would send the others a clear message.

Jonah fired. The Winchester's roar split the night. The man with the rifle pitched forward, arms outspread, a scream dying in his throat before it was even born.

The woman made up for it. Josie Bates sat upright in her bedroll and let out a wail that could have cleared several of the nearest Apache burial grounds. Jonah ignored her and stalked toward the firelight, levering out the empty and filling the chamber with his next bullet, eyes flicking this way and that, watching for whoever would make the next move. He carried the rifle easily, finger on the trigger, ready to swing it in any direction. The sleeping man stirred, sat up, rubbed his eyes.

"I ain't here to make trouble," Jonah announced as he entered the circle of light. "I just want two hundred dollars what's owed me, from Fred Bates's roll."

"Jonah?" Josie said. She put her hand over her eyes as if it would help her see through the gloom. "Is that you?"

" 'Pears to be," he admitted.

As he came into the light, the man with the hand-rolled tossed it into the fire, and a look of disgust came over his face. "If you ain't the ugliest *cabron* I ever—"

The guy beside him punched him with the hand holding the tin cup, sloshing coffee over its side onto the first one's arm. "That's Jonah Hex," he said. "Lookit that scarred mug. Don't you know nothin'?"

"Appears as if you know who I am," Jonah said. *This might go easier than I suspected,* he thought, pleased at the idea. *One good thing about having a reputation.*

"You worked for my daddy!" Josie shouted. "You're here to rescue me!"

Before Jonah could deny it, the man who had been sleeping jerked inside his flea trap. Jonah saw the outline of a pistol under the fabric and fired before the man could take aim. One shot to the head, and he was out. Jonah worked the lever again. Two shots down, fourteen to go. Never did to lose count.

The man's action had set off the others. The man squatting by the campfire threw one hand down to steady himself as he drew iron with the other. He hadn't reached his feet when Jonah's next shot buried itself in his chest, and, off-balance, he flopped forward into the flames. The man who had been drinking Arbuckle's tossed aside his cup and pawed for his holster. Jonah's slug tore a new hole between his eyes. Blood spurted from the back of his head, and he went over sideways, his hogleg still encased in leather.

The last man, the one who'd tossed his quirly into the fire before his *compadre* had started in to cooking himself, still sat against his saddle. He had raised his hands to shoulder height, revealing them to be empty.

"Now mebbe you and me can jaw a while," Jonah said. "About that money I'm owed."

"Sure," the man started to say.

From off to the side, Jonah heard Josie's voice again. "Let me, Jonah," she said. For a second, her meaning was unclear. When he did realize what she meant, he flicked his gaze toward her for a split second. She had already picked up the first dead man's Colt and was pointing it at the survivor, holding it in two hands as if it might lurch away from her.

"Josie, don't!" Jonah shouted. He wanted to tell her that he understood the impulse, but that she was no killer, and if she tugged that trigger, she'd surely regret it. There was no time, though, for any of that. She fired. The weapon kicked her hands backward so they struck her in the chin, and she gave a yelp of surprise.

The man she had shot had fallen back, slumped over his own saddle, the life's blood flowing out of him and staining the dirt.

Five men dead in the space of a couple of minutes, and no one left to tell him where the money was cached, unless Josie knew.

"You got any idea where they carried your pa's money?" he asked.

"I think Slender Bill had it in his saddlebags, or maybe his tucker bag."

Jonah guessed Slender Bill had been the one with the rifle, but that didn't do much good as he didn't know which man's belongings were whose, except for the ones who had died on their own.

"Over there," Josie said, pointing. Jonah crossed the campsite, found a saddle and gear piled together. An empty saddle scabbard leaned against the saddle, which made sense as the man had died clutching his old Sharps. Jonah started with the leather saddle pockets, but found no money in them. Digging farther through the man's gear he found the war bag she had mentioned, an old flour sack he kept closed with a length of rawhide *reata*.

Hoisting it, Jonah realized it couldn't possibly carry the F Bar B's payroll, even if the outlaws had already divvied it into five shares. He tossed it aside, swearing quietly, before spotting a leather morral. This one, Jonah knew, was too heavy to contain oats, and if it had just been a nosebag, it probably would have been left with the horses instead of buried under the man's outfit. Working it open, Jonah found it full of coins, mostly eagles and half eagles, with some *reales* and a couple of fifty-dollar slugs thrown in. To make the lightest load, Jonah counted out the two slugs and as many ten-dollar eagles as he could, then filled in the rest of his two hundred with half and quarter eagles. When he was done he tossed the morral toward Josie.

As he threw it, he glanced in her direction. He had expected her to be quivering on the ground, the reality of having shot a man sinking in. Instead she walked toward him, naked, firelight glinting off the curves and planes of her young, firm body.

"You ought to put some clothes on," Jonah said. "It's like to get colder 'fore the sun comes up."

"Those men had me every which way," Josie said. "Said they was getting me ready to be sold, down Mexico way. Figured if you want a piece, too, you might as well take it now."

"All I want's my money," Jonah answered, "then to get out of here before the Apache come around. They no doubt heard all the shootin'."

"You don't think I'm pretty?"

Jonah couldn't help feeling sorry for the girl, kidnapped and used as she had been. Girl her age should have been married, or making plans to be, but she had stayed on with her pa after her ma passed, setting her own life aside to help him on the ranch.

"Pretty enough," Jonah said. He turned the scarred side of his face toward the firelight, knowing that the flap of skin that stretched from cheek to chin, where his mouth had been widened by a flame-heated tomahawk, and the rippled, ruined flesh below his exposed right eye socket, turned most decent folks' stomachs. "But look at me. You sure you want this mouth kissin' on you, or this face gruntin' over you?"

"I'd have worse down in old Mexico," she replied.

"Reckon so," Jonah admitted. "But you don't have to now, less'n that's the choice you make."

She stood there for a minute, hands at her sides, as if letting him see all that she had to offer might change his mind. He experienced a familiar stirring—she really was a beautiful girl—but couldn't bring himself to take advantage of her situation. He hadn't had a woman since Mei Ling, his Chinese wife, had taken their son and left him, and that had been months. He'd tried to suppress the urge, but it never went away completely. If he'd been paying for it, he would take her up on the offer in a heartbeat, but even with his two hundred dollars out of the nosebag, the remaining payroll was still far more money than he had. She wasn't a rich woman, but she was better off than him.

"Cover up, Josie," he urged.

"You say so," she said. "You won't get another shot."

"I'll live with that."

She went back to where she had shucked her clothing and began to dress again. Jonah watched, admiring.

"You got a lot of coin there, for a single woman," he said. "But if you go back to the F Bar B, hire some new hands, it won't last long. On the other hand, you could go just about anywhere, let this money stake you, and arrange for someone you trust back in San Angelo to sell the land for you. You ever think about goin' to San Francisco? Or back East somewheres?"

"All I ever thought about was running the F Bar B with Pa," Josie said. "Anyways, all my things are there."

"There's nothing there but ashes," Jonah reminded her. "This bunch burned your clothes and everything else."

"I don't care," she said, adamant. "I want to go back. Maybe I won't stay, maybe I will. But I want to see it for myself just the same, then make up my mind."

"I reckon I understand that."

"Take me home, Jonah. Please."

Jonah hesitated. He had already spent nine days on the trail of two hundred dollars, when he would have done much better financially using that time to chase after some wanted men for the bounty.

"I'll pay you," she added. "I have money now, you said so yourself. Whatever your usual rate is, I'll match."

"You won't have money for long, that's the way you strike a bargain," Jonah pointed out. "But all right." He had intended going back in that direction anyway, even if not all the way to San Angelo. "Five dollars a day, and I'll keep your pretty blonde hair on your head where it belongs."

Josie chewed on her lush lower lip for a moment. "That seems like a lot."

"You see anyone makin' you a better offer, Josie, go ahead and take it."

He was taking advantage after all. But in a different way, a way she could afford. The extra forty-five dollars would help make the trip out here worthwhile, although it wouldn't do the whole job.

He'd have a sight to look at on the way back that was easy on the eyes, though. And if she made that other offer again, after they knew each other better, he just might take her up on it.

CHAPTER FIVE

Where the hell is Lois?

She didn't like it when Clark worried about her. He did it anyway. He couldn't bring himself not to. This time, she was late—eleven o'clock had come and gone, midnight closing in—and she wasn't answering her cell phone, which rang and rang, then went to voice mail.

She had mentioned that she'd be late, but casually. Clark knew she was up to something—he hadn't spent years married to her without figuring out how to read her. But he also knew that if he asked for details, she would be angry, resentful. Lois knew how to take care of herself and never let him forget it.

Not that he could.

Lois was his world. He reached for her in the morning, touched her as he went to sleep, as if making sure that she hadn't gone anywhere. When she was away for a couple of days on a story—a rare occurrence, but not unheard of—he got antsy, like he was missing his tether to the real world. His sleep suffered, he didn't eat right, and he couldn't fully relax until he heard the familiar sound of the front door opening and her footfalls in the tiled foyer.

Tonight, it had only been a few hours. She had been missing for this long hundreds of times before. He couldn't have put his finger on just why this time seemed different, but it did. Clark paced through the apartment, tried to read a book, closed it and set it aside again. He had tried to make dinner, but then failed to pay attention to it, and the apartment still stank of charred garlic bread and the saucepan he had scorched. *Where is she?*

He picked up the phone, checked for voice-mail messages even though he knew he hadn't heard it ring. When he hung up, he checked again in case she had called while he was checking. Still nothing. He paced some more. Looked out the window at the nighttime lights of Metropolis, spread like a blanket of diamonds as far as he could see.

Clark remembered his dreams. If he could fly, he'd take to the air, scour the city that way. He could cover every block, every building.

What if she's out there somewhere, and she needs me?

Then again, what could he do? Call Public Safety? If she was investigating one of her antigovernment stories, that would only get her into worse trouble.

Presumably her phone had a GPS chip in it. If he could call in a favor, get one of his government sources to track the chip, on the q.t. maybe . . .

No, he thought. That would be like sentencing her to death. He didn't have any leverage over those people. They were sources, not friends. He couldn't confuse the two. He had friends, but none who could help him now.

A noise outside the door, in the hall. Lois?

A knock followed. Lois wouldn't knock, not unless she had lost her keys. Who, then? Public Safety?

Biting back his fear, Clark answered the door.

And turned his world on its head.

Two men stood in the hall. "Invite us in," one of them said quietly.

"Come . . . come in," Clark said, powerless to resist the stranger's demand.

"We could have simply appeared in your living room," the same stranger said when Clark had closed the door behind them. "But we wanted to create the appearance of normalcy, for your sake. And we understood that a sudden materialization would have been unnecessarily disturbing. I will warn you, Clark Kent, that what we tell you will disturb you nonetheless."

Clark's mouth opened and closed, but he couldn't seem to squeeze any sound out.

The one who had done all the talking thus far was tall and lean, attributes enhanced by a long, dark cloak, navy blue or black, held at the throat by a gold chain connecting two golden clasps. Beneath the cloak, he wore a dark suit with a white turtleneck. White gloves covered his hands. A golden amulet of some kind hung from a slender chain around his neck. A fedora hat the same color as his suit and cloak shadowed his face, making it impossible to see what color his eyes were—if, indeed, his eyes had eyeballs at all. Somehow, Clark couldn't quite bring the man's eyes into focus. His face was narrow and unlined, with a straight nose and a mouth that appeared never to have smiled.

The other man appeared somewhat more normal. He

was handsome, in a rakish way, square-jawed and solid, if a little shorter than the dark man. A white streak stood out in stark contrast to the rest of his reddish brown hair. Anywhere between thirty and fifty, he had laugh lines around his eyes and a ready grin. He wore more traditional clothes than the first, too—an expensive silk blazer, collared blue shirt, khakis, oxblood shoes that almost matched his hair. He looked like money, while the other man looked like . . . what?

Mystery.

"What is it?" Clark demanded, finally finding his voice. "What do you want with me? Who are you?"

"If this is the journalist's traditional five Ws, you missed a couple," the shorter man said.

"All will be explained, Clark Kent," the dark man said. He pointed at Clark's leather sofa. "Sit."

Clark started to obey again, then stopped. He'd had enough of these jokers. "No!" he shot back. "You want to explain, get started, or else get out."

"Want me to take over, Stranger?" the second man asked. "Your bedside manner is sometimes a little lacking."

"Better that I do it, Jason," the tall man replied.

"I was beginning to wonder if you always used first and last names," Clark said. "Although in this case both would have been handy."

"He is called Jason Blood," the dark man said. He stood perfectly rigid, making Clark wonder if his skeleton was made of steel. At least the shorter guy slouched a little. "And men know me as the Phantom Stranger."

"Easy to see why," Clark said, his anxiety and anger revealing itself through sarcasm. "But what's your name?"

"That's the best you're gonna get, Kent," Jason Blood

said. "I've known him for—I don't even like to think about how long—and that's all I know, too."

"So, Jason Blood and the Phantom Stranger, eh?" Clark couldn't resist a wry grin, despite the very real fear the men raised in him. "Even assuming I believe either one of those names, what do you want with me? If you have a complaint about your *Daily Planet* delivery, I'm not the guy to talk to."

"Our business with you is serious, Clark," the Phantom Stranger said. Was that the ghost of a smile flitting across his lips? Impossible to say.

"Tell me about it, then," Clark insisted. "I'm not in the mood for riddles."

"You really should sit, maybe," Jason said.

Clark folded his arms across his chest, defiant. "I'll sit when I'm ready."

"Very well," the Phantom Stranger said. "Then listen, Clark, and believe, however audacious our tale appears."

Clark nodded. Unthinking belief seemed like a lot to ask, but he'd give it a try.

"There are two Earths, Clark," the Stranger began. "There should only be one—after all that's happened, there should, by all rights, be a single true Earth. But there are two, and therein lies a tale, and a problem of the most monumental proportions."

"Losing me," Clark warned. He tried to sound flip, cynical, but something about the Phantom Stranger's deep, steady voice was indeed convincing. "I care why?"

"You should care," the Stranger said. "Everyone should, although most will never know. Only a select few could comprehend the truth without going insane, and I see now that I was right in believing you to be one of those few."

"I'm not losing my mind, just my patience," Clark said.

"He's like this," Jason Blood said. "Takes him a while to get to the point, and then it takes a while longer."

Clark turned his attention to Jason, who at least appeared relatively sane. "And how could he possibly know all this if no one is supposed to be aware of it?"

"You don't want to ask that question," Jason answered. "He knows stuff. He just does. It's what he does best, really, but his sources aren't the types of things you and I could comprehend."

The Phantom Stranger shot Jason a sharp glance. "The point, Clark, is that an artificial divergence in the Earth's time stream has been magically created. Think of time as a river, flowing from then to now, and beyond. But sorcerers meddling with forces they shouldn't have carved a new channel, so that instead of one mighty river, there are now two, almost mirror images of one another."

"Why's that a problem?" Clark asked.

"Key word, 'almost,'" Jason said.

"Jason is correct," the Stranger went on. "While the two rivers—or, to return from the metaphoric to the concrete, the two Earths—might look similar from space, on the ground things are very different. The other Earth, for instance, is a chaotic, strife-torn place, where there is almost always at least one war, and often several, in progress."

Clark finally took the Stranger's advice and sat. Jason had leaned casually against a wall, but the Phantom Stranger remained on his feet, ramrod straight. "Sounds like a nasty place," Clark said. "Glad I don't live there."

"Sure about that, Clark?" Jason asked. He still wore that grin, and Clark was beginning to feel like he had been left out of a private joke.

"You do," the Stranger explained. "Clark Kent does, at any rate. And before you pass judgment on that Earth, think about why this one does not suffer the turmoil and conflict of the other."

"Why don't you just tell me?" Clark said. "Since I get the feeling you will anyway."

"Control," the Stranger said. "This world is under the strict control of those sorcerers I mentioned before. They have divided it up into three regions, and each rules his own region with the proverbial iron fist. Because the three are in league, they manage international affairs between them, leaving no purpose for international conflict."

"Still," Clark said, "it seems to work pretty well. Clean, anyway."

"You only say that because you haven't seen the other," Jason suggested. "Well, not *this* you, anyway. There's nothing like a little spirited orneriness to get the blood flowing, if you ask me."

"No one did," the Phantom Stranger said. Clark suspected that the line was as close to a joke as he ever cracked. "But Jason's point is well-taken. That Earth has its share of conflict, but it also has enormous freedoms, a concept virtually unknown here."

Clark glanced about the apartment. "I don't see any soldiers in here, no listening devices."

"Perhaps not inside your apartment," the Stranger said. "Yet. Give it time."

Clark was playing devil's advocate, to some extent. He and Lois had spent hours discussing their society's lack of real freedom, although they had nothing with which to compare it. And wasn't he worried, even as these strange men spoke to him, about whether or not she had run afoul of the authorities?

"The differences between this world and that are legion, and we haven't time to go into them all," the Stranger continued. "But there is one very significant difference that I will name. That world—the true Earth, by the way, as it's this one which is the imperfect mirror image—has a yellow sun."

Clark tried to imagine what that would look like. "Isn't it blinding?" he asked.

"The people there are accustomed to it, and have evolved accordingly," the Stranger said. "The red sun you know is one of the intentional efforts made by the sorcerers to keep this world safely under their grip."

"How does that work?" Clark asked. He still imagined himself blinking furiously under the glare of a yellow sun.

"I'm glad you sat down," Jason said. He cocked his head at Clark, looking expectant.

"It works because on that Earth, under a yellow sun, you are an entirely different being," the Phantom Stranger said. "You were not born on Earth—this, or any other. You were born on Krypton, a planet doomed to suffer a terrible calamity. In your homeworld's final moments, your parents sent you, an infant, in a small starship, which carried you to Earth. The magic that created the two Earths could not change that simple fact of history, so instead it created two of you, two tiny Kal-Els who crashed into fields outside Smallville, Kansas, and were adopted by Jonathan and Martha Kent."

Clark suppressed an involuntary shiver. How did this stranger know the names of his parents?

The Phantom Stranger kept talking. "Krypton, like this

Earth, had a red sun. Under a red sun, your powers are suppressed. You grew to adulthood as a normal human being, just like those around you."

"This is where it gets good," Jason tossed out.

"You say that like there's something wrong with being a normal human being."

"Not for those who are meant to be," the Stranger replied. "But your potential is so much greater. On the true Earth, it has been realized. Here, it can never be."

"And what's so different about that other me?" Clark asked. The whole thing sounded crazier by the second, but he suspected he ought to go along with their delusion in case they turned out to be dangerous psychopaths of some kind. He was already trying to figure out how to alert the authorities, though.

"Under a yellow sun, you have incredible powers," the Stranger said. "Strength, speed, flight. You can see through things, see for thousands of miles, use your vision to generate extreme heat. I won't detail everything you can do, and I'm sure your limits have yet to be fully tested. But you are a unique, powerful individual, a champion of freedom and justice, an inspiration to the world that has adopted you."

"And a generally all-around special guy," Jason added.

Clark waved an impatient hand at Jason Blood. What the Phantom Stranger had said sounded impossible, absurd.

And yet—those dreams of flying. He'd had them his whole life, it seemed, and they were so *real*, as if he knew what flying truly felt like.

Confused, he didn't answer for a moment. Instead, he sat with fists clenched, tense, face worked into a frown.

"You know it's true, although every fiber of your conscious mind resists it," the Stranger said.

"Now you're saying you can read minds? I thought I was the alien with freakish powers."

"Mind reading is not necessary to see what you're thinking, Clark. And in that world, there are many individuals with extraordinary powers and abilities," the Phantom Stranger replied.

"But here, they're all affected by the red sun? Or is it these . . . these magicians you're talking about? In addition to turning a yellow sun red, they did whatever was necessary to keep the others from gaining their powers?"

"Nothing that simple," the Stranger said. "This Earth didn't evolve in the same way as that one. Because freedoms are limited, because the state so rigorously controls the sciences, the economy, and so on, because of a thousand other events, large and small, those who might have gained powers did not do so. Most significantly, your arrival from outside the solar system, when it happened, was something their magic could not prevent, as I mentioned. And because you, symbolically as well as physically, stand head and shoulders above most of Earth's other heroes, however powerful they may be, your leadership and example set many, many others on a path they would not otherwise have chosen."

"You've got to understand how ridiculous this sounds," Clark said. He rose to his feet, spread his arms, turned around. His shirttails were rumpled, tie loosened at the throat, dress pants wrinkled from the day. Worried about Lois, he'd been running his fingers through his hair so it was shaggy, unkempt. "Do I look like some kind of hero? Some great example for the world?"

"Not so much, at the moment," Jason said. "But when you're on, in that world . . . even I'm impressed."

"On?" Clark asked.

"It is not Clark Kent I'm talking about," the Stranger said. "The people of that Earth, those who know of Clark Kent at all, know him as a newspaper reporter. That much is the same. But the one who is recognized around the world, the one who stands as a symbol of freedom and strength and decency—he is known as *Superman.*"

CHAPTER SIX

Clark suppressed a guffaw at the name the Phantom Stranger spoke. "Superman? How subtle."

"Perhaps not," the Stranger said. "Nevertheless, the name—and the person—are universally admired."

"And he—I, whatever . . . this 'Superman'—hasn't become a global dictator?"

"The Stranger did mention decency, right?" Jason asked. "Superman just isn't the kind of guy who's after power for its own sake."

"Superman is a fundamentally good man," the Phantom Stranger said. "The kind who are rare, on either Earth. Anyone with incredible power must always be tempted, but Superman resists the call to use his abilities except in the service of causes that are right and just. This is because Kal-El is a good person at the core, which means that you are, too."

"I'm sure there are people who'd disagree with you," Clark said. "But I suppose that brings me to my next question. Even assuming that everything you say is true, which is a stretch I'm not prepared to make, why tell me about it?"

"We've come because the universe is not a stable place," the Stranger answered. "Things change, the river of time flows onward. I have described two worlds where there should be one. What I haven't told you is that a convergence of these worlds is imminent. The two paths of the river are coming together again, soon. And thanks to the power of the sorcerers I've mentioned, when they do, when the time streams join, only one Earth will remain. That Earth will be this one—the false Earth, the magical construct. The true Earth will cease to be."

"The true Earth being the one with Superman on it."

"And freedom, and humanity," Jason replied. "The Earth that hasn't been divvied up between three of the baddest bad guys you could imagine, like three binge eaters with a pie."

Clark glanced at the clock—12:40 and still no sign of Lois. The arrival of these strange visitors had helped pass the time, but he was more anxious than ever about her. He paced over to the window, drew back the curtain, and peered out at the lights. "Okay, I grant you, that sounds like a bad thing. Especially for the people on that Earth. But it doesn't explain why you came to me. What can I do about it? Why not go to this Superman and let him fix things?"

"Superman cannot travel between the two Earths," the Stranger explained. "No one from that world may come to this one, yet it may be necessary, to solve the problem. The sorcerers established that rule when they branched the time stream, and it is not something that can be ignored, even by us. We two, because of our own unique natures, are able to make the trip, but no others. And only then by bridging the gap between worlds with a journey through Hell. A journey I, for one, would be happy never to make again. But I have, because this is so important. Billions of lives are at stake. All history, past and future, really. This Earth's history is borrowed, its future predetermined. This fate cannot be allowed to come to pass."

"But I still don't see what help I could be," Clark protested. "And why you expect me to care about the people of an Earth I've never even known about until just now, if it does really exist. I'll tell you what, at this moment I'm more concerned about my wife, who's a few hours late getting home, than I am about theoretical billions who may not even be there."

The Phantom Stranger's hand came down firmly on Clark's shoulder, warm and somehow comforting, even though he had thought the Stranger was all the way across the room. He heard the Stranger's steady, even breathing. And then the dark man spoke again, and his words shattered Clark's soul.

"Lois will not be coming home, Clark," the Stranger said. "She has been murdered while trying to investigate, to prove, what we already know—that this part of the world is under the sway of the one called Vandal Savage."

Clark's eyes filled with tears. "No," he said, not willing to accept the Phantom Stranger's words. He shook off the man's hand. "No. She's just late, that's all. She's just—"

"I can show you, if it would help," the Stranger said.

"Show me what? You were there?"

"No, we were not," the Stranger replied. "But that doesn't mean we can't show you the events as they happened."

"Some kind of hocus-pocus?" Clark asked.

"Call it whatever name you will," the Phantom Stranger said.

"He's just trying to help, Kent," Jason put in. "We both know this is hard on you. But if it'll help you accept the truth, then you should let him show you what happened to her."

"When?" Clark asked. "If she's . . . if she's dead, when did . . . when did it happen?"

"One hour and thirty-two minutes ago," the Stranger said.

"And you couldn't stop it?"

"Even had we known of it beforehand, we couldn't have. This is not our world, Clark. Our powers are very limited here, circumscribed by the might of Vandal Savage, Felix Faust, and Mordru."

Clark felt as if the floor was spinning around, like some kind of mad carnival ride, lurching toward him, then dropping away. Dizzying. Nauseating. He made his way unsteadily to the couch, dropped onto its cushions. He had bought this couch with Lois, four years before, at a funky furniture store on Siegel Avenue. They had tiptoed around it for days, even refusing to drink coffee on it, afraid of spilling a drop on its rich black leather. Finally, after a week they gave in and christened it, making love on it, and after that it had been a favorite piece, comfortable and luxurious.

He was ill at ease, sobbing, while Jason Blood looked on with sympathy and the Phantom Stranger gazed with that unreadable, blank expression of his. Clark couldn't help himself, though. Something about the way they both spoke made him believe their claim, no matter how hard he tried to do otherwise.

Finally, sitting with his legs spread, arms resting on his thighs, head hanging down, he realized he had to see, had to know for sure. Uncertainty would destroy him. "Show me," he said. "Go ahead, let me see what happened to Lois."

"Look, then," the Stranger said. Clark raised his head. The Phantom Stranger inscribed a design in the air with his hand. The space there shimmered, then a vision appeared, as if seen through some dark, viscous liquid.

Lois, sitting down in a chair somewhere, in front of what looked like a desk. A corona of light surrounded her, as if the darkness itself hemmed her in, pinning her to the chair. Clark could see but not hear as she made what looked like spirited declarations of some kind. She was afraid, he could tell, but she covered that fear, didn't give in to it.

Then her body jerked. Pain etched her face, and a rosette of blood blossomed on her dark sweater, slick and wet against the fabric. Clark watched the life ebb from the woman he loved, watched her face go slack, the spark fade from her eyes.

"That's enough!" he shouted, and the image vanished. "Why . . .?"

"As I said, she sought to reveal the truth," the Stranger said. "She was closing in on Vandal Savage, and he could not have that. Those three rule this Earth, but keep their own names, their identities, shielded behind others, puppets. They fear the spirit of humanity rising up against them, even from a humanity wholly manufactured by them.

Their goal isn't supremacy over this Earth, after all, but over the *only* Earth, once the convergence takes place."

Clark squeezed his hands together so hard he thought he would crush the small bones. "But . . . but I live on this Earth, and now I have to go on living without her, without—"

"But you don't," the Stranger interrupted. "It is only *this* Earth's Lois who has been killed. On the true Earth, Lois yet lives. There, too, she is married to Clark Kent. What we ask of you will not be easy, Clark. There are no guarantees that it will work. But what we want you to do is to accompany us, back through Hell, back in time. We need to find the point at which the branching of the time stream can be stopped before it even starts. Only that way can we keep this Earth from ever having existed. Don't think of it as wiping away billions of lives, because those lives are not real—not yet. If they are allowed to become real, to supplant the true lives on the true Earth, then a genocide of the worst order will have occurred. The future Earth could have had will be eliminated, and in its place you and those around you will continue to live under the rule of tyrants."

"I still don't . . . don't quite get it," Clark said.

"I'm not surprised," Jason answered. "I'm not sure I do either. Time travel is always tricky, and when you add parallel dimensions, then it just gets a little too far into Stephen Hawking territory for me. But what the man's getting at is this. When we go back in time—back into the real Earth's past—then you and our Clark, our Superman, will merge somehow. You'll have Lois back, good as new, because that Earth's Lois is fine. Quite literally, what we're asking you to do is to help us save the world, save history. And just maybe repair your broken heart in the bargain."

"Your problem is that you think of time as a one-way street," the Phantom Stranger commented. "That is inaccurate. Time is a dimension, like the other three you commonly think of. Yesterday is no more gone than you are a two-dimensional drawing on a page one day and three-dimensional bulk and solidity the next. It is not easy to visualize, perhaps, and harder to explain, but compared to some of the other dimensions—including Hell, which intersects with all of them—it is not so impossible to understand."

Clark swallowed, sniffed, rubbed his eyes. "I guess . . . I guess I've got no good reason to stay here. So why not, right? Let's do this."

Jason Blood grinned broadly, and Clark thought the Phantom Stranger's face even turned less severe for a moment. Nothing made Clark want to smile, just then—nothing could.

But if these men were right, then maybe he could channel his grief into something constructive, something useful.

A task of which, he was certain, Lois would have approved.

CHAPTER SEVEN

February 560

Three men trod unseen through the smoke cast adrift by the flames of war. Not entirely unseen—Felix Faust could look to his left and his right and see Vandal Savage and Mordru—but the people among whom they passed, the serfs and farmhands of the countryside surrounding Camelot, could not. More to the point, neither could the invading armies, human or demonic, of Morgaine Le Fey.

Savage did, Faust had to admit, cut a striking figure. The shortest of the three—Mordru, towering to seven feet, was by far the tallest of them—Vandal Savage still had a broad, powerful chest and shoulders wide as an ox yoke. His hair and long beard were as black as his heart. Thick black brows arched over brown eyes that seemed constantly in motion, as if worried they might miss something. His black robes, ornamented with red, flapped in the wind. Around his neck and on his chest he wore a massive chain of gold medallions, and a larger one, demon-headed, hung from his belt. He carried a scepter with a glass globe at its head, which glowed to illuminate their path.

Faust understood that, while Vandal Savage talked about the three of them being equal partners, and stressed the balanced aspects of the three-sided triumvirate, he really wanted to be more important than the others. It was his plan, after all, his research that had pointed the way. Faust had no objection to that. He would bide his time, watch for his opportunity. All three were long-lived, all three ambitious. Over the centuries, he guessed, alliances would form and break apart, each of them would scramble for supremacy from time to time.

Knowing that, Faust would be prepared to seize the advantage when it was presented to him. Power was grasped only with difficulty, but once captured, it could be held if the owner's resolve was sufficient and his preparations adequate. To Felix Faust, what mattered was not so much who held the power when the alliance was formed as who did when it ended.

As they walked, flames licked toward the sky from fields and outbuildings set afire by Morgaine's forces. Arthur's half sister, Morgaine Le Fey, had made it her life's goal to destroy Camelot. She hated Arthur and all he stood for. Camelot, to her, represented light, the power of good. The knights of the Round Table, Lancelot, Gawain, and the rest, took up noble causes, and Arthur supported their efforts. But while Arthur's mother and father were both human—although only married after his bastard birth—Morgaine was the spawn of Arthur's father Uther and a child of Faerie, who had enchanted Uther into believing her human. Upon learning of the deception, Uther had them both cast out of his kingdom and denied all responsibility for them. Raised by her mother, Morgaine had learned to despise everything that reminded her of her father. Arthur, the favored child, most especially.

After years of smaller-scale attempts, she and her cousin Mordred had finally amassed an army. She brought together soldiers from Gaul, from Rome, from Germania and the northern regions, and promised them the plunder of the richest kingdom in Britain, if not the Earth. To supplement these legions she added armies from Faerie and more from Hell—demons and pixies and sprites, monsters of every type and description. Together, her soldiers surrounded Camelot, put the torch to the fields outside its walls, and hammered incessantly on the castle itself.

Savage interrupted Faust's reverie by stopping and pointing with the scepter. "There!" he declared. "He is the one we seek!"

A small hut, its thatched roof half-scorched but its mud walls yet standing, loomed through the gloom and smoke. Through a doorway Faust could see the glowing red of a forge, and he heard the clank of steel striking steel.

"Who is this one, that Morgaine has spared his worthless life?" Mordru asked.

"A peasant," Savage explained. "But a smith, who can make weapons to replace those lost in battle, repair mail, and the like. He is useful to her, so she allows him to live." The sorcerer laughed. "Although, should his usefulness expire, I would not like to wear his boots."

"And why have we come to him?" Faust asked.

"Because there is something we require of him," Savage said. "Him, and his forge."

They walked up a bare, burned slope and into the hut. The smell of burning coals and hot steel competed with the fetid stink of burned fields. At the forge worked a man with the muscular arms common to smiths and a white streak in his brown hair. His arms and forehead were slicked with sweat. He looked up when the trio entered, surprise widening his eyes and elevating his brow. He was the first mortal to see them since they'd left Camelot, Faust knew. He gave a bow—not low enough for Faust's satisfaction, but since they had come to make use of his skills, the sorcerer was willing to forgive it.

"My lords," the smith said, by way of greeting. "What is your pleasure?"

"Word of your skill with the forge spreads widely, Jason Blood," Savage said. He smiled at the peasant—but then his smile, Faust thought, was enough to make women hide their young. "We three have need of your abilities."

A second bow. "Of course, my lords," the peasant called Blood said. "Whatever you desire."

"Three triangles," Savage told him. He touched the tips of his thumbs together to make a lower line, then brought the ends of his first fingers toward each other, forming a triangle. "About this size. Iron. The three must be identical in every aspect, size, weight, coloration. Is that understood?"

"Certainly, my lord," the peasant said. His voice was as uncultured as all his kind, as if someone had given the power of speech to the beasts that had grazed these fields before Morgaine's forces had torched them. "When will you need these, pray tell?"

"We shall wait," Savage said. "Outside, where the air is some fresher than in here. Tarry not."

"Not I, my lord." The man bowed once more and set to work immediately. Savage ticked his head toward the door, and the three left him to his labors.

* * *

Before the sun set, the three of them were back inside Camelot. Vandal Savage had refused to explain what he wanted the triangles for, but promised that all would become clear soon enough. He had led them back to the room in which they had first met. A fire blazed in a fireplace tall enough to stand in, and the three had drawn chairs around it. Savage bade each one lay his own triangle on the stones between them and the fireplace, and he arranged them, overlapping one another, to form a nine-pointed star.

Then, as Faust and Mordru looked on, Savage stood before the fire and threw his hands into the air. "Wizard, I, ere time began, I summon the demon, Etrigan!" he shouted.

Faust caught Mordru's gaze. The big mage nodded, almost imperceptibly. So he agreed—Savage had gone a little mad already.

Vandal Savage simply waited, fists on his hips. Within seconds, a puff of smoke, less substantial than a child's breath on a winter's day, had formed in front of him. As Faust and Mordru looked on, the smoke grew in size and solidity, until, moments later, a yellow-skinned demon crouched on the stones there, accompanied by the stink of sulfur and ozone.

Faust blinked twice. He had seen plenty of demons in his time—one couldn't look out the castle walls without spotting some. But this one glared at them with a fierce, red-eyed intelligence that the others lacked. Massively built, with arms and legs like the limbs of a giant tree and a muscled torso as thick as the tree's trunk. All he wore was a red bodice, long-sleeved, with ruffles at the wrists, braceleted at the forearms, belted at the waist. Below the waist, the cloth continued, covering his privates and little more and leaving his legs bare. Soft-sided red-leather slouch boots protected his feet, and a blue cape, verging on purple, was clasped at his neck by what looked like a broken medallion.

The outfit was odd enough. Odder still was the creature wearing it. His skin was yellow, dotted here and there with big, protruding welts. His head was huge and mostly round. His eyes glowed red, like burning coals. His wide mouth revealed gigantic, jagged teeth, with pronounced upper and lower canines, like fangs. Ears like bat wings jutted out to the sides. Above a ridgelike brow rose two short, sharp horns.

The demon seemed to know who had summoned it, because after regarding the room, he settled his gaze on Savage.

"Whosoever summons me'd best be prepared, if his life he would like spared," the demon said. His voice sounded like the scrape of a portcullis sliding toward the ground. *With innocents bound there, to be spiked by its points,* Faust thought. The demon continued. "Of tasks at hand I have too many, while of time and patience I haven't any."

"Calm yourself, Etrigan," Savage said. "What I've in store for you will be quick indeed, and shall not task you o'ermuch."

"A Rhymer, eh?" Mordru asked. "Curious."

The demon's face turned ferocious as he glared at Mordru. "No Rhymer I, at least not as yet. But practice breeds virtuosity; better and better will I get."

Faust couldn't contain a roar of laughter at the beast's

response, and the thing fixed his red glare on him. "There once was a wizard from Kent," the demon said dismissively. "Whose mind had a sinister bent. His spells were so weak, naught but bubble and squeak, his incantations seem'd flatulent."

Savage and Mordru broke into laughter at that. Felix Faust felt his face flush, his hands draw into tight fists, but the anger broke, and he joined in with the others, throwing his head back and roaring. Even the demon seemed to smile, but the expression was repugnant, and he might just have been opening his mouth to pick the flesh of infants from his teeth, as far as Faust could judge.

Impatient, the demon whirled back to Savage. "What is it you want done, then?" He leaned very close to Savage's face, so that the mage drew back reflexively. "And keep in mind, I do this boon because you summoned me, but it's one and one only you'll get."

"A simple task is all I ask," Savage said with a grin at his own rhyme. "These iron triangles you see? I need them forged into one by the heat of your breath."

"In this configuration?" Etrigan asked.

"Aye," Savage replied. "Just so."

"Stand back, then," the demon commanded. All three sorcerers stepped away from the fireplace, in front of which the triangles lay on the stone floor. Etrigan sucked in a great breath, puffing out his chest, then bent forward at the waist and blew out a thunderous plume of flame directed straight down toward the shapes at his feet. The room filled with an odor like that of the peasant's forge, but more concentrated and with an undertone that reminded Faust of the spoiled meat the three had eaten at their first encounter, only more intense, as if he found himself inside a rotting bull.

After the flame died away, the demon reached down and lifted the iron, now fused in the nine-pointed star shape Savage had indicated. The metal still glowed, white-hot, but the demon paid no mind. "Like this?" he asked.

"Aye," Savage said again. "That's it exactly, Etrigan. Well done."

"Save your compliments," the demon said. "I've stayed too long; Merlin'll be wondering where I've gone."

"Leave it on the floor, then," Savage instructed him. "It's too hot to touch with our hands."

The demon set the iron star back where he had been told to and walked to the door. Faust had expected him to dematerialize, perhaps. But he had been drawn here by Savage's spell, and apparently would leave under his own power.

When Etrigan was gone, Savage beckoned the others nearer to the star. It had faded from white to red. "The time has come to formalize our bond," Savage said. "To set into motion events that will take centuries to bring to full fruition."

"Fortunately, centuries mean little to us," Mordru said. "Else my patience would be sorely tested."

"I never promised a speedy result," Savage reminded them. "Something on this enormous a scale is, by nature, a slow process."

"Yes, yes, we're all agreed on that," Faust said. He knew the changes they sought would take time to come about, but his patience waned at the incessant jabbering of his fellows. He wanted to get started. "What comes next?"

"The bond of brotherhood," Savage answered, blessedly succinct. He lowered his gaze to the iron star once more. The glowing red had faded in spots. "We must all grasp it together," he said. "And lift it above our heads."

"But . . . it's burning hot," Faust pointed out.

"Are you a weakling, then," Mordru asked. "To be dissuaded by mere physical discomfort?"

"Not I," Faust said quickly.

"Let's do it, then, my brothers," Savage said. He reached for the star. The others joined him, and three hands touched it at the same moment. Faust bit the inside of his cheek, trying to ignore the burning pain that lanced up through the palm of his hand. Tasting blood, he straightened and, with the others, held it high. Only Mordru did not extend his arm to its full capacity, or else Faust and Savage could never have held on.

"By this act are we bound, three into one," Savage recited. A cool wind blew through the room, although the door remained shut, and it was an interior space without windows. The wind picked up as Savage continued, whipping the hair and robes of the sorcerers, whisking Savage's words into the ether the moment he spoke them. "By this act, we rouge the sun. Time's course flows as we desire, Earth dances to our triple choir."

Faust could barely hear the words now, so powerfully did the wind batter them. In response, Savage raised his voice, shouting the words toward the ceiling, toward the heavens, as if in challenge. "By this act, we three shall reign, man's future's ours to free or chain."

The wind redoubled, carrying the scents of sage, of copper, of freshly turned earth. Faust, knocked off-balance, had to take a step to one side, spreading his legs wider to remain upright against the furious gale. Mordru bent like a willow, while Savage stood his ground, feet far apart, letting it buffet him. "By this act does Earth divide, to merge again when we decide!" he shouted.

At that, the wind died instantly. Savage grinned like a mad bear and released the star. Faust and Mordru did the same. The nine-pointed object hovered by itself for a moment, revolving above them, its points catching firelight and flinging it to the corners of the room. Then it fell to the stone floor with a dull clank.

Savage held up his right hand, palm out, displaying the seared flesh where he had gripped the star. Faust copied his act, then Mordru. The three of them clasped fists, all together, and held tight. "It is done," Savage said.

"Begun, at any rate," Mordru corrected.

"As good as," Faust said. "From here, brothers, though our schemes may suffer defeat, all remember that in the end, we shall prevail. Earth—the one and only true Earth—shall belong to we three."

Savage chuckled, a horrible, sinister sound. "And what a glorious time we'll have with her," he said. "Glorious, indeed."

CHAPTER EIGHT

May 1872

In the dream, Wise Owl saw a wolf running away from the wind, instead of facing into it sniffing the scents it carried, as he would naturally prefer. He was an old warrior of a wolf, gray and black, with nicks in his ears and a scar running from his lip halfway across his muzzle, but he ran with his tail down, afraid. From this, Wise Owl knew that something was not right. Nothing he could do would change this, though; he was an observer in the dream, not a participant. At different moments he saw from the vantage point of an eagle soaring over the land, or a field mouse peering nervously from its den beneath the roots of a creosote bush, or a coyote nosing its way through the rabbitbrush and thistles.

After the wolf had passed, Wise Owl saw why it ran. A face scowled down from the heavens, from the wind and the clouds and a sky that had turned crimson although sunset was hours away yet and sunrise long since past. The face was filled with rage, although Wise Owl couldn't see why.

But as he watched from those shifting viewpoints, the

sky turned darker and darker, traces of blue mixing like the juice of berries in with the red until it was a fierce violet, and then the rain started to fall, fat drops spattering the dry desert ground like tears of blood. A raven huddled under a saguaro arm, feathers puffed out, afraid to fly.

Within seconds, the ground was saturated, and then some. Trickles became torrents, flash floods filled the washes and splashed over boulders, churning the dun earth, carving muddy rivers. When the water receded, the detritus was not just measured in uprooted bushes and downed trees. Wise Owl saw eagle feathers and beaded shirts, scraps of buckskin and velvet, ornaments of turquoise and silver, all caked into the mud. Spears and arrows poked out as if warriors had tried to fight the blood river, and failed.

When he woke up, Wise Owl's bed was wet with perspiration. He trembled, and not just from evening's chill. Images from the dream stayed with him—the raging skies, the tears of blood, the unstoppable river. Crossing to the window of the hacienda, he looked out. A peaceful moon shone down on tiled roofs and the scent of bougainvillea tickled his nose. The courtyard was empty, its central fountain trickling gently. In a few hours, the sun would rise. Chickens would scratch and claw at the dirt there, clucking and squawking. People would hurry across it to their chores, or dawdle by the fountain, enjoying the play of sunlight on the water.

He could not wait that long.

Wise Owl was a shaman, wise in more than just his name. He had learned at the knees of his grandfather and his father how to read the signs nature offered. He understood magic, and portents, and visions.

He understood that the dream had been more than just a dream.

It had been a warning.

Something was coming—not here to Puerta Del Sol, California, but to his ancestral homeland. The landscape he had seen in the dream had been that one, not the rolling hills here that led down to the ocean's edge. And whatever it was—in this regard, the symbolism was admittedly murky—it was not something good.

The dream would not have been sent to him if he were not expected to try to do something about it. Since he didn't know exactly what the threat was, when it would arrive, or how to combat it, his options were limited.

Only two things were certain. One was that he could not stay here in California. He had to go home—to his ancestral homelands, the Apache country—as quickly as possible.

The other was that, as an old man, even one attuned to the forces of magic that swirled around him, there was much that he could no longer do by himself.

But that was not a problem. There was one who could do all the physical things Wise Owl could not, and more. To look at Lazarus Lane, immobilized, spending his days in a wheelchair with a blanket over his lap, one would think him incapable of standing upright, much less anything more demanding.

And one would, Wise Owl knew, be correct.

It wasn't Lazarus Lane who would help him fight whatever threat loomed over the Apache country. It was the one known as El Diablo, who was a physical manifestation of Lazarus Lane's spirit. Although Wise Owl's old friend Lazarus had been left in a perpetual coma by a bolt of lightning, his spirit had been strong, and with Wise Owl's help and ministrations, a new kind of balance had been achieved. Lazarus Lane no longer moved of his own free will, but the strength that burned inside him found expression in the deeds of El Diablo, who emerged to fight for the weak, the oppressed, and the powerless whenever Wise Owl summoned him.

El Diablo could help Wise Owl protect the sacred lands of his birth, even if Lazarus Lane could not. But Lazarus had to be taken east, into Apache country. Wise Owl readied a buckboard and two horses, then went into the room where his old friend slept.

"Lazarus," he said softly. He had never been sure if Lazarus could really hear him or just how much consciousness remained in his still body. El Diablo heard, though, so Wise Owl spoke to Lazarus just as he had before the man's accident. "We must go, at once. Something threatens the Apache people, something I fear will require all the skills and strength of El Diablo to defeat. I'm sorry to disturb your slumber, my friend. Come, let me help you up."

Youth had left Wise Owl behind. His hair was straight, still black but with traces of gray, framing a face that could have served as a map to the Arizona Territory's canyonlands. His muscles were lean and stringy, not as strong as they had been in younger days. Lazarus's body had become as light as a bird's, though. If his bones weren't hollow, they might as well have been. Wise Owl was able to dress Lazarus, gently wiping a bit of spittle from the man's lips with his own callused hand, then he scooped Lazarus up in his arms and deposited him carefully in the wheeled chair, whispering meaningless words of comfort.

With Lazarus in the chair, Wise Owl quickly threw

more clothing and a couple of blankets into a carpetbag for him. Resting the bag in Lazarus's lap, he wheeled the chair outside into the courtyard where he had left horse and buckboard.

In the wagon he kept two sturdy planks. He drew them out so that they leaned from the wagon's bed to the ground, and used them as a ramp for Lazarus's chair. Inside the bed, he rolled the chair to a point just behind the seat, looking forward, so Lazarus would feel—if he felt at all—like a passenger instead of cargo. Wise Owl lashed the chair to the buckboard and Lazarus into the chair, with a blanket wrapped around him for warmth against the nighttime chill.

"Another journey for us, Lazarus," he said as he climbed up onto the driver's seat, behind the pair of horses. He held the reins in one hand and gave them a shake. The horses nickered softly and set out as one. "One of many. Any luck, this one will be brief, eh, and we'll be home in no time."

Even as he spoke the words, he knew they were probably not true. He would drive the wagon to Apache country as fast as he could. He would pray, along the way, that they arrived soon enough to help.

But it would be no easy trip, and if they made it back to Puerta Del Sol at all, he would be glad.

There was every chance, however, when he looked back on the hacienda from the crest of the hill, in the first glimmerings of dawn, that it would be the last time he would ever see it.

CHAPTER NINE

The Phantom Stranger had learned many, many things during his extended lifetime. One lesson, reiterated in different ways nearly every day, was that while human nature could be predicted or anticipated, it could never be known. Coming to this alternate time stream's Earth had been a gamble. Clark Kent might well have turned them down, rejected their offer outright, even summoned the authorities.

That Clark had not was a fortunate turn of events—the one he and Jason Blood had hoped for without quite daring to expect. Of course, the other thing the Stranger had been unable to anticipate was the murder of Lois Lane. Whether that had been providential or coincidence, he did not want to speculate. It had, however, sealed the deal for Clark better than anything the Stranger and Jason could have said.

Jason had been the first to discern rumblings about the other time stream. He made a point, as did the Stranger, of keeping attuned to the occult world, to Earth's ley lines and the points at which dimensions collided with one another. But the Stranger had been busy with other matters, and so Jason had come to him with his concerns. The two spent two days in research, studying what had likely happened and what might be done about it, and they had reached the conclusion that they needed Superman's help.

But not just Superman's. They also needed Clark's. Superman alone would not have the flexibility they needed to move between worlds, dimensions, times. The protective spells cast by Savage, Faust, and Mordru would block him, or worse.

So here they were, doing their best to sell this Earth's Clark Kent on making a visit to the other Earth. Just when it looked as if they would be successful, however, the Stranger realized that they were about to be interrupted.

And not in a good way.

"We need to go," the Phantom Stranger said abruptly.

"What is it?" Jason Blood asked.

"We have been detected," the Stranger said. "Vandal Savage's magic, no doubt."

"Go where?" Clark Kent asked. "I'm still not sure exactly what it is you're asking me to do."

"We can explain on the way," the Stranger answered. "There isn't time now."

"What do you mean, detected?" Clark wanted to know. He had agreed to go along with whatever plan these two had in mind, but he had hoped to know more about it before he was thrust into the middle.

"Most people on this Earth are simply duplicates of ones who also exist on the true Earth," Jason explained.

"Or the descendants of duplicates, anyway, since this one was created long ago. But the Stranger and I—we're unique. We've never existed in this time stream, and we're alien to it. Savage no doubt has sensors watching for just this sort of thing, unfamiliar magical signatures."

Clark had sensed there was something unusual about Jason Blood, but this was the first time the man had hinted that he, as well as the Stranger, was some sort of magical being. "What will he do about it?"

"There are already shock troops in your neighborhood, Clark," the Stranger said. "They approach, even now."

"Shock troops?" Clark echoed. "What's that mean?"

"You don't want to know if you can help it," Jason said.

"But . . . what are they going to do?"

Before anyone could answer, the building vibrated. The rapid pop pop pop of small-arms fire sounded outside.

"It's already begun," Jason announced.

Clark ran to the window, looked down. In the street below, illuminated by his building's own floodlights, soldiers moved toward the apartment like a tide surging into shore. Again, he heard the staccato of firing, accompanied by shrieks of fear and pain.

"They're shooting people!" Clark shouted. "My neighbors! They're looking for you two, you've got to do something. Give yourselves up, something!"

"Clark, we can't risk that," the Stranger said.

"Do I really have to remind you, Kent?" Jason added. "None of these people, your neighbors, were *meant* to exist. When the worlds converge, they won't anyway. They're all doomed. I'd rather spare them the pain of this, but the fact is, the sooner we get going, the better off everybody is, on both Earths."

The building shook again, from the heavy footfalls of many armored soldiers.

"Okay," Clark said. "Let's go, then. I can't stand here and listen to this."

"Very well," the Phantom Stranger said. He started toward Clark, one hand outstretched, but before the two made contact, Clark's front door was blown off its hinges by an explosive charge. Acrid smoke filled the room, and soldiers in gray, olive, white, and tan urban camo-patterned uniforms and body armor flooded through the door.

"You men! Freeze!" the first soldier inside commanded.

"Hold them off, Blood!" the Stranger said. He raised a hand toward the soldiers, as if dismissing them, and the men stopped in their tracks, horror showing on their faces. Clark couldn't see what they saw, but they stared at their weapons as if they had become some sort of alien entities clutched in their fists.

"I think there's someone who can do that better than I, Stranger," Jason Blood said. "But thanks for providing a distraction."

Blood's face took on a grim expression and he uttered words which made no sense to Clark.

At first, anyway.

"Gone, gone, the form of man," Jason intoned. "Rise the demon Etrigan!"

The transformation happened so fast that Clark couldn't follow it with his eye. Jason Blood stood there, then he was gone. In his place was a massively muscled, hulking, horned yellow beast, wearing a red body stocking and briefs, with a purplish cape.

"Umm . . ." Clark said. He didn't believe in magic, but couldn't think of any other reasonable explanation for what he'd seen. Except, perhaps, temporary insanity. "Is that *supposed* to be here?"

"That's Etrigan," the Stranger said. "I need a minute here, and he can give it to us."

The soldiers were already recovering from whatever the Phantom Stranger had done, which Clark guessed was simply casting an illusion of some kind. They surged forward, but Etrigan leapt past Clark with a huge bound, right into the thick of them. Deafening gunfire sounded, and bullets bounced off Etrigan's hide as if he were made of Kevlar. He tore into them like an enraged lion, snarling and spitting, and for a moment Clark felt sorry for the soldiers, facing an implacable foe with weapons that had no effect on him. Finally, he looked away, aghast at the carnage he saw.

The Phantom Stranger, meanwhile, was busy with his own activity. He had created another shimmering section of space, bigger than the one through which Clark had watched Lois die. For a brief moment, the soldiers' attack had driven that memory from his mind, but now it rushed back, smashing into him with the physical effect of a two-by-four in the skull. Clark's knees turned to liquid, and he dropped back onto the leather sofa.

None of what swirled around him made any sense. A monster the color of gourmet mustard ripped a bunch of American soldiers to shreds—soldiers who seemed to have been sent to kill or at least arrest the two freaks who had shown up in Clark's apartment, and who might, in fact, have been sent to save Clark. Lois was dead. The Phantom Stranger busily did . . . something, which Clark didn't understand, but he was totally immersed in it, paying no attention whatsoever to Etrigan or Clark. If what they said was true, then not only was Lois gone, but soon, with no chance for good-byes, he would lose his parents, boyhood sweetheart Lana Lang, Perry White, his boss at the *Planet,* Jimmy Olsen, his coworker and friend, and everyone else he had ever known.

Clark couldn't shake the feeling that it was all a surrealistic nightmare of some kind, and he willed himself to wake up, to find himself writhing in his covers, back in the normal grind that was his everyday life.

Instead of waking up, he saw everything in excruciating detail. The demon that Jason Blood had become dug his claws through a soldier's uniform, into his arm, and wrenched it off. Blood fountained from the wound, splattering Clark's ceiling and carpet. Etrigan swung the arm in a circle over his head and used it to club the injured soldier in the face, knocking him back into his terrified comrades.

Across the room, the Phantom Stranger worked feverishly, silently, mouth compressed into a grim line. The space he had demarcated with his hands had turned darker, and Clark thought he could see flashes of light within it, like distant lightning viewed through heavy storm clouds.

As Clark looked on, the Stranger turned to face him. "Clark, Etrigan," he said, urgency in his voice. "Time to go."

"Go?" Etrigan echoed. His voice sounded like a food processor full of broken glass. "No! I've just begun to have my fun, as this garrison strives to overrun. Some simpleton thought to shoot poor Etrigan with his puny gun, now he's sent to oblivion. And if you think my rhyme is done, then you'll soon see—"

"Etrigan!" the Stranger shouted, louder and with more force this time. "Now!"

Etrigan tossed a shrug and a frown toward Clark. "He thinks that I'm some myrmidon," he said softly. Then with a single leap he crossed the room, astonished soldiers left behind, and dived through the flickering, wavering spot the Phantom Stranger had made.

"It's a portal of some kind?" Clark asked.

The Stranger beckoned him anxiously. "I cannot believe there is someone more stubborn than Etrigan," he said. "Go through!"

Clark started toward the Stranger, worried about what the soldiers might do without Etrigan's bulk shielding him from their weapons. "To where?" he asked. "Where does it go?"

The Phantom Stranger grabbed Clark's arm to help push him through the portal.

"To Hell, Clark," he replied. "It goes to Hell."

CHAPTER **TEN**

Clark didn't believe in magic, but he had seen it on prominent display, right in front of him. He wasn't so keen on the concept of Hell, either. Once again, however, he couldn't bring himself to deny his own senses.

And Hell was nothing if not a sensory overload experience.

The first thing that struck him was the sound. He had just gone through the Phantom Stranger's portal, and was disoriented, his stomach heaving, his vision blurred. But he could hear.

It took several seconds to understand just what it was he did hear, to isolate meaning from the overall din. What seemed to be just ear-shattering noise, without form or purpose, gradually revealed itself to be voices raised in wails of pain and horror. Not a few voices, not even a thousand, but billions. Tens of billions. Clark clapped his hands over his ears. Useless. The voices penetrated as easily as if they were inside his skull. He could barely think, and already dizzy from the portal, he feared the noise would knock him off-balance.

"You will get used to it," the Stranger said. He didn't seem to shout, to raise his voice at all, but Clark heard him as clearly as if they were still back in his apartment.

"Are you sure?" Clark said, not at all certain he was making a sound.

"For some of us, it feels like home," Etrigan said. "Friend Cerberus's dear catacomb."

The sound of their voices—not yet familiar, but more so than anything else in this place—acted as a kind of grounding agent for Clark. He regained his balance, and his vision began to clear. He could identify scents—sulfur and molten lead and ammonia—and could make out others he couldn't quite determine, which reminded him of burning oil and seared meat. He had expected heat, as soon as the Phantom Stranger revealed his portal's destination, but was surprised to discover that it seemed no hotter than a Metropolis summer day, even though, all around him, flames licked up from gaps in the floor, dripped like liquid from above, and he realized that underneath the cries of the damned was a roar of constant, raging fire. He could taste the heat, like sucking in a big breath just as the lighter fluid ignited, but although he started sweating almost immediately, he didn't fear incineration.

What surprised Clark the most was how much it looked like what he would have expected. The effect was of an enormous cavern: the world turned inside out. Flames coiled down stalactites and dripped toward the floor, but from such heights that they burned themselves out before ever hitting. Stalagmites thrust upward, raw and jagged, some looking slick with ooze. Fire everywhere, the flickering light Clark had seen through the Phantom Stranger's doorway. And shadows, thrown by firelight, wavering and unsteady. The shadows, utterly impenetrable, might have been as deep as the Grand Canyon or as shallow as a closet.

Clark realized he had been turning in a slow circle, revolving like a top on its final, diminutive spins, trying to take in the incredible landscape. Even the keening noise seemed to have faded into background, so he could speak and hear. "So this is it," he said, full of wonder. "This is really Hell? The one in the Bible?"

"I would rather not enter into theological discussion just now," the Stranger said. "That question has more answers than we have time for."

"Why are we here?" Clark asked. "Not exactly a tourist destination, is it?"

"We are not exactly tourists," the Stranger said. "Or particularly welcome here. We are just passing through—it's the best pathway between the two Earths."

"The Hell you say," Etrigan called out. He scampered across the rocky outcroppings like a puppy exploring a new home. "You spoilsport. I want to play; you live to thwart. Now I inveigh, let me cavort, then we'll away, with my support."

The Stranger glanced toward Clark—a strange effect, since his eyes were still invisible in the shade of his hat's wide brim. "He is like a child when he comes back here. He'll settle down shortly."

"He said he was born here?" Clark asked.

"That's right. Etrigan, son of Belial, half brother to Myrddin, whom you may know as Merlin."

"Merlin the magician? King Arthur, all that?"

"That's the one," the Stranger said.

"So that's all true, too?"

"Again, not so easily answered, Clark. There are legions of stories about Arthur and Camelot. Some are certainly true, others are not. And then there are other aspects, like Etrigan's contribution, that are ignored by legend."

Clark shook his head. This was all too much to take in. "So he's, what, some kind of devil?"

"A demon, to be precise," the Stranger replied.

"And Jason Blood is just a disguise?"

"Not at all. He would, more accurately, be described as a host. Blood was chosen by Merlin himself to be joined with Etrigan. Sometimes it is easier, particularly in the human world, to take that form, and Blood helps keep Etrigan in check. Believe me, you would not want to live on an Earth where Etrigan roamed free. Here, however, Etrigan's demonic aspect is more useful." He looked toward where the demon leapt and capered. "Do not let his appearance deceive you. He is deadly serious when he needs to be, and although it takes all my will and power of persuasion, he will make this transit with us. And we will be glad for his presence."

"If you say so," Clark said. "So far he looks more like a nuisance. And does he always do that rhyming thing?"

"He is a Rhymer," the Stranger said. "It is an exalted position in the pantheon of the underworld. He worked hard to attain it."

"So yes, in other words."

"I have been described as occasionally loquacious," the Stranger admitted.

"I'll bet."

The Phantom Stranger looked toward the ceiling, so far away it couldn't be observed, like a man judging the time by the position of the sun. "We should be on our way," he said. "It does not do to spend too much time motionless in this place. People have been known to grow roots."

Clark decided it was safest not to assume the dark man exaggerated.

"Can you rein him in?" Clark asked. There was still so much he wanted to know—about Etrigan, and the Stranger himself, and what they were doing in Hell, how he could even be alive, and conscious, and walking through it. Apparently this wasn't the time to sit down for a cup of coffee and a long chat, though. He would have to resign himself to asking what he could, when he found the chance.

"Usually," the Stranger said. *Great,* Clark thought. *He's admitting that sometimes he can't.*

Etrigan was nearly out of sight behind a waterfall of flame. "Etrigan!" the Phantom Stranger called. The demon either didn't hear, or pretended not to, so the Stranger repeated his summons, louder. "Etrigan!" The Phantom Stranger's voice boomed like a fighter plane breaking the sound barrier. Clark thought that the keening of the damned stopped for a moment, but that might have been his skewed perception of the unearthly noise, which seemed to grow ever fainter the longer he stayed in Hell.

Etrigan noticed. His huge round head snapped around as if it had been attached to a rubber band. "Caution, Phantom Stranger, lest you put us all in danger," he said in a loud stage whisper. "Clichéd walls have ears, and one never knows what hears!"

He sounded genuinely worried, which concerned Clark. If Etrigan, a native of Hell, was scared by the place, then what chance did he have? For all the talk about some alternate version of him being Superman, he, decidedly, was Clark Kent. Etrigan could knock the stuffing out of him like a toddler with a piñata. He didn't even want to see anything that could pose a threat to the big demon.

"He's right," the Stranger said, to Clark's dismay. "It would not do to call unnecessary attention to our presence here."

"But . . . you've been through here before, right?" Clark asked.

"Of course," the Stranger assured him. "This is the route we took to your Earth in the first place. Roughly. Our destination is different than our starting point, so we will be adjusting accordingly."

"We're not going to Metropolis?"

The Phantom Stranger offered that not-quite-smile again. "Hardly."

Before Clark could ask for clarification, Etrigan bounded to their sides, a troubled look on his face. "Ungetines!" he said. "They fill a ravine, careen toward us 'crost lands subterene!"

"Ungetines?" Clark repeated.

"You do not want to know," the Stranger said. "Come quickly."

The Phantom Stranger and Etrigan started to run, and Clark joined in. He had no sense of direction here—everything looked the same, cavernous and lit only by flames that came and went capriciously. Becoming separated from them was the last thing he wanted.

As they ran, Etrigan kept glancing over his shoulder.

Clark, afraid to look, finally let curiosity get the better of him and was immediately sorry he had done so.

The Ungetines, if that's indeed what they were, had emerged from the ravine Etrigan mentioned and charged toward them across a relatively flat plain. Their numbers were such that at first glance they looked like a single, undulating mass. Clark's right foot struck a protruding rock and he nearly stumbled, but caught himself before he went down. Regaining his balance, he risked another quick peek back.

As they were closer now, Clark could make out individuals, although he wouldn't have been able to tell one from another. They all shared certain characteristics. All were naked, it seemed, with flesh of a pale whitish gray. They had four limbs, but it was impossible to distinguish arms from legs. All four limbs depended from a trunk barely bigger around than the limbs themselves, and shorter, like a stub of a cigar with four longer, slightly thinner cigars jammed into it. The front limbs were shorter than the rear, so the torsos seemed to recline even as they dashed forward. Each of the limbs ended in a many-fingered "hand," the digits of which clutched at the ground, then pushed off, helping the creatures attain speed on the rocky surface. Small tentacles, maybe the thickness of garden hoses and ranging from nine to twenty inches in length, hung in seemingly random spots around their trunks and limbs, coiling and reaching and snapping like tiny whips.

Worst of all, they had no heads. None visible, at any rate. No facial features of any kind, nothing that looked like sensory organs. The trunks tapered to rounded, fleshy points.

At least they won't be eating us, Clark thought as he

hurried to keep up with the Stranger and Etrigan. The absurdity of the thought almost made him laugh in spite of the situation.

The Phantom Stranger's next words knocked any thoughts of humor from him. "No use!" the dark man announced. "We cannot outrun them!"

We sure can't outfight them! Clark thought. He hadn't counted, but guessed there were somewhat fewer than a hundred of the beings.

Not many fewer, though.

The Stranger pulled up short, and beside him, Etrigan spun around, his substantial knuckles resting on the ground, apelike. He glanced over at Clark and grinned. Clark wondered if the demon had gone completely insane.

"We get to fight 'em, use our fists to kill and smite 'em!" Etrigan said.

"And that sounds like fun to you?"

"You'd do what, try to gaslight 'em?"

The demon didn't wait for an answer, but rushed forward to meet their charge, a horrific roar escaping from his lips as he did. The Stranger put a hand on Clark's shoulder, as if he might have to restrain Clark from joining Etrigan's attack.

No chance of that.

"What can he do against all of those things?" Clark asked.

"More than you think," the Phantom Stranger said. "I'll do what I can to help, but using magic here is a tricky proposition. It does not always work out the way one intends."

"What are they?" Clark wanted to know. The reporter's curiosity, even in the face of almost certain death. No official press releases would be forthcoming explaining this phenomenon, he was sure.

"The souls of those who've lost all hope," the Stranger replied. "They have been here so long, with no way out, no hope to change their status, no chance for advancement in Hell's class structure, that this is what they become. This is a small group of them, of course, but they tend to travel this way, in packs. Hell's regents prefer it that way, since together they number in the trillions."

Etrigan didn't hesitate when he reached the surging rush of the Ungetines. Within seconds, he was out of sight. Clark feared that he had gone down, overwhelmed by their sheer numbers. But then, in the midst of the faceless creatures, he saw an upset in the ranks. It didn't take long to realize that when he'd been fighting the soldiers, back at Clark's apartment, the demon had been pulling his punches.

If they'd had mouths, he was sure the Ungetines would have been screaming. As it was, except for those of Etrigan's utterances that made their way across the distance, the battle was conducted without vocalization. The impact of fist upon flesh made noise, as did the rending of tissue and spattering of blood, so pale green it almost seemed to glow.

More and more of the creatures swarmed toward the spot where Etrigan had closed ranks with them, as if forgetting that Clark and the Phantom Stranger stood watching, seemingly unprotected.

Which was okay with Clark. His journalist's curiosity didn't extend to wondering how it might feel to be torn apart by faceless hell-beings.

The Stranger didn't wait around for them to remember.

He gestured toward the unseen ceiling and spoke a few words Clark didn't recognize. But the impact of his words made itself known almost immediately.

A groaning noise sounded overhead, and then from the shadows a huge stalactite plummeted into the midst of the Ungetines, landing with a thunderous crash. Dust kicked into the air, almost obscuring the battle. "Be careful you don't hit Etrigan!" Clark warned.

"He can take care of himself."

The darkness erupted again with a resounding cracking sound, and more missiles fell toward the scrambling creatures. This time, several dropped at once, different sizes, and Clark saw Ungetines smashed by rocks as small as cars and as large as buildings. Rubble tossed aside by the falling stalactites hit Clark's chest and face, even though the action took place a considerable distance away.

"Clark," the Stranger said, his voice tight. "This isn't good."

I hate it when he says things like that, Clark thought. He was about to ask what the problem was when the ground shifted beneath his feet. "Earthquake?"

"Worse," the Stranger said. "Hellquake!"

The Ungetines—those not already destroyed by Etrigan or falling rock—scattered, most heading back in the direction from which they'd come. Clark would have been happier about the retreat if the ground hadn't been rolling underneath him like a flimsy rope bridge in a powerful wind.

Etrigan emerged from the mass of bodies and roiling dust, scurrying back toward Clark and the Stranger, luminous green blood smeared all over his body and clothing.

"This way!" the Phantom Stranger urged, tugging

Clark's arm. He and Clark started running before Etrigan reached them, though they had only gone a few steps before the demon caught up. The Stranger directed them toward a narrow gap Clark hadn't seen before, a kind of canyon of dark, porous rock. Just behind them, the noises grew louder, as if the very walls of Hell itself were collapsing, its floor splitting apart. Clark glanced back to see if he was right.

Mistake.

When he looked forward again, the Phantom Stranger and Etrigan were out of sight. Had they already reached the canyon? It seemed far away still—farther now than it had a moment ago.

It took Clark a second to realize it was not the canyon's position that was changing, but the light. Where before Hell's intermittent flames had provided enough light to see by, the Hellquake seemed to have extinguished all the fires in the immediate area. The effect was like late dusk, and getting darker by the second.

"Phantom Stranger!" he called. "Etrigan!"

No response reached his ears. The ground beneath his feet warped and wavered, making him unsteady on his feet. They had been headed toward the canyon, so that was still the best course of action. The darkness, though, descended like a curtain, from the roof down, and in moments he was wrapped in it. "Phantom Stranger!" he shouted again.

The canyon had been directly ahead. He'd turned around, however, to look behind. Had he returned to exactly the same position? If he simply headed forward, would he reach it? Since he didn't know how far away it was, he didn't know if a degree or two of difference would send him a few feet out of his way, or a thousand yards.

He had to chance it. The Hellquake, or its aftershocks, continued to reverberate. Debris fell from overhead, huge rocks that, from the sounds they made, could crush him in an instant. If the canyon led to safety he needed to get there.

Why did I agree to this?

Truth be told, he hadn't had a lot of choice.

Clark put his right foot in front of his left. The nauseatingly churning earth made walking difficult, and walking in a straight line almost impossible. Another step, and another. His foot caught a small rock sent rolling by the Hellquake, and he slipped. Went down, caught himself on his hands and one knee. Forcing himself upright, he continued.

His knees felt like jelly, his gut seethed as much as the ground. Sweat coated his shirt, soaked his hair as much as if he had just showered. The idea struck him that he could just give up. He'd been recruited into someone else's war, after all. He had no stake in the outcome, especially now that he'd lost Lois. This was all just too much effort.

He tried to force himself to stop, just to sit down and let a boulder smash him like a bug beneath someone's shoe.

And discovered that he couldn't.

Seemingly without his active participation, his legs kept moving unsteadily toward where he thought the canyon was. Quitting, it seemed, was not an option.

So he forged on. One foot, then the next. The darkness and the roar of falling rocks and the shifting, unstable ground terrified him, but he fought back his fear and kept going, heading in the direction he believed the canyon was.

Ahead, through the blackness, a glow appeared. He shifted course, heading toward it. It took a minute before the glow resolved itself into something he could make out—the Phantom Stranger, standing still, arms by his sides. The sight lifted Clark's spirits. The ground continued to shake, but with the Stranger there, a beacon in the gloom, it didn't seem so bad. Clark pushed ahead, and within a short time he stood with the Phantom Stranger, and Etrigan, who he could make out in the incidental illumination of the Stranger's glow. "I thought I was lost," Clark said when he reached the others.

"You very nearly were," the Stranger said. "Come, we need to hurry."

Clark didn't argue. He stayed close behind the Stranger, keeping his eyes locked on the man all the way, as they entered the canyon. Once they were there, almost imperceptibly, the Stranger's glow faded, and the natural background light cast by Hell's fires returned. Clark could make out the canyon walls, steep and sheer. The landscape remained horrific, but Clark found himself beginning to relax, back in the proximity of his guides.

The canyon, only a couple dozen feet across when they entered, constricted more as they progressed. Clark started to worry that it would come to a dead end, leaving them at the mercy of the Ungetines or whatever other dangers dwelled here. Overhead, he could even see the ceiling now, lowering as if to meet the walls.

"As I said, magic doesn't always work quite right here," the Stranger said.

"So that wasn't what you intended?"

"Not precisely, no. I did want to drop some stalactites on them, to even the odds a bit. But the rest of it was Hell's way of reminding us not to underestimate it."

"I'll keep that in mind," Clark said.

As they continued up the canyon, its passageway twisted left, then right, then left twice more. Clark hoped they weren't traveling in a big, uneven circle. The ground's shaking seemed to have stopped, though, its effects not reaching this far back, so all things considered, he thought their situation had improved somewhat.

Until they reached the dead end, anyway.

Just before they came around the last bend, Clark found himself looking at the Phantom Stranger's back and finding it strangely familiar. Not just from the events of the past—what, hours—but from what seemed like long acquaintance. It was an odd sensation, akin to déjà vu, Clark supposed. A trick of the time they had been together, coupled with the disorientation that had struck him since they'd been in Hell.

All thoughts of that vanished when he looked at the solid wall of rock that met them around the turn. If the Ungetines, or any other threat, had followed them into the canyon, they'd be trapped here.

The Phantom Stranger and Etrigan regarded the huge wall, which towered before them, so high that Clark couldn't see its top. Looking closer, Clark realized that the wall wasn't really rock at all, but made up of human faces, tens of millions of them, all jammed together. Many were frozen in horrific screams, others as blank as if their previous owners had been asleep, or comatose. Some were screwed into visages of rage, some laughing, some perhaps speaking quietly, yawning, kissing, smiling. Clark couldn't help wishing the darkness would envelop them again so that he wouldn't have to look at them.

"Guess I should've taken that rock-climbing class with Jimmy," Clark said. "Although I'm pretty sure they didn't have any practice walls like this. We have to go up that?"

"You do not want to climb it." To demonstrate his point, the Phantom Stranger held his hand near one of the immobile faces. To Clark's surprise, it came to life, snapping at the hand, its teeth barely missing the Stranger's glove.

"Then how do we get out of here?"

"There is a way, Kal-El," the Stranger said. "There is always a way."

fly

"Are we even close to our destination?"

"Closer than you think," the Stranger said. "Over this wall, and we're nearly there."

"Easier said . . ." Clark began. "Wait, what did you call me?"

"Kal-El," the Stranger answered. "Your real name."

Clark started to protest, but then stopped. Something about what the Phantom Stranger said made sense, even though it shouldn't have. "So how do we get up there?"

flying

"How do you think, Kal-El?"

swooping soaring sailing

Clark started to say something about his dreams, but the walls suddenly spun around him. Dizzy, he maintained enough presence of mind not to lean against the wall of faces. But the spell grew worse, until he couldn't see the Phantom Stranger or Etrigan at all. Instead, his mind was flooded with images, memories.

Lois, of course, sitting in Shuster Hall with him, watching a play.

Their wedding day—after he had almost given up hope that it would ever happen. Everyone had been there, even Lois's father, dead set against it, and against him, from the start.

His parents, Jonathan and Martha Kent. They walked along Center Street together, each holding one of his hands. He couldn't have been more than four or five years old. He tugged at them, drawn by a red bicycle with silver trim and streamers trailing from the ends of the handlebar grips, standing in the window of the Smallville General Store.

Sitting with Pete Ross at a table in Smallville High's lunchroom, watching Lana Lang carry a tray toward her own table. He could taste the peanut butter and jelly sandwich he'd been eating, and he could hear Pete's low whistle.

Lex Luthor. Doomsday. Brainiac. Mxyzptlk. Parasite. Ruin.

His Fortress of Solitude. Kandor. The Phantom Zone.

These were not his memories. They belonged to someone else. He shook his head, trying to clear it. Blinked, rubbed his eyes.

"Are you all right, Kal-El?"

"Fine. I'm . . . fine. Just disoriented."

During the seconds or minutes his attention had been elsewhere, he saw, another danger had appeared from down the canyon. Two beings, their purple skin looking like the very rock that formed the canyon walls. They were at least a dozen feet tall, with gigantic arms and short, stubby, big-footed legs. Mostly, they were mouth—

huge gawping holes that must have accounted for six feet of their height. The teeth in those mouths, rows and rows of them, were the size of bowling pins, but sharp. Each mouth had three tongues that Clark could make out, licking and flicking.

"Good to hear," the Phantom Stranger said. "Because we should get going."

"But . . . how?"

"You know, Kal-El."

Clark shook his head. "Don't call me that! I don't know what you're talking about, Phantom Stranger. Make sense for once!"

"You know," the Stranger repeated. "Just let it come."

"I don't—"

"Open your shirt, Kal-El."

"What do you—"

"Just try it."

The giants moved closer. They looked hungry, and they looked like three people—or two people and a demon—would barely make a decent appetizer.

"Hurry," Etrigan urged. "Find your true affinity, ere we learn fatality and relinquish our infinity."

Clark resisted the Stranger's suggestion until he could smell the creatures' breath, foul and fetid.

"Whatever," he said. He tugged his tie to one side, then yanked on the placket of his shirt, popping buttons. *There's sixty bucks I'll never get back.*

When he had the shirt open in a triangle shape, point down, he realized that there was another shirt beneath that. He hadn't put on an undershirt that morning, and anyway, he didn't own any like this: blue, with a red-and-yellow design on the chest.

An "S" insignia, like a partially coiled snake.

Superman.

Faster now, he tore the rest of his clothes off, revealing the costume beneath.

Red boots with a V-shaped notch in front, red trunks held by a yellow belt, a red cape tucked into his neckband.

"I'm Superman," he said.

"Welcome back, Kal-El," the Stranger said. "And now, if you wouldn't mind . . ."

Kal-El—Superman—nodded. Taking Etrigan under one arm and the Phantom Stranger under the other, he hoisted them gently off the ground just before the big purple mouth-monsters reached them. He turned in a lazy spiral as he flew up and up, examining the wall of faces, using his telescopic vision to explore what he could of Hell.

At the cliff's top, he set his two comrades down and hovered an inch off the ground.

Just because I can, he thought.

Just because I'm Superman.

CHAPTER ELEVEN

May 1872

Elfego's Saloon was just a block off the Plaza that marked the center of Santa Fe, which was, to Bat Lash's mind, the center of civilization in the raw, untamed New Mexico Territory. Santa Fe contained drinking establishments, gaming establishments, dining establishments, and a man could even indulge the pleasures of the flesh, if he was so moved. The best places, like Elfego's, offered all the aforementioned delights in combination. Bat's emphasis on this particular night was cards, because that was how he intended to finance the other three.

The saloon was one big room, adobe-walled, with a carved, polished-oak bar extending most of its width at the back and plank floors. Beside the bar was a rear door leading into an open courtyard, where Elfego himself kept a fire going over which he cooked whatever meat his clientele brought him—often beef, but sometimes duck, pheasant, bear, or something else. Arranged around the courtyard, six cribs, smelling of the roasted meat and mesquite logs of the fire pit, allowed the saloon's soiled doves to entertain customers.

A sweet-faced redhead with formidable curves and a syrupy voice caught Bat's eye when he first walked in the place. She asked if he'd like a poke, but he suggested waiting until he had earned her price and then some. While he played five-card stud, she left with half a dozen other men, always returning and casting an inquiring gaze in Bat's direction. He kept putting her off, devoting his immediate attention to his cards.

Bartholomew Aloysius Lash loved the sensual aspects of the game, the stuttered riffle of cards being shuffled, the green baize of the tabletop, the aroma of the fine cigars and whisky in which he and his opponents indulged. Faro was his preferred game; its elegant simplicity appealed to his sense of order. No worries about full houses or three of a kind or any of that, just the turn of the cards and the thrill of the win. But tonight the faro table sat empty, so he joined the "cheating game," or poker.

Around them the big room was full of activity. A pianist, enthusiastic if unskilled, banged away in one corner. Men and a few women drank and laughed and argued. Chairs scooted loudly over the plank flooring, mugs slammed against wooden tables. It sounded like life, like enjoyment, and Bat smiled even though his hand, to put it frankly, stank. On the table were the two of clubs, four of diamonds, nine of hearts, and ten of spades. His hole card was the five of diamonds. When the two and four turned up, he'd hoped for the low straight, but it hadn't come to pass.

But two of the men at the table had already folded, and he thought he could read Sam Gordon's tells. He believed Gordon had something in his hand, but probably no more than a pair of something. He also thought he could bluff Sam into folding, and take the pot.

He thumbed his coins, slid five dollars toward the table's center. "I'll raise you . . ." Before he released them, he drew them back, as if reconsidering. "No," he said, adding another five. "Ten dollars."

Sam Gordon looked at the stack of coins, swallowed, looked at Bat. "You're bluffing," he said. The table cards were weak enough that he had to know there wasn't much Bat could have. But maybe he had a pair of twos, and Bat a pair of tens. Unless he had tens himself, he couldn't know otherwise.

Bat just held the smile steady on his lips. "Could be you're right, Sam," he said. "Then again, you've been mistaken before. Unless I'm mistaken, that is."

Sam's deep-set brown eyes blinked a couple of times. He was a thin man with a scruffy growth of brown beard on his chin, cheeks, and down his neck, which otherwise resembled a turkey's. His hat, battered and hole-punched, dangled from the back of his chair.

"Reckon I have," he admitted, laying his hole card down and picking at the hairs on his chin. "Time betime."

Even though Sam Gordon had already put nine dollars in the pot, Bat was betting that the extra ten would be enough to force him out, make him decide to cut his losses. Five wouldn't have done it.

The other players, Chinese John and Paddy McCain, watched intently. Bat's run of luck had been remarkable, especially while he had been dealer, and their coin piles had diminished as his had grown. Sam had played cautiously, for the most part, and was still in the game in a larger way.

Not for long, if Bat had his way.

Chinese John's real name was Jun, and he wasn't even Chinese. Bat couldn't remember where he was from, Japan or Korea, but most folks just assumed he was Chinese because of how he looked, and the name had stuck. He was a heavy man who dressed like a gentleman, in a vested, striped suit and a derby hat, and he kept his whiskers trimmed into a neat goatee. Paddy McCain, on the other hand, was as Irish as he sounded, with a shock of bright red hair and a ruddy face that flushed brighter the more he lost. He drank heavily but never seemed to show the effects of it.

Of the four players at the table, Sam Gordon was the slob. His leather vest was stained and torn, his shirt coming apart at the seams. He didn't seem to have bathed in recent memory.

Bat bathed whenever he could, had his clothing laundered regularly, and tried to dress well when possible. A hard life, with his parents murdered when he was just a teen and the responsibility for tracking down their killer landing on him, had convinced him early on to indulge himself in life's finer things whenever possible. Now that he was grown, he did just that. Tonight he wore his favorite vest, yellow with a floral pattern, over a white shirt, with blue pin-striped pants and brown boots. His hat was white, or had been when it was new, and there was an orange flower tucked into the band. A red wild rag was tied around his neck.

Sam spat and shoved his hole card toward the center of the table. "Dammit," he said.

Bat tossed his five in, facedown so the others couldn't see. Chinese John, who was dealing, scooped up the cards as Bat scraped the pot toward himself. "Thank you, Sam," he said, "for recognizing the wise course of action."

"Dunno about wise," Sam said. "I'm beginnin' to distrust you, Mr. Lash."

"I already did," Chinese John said. His English was every bit as good as Bat's, maybe better on account of Bat's having been born in Texas. "Bat, your luck has been frighteningly good. Even when you're not dealing, but especially when you are."

Bat shrugged, smile plastered onto his face. "What can I tell you, gents? Lady Fortune has always smiled on the Lash household." A lie, of course, but then wasn't that what the game was about?

"I ain't so sure a lady has anythin' t'do with it," Paddy said. "'Less'n y'got a queen tucked up that sleeve."

At the tables nearest theirs, Bat heard the sharp intake of breath. A man had been accused of cheating, and that was never an accusation taken lightly. Everyone at the nearby tables waited to see how Bat would answer Paddy McCain.

Bat kept smiling, kept his hands on the tabletop, although he slowly drew his right one back toward the edge. Just in case. "Let's don't be hasty," he said. Keeping his tone casual. "I've won a few more than I've lost, sure. That happens, right?"

Paddy's hands both disappeared beneath the table. "But when you win, you win big, and when you lose, you don't lose much."

"That's called good poker, I believe," Bat said.

"T' some," Paddy went on.

"Chinese John, Sam, either of you gents think I cheated

you?" Bat asked. He had, during the evening, been squirreling coins away into his pockets rather than leaving them on the table, both so he wouldn't look like he was winning too much and in case a quick getaway was called for. Looked as if the latter might be the case after all.

"Are you asking me?" Chinese John said.

"I think that's what you'd call it."

"Then yes," Chinese John said. His hands, Bat noted, remained flat on the table. Sam Gordon's hovered about an inch above it, quaking with anxiety.

Paddy would draw first—probably already had iron in his hands—but Chinese John was more dangerous. He didn't even wear a holster, but Bat was sure he had a derringer or two tucked away on his person, and maybe a hogleg in his pants, hidden by that jacket and his own bulk.

Bat wore a .44 Smith & Wesson Army in a holster that sagged below his waist, with a tie-down string lashed around his thigh from the holster's toe, so it didn't ride up when he jerked the weapon out. He had hoped not to use the .44 tonight, or anytime during his stay in Santa Fe, but was pleased just the same that Elfego didn't object to armed men in his saloon.

"Let's just be real clear about this, Chinese John," Bat said. "You and Paddy here, you're both callin' me a card mechanic?"

"Your words, Bat. But for the sake of clarity, yes. I think you're cheating."

"And I'm sure of it," Paddy added.

"Sorry to hear that," Bat said. With his left hand, he snatched up as much of his winnings as he could, knowing the move would also mask his right hand dropping to his persuader. "Guess I'll just find myself a more hospitable game."

"No you don't!" Paddy said. His eyes narrowed, and his mouth dropped open slightly as he made his move.

As Bat had expected, Chinese John moved faster, in spite of his bulk. Bat's hand had barely cleared the tabletop when he saw the derringer appear in Chinese John's meaty fist. *A sleeve rig,* Bat marveled. *Clever.*

Bat almost hated to kill the man.

He didn't have time to wound him, though. Paddy may have been slow, but he wouldn't take all night.

Bat drew his weapon and while it was still under the table, fired the first shot. The bullet slammed into Chinese John's gut, and the man's mouth made a little "o" shape as his skin paled. Bat brought the revolver up, then fanned the hammer and fired as fast as he could. Accuracy be damned, at this range he could hardly miss. Paddy jerked backward as if his chair had been kicked over and his unfired six-shooter sailed into the air. Bat put a bullet into Sam Gordon's chest, just above where his shabby vest closed, and a second into his forehead, then swung back toward Chinese John, just in case. Chinese John was down, so Bat ceased firing.

Blood stained the green baize.

What a waste.

Recognizing that his welcome in Santa Fe had been abruptly worn out, Bat hurried to his hotel room and packed his few belongings into his saddlebags. Faro, his tan cayuse, a wild-born, Indian-trained pony Bat had purchased in El Paso, had been stabled at a nearby livery. He collected Faro, saddled him up—over the horse's objections, since he was essentially a diurnal creature who appreciated a good night's sleep—and rode out of town under a blanket of stars. The night was cool and scented with woodsmoke until he got into the hills outside of town.

No one followed or gave chase. Witnesses at Elfego's had confirmed that they believed he had acted in self-defense, so he wasn't too worried about the law. Chinese John owned some businesses in town, though, while Bat was only passing through, a fact that inspired Bat to caution. By the time he stopped to get some sleep, the eastern sky had started to go gray. Bat tied Faro to a tree and laid out his bedroll on a flat stretch near the bank of a stream, wishing it was a real bed in a hotel or house. Like his horse, Bat enjoyed creature comforts, and sleeping outdoors with weather, insects, and other varmints was something he preferred to avoid when possible.

The sun had climbed about a quarter of its way into the sky when he opened his eyes again. From not far away, Bat could hear the shuffle, creak, and clank of riders. He washed his mouth out in the stream, splashed some water into his face, and climbed the little ridge he had slept by to see who made the noise he heard.

A cavalry unit cut through the center of the valley, men arranged in a single line led by a desultory color-bearer. His lance held the blue standard and stars-and-stripes guidon high, primarily because it rested in a socket in a right-hand stirrup. He clutched the pole with his right hand, his reins held loosely in his left, but his shoulders were slumped and his head drooped. The men behind him were much the same. They rode at a steady clip, and Bat guessed they were partway through a long journey, with a ways left to go.

They rode west-southwest. Same way he was bound. Deeper into Apache country than he liked to ride alone.

And soldiers did enjoy gambling, from time to time.

Might just have to join them for a spell, Bat thought. *See if I can get a game or two going.*

CHAPTER TWELVE

Superman found himself confused by the memories of a different Clark Kent—confused and disturbed, particularly at the cold-blooded murder of that Clark's version of Lois Lane.

They had just passed over the Bridge of Failed Expectations and into the Valley of Regret, and with no immediate threat, other than a general sense of depression and loss that slowed their steps, he asked the Phantom Stranger about it.

"Both versions of you cannot coexist in one reality," the Stranger said. "Etrigan and I can go back and forth because we have no doppelgangers in the false reality, but there's a Clark Kent in each place. You can't go there, and he had to merge into you to come here. In your world, you will be in charge, have no fear about that, but you will likely have his memories floating around in your head. And if we have to go back into his world, you'll find that the reverse is true. We can hope it doesn't come to that, since his Earth has a red sun and you would be powerless there."

"Let's hope it doesn't come to that for a lot of reasons," Superman said. He blinked away a memory of an angry fight he'd had with Jonathan Kent, during his teen years—a memory inspired, no doubt, by the Regrets that hung like ragged sheets across the valley. They passed through the Regrets, no more substantial than fog, but with each one came a wave of unpleasant recollection. "It's pretty disconcerting right now, and a little disorienting."

Since he'd flown them away from the mouth-monsters, they hadn't had to fight anything. The Stranger and Etrigan had chosen as safe a path through Hell as could be found. Superman took advantage of the time to try to figure out just what was going on. In his Clark Kent identity, he had been at his desk at the Daily Planet, filing a story about Metropolis's Special Crimes Unit. He had stepped over to a filing cabinet for a second, and the next thing he knew, he was standing in Hell with the Phantom Stranger and Etrigan, carrying someone else's thoughts in his head.

The Man of Steel could think on his feet, but an experience like that was a little bewildering, even for him.

"We are very nearly out," the Stranger said. Etrigan capered ahead of them, his cape fluttering, like an enthusiastic child in a toy store.

"Where will we come out, exactly?" Superman asked.

The Valley of Regrets fell away behind them and the Stranger waved a gloved hand toward a short tunnel that ended in a cavelike opening. Beyond the mouth, Clark could see actual daylight. Etrigan had paused at the beginning of the tunnel, waiting for the others. "There it is," the Stranger said.

"Our destination," the demon said, "is no vacation, but likely botheration and altercation. Of preparation there's been no communication, no consultation or cerebration. We count on you, O' man in blue, to beat our foes to supplication."

Superman couldn't suppress a smile at Etrigan's rhyme. Even so, he hoped he wouldn't be called on to fight, especially since he still didn't know for sure where they were or why.

He would find out, he guessed, soon enough.

February 560

"Camelot?"

The Stranger nodded. "That's right, Kal-El."

Smoke roiled in the air as they emerged from the cave, choking off sunlight. With his X-ray vision, Superman could see the castle's defenders working frantically, preparing what looked like last-ditch defensive measures. Some fletched arrows, others boiled water in huge vats to be hurled over the walls. Still more tended to the wounded. A knight on a winged horse flew out from behind the wall to battle airborne demons.

Surrounding the castle like rising floodwater were a host of demonic and human warriors in plate armor or mail shirts. To Superman, the place looked like it had already fallen and just didn't know it yet.

"What's the plan? Do we somehow get to the bad guys before they perform whatever spell they did and stop them?"

"Unfortunately, that is not possible," the Stranger answered. "That magic has happened and cannot be undone. The best we can do is try to counter the effects of the spell. Whether we can accomplish that here and now remains to be seen, but if we can find the sorcerers, then at least we have a chance."

"And they're here somewhere?"

"We need to get inside the walls of the castle," the Stranger added. "Unfortunately, the passageways through Hell do not always allow for pinpoint navigation."

"And we can't take sides in the battle going on down there," Superman pointed out.

"Of course not," the Stranger agreed. "We all know what the conclusion is, at any rate."

"Come on, then," Superman said. "I'll fly us in."

Before Etrigan and the Stranger reached his sides, a winged beast—some kind of fleshy dragon, Superman thought, with a horned head and a distended but humanoid face—let out a screech and stooped toward them, talons out like a hawk diving at a rodent. Superman left the others where they were and darted up toward it, right fist out. *Shouldn't take much to discourage this thing,* he thought.

Its mouth opened and a gout of black flame burst forth. Superman braced himself for the contact, not expecting anything harmful, but when it struck him, it burned like liquid fire. He screamed and shifted course, dodging the rest of it.

"It's magic, Kal-El!" the Phantom Stranger called from below.

Of course. The creature was one of Morgaine Le Fey's minions. Superman had few weaknesses, but his powers proved useless against magic. He was just recovering from the first blast when another of the flying beasts slammed into him in midair, knocking him over.

Taking sides is one thing, he thought. *Self defense is something else entirely.*

Not that there's much I can do to defend myself against them. But where there's magic, there are usually magicians.

Flying higher than the mystical creatures, he cast his gaze about, looking for whoever was in control of the strange, fleshy dragons. Below, the one that had attacked him was spitting its flame at the Phantom Stranger and Etrigan, but the Stranger blocked the black flame with a spell of his own. The cave through which they had exited Hell was high up on a rocky slope overlooking the castle, and most of Morgaine's army thronged on the plain at the slope's base. Some were charging up toward the three interlopers from the future. In all the chaos of war, Superman couldn't determine who, if anyone, directed the weird dragons, or if, once created, they were left to their own devices.

But the Stranger and Etrigan were about to be overrun by others of Morgaine's army. Superman abandoned his search, for the moment and zoomed past the flame-spitting dragons, back to ground level, where he could do some immediate good.

The Stranger continued to hold off the winged beasts, while Etrigan engaged the ones on the ground. Superman flew into the midst of an oncoming mob of armored knights, ignoring the swords, pikes, and axes that slashed at him. He didn't want to do enough damage to make a difference in the battle, so he pulled his punches, contenting himself with scattering the soldiers without doing serious injury.

Etrigan didn't similarly restrain himself. He opened his mouth and spat Hellflame at the knights, showing no mercy. Superman cringed to hear the cries of pain and groans of the dying. In an instant, he had condensed oxygen inside his own lungs to a supercold state, then he blew out the freezing air in a massive exhalation. The knights in the path of the blast of air were flash-frozen in their tracks. Superman had kept it warm enough not to freeze the people inside the armor, but until the metal thawed they wouldn't be going anywhere.

That done, he landed next to the Phantom Stranger, who had discouraged the dragon-creatures. "Wouldn't he be more helpful as Jason Blood?" he asked, eyeing Etrigan.

"More helpful?" the Stranger echoed. "I don't know about that, but less destructive, certainly."

"Good enough for me," Superman said. "If we've got something to do inside the castle, let's get to it instead of wasting time out here. Can you make him change?"

"He hates it when I do," the Stranger said. "But then, when he's Etrigan, he hates just about everything I do." He looked toward where the demon battled the few remaining knights of the ones who had charged up the hill toward them. Below, as if in answer to the demolition of their initial force, a larger one composed of human and nonhuman soldiers readied for a second assault. "Vanish, vanish, Etrigan!" the Stranger shouted. "Return again in form of man!"

With a burst of flame and a swirl of bitter smoke, Etrigan disappeared, replaced by the very human Jason Blood.

Etrigan had been unarmed, however, and the pair of knights bearing down on Blood were not. Reversing his earlier tactic, Superman used his heat vision to fuse metal to metal, paralyzing both knights. One gave a panicked shout and fell over, knocking down the second one.

"Let's get to the castle," Superman suggested. He lifted the Phantom Stranger and swooped over to Jason Blood, hoisting him up as well. The next batch of Morgaine's soldiers protested, hurling stones and shooting arrows, but Superman easily dodged their missiles and flew over their heads, dropping down into the castle.

As he did, he realized it was already too late for Camelot. To the west, the walls had been breached. Morgaine's forces flooded through the gap in the wall, putting steel and flame to everything and everyone in their path.

"We had best be quick about this," the Stranger said.

"I'll do my part," Superman offered, landing them on an empty cobblestone street not yet threatened by the invading army. "But what are we looking for?"

"This is where we believe Vandal Savage, Felix Faust, and the Dark Lord Mordru sealed their bargain and began the process that resulted in two separate time streams," Jason explained. "We didn't know precisely when they did it, or where, but I hope we're not too late."

Superman started scanning through the walls, looking for the three sorcerers. Only lead could block his X-ray vision, and the natural lead content in the stones of which Camelot was built was too low to hamper him. Within a few seconds, though, he had spotted something else that concerned him. A wizened, bearded old man carrying a tall wooden staff in his scrawny hand, accompanied by a familiar yellow demon.

"I see someone who must be Merlin," he said. "And Etrigan."

"Of course," Jason said. "This is why Merlin brought him into this world, to defend Camelot against Morgaine. You might see another one of me around someplace, too, Superman."

"I'll keep my eyes open," Superman said. "We should keep you away from your local counterpart if we can."

"True," the Stranger said. "It doesn't do to raise eyebrows unnecessarily."

"One thing, though," Jason added, his face grim. "I should probably change back to Etrigan. With Morgaine's army having breached the walls, this isn't a very safe place for mere humans. And I'd hate to have you guys distracted by looking after me."

"He's right," the Stranger said. "Very well, Blood. Just be cautious."

"Aren't I always?" Jason said. A quick smile flashed across his square face, then vanished. Superman knew that he didn't enjoy the transformation, and always worried about what mischief Etrigan might get into when he was released. "Gone, gone, form of man!" he shouted. "Rise the demon Etrigan!"

Once again, a puff of smoke marked the transformation, although there was no flame when he changed in this direction. Where he had stood, the demon Etrigan crouched now. "Much better," Etrigan said. "No reason, in battle, a demon to fetter."

"We're not in battle," Superman reminded him. "With any luck, we won't have to be."

"Do you see Savage?" the Stranger asked. "Or the others?"

Superman went back to scanning for the sorcerers. He felt like he was prying when he used his X-ray vision in this way, scattershot, instead of focusing on one particular spot where there might be trouble. Fortunately, in this moment of crisis, most people weren't engaged in private or intimate activities. Word had spread through the walled city that the invaders had broken through. Panic inspired motion that was not always useful—he saw a woman tearing hangings from a wall and bundling them in a corner, for no apparent reason, with tears streaming down her cheeks. A man shouted at three small children, trying to hurry them out the door, even though they would be much safer inside.

Seeing people dying and others no doubt about to die horrified Superman. He had made it his life's work, his mission—once he had understood that he was different, powerful in ways that others weren't—to try to prevent unnecessary death and crime and the victimization of the weak by the strong. He couldn't stop all death, of course. Nature had its cycles, and death was part of life. But where he could, he prevented murder and wholesale massacre. Earth was a big place, governed by forces that were more powerful than he. Still, he contributed. He saved lives. He helped.

Here, he could do nothing.

The past had already happened. Time's river flowed on. With great difficulty, one could visit moments that had come and gone. What one could not do was interfere with the past as it had happened. Simply visiting was dangerous. The smallest deviation from history could have unintended consequences. Larger differences—if, for instance, Superman, the Phantom Stranger, and Etrigan decided to intervene and defeated Morgaine's army, saving Camelot, everything from that moment on in British history would be different, and those changes would also impact the rest of the world.

The triumvirate of sorcerers had messed with the time stream, and now Superman and his allies were here to set things right again. They had to be careful not to compound the problem during their visit. Painful as it was, Superman could not act to prevent the carnage he witnessed. He swallowed bitterly and continued his search.

From around the corner of the narrow road came a roar and the thunder of rushing feet. Superman adjusted his vision and saw them just before they cleared the wall—about twenty demons charging toward them. Some carried swords or short spears, others were armed only with claws and sharp, gnashing teeth. No two looked alike. Skins were red and green and orange and violet. Some had four limbs, some more; one seemed to have none but propelled itself forward on thousands of minute bulges in its bell-shaped body that all worked in unison. It kept up with the others, and a mouth big enough to swallow a basketball, lined with needlelike teeth, revealed its dangerous potential.

"We have company," Superman said. Before shifting focus, he thought he'd caught a glimpse of Vandal Savage. In the split second between observing the oncoming demon force and the time they came around the corner toward them, he returned his focus to that spot.

"And I've found Savage," he added. "All three of them, in fact."

The sorcerers hurried down a dark interior corridor, deep in conversation. Superman could have used his super-hearing to listen in, but at the moment the onrushing demons seemed more important. They had turned the corner and hurtled straight toward the three allies.

The Stranger threw his hand into the air like a fly fisherman casting far into a lake, and a wall of flame leapt up from the cobblestones. The demons didn't hesitate, bursting through the fire. Flames clung to clothing, licking at the tails of cloaks and the heels of cloth boots, but they came on just the same. Etrigan tensed, dropping into a coiled crouch, ready to spring. Superman restrained him with a hand on his left shoulder. "Let me try something," he said.

Etrigan glanced at him, silent.

The Man of Steel sucked in a great breath and blew it out in one mighty wind. The demons staggered, their feet finding no purchase, and flew backward, plowing into a stone wall at the end of the street. The first ones to hit crumbled the stone, and the ones who came after, those who had been closest to the front, smashed into their fellows.

"That works," the Stranger said.

"I know some of those jerks," Etrigan added.

"I didn't know you could rhyme other people's words," Superman said.

"The rules are few which govern my rhymes," Etrigan said. "To borrow a phrase is committing no crime."

"Dropping the plural is okay, too, I guess."

Etrigan shrugged. "So it would appear. For poetry, you've a decent ear."

"Not my long suit," Superman said. "But I know my way around a keyboard, so I guess it's similar."

"You said you saw our quarry," the Stranger reminded him.

"Yes," Superman said. "Still do. Shall we?"

"Afoot or by air?" Etrigan asked. "Either way, I don't much care."

"Let's walk," Superman suggested. "They aren't far off." He led the way, past the dazed, furious demons embedded in stone, around another corner. Along their path they encountered others of Morgaine's army, intent on laying waste to the walled city, and some of Camelot's defenders. When they had to, they defended themselves, but they tried to keep their distance.

A few minutes later, they waited in a great hall, outside a heavy, carved, wooden door, lounging almost casually in wooden chairs. When the door opened, Vandal Savage, burly and bearded, stared at them in disbelief. He stopped short, and the other two mages crowded into him from behind.

"What manner of men are you?" he asked, his tone reflecting anger at being surprised. His pronunciation of English was almost as alien to Superman's ears as if he'd been speaking Latin.

"Never mind that," the Stranger said. "We have an important matter to discuss with you."

"Savage," Faust pointed out. "Look, it's him! Your pet demon!"

"Merlin's pet," Mordru corrected.

"As good as mine," Savage said. He held up a strange, nine-pointed iron star. "He's bound to this now, and therefore to us."

"No pet am I, and no one's minion," Etrigan responded with a growl. "O'er me no man can claim dominion."

Tension gripped Superman during this exchange. He wanted to shake the three sorcerers until they gave up whatever their plot was. But this was the Phantom Stranger's play, and at any rate, he would be powerless against any magic they might employ. Better, in this case, to wait and see how things played out. Taking the cautious approach was rare for him; usually he could count on his strength and invulnerability to carry him through any encounter, but he liked to think he was smart enough to know when to hold back.

"I care not for the looks of these others," Faust said. "If the demon bows to your authority, then put him to work. I'd not like to be delayed at this point."

"Hold," the Stranger said. "We've come to talk, nothing more."

"We've nothing to talk about," Savage replied. As if sensing that the demon was about to spring, Savage directed his next comment toward him. "Etrigan, you obeyed me once, now do so again. It be my wont that you kill these men."

Etrigan lunged for Savage, clawed hands grasping, mouth dropping open in a furious roar. But halfway to his prey, he stopped, turning slowly as if fighting his way through some viscous liquid. "I can't control my own four limbs," he said through gritted teeth. He appeared to be in excruciating agony. "For on the whole, I'm ruled by him!"

"How . . .?" Superman began. He didn't bother to finish the question. Etrigan dived with no further warning. As slow as he'd been a moment before, he was quick now, as if giving in to Savage's demand had freed him from unseen shackles. Superman moved with superspeed, inserting himself between Etrigan and the Phantom Stranger, who had been the demon's first target.

Forgetting for the moment just how strong Etrigan was when he went all-out, Superman hadn't braced for the impact. The demon slammed into him with the force of a small bomb, knocking him backward. The Stranger dodged them both, but Superman's outflung arm clipped him, sending him sprawling on the stone floor.

Superman recovered his balance and hurled a right jab at Etrigan's midsection. Still not sure how far he could push it, he pulled his punch a little. The blow landed hard, knocking the wind from Etrigan but doing no serious damage. Etrigan wiped his mouth with the back of one hand, scowling at Superman, then closed again. One of his clawed hands raked Superman's cheek, stinging him, the impact momentarily blinding the Man of Steel. Superman swatted the hand away and followed up with another, more powerful blow. His fist crashed into Etrigan's jaw, and the demon reeled and went down.

Superman closed in to finish Etrigan, figuring he could knock the demon unconscious and get back to the three wizards. But Etrigan had different ideas. As Superman neared, he dug his claws into the floor and ripped up a swath of solid stone. He hurled the chunk at Superman, who blocked it with an upraised hand. Doing so spread flying bits all over the room, however, and worried about the Stranger, Superman darted about at superspeed, catching each one and dropping it harmlessly to the ground.

By the time he finished that, Etrigan had launched a

heavy wooden chair at him. Superman batted it aside and braced for the next missile.

None came. The demon was nowhere to be seen. Superman listened for Etrigan's heartbeat, his ragged breathing.

Instead, he heard the soft footfall of the Phantom Stranger, at his shoulder. "They're gone, Superman," he said. "They're all gone."

CHAPTER THIRTEEN

The Phantom Stranger was right.

The three sorcerers had taken advantage of Superman's distraction—and that of the Stranger, whom Superman had knocked down—to vanish. And while Superman was blocking thrown objects, Etrigan had slipped out a door into the castle.

"They can't be far," Superman said. "It's only been seconds."

"If they move only through normal space," the Stranger reminded him.

Superman nodded. If they had departed magically, through some kind of portal or mystical doorway, his X-ray vision wouldn't pick them up. He peered through walls, again viewing things he wished he hadn't, but not spotting the mages again.

Etrigan was another matter. He had run away within the castle and didn't prove hard to find. Catching him, however, might be another matter.

"There are two of him," Superman reported. "He's met up with his contemporary counterpart."

The Stranger groaned. "He should know better."

"I'm sure Blood does," Superman said.

"Etrigan is no idiot," the Stranger said. "Childlike, yes. Poor impulse control. He probably thinks it's a big lark."

That was how it appeared to Superman. The twin Etrigans amused themselves romping through one of the palace's kitchens, overturning racks of pots and pans, terrifying cooks and scullery maids who had tried to pretend that their world wasn't crashing to an end. Instead of exiting through a doorway when they'd done their damage, they took turns running headlong into a stone wall until they smashed through it.

Superman described the chaos to the Stranger.

"Merlin brought him here to fight off Morgaine's army," the Stranger said. "He can't be happy about this either."

"I'm less concerned with Merlin's happiness than I am with finding those three sorcerers," Superman admitted. "But I can't pick them up anywhere."

"They have vanished," the Stranger said. "They could be anywhere. Even you can't scan the whole world for them. Especially if they're using magic to mask their location."

"So we just give up?"

"No, but we need a different tack. In the meantime, we've got to bring Etrigan under control before he does something terrible to the time stream."

"Can't you just turn him back into Blood?" Superman asked.

"If I could get near enough to him," the Stranger said. "But with two Etrigans it could be tricky."

Superman tried to imagine what could go wrong, but the trouble with magic was that you just never knew. Maybe it would turn both of them into Jason Blood, which might be worse for the time stream than two Etrigans. Maybe it would turn the right Etrigan into the wrong Blood. Maybe diffused by the double demons, it wouldn't work at all.

"Then we'll have to isolate ours," Superman said. "Tell you what, if you can get him here, I'll pen him up long enough for you to do your thing."

The Stranger agreed and left the room. Superman went to where Etrigan had begun tearing up the floor and continued the job, working at top speed. He peeled away rock, pressed it together, superheated it with his heat vision and flattened it into a solid surface. With more stone, he repeated the process, until he had three walls, a floor, and a ceiling, fused together by melting the corners and shaping them. Etrigan would be able to break through ordinary stone, so Superman condensed the material, making it thinner but incredibly dense, until he believed it would even hold the powerful demon. Finally, he made a fourth wall of the same stuff, but kept it separate from the first three.

He finished just in time. The door flew open, and the Stranger scrambled in. On his heels came Etrigan, followed by his doppelganger.

"The first one!" the Stranger shouted. Superman didn't question how he knew—that was just the sort of thing the Phantom Stranger did.

Moving at superspeed again, he hauled the cage he'd

built into the demon's path. Etrigan, moving too quickly to evade it, ran right in. As soon as he had, Superman slammed the fourth wall in place and fused it there.

"Now if you could get the other one out of here," the Stranger said. "Not so far away that he cannot do what Merlin needs him to, but away from the immediate vicinity."

"Done," Superman said. He took flight, catching the second Etrigan—who didn't know what to expect—around the middle, and carrying him out of the room, down the hall, through an exterior door, and up into the air. By the time they were airborne, Etrigan had regained some of his composure.

"I know not what you are, strange being," the demon complained. "By your garb I vow you're a stranger to Camelot, and perhaps Earth. But I've never seen your kind in Hell, either. Are you one of Morgaine's?"

"I have no stake in this conflict," Superman answered, surprised that the Etrigan of this time was not a Rhymer. He turned in midair and made for an empty battlement ringing a tall tower.

Etrigan aimed a gout of demon-fire at him. It burned, but Superman flew a little faster and blew a breath of icy air down the length of his body to extinguish it. A moment later, he had left the demon alone on the tower. It wouldn't take him long to get down, but at least he'd be out of the Stranger's way.

From the air, Superman could see that the tide of battle definitely favored Morgaine's armies. They had breached the walls in several spots, and Morgaine's soldiers met little resistance as they flowed into Camelot.

Even though he knew Camelot was destined to be overrun, had to fall for the rest of history to continue on its proper course, he couldn't help feeling a pang of sorrow at watching it happen.

In the compressed stone box Superman had so rapidly built, Etrigan hissed and snarled and spat like a cornered beast. He was no beast, the Phantom Stranger knew, but exactly what mental capability he had was something the Stranger had never been able to ascertain fully. He seemed nearly as capable of rational thought in his Etrigan guise as he did as Jason Blood, but without Blood's ethical compass. Etrigan was a bundle of reactions to external events, but making plans and carrying them out often seemed beyond his abilities.

The Stranger wondered what Etrigan thought now, having met himself. Not an ancestor, not an alternate dimension's version, but his actual self. Like the Stranger, Etrigan was long-lived, and from conversations with him the Stranger knew that Etrigan remembered the battle for Camelot. He had never mentioned meeting himself. Perhaps, since the Stranger had been present, he just assumed the Stranger remembered it, too.

The fact was, the Phantom Stranger had no memory of this visit. The Stranger had not been to Camelot before this trip through time, so these events had not happened before for him. Etrigan, though, had been here and was again, and had met and caroused with himself. What impact might that meeting have on him? This was the reason time travel had to be done carefully.

Of course, it was entirely possible that the Stranger would not have remembered visiting Camelot even if he had. His own origins were lost in the haze of memory, and he could not remember, any more than humans recalled their own births, how he had come to wander the globe. Other people had offered their own theories, suggesting that he was a fallen angel or had been sent to atone for some horrible sin. He didn't know. He knew only that he served the cause of Order, battling back the darkness of Chaos when and where he could.

Like Superman, he perceived the fundamental decency of humanity. Individuals were flawed, some embraced evil willingly, but overall humankind was good and deserving of protection against those who would do it harm. Superman's efforts were directed toward the sorts of threats that came from dangerous, powerful villains—people like Lex Luthor: wealthy, brilliant, and deranged, so full of hate that he devoted his considerable financial and intellectual resources to crime. The Stranger's war tended to be against more obscure, esoteric threats, the kind that used magic and mysticism to attack on a spiritual or psychological level.

Two sides of the same coin, though.

Even Etrigan, unpredictable as he was, fought for the right causes more often than not. He didn't like to think of himself as a do-gooder, but when he could be shown that it was in his own best interests, he was happy to perform good works.

Just now, the Stranger had to get him under control. Etrigan battered at his containment box, his fists thundering against its sides and making it bounce around the room. Every now and then, the Stranger could hear the roar of his Hellfire. Sooner or later, Etrigan would find a way out. Better to bring Blood back now, before he did.

"Vanish, vanish, Etrigan!" he shouted, hoping it would

work through the stone Superman had condensed. "Return again in form of man!"

After a moment, he knew the spell had taken effect. No longer could he hear the growling voice shouting complaints and curses, or the pounding of powerful fists against its sides.

In the demon's place was a no-doubt-confused, possibly terrified Jason Blood, who would have no idea where he was or how he had come to be imprisoned.

One way around that. The Stranger didn't know who he had once been, if anyone, or how he had come by his powers. Having no guide or mentor, he didn't even know if he had learned for certain the extent of his own abilities. But one thing he could do was pass through "solid" objects and take others through with him.

He did it quickly, barely thinking about it. Conscious thought could, after all, become a barrier to magical action. The Stranger simply willed himself into the dark tomb, took Jason's arm, and willed them both back out.

In the light outside, Jason's hair was plastered to his face, slick with sweat. "Thanks," Jason said, breathless. "What . . . what was that?"

"Superman built it, to contain Etrigan," the Stranger replied, careful not to refer to Blood and Etrigan as one and the same. "There were two of him—he met himself, and they were having a grand time terrorizing the castle. We needed to confine ours so that Superman could get the other out of the way. Trying the transformative spell with both of them here would have been too risky."

"Well, thanks again for getting me out," Jason said. "Is it bad, that both Etrigans ran into each other?"

"We shall hope not," the Stranger said.

"What about those magicians we came here after? Any sign of them?"

"After Etrigan distracted us? No, they're gone. Not just from the room, but from the area."

Jason was about to say more, but Superman rocketed back into the room.

"He's out of our hair for the moment," Superman said. "Welcome back, Jason."

"Thanks, Kal-El," Jason said. "I hope we weren't too much trouble."

"I don't think so," Superman said, cracking a smile. "Although I don't suppose we'll know until we get home and find that some major change in Earth's history has come about. You know, Lex Luthor winning the White House, something like that."

"Hey," Jason protested, "you can't pin that on me! Or Etrigan."

"Kidding," Superman assured him. "Seriously, I think we got the two of them separated before any significant harm was done. But we really won't know standing around here."

"I believe we have no reason to stay," the Stranger said. "Our quarry has gone. Best to get back to our own time and come up with a new plan."

"That's what I was thinking," Superman said. He knew he could fly through time—a difficult, draining process. He had even carried others with him, although that made it harder, and dangerous for his passengers. "Do you know a way back that doesn't require a trip through Hell?"

"Since our destination is our own Earth and not the alternate one, yes," the Stranger said. "It will be much easier. Not easy, mind you. But easier, definitely."

"Let's get a move on, then," Jason urged. "If there's a spare Etrigan running around here, I'd just as soon not meet up with him. Again."

"Very well," the Stranger said. He took Superman's arm in one of his hands and Jason Blood's in the other, then began to walk.

CHAPTER FOURTEEN

May 1872

Brian Savage, better known to those who knew of him at all as Scalphunter, or as Ke-Woh-No-Tay, a name which meant "He Who Is Less Than Human," to his Kiowa brethren, rode as he had never ridden before. He had nearly exhausted his pony. To push the paint much harder might kill her, but to give up now meant certain death for him.

The journey had begun on Oklahoma's panhandle, where tall grasses grew from red earth and hardy settlers worked themselves into their graves trying to eke a living from both. Scalphunter knew a woman there, a widow who enjoyed the company of a man from time to time. He suspected Mrs. Swain liked having him around largely because he was a taste of the forbidden, but safe. Although in his buckskin tunic and leggings, his long black hair tied down by a headband, he looked like any other Kiowa warrior, he was actually a white man, the son of rancher Matt Savage and his wife Laurie, kidnapped and raised by the Kiowa. He had adopted the ways of the Indian and left behind the trappings of so-called civilized people. She got what she wanted from him, and he enjoyed the time he spent with her, despite doubts as to the purity of her motivations.

He had been riding along over a grassy plain, on his way to her remote ranch, when he heard the distant rumble of gunfire. More than just a shot or two, he knew at once that he wasn't listening to a hunting party, but a battle.

More like a massacre, he discovered.

He had nudged his pony toward the sounds, but they came from a great distance, across two valleys and the low, rocky ridges that separated them. By the time he reached the source of the gunfire, the battle, such as it was, had ended. The guns he had heard belonged primarily to a cavalry patrol, and the bullets they left behind had lodged in the hearts and heads of a group of two dozen Kiowa women and as many children. Scalphunter dismounted, tears streaming down his face, and walked through the carnage, his tread gentle, his hands grasping at empty air as if he could reclaim the past and change what had occurred.

He found no men, or boys more than twelve years old. They were most likely off hunting. Which meant there was no reason for the massacre except the evil that resides in some men's hearts, and their hatred for all things foreign to them. These innocents had been murdered simply because they were Indians.

The men who had committed this vicious crime had left a track Scalphunter could have read in his tenth year, a wide swath through the grasslands. He followed the path, learning the individual hoofprints of their mounts. Half a dozen men in all. Out on routine patrol he guessed, and having run across an encampment whose people couldn't defend themselves, they decided to have a little fun.

As he neared the small settlement of Prairie Wind, the tracks became harder to make out because they were obscured by heavy horse and wagon traffic. Hard, but not impossible, especially for Ke-Woh-No-Tay, who had learned tracking from his Kiowa brethren as a young boy. Every time it seemed he had lost the trail for good, he managed to find one horse, or another, and in this way, painstakingly, he followed the killers all the way into town. He had expected they would make for the nearby fort, but dusk had fallen and apparently the men had decided to stop in town for a drink first. Ten horses had been tied to a hitching post outside the Crystal Gate. Scalphunter left his war pony across the street and walked over, checking the hooves of those near the saloon by the light of the gas lamps on the street.

All six horses he'd been following that day were there.

A few people on the street had noticed him. Most whites gave him a wide berth, but there was nothing illegal about a Kiowa man walking on a public road.

No, he hadn't done anything against the white man's law. Yet.

He would, in just a few moments.

Through the saloon's filthy window, Scalphunter could see six soldiers sitting at a round table. They drank and laughed as if they hadn't a care. As if they hadn't made widowers and orphans out of many Kiowa men and boys. One of the men, a young blond lieutenant, appeared to be the ranking officer.

That would be the one whose scalp he would take,

then. To serve as a lesson to the rest, and to all those in the town and the fort who supported his activities.

On one of the soldier's mounts a Henry rifle rested in a saddle scabbard. Scalphunter waited between the horses, hidden by shadows and their bulk, until there was no one on the town's dusty main road. While he stood there, he quietly released the reins from the post. When it was safe, he drew the rifle, checked to be sure there was a round in the chamber. One would be enough.

He knew the whites spoke about the necessity of "fair play," of not shooting someone until you knew he was looking at you and had a chance to draw his own weapon. But he also knew that they would shoot an Indian in the back—or massacre women and children—without hesitation. So he would apply their own rules. Still standing outside the window, he aimed the borrowed Henry at the young lieutenant and pulled the trigger.

The shot echoed down the covered walkway, sending the untethered horses into a panicked scramble. The bullet shattered the smudged window and hit the lieutenant in his left temple. Screams and shouts came from the saloon, and up and down the street doors and windows opened up as people came out to see what had happened.

Scalphunter didn't wait for people to react. While all eyes were still focused on the window, he ran through the batwing doors and into the saloon. Some of the people congregated inside saw him and shouted warnings, but he moved too quickly for the stunned onlookers to react. Within seconds, he stood beside the lieutenant, who had slumped over in his chair, blood running from the wound in his head. Drawing his scalping knife, Scalphunter sang an ancient chant and skinned off part of the man's head,

including a thatch of blond hair. He knew most of the
whites who watched viewed his action with utter revul-
sion, but he also knew that there were some who collected
Indian scalps and were paid to do so. Scalping a foe was
strong medicine, at any rate. It was a sacred ritual, and it
served as an insult to the scalped as well as to his tribe.

That was the intended effect this time. The bluecoats
had to be shown that senseless killing would not be tolerated.

When he had sliced through the last tendril of flesh, he
raised the scalp high. "This soldier and his men slaughtered a group of women and children today!" he called.
"Kiowa women and children, defenseless while their men
were away! For his crime, he has paid, but let all of you
know that such crimes will be repaid in kind!"

"Someone get Colonel Murray!" a man called. "That
renegade's killed his boy!"

Two shots rang out, both missing Scalphunter—thanks
to the medicine the scalping had bestowed on him, he was
sure. Without waiting for more, Scalphunter bulled his
way through grasping hands and back outside. As he burst
through the door, he gave a whistle. Hearing it, his paint
wheeled and ran toward him, meeting him before he'd
made it halfway across the road. He jumped on the pony's
back and rode. More shots zipped harmlessly past him,
and soon he was away from the town and out of immediate danger.

But the lieutenant had been the son of a colonel at the
fort. Although there was nothing he would have chosen to
do differently, he wished he had known that. The colonel
had apparently sent a troop after him, and they had not
slowed or given up, chasing him even across state bor-

ders. He guessed he should have been honored—it wasn't often the Army devoted so many men to chase a single brave.

But he was too tired to feel proud, and his poor abused mare was almost too worn-out to continue. He had passed through part of Texas and New Mexico Territory, and he was moving into Arizona Territory. Apache country. The Apache and Kiowa peoples had been allied from time to time—though they had also had their differences—because both groups understood the threat posed by the continued incursion of the whites. Every now and then, from high spots, he'd been able to glimpse the column of soldiers dogging his trail. The threat of confronting Apache warriors hadn't dissuaded them.

Ahead, Scalphunter saw a thin line of smoke against the deep blue sky. A ranch, maybe even a town. He prodded his war pony on. They could make it that far, then he'd have to rest the mare, get her something to eat. Maybe even something for himself.

When the soldiers caught up, he would be fed and rested.

The meeting might not have the outcome the bluecoats anticipated.

CHAPTER **FIFTEEN**

"What do you mean, you can't tell me where you've been or what you've been doing?" Lois exclaimed. Clark was glad the conversation took place by cell phone instead of in person. "Clark, even at the Planet they know you have a habit of wandering off, but they've been looking for you, paging you—"

"I know, Lois. I'll have to come up with a cover story."

"You've told more cover stories than you've reported real ones," she retorted. "Nothing new there."

The Phantom Stranger had insisted that Superman couldn't tell anyone—not even Lois—about the alternate Earth. Superman would be able to let her know about it eventually, but for the moment he agreed. The situation was in too much flux, the Stranger had said. The more people were aware of the other Earth, the more the balance might tip in that direction. Superman didn't quite see how, but that sort of esoteric knowledge was the Phantom Stranger's specialty, not his. All he knew for sure, dodging her questions, evading the truth, was that he caught a momentary glimpse of another Lois falling to a murderer's bullet. He knew it was a trace memory of the other Clark he carried inside himself, but the more time he spent on his own Earth, the farther away those memories seemed.

"Lois, I'll fill you in when I can. For now, it's important that I keep my mouth shut. Anyway, I made a promise."

A moment's pause. Superman could hear the gears turning in her head—not literally, but only because there were no literal gears. "Okay," she said. A promise is a promise, he had repeated many times before, and while she wouldn't appreciate it being used to keep her from knowing something—curiosity being one of her key driving forces, and its corollary, the pursuit of knowledge, being another—she would accept it and not press him further.

For now.

Ending the call, he turned to see the Phantom Stranger and Jason Blood waiting for him. For the same reason that he hadn't been able to tell Lois where he'd been, they had decided not to inform the other members of the Justice League of America, the super hero team of which Superman was a member, or to use the JLA's orbital Watchtower as a temporary headquarters. Instead, they were in Jason Blood's Gotham City apartment, waiting for the only two people of this Earth they were planning to tell.

Jason's apartment could have doubled as a museum, except that no one would pay to visit it more than once. Over the many years of his life, he had amassed an incredible collection of artifacts, mostly related to demons and demonology. He made his living as a demonologist, writing articles and scholarly studies, occasionally consulting for people willing to pay for his expertise. These included filmmakers, of course, but also academics and even the odd corporation or two. None of his clients knew that his expertise was born of long, hard experience with the real thing.

Jason and the Stranger sat at an ornately carved wooden dining table that seemed vaguely Oriental, although Superman was unable to determine its precise origins. Blood had his elbows on the table, his shoulders slumped, as if the day's events had already worn him out. The Stranger sat erect as ever, apparently without the capacity for fatigue or boredom. Musky-scented candles burned on the table.

"That sounded like it went well," Jason observed.

"As well as could be expected," Superman said. "She doesn't like not knowing things."

"In this instance, she is far better off," the Stranger said.

Superman examined what appeared to be a skull of incredible antiquity. Fangs jutted up from the lower jaw, and a pair—almost big enough to be tusks—hung from the upper. Eye sockets were deeply recessed under a sloping, overhanging brow. "Maybe I should have let you explain it."

"She will understand," the Stranger said. He sounded sure of himself, as usual. Superman considered himself generally a pretty confident guy—the result, he suspected, of having incredible strength and power, along with a realistic view of the world and his place in it. But even he second-guessed himself sometimes, had crises of confidence when he wasn't sure his decisions were sound. It never seemed as if the Stranger shared those concerns.

Superman's gaze passed over a series of portraits of Jason Blood—not ancestors, as he claimed when "civilians" came to visit, but Jason himself—painted at different times throughout history. One was a genuine Rembrandt, another an early Picasso. He was admiring its use of color to delineate form when a knock sounded at the front door.

"They are here," the Stranger announced. Easy call—they hadn't ordered pizza. But Superman was again impressed by his certainty.

Jason shoved himself away from the table and strode to the door, pulling it open with a flourish. Outside, a man and a woman, both clad in trench coats, waited for entry. "You couldn't just zap yourselves in?" Jason asked.

"We could have," the woman said. Her name was Zatanna, and she was beautiful, with pitch-black bangs above her eyebrows and hair that fell past her shoulder, framing a high-cheekboned, wide-mouthed, bright-eyed face. She let the trench coat fall open, revealing her usual working clothes: a tailed tuxedo coat, white vest, white shirt and bow tie, tight black briefs, and black fishnet stockings that vanished into black-leather boots, which reached above her knees. Zatanna worked as a stage magician—although, unknown to her audiences, her magic was no illusion—and the look helped keep the crowd's focus on her impressive physical form and off what she was doing. "But that's generally considered impolite."

"We did 'zap' ourselves, as you put it, here to Gotham City," Dr. Occult added. He had come from New York, Superman knew, and Zatanna from San Francisco. "Saves on plane fare, after all."

"Not to mention time," Zatanna said. "And you said it was an emergency. I was rehearsing a new trick."

Dr. Occult, lean but muscular, his old-fashioned fedora shading a squared-off face that always reminded Superman of Dick Tracy, was one of the few people Superman knew who could really understand what Jason Blood went through every day of his life. Superman carried the leftover memories of the other version of Clark inside himself, but they were beginning to fade. And most super heroes, like Superman, had alter egos, secret identities they wore like masks. He needed to be Clark Kent sometimes, or else he would have had no peace, no time to himself. The world contained enough misery, hatred, crime, and corruption to keep a hundred Supermen busy all the time. As powerful as he was, he couldn't do it all. If he hadn't had another identity to duck into, he would have been under constant pressure—more than just that which he placed on himself—to attack every single problem. He had a place of refuge, his Fortress of Solitude, to which he could retreat sometimes. But when he wanted to be in his adopted city, and informed of potential issues that might require his attention, the Clark Kent persona was the best option.

Dr. Occult, however, like Jason Blood and Etrigan, shared his physical body with another person. In his case, Richard Occult and his partner in a private detective agency, Rose Psychic, had been fused into the one body. They could appear in male or female form at will, although on the occasions Superman had met them, they had usually used the male one, and Superman tended to think of Occult as the more dominant personality. They still had the agency in New York, with offices in Chicago,

San Francisco, Paris, and Hong Kong, specializing in cases with supernatural elements.

The decision to seek their help with the current dilemma had not been an easy one, and Superman, the Phantom Stranger, and Jason had talked it over for hours. They knew plenty of magic users, but had finally agreed that these were not only two of the most powerful, but also that they could be trusted with the information. The Spectre, probably the mightiest magical being in the known universe—bordering on omnipotent—had a habit of flying off the handle, and would probably insist on trying to fix everything himself. The Stranger believed that would only make things worse, and Superman was inclined to go along with that.

The Stranger rose from his seat. He shook hands with Zatanna and Dr. Occult, as did Superman—no reason super heroes shouldn't observe the social niceties—and invited them to the table.

"Anything to drink?" Jason asked, playing the good host.

"Etihw eniw, esaelp," Zatanna said. As if by magic—because it was—a glass of white wine appeared before her on the table. Her magic only required that she speak her spells backward, and that which she desired came true. Within limits, of course. Still, a handy talent to have.

"Scotch, neat," Dr. Occult said.

Jason smiled. "Got just the thing," he said, turning to his bar. "Nicely aged."

"In this crowd, we're the babies," Zatanna said to Superman. Nowhere near as old as the Phantom Stranger or Jason Blood, Dr. Occult had been born just before the turn of the twentieth century and had maintained his—and Rose's—apparent age that they'd been in the mid-1930s.

Jason brought Occult's Scotch in a chunky glass tumbler, along with one for himself. Superman, who knew he had a "Boy Scout" image but didn't care, stuck with water. The Stranger had declined anything to eat or drink, as he generally did.

"You're probably wondering why we called you here," Jason said as he sat down and scooted his chair toward the table. "Isn't that how the cliché goes?"

"I have been curious," Zatanna said. "There's nothing like a summons from the Phantom Stranger, refusing to give any details but demanding immediate attention, to pique one's interest."

"I apologize for any inconvenience," the Stranger said. "But secrecy is of the utmost importance."

"Speaking of clichés," Dr. Occult added.

The Stranger kept going as if Occult hadn't spoken at all. "We face a difficult situation," he said. "One that could result in the end of this Earth and everyone upon it. Everyone who has ever dwelled here, in fact."

"Are we talking 'Crisis' proportions?" Zatanna asked, referring to an event that few remembered, in which a multiverse of different worlds had been reduced to the single universe they inhabited.

"Not quite," Superman said. "But the effects locally could be just as dire, if not more so. If I understand it right, not only would our world no longer exist, but it would never have existed."

"Sounds like a pretty serious screwup," Dr. Occult said. *Master of the understatement,* Clark thought. *Occult isn't given to hyperbole.*

"How can we help?" Zatanna asked. Her head was tilted toward the table, but she looked up at the three who had invited her to this place. "You don't have to tell us what the details are if you don't want us to know."

"Absolutely," Dr. Occult agreed.

Implicitly trusting them, Superman knew. That fact alone made him believe that asking their assistance had been the right thing to do.

"We need to find three sorcerers," Superman explained. "Vandal Savage, Felix Faust, and the Dark Lord Mordru. We have no idea where they might be, or when, because there are time-travel elements to this . . . this situation, and they could be hiding in time."

Dr. Occult eyed the Phantom Stranger. "And you can't . . .?"

"I can locate no trace of them. They are as hidden from me as if they'd never existed."

Occult gave a low whistle. "First time for everything, right? As long as we're trading in clichés tonight."

"Not the first time," the Stranger corrected. "Albeit rare, I'll give you that."

"Is there anything else you can tell us about their activities that might be helpful?" Zatanna asked.

"I'm afraid not," the Stranger said.

"Because the last thing we know they did related to what we're concerned about now was in A.D. 560," Jason added. "We tried to get our hands on them then, but failed. They've no doubt moved things along since then, but we don't know what, or when."

"That really is a reach," Dr. Occult said. He drummed his fingers on the table arrhythmically. "So whatever they did back then has, let's say, tendrils reaching through the ages up to now."

"That would be a safe assumption," the Stranger admitted.

"And we can only speculate that it's of considerable urgency, or you three wouldn't have banded together and brought us here," Zatanna put in. "On top of what you already told us, of course."

"Definitely," Superman replied. "The highest urgency, if the Stranger and Jason are correct."

"Which we are," the Stranger said.

"Of course," Dr. Occult said. "Well, I'm in. Anything I can do, just give me the heads-up. As far as looking for those three weaselly magicians, let's get started."

"Are there any special materials you need?" Jason asked. "I have some stuff here."

"For this sort of thing, I don't think we need any tools," Zatanna said. "It's more of a fishing expedition than a spell intended to create a specific effect."

Of course, Zatanna didn't tend to use magical implements or tools in her spells anyway, Superman knew. If Dr. Occult wanted to speak up, he would—the pair inhabiting that body weren't known for holding their respective tongues. Instead of protesting, Dr. Occult opened his hands on the tabletop. "Let's get to it."

His intention was obvious. Superman, the only one who had not already taken a seat, did so now. He didn't like magic or particularly trust it, but it seemed he would now become a willing participant.

He held Zatanna's hand, small and warm, in his right, and Jason's meatier one in his left. To Jason's left was the

Stranger, then Dr. Occult, who had to reach across the table to grasp Zatanna's hand.

"You all have more familiarity with this sort of thing than I do," Superman said. "You'll have to walk me through it."

"Close your eyes," Zatanna said, her voice soft. He could smell hints of cinnamon and vanilla wafting from her. "And open your mind. Try not to think of anything in particular, just visualize what I'm saying. If that's okay with you, Richard and Rose."

"Take it away," Dr. Occult said.

"Very well. One more thing—you do have the Mystic Symbol of the Seven with you?"

"Always."

She referred to the talisman Dr. Occult carried to ward off magical assaults. Superman guessed that she was concerned that since they sought three powerful sorcerers, their prey could turn the tables and mystically attack them while they were engaged in the search and otherwise defenseless.

"We seek three who use the darkest magics," Zatanna said. She sounded calm, collected. "We know them by the names Felix Faust, Mordru, who calls himself the Dark Lord, and Vandal Savage. We can hold their visages in our minds, see them as they are—the personifications of great evil. We can imagine their sinister countenances and the darkness they hold close to their hearts. We wish to see their physical location, in this world or another, in this time or another."

Superman had done as she had suggested, emptying his mind. Now, in accordance with her words, he visualized them as he had seen them in Camelot, and as he knew

them in the present time. He had never before imagined
the three of them teaming up, and now that he did he realized what a dangerous combination they would make.

"Show us, o forces beyond the ken of mortal man,
where are the three we seek. Reveal them to us in the full-
ness of their fury. Disclose their whereabouts to us now.
Wohs su eht segam!"

Superman had kept his eyes closed, but now he seemed
to see a cloudy, amorphous shape. All the colors of the
rainbow floated inside the cloud, as if an oil slick had
settled there. Superman thought for a second that three
ambiguous forms would coalesce into the three sorcerers.
Before that happened, however, a bright flash of light
blinded him—even though his eyes remained shut. From
the gasps of others at the table he knew they had all experienced the same thing.

Zatanna released his hand. "It isn't working," she said.
Superman let go of Jason's hand and opened his eyes.
Disappointment etched itself onto Zatanna's pretty face,
her blue eyes downcast, a frown wrinkling her forehead.
She was sweating, he saw. *Afraid.* The realization sur-
prised him. "They're blocking us."

"That's what I got, too," Dr. Occult said.

"By blocking, you mean . . ." Superman began.

"They have defenses up," Zatanna said. "They detected
us, saw us. They know who's looking for them and where
we are. And those defenses aren't something we can
break through."

"So we've hit another dead end?" Jason asked. "This
case seems to be full of those."

"So it would appear," the Stranger said. "So it would
appear."

CHAPTER SIXTEEN

Lois Lane hated the way Clark had sounded. He might not have been aware of it himself, but to her, he seemed worried. Concerned, at the very least. *And he's a pretty tough guy,* she thought. *So anything that worries him scares the hell out of me.*

She thought of herself as a skilled judge of people, a human lie detector of sorts. So many people tried to bamboozle reporters that she had developed a sixth sense for it. The press had little legal standing, after all—its members weren't judges or juries, and couldn't prosecute anyone for perjury. All they could do was report the truth as they saw it. Lois had no respect for people who tried to play her, and she could tell the difference between someone who was scared or nervous and someone trying to intentionally mislead or obfuscate.

Clark had been among the former.

She tried to put it aside, to drop it into a mental compartment and close it away for now. She couldn't force

him to talk, and she had other things going on that required all her attention.

A fog swirled around the docks that night, moving up
Hob's River from the open ocean beyond, reaching with
cold, damp fingers between the warehouses, parking lots,
and watering holes that fronted onto the water. Lois had
parked a few blocks away and walked toward the docks.
Most of the streetlamps were out along her route, either
smashed or simply nonfunctional. The sidewalks, where
they existed, were wet from the thick fog, but much of the
time she had to walk on the street. She stayed close to the
buildings, ready to melt into the shadows at the approach
of vehicles or other pedestrians. Already the fishy, fetid
river smell worked its way into her consciousness.

She didn't think she was in any danger here, and she
wasn't breaking the law. At least, she hadn't yet. But she
didn't want anyone to know what she intended. Her destination was a crime scene, and while she could have asked
the Metropolis PD's public affairs officer for a tour, she
didn't want some cop looking over her shoulder the whole
time she examined the scene. If they allowed her in it at
all. The other option, of course, was that they would refuse
her access, and she'd have tipped her hand for nothing.

Nearer the docks there was more activity, even this
time of night. Lois could hear the shouts of working long-
shoremen, the growl of forklift engines, the hum of gen-
erators and the rattle and clank of chains. That would
complicate her mission, but she supposed the docks stayed
busy day and night.

She wore jeans, a dark sweater and jacket, and black
boots—a little clunkier than she preferred but good for
skulking around docks. It all helped her blend with the

night. As she neared the last corner before the dockside warehouse she needed to visit, bright light blasted toward her—the arc lights by which the dockworkers plied their trade. Nothing would keep her hidden where there were no shadows. She approached the corner cautiously. Getting caught here still wouldn't get her into trouble, necessarily, but it would make her job considerably more difficult.

There was a story here, she believed. More than that, it was the kind of story that mattered, that affected people's lives. Lois Joanne Lane—some of the Planet's interns had tried to start calling her "LoJo," but a few harsh words and intimidating scowls had ended that quickly—had built her reputation following such stories.

At the corner, she paused, peeking around to see if anyone might notice her. Dockworkers wrestled with a cargo container being lowered by a giant crane, but they were paying attention only to their own jobs. From here, she could see the entrance to the warehouse she wanted, blocked off by yellow CRIME SCENE tape. A uniformed cop stood about fifty yards away from the door, sipping from a Styrofoam coffee cup and chatting with a supervisor of some kind—at least, Lois assumed he was a supervisor because he wore a tie with his hard-hat and carried a clipboard.

She wouldn't get a better shot. Swallowing back her anxiety, she dashed across the damp pavement, ducked under the yellow tape, and ran through the open door.

Inside the vast, dark space were dozens of huge metal shipping containers, stacked three high. The smells of diesel, exhaust, and the river were less pronounced in here. She slipped a mini-MagLite out of her pocket and clicked it on. She hoped the container she sought had been left open, or she could be in here for a week. *What I wouldn't give for Clark's X-ray vision sometimes.*

She played the light around as she made her way down the aisles. The containers came in many colors, with orange, blue, red, and green predominating. They were all closed up tight. But four rows back, she found a container that had been left open, and another ribbon of yellow police tape spanned the gap. The container was sandwiched between a yellow one beneath it and a blue one above.

The doors on the closed ones were held shut by vertical bars running from top to bottom, each one locked with a padlock and a seal. Between those bars and the horizontal ridges of the container walls, a kind of latticework formed that Lois could climb, with difficulty. Dropping the flashlight back into her pocket, she gripped the vertical bars, stretched her right foot up nearly as far as she could without falling over backward, and hauled herself up.

She figured the crime-scene units had brought ladders, or even a scaffold, but those were gone now. And with them, most likely, anything that would help her own investigation. When she could reach the floor of the open container, she pressed her palms against it, drew herself up so her waist was level with it, and rolled inside, under the tape.

As she feared, the container had been emptied out. On the one hand, she was glad, because what she had heard was that it had contained eighty corpses, a couple of days before. She sniffed the air and thought she could make out traces of the odor that must have been indescribable when the container was first opened. A strange hint of sweetness, tinged with spoiled meat and raw sewage.

Eighty people. Mostly women. Each must have had a couple of feet of personal space, she guessed. Maybe room to sit down in. The ones against the walls would have something to lean on, but if you were stuck in the center then you only had each other. No way to stretch out, so they slept sitting up. Probably not much sleep—on the deck of a freighter, across open seas, the thing was probably pitching and rolling all over the place. Any food and water they had, they brought in with them. Any waste stayed in, too. Did they bring some buckets for toilets? Couldn't just use the floor, not without it sloshing all over themselves during the crossing.

She tried to picture the scene, tried to imagine the stench even before they started to die. They were all in it together once the container was sealed, but did they argue over things like space, or accidentally bumping into one another? Were there fistfights, brawls? Did the people carry knives or other weapons with them?

She walked to the back of the container, ignoring the unidentifiable dark stains on the floor. Her own footfalls, soft as they were, echoed faintly in the steel coffin. Without her flashlight, it was dark back here, little of the illumination from outside leaking so far inside. Closer to what it would have been like for the people trapped here. Lois could barely contemplate the steadily building tension, the fear, the creak of the ship and the thunder of the waves and the way every noise made inside would have bounced around, driving people utterly mad. Bad enough not to know exactly what they were in for when they reached Metropolis—if in fact they reached it, since once they were locked in, they would have no control over their actual destination. Bad enough to know they had paid for the privilege of being canned like sardines.

Causes of death were still being investigated, according

to the limited official reports she'd had access to. Thirst, probably. Hyperthermia, from being locked in a steel box on the deck of a ship, out in the summer sun.

Also according to the official version, the container originated in Kaziristan, a former Soviet territory fronting on the Caspian Sea. The eighty had been illegal immigrants, trying to escape a repressive regime and come to the United States in search of a better life.

Instead, they found horrible, slow death.

Lois had taken a risk, sneaking through the police line into the crime scene. Really, there wasn't much to see.

But someone had to tell their story. The risk these eighty people took was enormous, next to hers. Theirs didn't pan out for them. She found it tragic, heartbreaking. Inspirational, too, in a way. The fact that they would even make the effort, would think that crossing the ocean in a cargo box was a good way to build a new life. Or that it was the only way.

She would find out who these people had been, and more importantly, who they had paid to lock them in the coffin that killed them. Somebody had to be on the outside, closing the doors, putting on the seal. Somebody had to pay off inspectors, arrange the transit. Somebody had made a tidy profit on the deaths of eighty innocents.

That somebody will find his or her face plastered all over the front of the Daily Planet, Lois vowed. *And that's a guarantee.*

CHAPTER SEVENTEEN

Zatanna and Dr. Occult had gone back to their respective homes, each promising to keep trying to locate the missing sorcerers. The Phantom Stranger and Jason Blood ensconced themselves in Jason's apartment, researching the problem in some of the many mystical books Jason had acquired over the centuries. Superman, unwilling to sit around waiting, had flown home to Metropolis.

A bank robbery had gone bad on the West Side, the robbers holding hostages and threatening to kill them. An oil truck had flipped over in the hypersector, threatening to start a fire that could engulf the city's financial district. An airliner with 319 people aboard had lost power shortly after takeoff from Metropolis Airport and plummeted toward the LuthopCorp Tower. Superman dealt with all those emergencies, and more, then flew back toward Gotham and Jason Blood's apartment.

When he neared it, he saw that it had erupted in a massive blaze. Bright flames tongued the sky, and the building had almost disappeared behind them. Disappeared to most people—Superman peered through the flames, and the apartment wall, and saw the Stranger and Jason sitting inside, massive tomes open on Blood's dining table, oblivious to the fire.

Something was wrong, then. They weren't men who were ignorant of their surroundings. They would see the flickering flames, hear the fire's roar, smell it.

Superman slowed his approach, hovering just beyond the fire's reach. He could feel the heat. He smelled burning wood and the ozone stench of electrical wires sizzling. But if it was real, he would hear screams. He combed the other apartments, and in none of them did he see anyone who appeared panicked or even seemed to notice the blaze. Cars drove down the street, pedestrians passed unconcerned right through the walls of fire. This was Batman's city, but Superman's old friend was nowhere to be seen.

Which means it's for my benefit, Superman thought. *The fire's not really there—it's some kind of trap.*

He decided to ignore it, just to fly through the flames like the people on the sidewalks below walked through them. But as soon as Superman got close, the fire seemed to coalesce into a solid arm, which darted toward him, slamming into him like a giant fist. The force of the blow surprised him—hot, but also amazingly forceful— sending him spinning three blocks from the building. He caught himself and flew forward again, striking at the retreating arm of flame, but his hand simply passed through it. *Like it was fire. Go figure.*

He took a few more swings at it, but all he got for his trouble was an unpleasantly warm arm. As he prepared to make another effort to get inside, though, flame shot toward him again, this time driving into his sternum, forcing the air from his lungs. He flipped a few times in the air, recovered, and came back for more.

Only one reasonable answer presented itself. The fire had been created, and was being controlled, magically. That was why it affected him and probably why he couldn't fight back against it. He kept trying, slugging away at the flame every time it became solid enough to hit him, but without success.

He wasn't going to be able to beat it alone. Since it seemed to be causing no genuine damage, he wasn't really worried about it. But it prevented him from reaching the Stranger and Jason, so he had to get through somehow.

Using his X-ray vision, he took another look to see if they had become aware of the situation. They didn't seem to have, but they weren't reading any longer, either.

Instead, Jason Blood had been knocked to the floor, where he appeared to be unconscious, and the Phantom Stranger was wrestling with a creature that looked like a mammoth, hairless, pink-skinned bear. Although the beast's appearance was amusing, it was clear from the Stranger's desperate expression that he took the attack with all seriousness. The thing freed an arm from the Stranger's grip and swatted him across the face. The Stranger's hat flew off, revealing close-trimmed white hair. Claw marks on his cheek began to bleed.

Superman wanted to rush in, to help battle the beast, but he couldn't get past the fire. The Phantom Stranger could probably have helped with the fire, because of its magical origins, but he couldn't shake the creature. Jason Blood couldn't help any of them, unless . . .

What was the spell the Stranger had spoken?

It might hurt the ears of some of the neighbors, but with luck they would hear it as booming thunder without being able to make out the words.

"Gone, gone the form of man! Rise the demon Etrigan!"

As the fire batted at Superman, he watched the transformation of Jason Blood into the yellow-skinned, snarling demon. When it was complete, Etrigan, not unconscious like Jason, rolled quickly to his feet.

"Etrigan!" the Stranger called. "Give me a hand here!"

"A hand? A hand? For the one-man band? First you grandstand, now you demand, as if your wish is my command?"

Through flame and brick, Superman saw that, though Etrigan taunted the Stranger, the demon was already on the move. The naked bearlike beast glanced over its shoulder to see Etrigan leaping at it, and released the Stranger to defend itself against this new contender. It had moved too slowly, though, and Etrigan was already there, his claws biting into the thing's naked flesh. The beast let out a squeal of pain. While its back was turned to him, the Stranger clapped his hands over its ears. In agony, the creature bent forward, and Etrigan brought clasped fists up into its chin.

The thing gave a grunt and folded. The Stranger, clearly winded, put his hands on his knees and sucked in a few deep breaths. Etrigan looked at the downed bear-creature like he wanted to eat it.

As he watched the brawl, Superman tried to dodge the fire's punishing blows. It kept up its assault so that he couldn't get through. Now, though, there was a chance that the Stranger could help him. "Stranger!" he called, using a superwhisper that he could throw for long distances. "Outside!"

The Stranger heard his plea and hurried to a window. Etrigan, curious as ever, followed him. Outside, Superman weaved and bobbed, trying to avoid yet another solid tendril of flame shooting toward him like Muhammad Ali's fist. Unable to see the fire, they must have thought he had gone completely insane.

"What's going on, Kal-El?" the Stranger asked. Knowing about Superman's superhearing, he didn't bother to shout.

"There's a magical flame," Superman explained, still using his whisper power. "It can become solid—and strong—when it wants to hit me, but it's nothing but fire when I hit back. I can't get through to you. Anything you can do to help?"

"Give me a moment," the Stranger said. He vanished from the window, although Etrigan continued to stare out. Another wisp of flame suddenly solidified and plowed into the side of Superman's head, smacking him so hard he saw stars.

True to his word, the Stranger reappeared several seconds later. He had recovered his hat—even when it was gone, Superman realized, his eyes still had not been visible—and seemed more composed. He recited a string of words in a language Superman didn't recognize, and when he reached its end, the flames vanished.

Superman flew in through the open window, hoping his antics and eventual entry had gone unobserved by the neighbors. Then again, this was Gotham City—a guy in a bat suit was its most famous hero, and the grinning, green-haired Joker seemed to be able to travel about the city without raising eyebrows.

"That was curious," the Stranger said, when Superman had floated to a gentle landing. "One moment we were sitting here reading, and the next that creature had knocked Jason out and attacked me."

"All while I was outside, prevented from getting close," Superman said.

"Sinister magics," Etrigan added. "Savage's tricks?"

"Or the three of them together," the Stranger speculated. "Zatanna said they were aware of our search and our whereabouts. So without coming here in person—thereby making themselves vulnerable—they sent these mystical champions to do battle in their stead."

"Very clever, those three," Etrigan said. "They hope to beat us absentee."

"Still," the Stranger said, "if that's the worst they can throw at us—"

"I have a feeling that's far from the worst," Superman interrupted. "A first shot over our bow. A warning shot. There'll be much worse to come, I'm convinced."

The Stranger nodded. "You're no doubt correct, Kal-El. We'll just have to play it as it comes and keep in mind that together we're stronger than any of us alone."

Superman folded his arms over his broad chest, his mouth held in a tight, grim smile. He had taken partners many times—the whole point of the Justice League was that as a group, its members could vanquish almost any foe—but he preferred to work solo. "That's for sure," he said, as much to himself as to the others. "When it comes to magic, I need all the help I can get."

Etrigan looked like he was about to say something—from the smirk on his homely face, a snide remark of some kind—when he shimmered, as if a sheet of shiny water had appeared between him and Superman. Etrigan stopped, mouth open. A glance at the Stranger revealed that he had seen it, too.

Superman swiveled his head, looking around the whole apartment. Its walls did the same thing, wavering for a moment, then taking their original, solid form again.

"Any ideas?" Superman asked.

"One," the Stranger replied. "You won't like it."

"Because it has to do with magic?"

"Because it means that the convergence is beginning. We are running out of time, Kal-El. If we don't do something quickly, then the alternate Earth conjured up by our enemies will become the one and only Earth—and everything we know will be gone forever."

CHAPTER EIGHTEEN

May 1872

Jonah Hex stood at the bar of the Willson Grand Hotel and Saloon, an expansively named place that didn't live up to its billing. Willson was a dusty little town that had sprouted up near Fort Bowie, a military camp located along the Tucson-Mesilla road and close to an important spring—fresh water being hard to come by and vital to survival in this arid land. Taking a second sip of the whisky he'd been handed, he guessed it had not been made with fresh water, but more likely with muddy rainwater, possibly mixed with a little effluent along the way.

But he would sleep in a bed tonight, with a roof over his head. Josie Bates already was—he had passed her room a few minutes before and heard her snoring away inside. There was enough alcohol in the whisky to kill anything unpleasant that might be living in it, and the smell of it covered up that of unwashed men. He drained the glass and clapped it on the unpolished, water-stained bar. The bartender, a skeletal man with a drooping mustache and sad eyes, raised a bushy eyebrow. "Again?"

"Again," Jonah confirmed. There were a handful of other men at the bar, and two dozen or so more scattered about at tables. Two fairly plain women worked the crowd. Jonah had been told that Willson hadn't even attracted a decent whorehouse yet, but as the fort grew it wouldn't take much longer. The bartender poured more whisky from an unlabeled bottle into Jonah's glass. His mustache twitched once, which Jonah reckoned might have been a smile.

He and Josie had been traveling for a couple of days. She'd had enough of racing across the landscape, she said, and wanted to return home at a slower pace in order to give her behind a rest. Since Jonah had persuaded her to pay him by the day, the pace suited him just fine. He wasn't a man who paid a lot of attention to scenery, but he had to admit that riding a little slower, really looking at the gradation of the various mountain ranges marking the horizon, browns and sage greens and grays and purples and blues, enjoying the starkness of the tall yucca stalks standing out against the deep blue skies, made the journey much more pleasant than the sprint out had been.

Now, sipping bad whisky and listening to the comfortable bustle of a crowd of drinkers, he was feeling downright contented.

With no notice, the crowd noise suddenly stopped. Jonah heard the slap of the front door as it closed, then a creaking sound. He instinctively looked toward the back of the bar, but no mirror hung there. Shifting his drink to his left hand, he let his right drop to within a quick yank of his hogleg and turned around.

Easy to see why conversation had ceased. Through the saloon—almost in the shadow of an Army fort built to combat the ever-present Apache threat—an old Apache man pushed a white man across the room in a wheelchair.

Jonah heard the sigh and creak of weapons being slid from leather.

If people started firing, the old man was done for. So, most likely, were several of the people doing the shooting. The old Apache rolled the chair through a gap in the tables that ran right up the center of the saloon, from the front door to a staircase that led upstairs to the hotel rooms, and if lead started flying some folks were bound to lean into bullets going past.

"Easy, gents," the bartender said. His voice was deep and carried easily through the room. "These men are payin' guests, and don't mean no one no harm." Through his contented warmth, Jonah was glad to know he was in the presence of an enlightened hotelier.

This announcement was greeted with a few curses and the wind-through-dry-leaves rustle of whispered complaint. "Lucky if we don't all wake with our throats slit!" one old codger groused.

The Apache ignored the comments and made his way to the stairs. There he stopped the chair and gazed at the seemingly insurmountable obstacle before him. The man in the chair, crippled or paralyzed though he was, had to outweigh the scrawny Indian by almost double. Jonah figured maybe the Apache could unload the cripple, drag him up the steps, then return for the chair. Hoisting both up at once would be impossible.

"Let's help him with that," a fat man in a red vest called

out. "Someone string a rope around the Indian's neck, and the rest of us can pull on it!"

This suggestion was greeted with raucous laughter, and inspired others of similar helpfulness. "Both fellers'd be a lot lighter with a few bullet holes in 'em!" someone offered.

"That 'pache didn't have legs, he wouldn't feel like he had to push the other *hombre* around!"

The saloon erupted with more laughter. Jonah realized the whole thing steamed him. He had just enough whisky in his gut to feel a kinship with the underdog. As a boy he had been teased mercilessly by his peers, who called his mother a tramp and worse. She was—driven into the arms of other men in a desperate attempt to find the love her own husband denied her, since he was too busy drinking liquor and selling it to Indians to pay her any mind at all—but that didn't make the teasing any easier to deal with. Then, of course, Jonah had driven off his own wife and child, so he reckoned the apple didn't fall too far from the tree.

As an adult, too, he had been teased and harassed plenty of times for his own disfigurement, and he hated to see such things happen to anyone else. Setting his glass down on the bar, he crossed to the Apache man's side. A hush fell over the saloon again, everyone watching to see what he would do.

"You take the back," Jonah said quietly. "I'll get the front."

"Thank you, stranger," the Apache said.

Jonah knew he'd get the worst end of this deal. He was far stronger than the old Apache, although the Indian's stringy muscles looked like they had more power in them than he'd guessed at first blush. So Jonah would take the front end, and most of the weight, and try to keep the old man from having to do much of the lifting. He almost regretted even making the offer, at least without downing another drink first. But he was stuck now, and every eye in the place rested on him, so there was no backing out of it.

He gave the crippled man a brief once-over. Fire burned in the man's dark eyes, a kind of intelligence that let Jonah know that although he could not move or speak, he was fully aware of his surroundings and situation. Jonah nodded, then squatted down and grabbed the wheelchair's front rails. "Pardon," he whispered to the silent man. "Realize this is a mite personal, down here." With that, he stood and lifted the chair off the ground. Behind it, the Apache man grabbed the back end, and Jonah began his backward lift up the staircase.

A couple of awkward, sweaty minutes later they had reached the top. Jonah set the chair down on the wooden floor. The Apache man brushed sweat away from his eyes and smiled. "Thank you, mister," he said. Even in those three words Jonah could hear the singsong speech patterns many Indians displayed.

"You're welcome," Jonah said. He touched his hat brim and turned away, happy to let the Indian finish the job.

As he started down the stairs, however, he was greeted by hoots and catcalls. "You tuck him in nice and tight?" the fat man in the red vest asked.

"Funny how he was drinkin' alone until an Apache showed up," another said.

"Reckon a feller that ugly don't get along none too well with white men!"

Jonah was willing to go back to his drink, which still

rested on the bar, waiting for him. He was in too fine a mood to spoil it by shooting anyone he didn't have to. He could take a few rude comments if it would let him get back to drinking sooner.

But he hadn't quite made it all the way down the stairs when a stranger rose from a table near the door. The man was young, dressed fancy in a striped jacket over a yellow, flowered vest and an open-collared white shirt. He wore a red wild rag around his neck, and a white Stetson kept a bottle company on his table. His hair was a sandy brown color. "I think y'all are bein' unnecessarily unkind," the man said. "What did this stranger do, except offer the hand of kindness to those less fortunate than himself? I ain't no preacher or religious man, but seems to me that's just the biblical way of doin' things, and I'm ashamed of all y'all for not helpin' him out. And I include myself in that, too."

A man at a table near his scooted his chair back and fixed the fancy-dressed man with a fierce glare. "You callin' us un-Christian?"

"I'm merely describin' what I saw, best as I can," the standing man said. "You want to apply a name to it, that's up to you."

The angry man stood up, and a couple of the other fellows at his table followed suit. "I didn't come here to be insulted," the angry one said. His hands were bunched into tight fists.

"Judgin' from your attitude, it ought to come right natural to you."

From that moment, Jonah knew, there was only one way things could go. The stranger in the flashy vest had just called the other man out. The other man had friends who would not sit by and watch their *amigo* get tromped by a pistol in a flowered vest. They would pile on, and men at the other tables would choose up sides, and Jonah, who had tried to avoid a fight, would have to join in on behalf of the man who had spoken up for him.

The only thing he misjudged was just how good the fancy-dressed stranger was.

The angry guy lunged at him, kicking his chair over as he did. One fist flew toward the fancy man's square chin. But it missed its mark by a wide margin because the man shifted his head to the side at the last possible second. At the same moment, he scooped up the bottle on his table— still half-full, Jonah noted—and swung it. His aim was better than his opponent's, and the bottle smashed against the side of the angry man's head. Amber liquid—mixed with some red—flew into the air and pattered against the floor. Jonah found himself sorry for the waste, even though the whisky had tasted more or less like horse piss to begin with.

By the time glass and liquid finished raining down, the brawl had begun in earnest.

The stranger in the yellow vest had three men piling on him, arms swinging, pummeling him with fists. All across the saloon floor, others had leapt to their feet and started in on one another. Jonah saw hair-pulling and kicking and a short man wearing a black slouch hat biting the ear of someone who looked like a gold miner just in from the fields. Then light from the overhead gas lamp glinted on steel. A tall fellow had drawn a knife, elevating the stakes, and he was fixing to bury it in the back of the fat man in the red vest. *Probably some old feud he figures he can settle now,* Jonah thought. He launched himself off the third step, sailing over two men wrestling on the floor, and landed on the tall guy's back.

The impact knocked the man forward, so he plowed right into the fat man. Jonah managed to grab the arm with the knife in it, however, so the man couldn't use the weapon. The fat man spun around and snarled at the knife-wielder. "Kanigher!" he said. "What the hell you up to now?"

"Lookin' to stab you in the back," Jonah explained, still gripping the knife arm.

The tall man wriggled, trying to shake Jonah's hold. He was strong, with broad shoulders and the muscles of a man who worked outside, likely with animals. "This ain't got nothin' to do with you, mister," he argued.

"You pull a knife in a friendly saloon brawl, I figger it's everybody's business."

The fat man smacked the hand holding the knife, causing the other one to drop it. It clattered onto the floor. "I'll take care of him," the fat man said. "Thanks for your help."

Jonah released the man and dived for the knife. Once he had palmed it, he stuck it into his holster, between the Colt and the leather, for safekeeping. He didn't have any time to savor that small victory, though, as a fist smashed into the back of his head. Jonah spun around to see a burly guy, blood already trailing from a cut on his forehead, shirt open to reveal a thick thatch of black hair. He was an inch or so shorter than Jonah but outweighed him by a good thirty pounds, and his arm was cocked to throw another punch.

"I don't like your face, stranger," the man said. Even as

he spoke his shoulders were in motion, that big fist driving toward Jonah's jaw.

Jonah sidestepped and kicked up with his right foot. The boot landed squarely between the man's legs, and his face turned red, then purple, as he folded in on himself. Jonah followed with a jab to the man's nose. The burly man went down, blood spurting, and writhed on the floor.

"I seen that!" another man shouted. "You kicked him right in the jewels, you durn jayhawker!" This man was taller than Jonah, wiry and bowlegged. His neck was corded with muscle and his face flushed with rage. "I ought to give you jesse!"

"Feel free to try," Jonah replied. "You happen to notice he bushwhacked me first?"

"That don't make no nevermind," the guy said. He spat on the floor at Jonah's feet. "A real man don't fight that way."

"A real man takes whatever advantage he's got and is glad of it."

"Try it on me, and you'll find out," the man said. He moved on Jonah, hands curled into claws. Jonah blocked them and threw a fist toward the man's gut, but the man stepped back and it missed. The other man closed again, and this time his clawed hand struck Jonah's good cheek, drawing blood. Jonah backhanded him across the face. The man spat teeth and blood and charged again. This time Jonah's foot slipped in some spilled liquid, and despite his small stature, the man knocked Jonah over backward.

The two rolled around on the floor, trading blows. The other guy's fists were lean, his knuckles hard, and he delivered some punishing shots. Jonah gave as good as he took. The man's cheek split under his fist, and blood seeped from the opening. Another blow raised a knot over the man's right eye that started to swell almost instantly. Jonah took a fist in the throat that choked him, and the man followed up by closing both hands around Jonah's neck.

Jonah kicked and rolled and tumbled, but the guy clung to him like a leech. The saloon started to look dark, as if someone had blown out the gas lamps. Finally, knowing that losing to this *hombre* would rile him enough to eat a horned toad backward, Jonah rolled again so that the other man was on the floor, and he pushed himself off with both hands, then released and let his full weight slam down on the guy. This broke the man's grip on his neck, and Jonah grabbed two handfuls of hair and slammed the guy's head on the floor five or six or ten times.

Finally, he eased off the man. Blood stained the floor. The man's eyes were open and moving, but he was out of the fight. Jonah stood quickly, ready for more.

"Vicious," someone said behind his back. "Laid him out colder'n a meat hook."

Jonah glanced toward the voice. The speaker was the fancy man in the yellow-flowered vest. "Just do what it takes," Jonah replied.

"Makes sense to me."

Jonah and the other man had their backs almost together now, and they threw punches at those brave or foolish enough to come at them. Between blows, the man seemed anxious to get acquainted. "Name's Bat Lash," he said. "Appreciate you gettin' into this thing."

"You spoke up for me," Jonah said. "Many's the man wouldn't'a done that."

"You got a moniker?"

"Hex," Jonah answered, driving a young soldier down with a left hook. "Jonah Hex."

"Bounty hunter?" The man who called himself Lash sounded impressed.

"That's right."

"Heard tell of you."

"Figured maybe."

They kept at it for a few more minutes, fighting and talking at the same time. Jonah only remembered twenty-some men in the place when the fight had started, so he wondered if the rest of the town and fort had heard about the fun and decided to join in.

"Hex?" Bat Lash said shortly.

"Yeah?"

"You notice that there don't seem to be anybody takin' our side here but us?"

"'Pears that way."

"And that they got us outnumbered by a far piece?"

"Seems so."

"You think we should start burnin' iron? Or maybe powwow?"

Jonah knew that drawing weapons would mean people would die. And he wasn't at all sure that other men would sit down for a peace pipe. Bat had a point, though—for as many men as they had already taken out of the fight, there seemed to be plenty more coming. At some point, unless the odds were evened up, Hex and Lash would have to go down under their numbers.

Before he could mention this to Bat, a commotion from another part of the saloon kicked up. Jonah looked past the men crowding in front of him and realized that a man he had barely noticed, sitting by himself at a corner table, had finally joined the fight. Tossing aside his black, flat-brimmed, dome-crowned hat and a gray topcoat, he revealed himself to be an Indian. Kiowa, from the looks of his outfit. He was tall, with shoulders you could lay an axe handle across and have room to spare. Jonah couldn't tell if his fists or his appearance had more impact, but the men he faced down seemed to fall awfully quick. He flashed Jonah a white-toothed grin as he fought.

"Looks like we got us some help," Jonah pointed out.

"None too soon," Bat replied. "Didn't know that feller was here, but I'm glad to see him. That Kiowa's an old saddle pard, and I'm runnin' down faster'n a two-dollar watch."

"Feelin' a mite peaked myself," Jonah admitted.

Even with the tall Indian's help, the tide of battle had turned against Jonah and his allies. The townsfolk seemed to have banded against the strangers, and as the fight wore on, what had started as a good-natured brawl had turned into a vengeful, bitter contest.

Jonah knew it had become deadly serious when he saw iron in the hand of a man near the back of the pack. He had two guys hanging on to his arms, but he shook one off and reached down for the Colt at his right hip. Before he could even draw it, a whip cracked and the hogleg that had been pointed at his head flew into the air. Its wielder let out a yelp.

Jonah couldn't say as he blamed the man. Standing behind him was a lean, dark man in a black cloak with red lining, a black mask similarly adorned with red, and a low-crowned, wide-brimmed black hat. The rest of his clothing was just as dark, and he blended with the shadows.

His skin was dark, too, almost nut brown, his face impassive, except that the eyes behind that mask fairly glowed with life and fury. He still held the braided leather bullwhip with which he had disarmed the *pistolero*.

"Who the hell . . .?" Bat began.

"Never seen anythin' like him," Jonah said.

The townsfolk threw a few more listless punches, and another one tried to pull a six-shooter on the Indian, but the spirit had gone out of them. When the sheriff and a handful of deputies threw back the door and roared in with shotguns in hand, the fight was mostly over.

"Everyone lay off!" the sheriff shouted. He was a round man with a prominent gut that a leather vest couldn't entirely contain. Beneath the brim of his hat, Jonah could make out small, pale eyes and a trimmed mustache half-shaded by a large, red nose. *A hard drinker,* Jonah guessed. *Probably peeved that we busted up the town's only saloon.* "Hands down!"

The townsfolk, those still upright at all, complied. So did Jonah, Bat Lash, the Indian, and the cloaked stranger. The deputies fanned out through the crowd, and it didn't take long for them to identify the troublemakers. They drew the outsiders together. Handing his scattergun to a deputy, the sheriff approached Jonah.

"You, mister," he said. His breath stank of fish, and there were flecks of it in his mustache. "I understand you started this fracas."

"That's right!" one of the townspeople called out.

"Not hardly," Jonah said.

"Actually, I landed the first punch," Bat admitted. "Well, bottle. But that was after I dodged one."

The sheriff barely glanced at Bat. "You got a reputation, Hex, and it ain't a good one. Where you go, dead bodies pile up. We got a lot of blood spilled in here tonight, but it don't look like anybody's got to be put to bed with a pick and shovel. Yet."

"Tried to keep it from goin' that far," Jonah said.

The sheriff might have gone deaf, for as much attention as he paid. "You goin' to come peaceably, or do I have to put the irons on you?" he asked.

"You're arrestin' me?"

"Smart as a bunkhouse rat, ain't you?"

Jonah heaved a sigh. This was always the way. Law dogs didn't much like men who earned their keep doing what they couldn't. Add in the scarred face, and Jonah had seen the wrong side of a lot of jailhouse bars he shouldn't have had to. It appeared that tonight would be no different.

"Save your shackles for them as need it," Jonah said. "I'll come quiet."

As he was being led out by the shotgun-toting deputies, Jonah caught the eyes of Bat Lash and the tall Kiowa brave. The dark man seemed to have faded back into the shadows he'd come out of. Both of his allies ticked their heads toward Jonah, acknowledging him, but then he was outside under the stars, a cool breeze blowing in off the desert, headed toward the lights of the sheriff's office across the street.

CHAPTER **NINETEEN**

Time, Felix Faust understood, was like the lane markings on Gotham City streets: more of a suggestion than an absolute law. He had been partnered with Vandal Savage and Mordru since the sixth century, A.D., as those who made the calendars liked to call it. He had not actually been born yet, but when one knew the ins and outs of magic as he did, that was not the obstacle it might have been to others. Vandal Savage had already been alive for aeons by that time, he knew. Savage, whose original name was Vandar Adg, had been one of the first modern men, the Cro-Magnons from which the rest of the race had descended. Radiation from a meteor bestowed immortality and incredible intellect upon him, and he used his many aeons to amass a wealth of mystical knowledge. He claimed—and Faust had no reason to doubt him—that he had been one of the Caesars of Rome, the Mongol war leader called Genghis Khan, a captain of the Spanish armada and an advisor to Napoleon, and the mass murderer history came to know as Jack the Ripper.

His other partner, the Dark Lord Mordru, may have been older still. Mordru didn't remember his childhood at all, and the legend surrounding him was that he had never been born and could never die. Like Savage, his memories included all the ages of mankind, and, like Savage, he had spent a goodly portion of those centuries as a student of the darkest arts.

Faust, younger by far than either of those, had extended his time and influence on Earth in other ways. He had lived millennia ago, but was slain in a vicious magical battle. During the twentieth century, he was finally reincarnated, in the body of a small-time sorcerer named Dekan Drache. Some part of him recognized that great power flowed in his veins, and he worked and studied and fought to regain that which had been so unfairly denied him. In quest of the immortality that defined his partners, he allowed his body to be possessed by master mage Hermes Trismegistus. That effort had been ill conceived from the start, and Faust had long since broken free of that sorcerer's influence. He was his own man once again—third in power and influence to his partners, but that was third among three of the most powerful beings Earth had ever seen. No small status in anyone's estimation.

Many years on Earth and a long view of events taught patience. Faust, younger than his cohorts, was not as patient as they, but he could bide his time when he had to. When it was important. Sometimes he wore the guise of a modern man and went into Metropolis or New York or Paris for one reason or another, and standing on a street corner in a cold rain trying to hail a cab, he could be as impatient and easily vexed as the next guy.

Except the next guy, for the most part, couldn't cast a spell of slow, painful death on anyone who dared to snatch a cab from a position down the block.

But when it came to their plan finally to take ultimate control of Earth—and to merge the Earth they had caused to come into being with the other, original Earth—he could be as patient as necessary. He could wait and wait.

Using their combined powers, he, Savage and Mordru had built a kind of sanctum between dimensions, a little home away from home, protected from being seen or otherwise detected by any of the hated super heroes who might have tried to stop them. It was here that they had gathered to wait for the end game, now that it had begun. "Now" being a flexible concept, he knew, since the events that made it happen took place centuries in Earth's past, and the split, the division into two separate Earths, also came about more than a hundred years ago. The convergence, though—the culmination of their plans—that was *now,* by any definition.

Although he had waited for centuries for the final victory, Faust found that these few days before the end were the hardest. During the intervening years, since they had no way to know for sure if their plans would play out just as they hoped, they had continued trying new schemes to defeat their foes and grab power on the original Earth. Controlling both Earths would guarantee their success, of course.

For the moment, there were no major efforts in the works. They tried to keep a low profile, not counting the occasional assault on Superman, the Phantom Stranger, and the demon Etrigan, who had teamed up in these last hours to try to thwart their long-term plan. Faust found himself watching TV, which he almost never did, and playing cards with the others, sometimes reading through popular novels or ancient, mystical tomes. The sanctum wasn't stylish in the least, although it was functional. Each conjuror had his own suite of rooms: bed and bath and library, where he could escape from the others when need be. A common area contained a fireplace and more books and a few comfortable couches to lounge on. There was a kitchen, although no one cooked much when they could simply conjure meals at will. The walls, if they had existed in the real world, would have looked like pine paneling, and the furniture would have been aged but not antique, simply broken-in and ready for use.

Mordru, as it turned out, was hard to live with. He demanded almost constant attention, apparently uncomfortable with his own company. Savage had no problem being alone, and sometimes even when they were all in the same room he paced and muttered to himself as if formulating pernicious plots.

If it hadn't been for Savage's scheming, however, they would never have made it to this point. It had been he, after all, who had first discovered the slipstream nature of time and suggested the idea to his past self. It had been his idea to forge the nine-pointed star that sealed their partnership and created two Earths where there had been only one. It had even been Savage's foresight that caused him to enlist Etrigan to help forge the star, allowing them to control the demon when he—or a later incarnation of him—tried to stop them, back in Camelot.

Those last few days in Camelot had been wild ones.

With Morgaine's forces attacking and Arthur's knights—
even assisted by Merlin—unable to resist, the safety that
Faust, Mordru, and Savage had found inside her walls had
proven only temporary. In the end they had been forced to
separate and flee for their very lives. Savage had explained that they didn't want to keep the star with them,
because any one of them who spent too much time in its
proximity would risk being driven mad by its power and
influence.

The three had met up a few years later, then again at ir-
regular intervals over the succeeding centuries, to keep
tabs on the star. From Camelot, it had been carried deep
into the trackless forests of Britain with other souvenirs of
Camelot, some valuable and others not. It sat in a cave beneath a rocky crag with that hoard for years, until Norse
reavers bore it away, having slaughtered the tribe of Celts
who protected it. The Norsemen took it with them on
longships to a massive-beamed wooden building on a
frozen shore in their forsaken homeland. Finally, after
more years there, it was traded with other baubles, their
origins forgotten by now, to Carolus Magnus, known as
Charlemagne to the world at large.

Having entered Gaul, which would become France and
fall under the sway of the Holy Roman Empire, the star
and some of the other treasures of Camelot were claimed
by the Pope during the time that Avignon was the seat of
the Church. When that position shifted to the Vatican,
within Rome, the hoard moved there, including the star.

And there, protected by magic and the soldiers of the
Papal Army, it stayed for a long, long time. Faust worried
about it occasionally, wishing he could gain access to it,
touch it. Savage tried to calm him—and Mordru, whose

patience even then was thinner than a fraying knot in a narrow, braided rope—with only modest success.

They couldn't get to the star, and it would do them no good if they could, Savage reminded them. The thing's usefulness was at an end, for now. It had done what it needed to do, had set in motion the course of events that would end the way they needed it to. The second Earth had been created, and they would run that world, returning to the original one only as necessary to make their attempts to conquer it as well and retreating when they had to. Not until it was time to finalize the convergence would they need it again. When that time came, Savage insisted, they would find it, reclaim it, and use it again. Until that time, it was as safe in the Vatican as anywhere else on Earth.

And their enemies would *never* think to look for it there.

As with most of this long-term plan, Savage had been correct.

CHAPTER **TWENTY**

Some things, it turned out, Clark Kent could do more easily than Superman. Getting inside Gotham City's Club Mysterium was one of those things. Sure, he could have bulldozed his way in, but that would have resulted in piles of cinder block and twisted steel, angry members, and no information. He tried listening from far above, but although the conversations he heard were intriguing, he couldn't learn specifically what he was after.

Clark Kent, however, could go inside peacefully—an invited guest—and even ask pointed questions. Not only could he, but it was expected of him. His first inclination had been to suggest that the Stranger or Jason Blood go, but they would both be recognized there, they said. Clark would be recognized, but that would work in his favor.

Convinced, he stood outside the club's Art Nouveau–style metal door, eyeing its façade. Three stories tall, the windows faced only onto the street and were painted black.

A couple of spotlights mounted on metal sconces washed the black cinder blocks.

As if to block Superman's prying eyes, the inside of the block walls had been coated with lead.

Clark had dressed in a black suit for the occasion, with a white shirt and a red-patterned tie. Black had been the right color choice, judging from the outfits he saw on those who came and went during the evening, but he might be the only one in a white shirt or a necktie. The clientele appeared to be mostly young and well-off. He saw a lot of Goth-looking people, but not exclusively those. Bearded men, long dark hair on both genders, women wearing cleavage-revealing tops, short skirts, fishnets. Zatanna might have fit in, although Clark wouldn't. Fitting in, however, wasn't the point.

The people who did go in first knocked on the door, where they were met by a bouncer with a shaved head and arms as big as Superman's—although he had probably been born under the yellow sun and so didn't have Superman's strength. He admitted everyone with a smile and a friendly greeting. Clark got the idea that strangers didn't even try to get in. Why would they? Nothing on the building gave any indication of what was inside.

According to the Stranger, Club Mysterium was the hot gathering place for magicians and magic users—not the stage kind, but real magic, as practiced by Zatanna and Dr. Occult. They and a few others worked with Earth's heroes. The magicians who frequented Club Mysterium were more likely to have other allegiances.

Clark had phoned ahead for an appointment with the club's manager, a woman who called herself simply Janna. Having watched the comings and goings for a few minutes, he walked to the door and knocked. The same huge bouncer opened it. He wore a black tuxedo shirt and snug black pants. This time, recognizing an outsider, his expression was far from friendly. "Yeah?"

"My name is Kent," Clark said. "I have an appointment with Janna."

"Wait here," the bouncer said, slamming the door. Clark stood on the sidewalk outside the door, feeling strangely vulnerable. He guessed that the sensation was partly because he'd been left standing out in the open, where anyone could be watching him, and partly because he still carried traces of that other Clark around with him, the one who wasn't Superman, and who'd had to watch helplessly as his Lois was murdered.

A few minutes passed, and the door opened again. This time the bouncer smiled, gold teeth glinting in the glow from the spotlight over the door. "Come on in, Mr. Kent," he said, waving a hand as if to illustrate the proper direction. "Sorry for the wait. Janna will be right down."

"Thanks," Clark said, entering into a small, dark lobby. The phone the bouncer had used to call Janna sat on a small counter in one corner. A TV monitor showed the empty street where Clark had just been standing. On the back wall the club's logo had been painted, in the same curlicue Art Nouveau style as the wrought-iron door, and a small ceiling-mounted spotlight shone down on it. Clark could smell the bouncer's sweat, the cup of black coffee sitting beside the phone, and the garlic he'd had in his dinner. "You recognize all the members?"

"Doesn't take long," the bouncer said.

"How many are there?"

"Maybe Janna will tell you that. Not me."

"Guess I'll wait for her, then."

The bouncer flashed him the gold-filled grin, but didn't speak again.

A minute later the back wall opened up, hinged at the corner. Behind the door was a lit staircase. Descending footsteps sounded, and the sharp tang of ozone, maybe mixed with a little brimstone, filled the lobby.

Clark saw Janna's legs first as she came down the stairs, long and slender, with nicely turned ankles and firm calves. Her dress was black, as expected, with an uneven, pointed hem, almost batlike. *Or Batman-like,* Clark mentally amended, given that he was in his old friend's town again. A slender waist was wrapped in the same fabric. Above the waist, the dress swelled like an inverted bell, its scooped neckline barely containing an expansive bosom. Janna's hair was as black as her dress, straight and falling to the tops of her breasts. It framed a narrow, oval face with full, red lips, an angular nose, and large, luminous green eyes. Her smile crinkled the skin around those eyes and carved dimples at the corners of her mouth.

"Mr. Kent," she said. "Please forgive the wait."

"No problem, Ms. . . ."

"Just Janna."

"Janna."

"Won't you come up to my office?" she asked.

Clark felt a little like the fly being invited into the spider's web—Janna's office being the command center of a private club dedicated to magic. He'd come this far, though. "I'd love to," he said.

She led him back up the staircase she had just descended. It was lit by flickering oil lamps mounted at intervals on wall sconces. At the top an open, arched doorway led into her office. She passed beneath the arch with a glance back at Clark, a hint of a smile over her shoulder. By the time Clark reached the top of the stairs and followed her in, she had taken a seat on a mound of silky pillows. Her knees were pressed demurely together, her hands resting on them, but the whole scene—candle-light, cushions, the slits in her dress riding up her thighs— spoke of sensual invitation.

This was, he reminded himself, a magic club, not a sex club. He also knew enough about magic to realize that for many practitioners the two were interchangeable—that sex released powerful emotions that could be channeled into magical energy.

"Have a seat, Mr. Kent."

There wasn't a chair in the place. A few piles of cush-ions like the one she lounged on, a low wooden table to her left that held a cordless phone and a laptop computer, turned off and folded shut, and some drawers built into one dark wall that held file folders, business records and the like. Clark sat on one of the piles, crossing his legs at the ankles. He pulled a small pad and a pen from a jacket pocket. "Please, call me Clark."

"Very well, Clark," Janna said. Her voice was soft, kit-tenish. "I do have a few things I'm curious about, before you start asking your questions."

"That's fine, Janna."

She smiled again, then let her face go blank. All busi-ness suddenly. "First, I wondered why the *Daily Planet* would be interested in a Gotham City club."

"Simple enough," Clark replied. "We don't have any-thing like it in Metropolis, but I'm sure some of our resi-dents belong to the club, right?"

"Yes, that's true."

"And it's unique enough to be interesting on its own merits."

"I like to think so. But why send Clark Kent? Surely we're not on the crime beat."

"To tell you the truth, I'm off the crime beat." He didn't like lying under any circumstances, so tried to stick to the truth where he could. And he hadn't exactly claimed that he'd been assigned to write about Club Mysterium. He wasn't sure he'd get time to do so, but if he had the time, he'd write the story and at least submit it for publication.

"By writing a feature story on us? We're not exactly hard news."

Clark shrugged. "But you're a story," he said. "And I think a compelling one."

"That I can't disagree with," Janna said. "All right, you've satisfied my curiosity." She looked at her own fingernails, as if suddenly shy. "Some of it, anyway. All right then, Clark, what would you like to know?"

That invitation was also the tricky part. What he really wanted was to know if any of the members had information on the current whereabouts of the three sorcerers he sought, or what exactly they were up to. But he couldn't ask that outright. He would have to put the reportorial skills he had developed over the years to good use, to try to sneak in on his questions without tipping his hand. "To start with, as I suggested before, I'm sure your members come from all over, not just from Gotham, correct?"

"That's true."

"Can you give me some general guidelines? Regional? Nationwide?"

"International," Janna said. "If there are any other groups quite like ours, I don't know of them."

"How did it come about? Were you the founder?"

"One of them. I started the group, I guess nine years ago now, with my late husband Jerry. We were both involved with ritual magic, and realized that there had to be other people around who shared our interest but we had no way to reach out to them. So we started the club in our own home, advertised a little, and before we knew it we were deluged with responses. We rented a small building after that, and a year later bought this one."

"Remarkable growth," Clark observed. "How many members do you have now?"

"You understand, Clark, that I can only talk about our membership in the most general terms. Membership information is strictly confidential, and, well, there are those in the outside world who might think that membership in such an organization is indicative of low moral standards."

"I'm sure that's true," Clark replied.

"But in numerical terms, I can tell you that we now have more than three thousand members, representing five continents. Some members only visit in person once a year, some less often than that, but they keep their memberships current just the same. Others, particularly the local ones, might be here two or three nights a week."

Clark jotted a couple of notes, just so it would look like he was doing something. He would remember the pertinent information without notes. "In what sorts of activities do they engage while they're here?"

"We're mostly a social club," Janna explained. "A place where people with similar interests and pursuits can get together. There are two fine restaurants on the premises, three bars. A library, various smaller sitting rooms. We hold workshops and seminars. Anyone interested in what some might call the Dark Arts will find kindred souls here to talk with, share ideas and experiences."

"So it's pretty much like other private clubs? A few drinks, maybe a meal, and some conversation about the last demon you summoned or prosperity spell you performed?"

"If you're trying to bait me, Clark, it won't work," Janna warned. "I recognize that outsiders won't always think much of us and what we do here. And yes, some of our membership may summon demons from time to time. They don't perform ritual magic here at the club, though, and I'm not going to comment on or reveal what they may do away from here."

"That's fair," Clark said. "What about membership qualifications, then? Is there an application procedure? How do you keep out the merely curious, or the actively hostile?"

She tossed him a smile and rubbed her knee. "There's a lengthy process," she said. "Any new member has to be recommended by an existing one. Then there's a written application and a fairly substantial membership fee. After that all checks out, there's a personal interview, which I conduct."

"So you've met all the members?"

"Every single one of them. Three thousand and some people is quite a few, and I wouldn't swear that I'd recognize all of our members at the mall or in a grocery store. But most of them I would. As would Alex, whom you met at the door."

"Any celebrities?" Clark asked. "People who are known to the general public outside the magical community?"

Janna's tone had turned cool when she replied. "I told you, I'm not talking about specific members."

"I mean in general. I'm not asking for names."

"In that case—and I don't want to draw attention to them, because we're about protecting privacy, not exploiting our members—but yes, I'd venture to say there are some famous names on our membership rolls."

"Care to give categories? Politics, sports, show business . . . ?"

"Next question," Janna said flatly.

"Next question? I guess you've already answered it. If someone is interested and wants to apply . . ."

"Then they need to know a current member."

"So you're not looking to expand at this point."

"It's already hard for me to keep up with all the work, Clark. Not to mention trying to find time for my own magic. We don't need more members. We wouldn't turn anyone away who is sincerely interested and meets the other qualifications, because the club's mission remains the same as it was when Jerry and I founded it."

"Do your members engage in magical practices of which you disapprove?"

"I told you, I don't comment on what any member does away from our premises. It's not my place to be judgmental. You don't have to be involved in magic for long to know that judgmental people are one of our greatest problems—that's been true since the Inquisition, if not before, and I'm certainly not going to go out of my way to make it worse."

"I guess what I'm getting at is, I know from my crime

reporting that some super-villains, the kind who Batman and Superman and the Justice League deal with, are magic users. If you had anyone like that among your membership—people who used magic to break the law, for personal gain, or to commit acts of violence—would that be tolerated?"

"Is there an echo in here? I could swear I just heard someone say that she wasn't going to comment on or judge on members' activities."

"You did," Clark admitted. "But you can't blame a guy for trying." He set the pad down and retied his shoe, which had not been untied in the first place. "Only reason I ask is that I heard a rumor that Felix Faust was a member here, and he's got quite a reputation as—"

Janna cut him off. "Mr. Kent, whether or not Felix is a member here is none of your business, and certainly nothing I'm going to discuss with you. I thought I had made myself very clear."

"Yes, you did. I'm sorry."

"I think that concludes this interview, Mr. Kent." All the earlier flirtatiousness was gone now. Clark could see by the set of her jaw and the angle of her head that she was serious. "Whatever publicity the *Planet* may offer, I don't need."

"I'm sorry if I pushed too hard, Janna," Clark said, getting to his feet and putting away his pad. "I have to follow where I think the story is, and I know it can get annoying sometimes."

"That's certainly true. Unfortunate, too, since at first I was thinking you might be kind of fun to have around."

Clark didn't bother to point out that he was happily

married and not planning to be around beyond this one brief encounter. He knew when he'd been dismissed.

With only the most halfhearted pleasantries, she let him show himself out. Hearing Janna's instructions to Alex the bouncer, he didn't linger downstairs or try to ask any more questions. Instead, he went out into the street and walked three blocks down until he found an alley dark and isolated enough for his needs. There, he stripped out of his street clothes, compressing them in his hands and tucking them into a pouch inside his cape.

The whole time, he listened in using his superhearing. For the first few minutes after he'd gone, Janna ranted to Alex, whom she had summoned up to her office, about what a jerk that Clark Kent was. Finally, she got around to describing specifically what had upset her, including his question about Felix Faust.

"Felix is the only one he mentioned by name?" Alex inquired.

"That's right. There might have been more if I hadn't shut him down right away."

"Are you going to tell him?"

"I can't exactly call him on the phone."

Damn! Superman thought. That was exactly what he had been hoping for—a phone call on which he could eavesdrop.

"But I can get a message to him another way. He should know there's a reporter snooping around."

"Anything you need me to do, Janna?"

"Just be sure I'm not disturbed," Janna said. "I'll need the ritual room for the rest of the night."

Ritual room. After she had assured him that no magic was practiced on the premises.

And, of course, she would use magic to contact Faust, guaranteeing that Superman could not listen in.

But he knew someone else who might be able to.

With a quick two-step, he took flight. Less than a second later he had passed two hundred miles per hour and sped up steadily from there. By the time a full second had gone by anyone looking directly toward him would have seen nothing more than a streak, a wavering of the light in front of their eyes.

Two minutes after that he was back inside Jason Blood's apartment, explaining the situation to Jason and the Phantom Stranger.

"I think I know what she has in mind," the Stranger said. "And I should be able to intercept. It won't help us a lot—all we'll get is whatever message she's sending, which is that you're a pain in the neck. We already knew that."

Superman grinned, knowing the Stranger was making—for him—a hilarious joke. *This guy and Batman,* he thought. *I sure can pick the humorless ones. Good thing Booster Gold's usually around the Watchtower when I need a laugh.*

"If Faust replies?"

"Then I'll be able to pick up his message, too," the Stranger answered. "Which might be a little more helpful."

"But then again, maybe not," Jason added.

"True."

"I guess we get what we get," Superman said.

"Truer words . . ." The Stranger let the thought fade out. "Jason, why don't you tell Superman what we've been up to while I take care of this?"

"Sure thing," Jason said.

The Stranger nodded toward a closed door. "I'll be in there." Superman hadn't been in the room on the other side of that door, but he had seen through the door that it was a kind of inner sanctum of Jason's, filled with more demonic memorabilia but also other types of magical implements. He guessed the Stranger would be conducting a ritual of his own and didn't care to have it observed by anyone.

Fine with Superman. He didn't want to watch.

Jason Blood bade Superman sit down on his comfortable couch, while he took a straight-backed chair across from him. "We've been doing a lot of studying tonight," Jason said. "We've come to a few conclusions about what our little threesome is up to. I warn you, it's not pretty."

"I wouldn't expect it to be, given the participants."

Jason leaned forward. "Doing what they've done— creating an entire new world, branching the time stream, changing its sun to red, then merging it with ours—this is some powerful magic."

"Clearly," Superman said.

"Powerful magic requires powerful emotional energy. Magic sucks energy like one of those big flashlights sucks battery power. This kind of ritual—well, slicing open your palm or cutting the throats of a couple of goats doesn't cut it. Not on this scale."

"We're talking ritual sacrifice?"

"We're talking ritual sacrifice on a scale never before seen on Earth," Jason replied. His eyes were glistening with intelligence and emotion.

"So we need to be on the lookout for some kind of mass murder?" Superman asked.

"That's the thing," Jason said. "The worlds are already merging, which means the magic has already happened."

"But wouldn't we know about the sacrifice?"

"We do, but we might not recognize it as such. There have been plenty of cases of wholesale slaughter in our history, sadly," Jason reminded him. "We need an occasion when deaths were counted by the tens of thousands. Maybe the millions. We wouldn't have seen the ritual aspect because we would never have looked for it. But it's there, somewhere. With any luck, the Stranger will get a clue as to where we should look from 'listening in' on Janna and Faust."

"And when we find out which of history's greatest tragedies took place in order to further the sinister ends of these three villains," Superman said, "we won't be able to do anything to prevent it."

"It's already happened, Kal-El. You want to change history on that kind of scale?"

"Of course not. I just hate to sit back and let it happen."

"You and me both. I know the Stranger feels the same way. We can't save everyone, Kal-El, no matter how much we'd like to. What we have to focus on is saving everyone who's left—everyone alive right now. Because if Savage, Faust, and Mordru have their way, they're all doomed. The whole world is doomed. That's the prize we need to keep our eyes on."

Superman nodded. Jason was right. Millions might have died to set their evil scheme in motion. Nothing could be done about that now.

But he would not let billions more follow.

CHAPTER TWENTY-ONE

May 1872

When the lawmen broke up the brawl, El Diablo melted into the shadows at the back of the saloon and vanished up the stairs. He preferred to work in darkness, to let the mystery of his existence keep his foes off-balance. By the time Jonah Hex was hauled off to the sheriff's office, El Diablo was already on the hotel's roof, listening and watching. He stayed there, unobserved, while Bat Lash and the big Kiowa warrior spoke in the street, in hushed tones. A moment later, a white man in a neat gray suit joined them from inside the saloon. The newcomer's blond hair was neatly combed, his face clean-shaven, and he wore small, round-framed glasses. He couldn't disguise his height or the spread of his shoulders—he was a big man, although he carried himself like one who was weak and frail. El Diablo was at a bad angle to judge a person's height, but the blond man looked even taller than the Kiowa.

"Gentlemen," he said. His voice was just as high as one

would expect, to look at him—but El Diablo suspected it was no more real than his feeble appearance. "I hate to observe a gross miscarriage of justice, but in this case I fear that's what has transpired."

"I think I agree with you," Bat said. "It's just I'm not entirely sure what you said."

"A raw deal," the stranger clarified. "Hex got a raw deal."

"True," the Indian agreed.

"We were just talkin' about that very thing," Bat said. "What's it to you, stranger?"

"I was inside the saloon," the blond man said. "I kept away from the fisticuffs, naturally—I'm a schoolteacher from up Mesa City way, not a fighting man. But should Mr. Hex need a witness to testify as to his innocence, I would be more than happy to speak up."

"Why, Hex'd surely appreciate that," Bat said. "If his case comes to trial."

"My name is Tane," the stranger said. "John Tane."

Bat stuck out his hand, and John Tane gave it a shake. "Bat Lash. Pleased to make your acquaintance."

"Likewise, Mr. Lash."

The big Kiowa didn't say anything during the rest of the exchange, just looked at John Tane with his arms crossed over his chest. In another couple of minutes, Tane had gone back into the hotel.

After he was gone, Bat chuckled softly. "Big help he'll be."

"More to him than it seems," the Kiowa said.

"More to you as well, I reckon, Ke-Woh-No-Tay," Bat said. "Been a few years since I laid eyes on you, then you turn up on the right side of a brawl here in the middle of nowhere."

"Don't like to see brave men outnumbered," the Kiowa said.

"You never did. But I'm surprised you're anywhere's near a white man's saloon, much less a cavalry fort," Bat said. He paused, regarding the Indian. "We go back a ways, you and me, and I always liked you, even though you always got us in trouble, seems like. But now I'm gonna ask you for another favor."

"I rode hard to escape a cavalry troop," Scalphunter explained. "It is a thirsty business. As for this favor, what is it?"

"We can't let Hex stew in that jail cell. I don't know what it means, the three of us turnin' up in this little town all at the same time, but there's a reason for it. Things like this don't happen for nothin'. And whatever's comin', we'll wish Hex was beside us."

El Diablo lashed out with his whip, catching the balustrade of a balcony below him. The moment the end of the whip had circled around it four times, he launched himself into the air, still holding the whip's handle. When the whip was fully extended, his angle of descent changed. The whip slowed him just enough to enable him to land safely on his feet, then it loosed itself from the balustrade and dropped into his hands.

"This is what I have been wanting to hear," he said when he'd landed. He agreed that there must have been some purpose for them all showing up in the same small town, and suspected that it might have something to do with the vision of which Wise Owl had told him. "If you plan to break Jonah Hex out, I'd be happy to be part of the plan." He gave a half bow to Bat and Scalphunter. "I am called El Diablo," he said. "The reputations of both of you gentlemen, as well as that of Jonah Hex, are well-known to me."

"Reckon I've heard some campfire stories about El Diablo, too," Bat said. "Always figured you'd have goat hooves instead of leather boots, though."

"I hope I do not disappoint."

"Entrance like yours? You'd have to go a long way to disappoint me after that."

El Diablo smiled. As paralyzed Lazarus Lane, he met precious few new people. Those El Diablo encountered were usually on the wrong side of the law. He thought he might enjoy this adventure, and these new *compadres* would prove entertaining at the least.

"Come," Scalphunter said. "If we plan to free Hex, we should not do it standing in front of the jail."

The street was dark, but still the Kiowa's point was well-taken. He, Bat Lash, and El Diablo hurried to the end of the block. The town essentially ended at that point. Beyond, dark hills rolled toward mountains that could only be discerned because their jagged peaks cut off the sky full of bright stars. A handful of ranchers dwelled out there, struggling every day against dry country and Apache raiders, but from the edge of town no sign of those ranches could be seen.

As they walked past it, El Diablo examined the sheriff's office and jail as closely as he could. He'd need a better look before they actually moved against it, but from across the street it appeared secure enough. It was a building separate from the others in its block, not even connected by the covered boardwalk that passed before the rest. A single story, it was built of adobe brick that must have been sixteen inches thick judging by the depth of the windows. A large glass window faced onto the street, and through it El Diablo saw the sheriff and some of his deputies sitting around a desk, gas lamps burning, passing around a bottle. Behind them, barely visible, were cell bars. On the one side he saw as they passed, toward the back of the building, a small barred window opened onto the alley that separated the jail building from its neighbor.

"Way they're exercisin' their arms on that mescal bottle, we might could wait till they're either asleep or out in the street shootin' at snakes that ain't there, then just waltz in and unlock Jonah's cell," Bat suggested.

"Unless they decide to shoot Hex instead," Scalphunter added.

"Which they might well do," El Diablo agreed. "Who knows when a circuit court judge might come this way again? Less'n they turn Hex over to the military, they may have him in their cell for some time."

"On account of which we need to get him out," Bat said. "Whatever it is we've been drawn here to do, I doubt it can wait until some circuit rider comes around."

"That's most probably true," El Diablo said. "We should free him tonight, if at all possible."

"Any suggestions?"

"I got one." This comment came from the shadows at the corner of the block. The three men drew iron and spun to face the newcomer. "Easy," he said in a deep, commanding voice. "If you're fixin' t'bust Hex out, I'm on your side."

The stranger was tall, with thick dark hair. His hat hung down his back, a stampede string holding it there.

He wore a fringed leather jacket, a long red wild rag tied around his neck, white leather gloves and jeans, with two gun belts crisscrossed on his hip. There was something familiar about him, even though El Diablo was sure he had never encountered the fellow before.

"Why should we trust you?" Scalphunter asked.

"Way I see it," the stranger said, "none of you knows the others. So you don't know me just's well. Folks call me Johnny Thunder."

"Well, Johnny Thunder," Bat said, "you make a good point. We've only just made each other's acquaintance, so I reckon you ain't too late to join the party."

Johnny Thunder smiled and stretched out a hand toward Bat, and in that moment El Diablo realized who it was. Most would have never noticed, but sitting in his chair all day, every day, Lazarus Lane had become a keen observer of men. When Johnny Thunder reached toward Bat, he tilted his arm out and then sharply up from the elbow. El Diablo had seen that same motion a short while earlier, when the schoolteacher named John Tane shook Bat's hand.

Somehow John Tane had colored his hair, and he'd changed clothes and discarded the glasses. But it was the same man, El Diablo was certain.

He didn't think any less of Johnny Thunder for that. After all, he had another identity as well, one even less like El Diablo than Johnny Thunder and John Tane. Almost no one thought that El Diablo could possibly be wheelchair-bound Lazarus Lane.

With introductions made, when it was his turn to shake Johnny's hand, El Diablo gave no indication that he knew the man's secret. He would want it the same way. "What is your idea?" El Diablo asked him.

"Way I see it, you need a diversion," Johnny said. "Those men in there are busy paintin' their tonsils, and it won't take too long before they're seein' double or triple. But then they'll like as not fall asleep where they sit, with those scatterguns close t'hand. We go in there to take Hex out, they might just wake up and start blastin'. But if some of us can draw 'em out into the street, thinkin' there's somethin' outside needs their attention, then the others'll be able to get in and free Hex."

"Might could work," Bat agreed. "You got anything particular in mind?"

A broad grin lit Scalphunter's face. "How about an Indian attack?"

The other men shared his smile. "We don't want to engage the entire town, or the Army," El Diablo pointed out. "But a fight between an Indian and a white man may well do the trick."

"Sounds like you three and Hex got some important business t'take care of," Johnny said. "I'd stay and throw in with you if'n I could, but I got to light a shuck out of here tonight, back to Mesa City. I'd be happy to fight old Scalphunter here, and then try to draw the sheriff and his boys after me so's the four of you can get on with it."

"What about it, Scalphunter?" Bat asked. "You'll be riskin' arrest or worse if they catch up to you."

"They won't." Scalphunter said it as casually as if he'd been ordering eggs for breakfast.

"Then me'n El Diablo here will go in after Jonah," Bat said. "You two try to lure 'em well away from the jail door so they won't see us goin' in and out."

"This is startin' t'sound like fun," Johnny Thunder said, with a grin. He and Scalphunter stepped aside to choreograph their fight, while El Diablo and Bat Lash tried to plot out their moves once the fight began. They could only anticipate so far, however, as their actions would depend on how many men were left behind inside.

Ten minutes later, they were ready to begin.

El Diablo and Bat Lash led five horses around to the alley behind the buildings. Bat had wanted to alert Jonah that they were coming, but El Diablo had convinced him that they ran too big a risk of accidentally tipping off the sheriff's men as well, since the jail building was so small. Their appearance would be just as much a surprise to Jonah Hex as to the deputies.

They waited back there, behind the building, for a couple of minutes. El Diablo enjoyed a comfortable tension, knowing that soon he would explode into action but for the moment, at least, simply waiting for it all to start. The alley behind the jail smelled of horses, urine, and spat tobacco. A bright moon cast ghostly shadows. He loved times like these, when his body was as alive as his mind and senses, instead of pinned inside the motionless form of Lazarus Lane.

Lazarus Lane's father had been a wealthy man, owner of ships and wagons, with friends in the Mexican government. He spoke perfect Spanish, and his wife, Lazarus's mother, had been Mexican nobility, of Spanish birth. Although most of the land of Mexican California was granted to Spaniards, Harold Robert Lane had been given lands there and had built himself a formidable hacienda. Lazarus had been born there, schooled in Mexico City, then Madrid. By the time he returned to California, it was falling into American hands, his mother was dead, and his father was weakening by the day. Lazarus had, he knew, been groomed to take over his father's position, overseeing the fertile farmlands. The idea brought him little joy, but he did as he was told. His father died before the family holdings had been legally transferred—under American law—into Lazarus's name.

Lazarus had been allowed to keep the hacienda, but not the lands or the wealth attached to them. He went to work at Puerta Del Sol's only bank.

And then the day came, in October of 1866. While Lazarus worked, a gang of bank robbers entered, demanding money. Lazarus raised his hands as he was told, but his friend Albert tried to fight back and was murdered for his trouble.

A week passed during which Lazarus became consumed with guilt for not trying to protect Albert. To get his mind off it, his girlfriend Nora persuaded him to take a wagon ride in the country. While they were out, the same bandit gang confronted them. This time, Lazarus refused to stand idly by, but when he tried to fight, he was knocked into a river, then struck by lightning. Only the intervention of Wise Owl had saved him—and split his being into two, the paralyzed Lazarus Lane and the powerful El Diablo.

In the street, the planned fight started. El Diablo heard Johnny Thunder shout out as if in fear and surprise, then Scalphunter raced past the alley clutching a tomahawk in his fist. As he and Johnny came together across the street, bumping into the posts supporting the covered boardwalk's roof, El Diablo and Bat rushed toward the front of the jail building, on the side of the door without the big front window.

The fight was a wild one, Scalphunter letting out some Kiowa-style yelps for effect. Less than a minute after it had started, the sheriff and a couple of his old boys stumbled out the door and into the street, shotguns in hand. "Here now!" the sheriff shouted. "Break it up there!"

Two men left inside, El Diablo believed. He nodded to Bat, and the two of them moved silently toward the door, which had been left hanging open. The deputies inside were riveted on the fight, watching through the big window.

El Diablo went in first, moving like a swift shadow. Bat came right behind him, and they had both passed inside before the men staring out the window knew they were there. One reached for a Colt at his hip but El Diablo's whip snaked out and stung it from his hand. He covered the man with his own six-shooter. Bat caught the other by the throat, spinning him away from the window and up against the cell door.

"Jonah?" Bat said. "This guy got keys on him you can see?"

Jonah grunted and checked the man's belt. "Sheriff has a set," Jonah said. "I think the others are in his desk."

"That a fact?" Bat asked. The deputy's pudgy face was headed toward purple. He nodded rapidly.

"Top drawer," he managed.

"I leave go of you, you won't make me sorry I did?"

"Nossir," the man gasped.

El Diablo shifted position so he could cover both men from where he stood. Bat released the deputy's throat and crossed to the desk, yanking open the top drawer. As promised, he reached in and came up with a ring of keys. He tossed the ring to the deputy. "Open it."

"Yes sir," the deputy said. His color was returning to normal, but he still spoke in a ragged, hoarse voice. He fumbled with the keys, but found the right one faster than Bat would have, and jammed it into the lock. When he turned it, Jonah shoved on the door, smashing it into the deputy's face. The man dropped back, hand going to his nose, which had already begun to leak blood. "What'd you do that for?"

"You ask yourself that when you kicked me puttin' me in there?" Jonah replied. He glanced at Bat and El Diablo. "Reckon I owe y'all some thanks for this."

"Save it till we're gone," Bat said. "We still got to get out."

Jonah's holster was coiled on the sheriff's desk, his spare Colt stuck on top. He quickly strapped on the rig, sticking the extra under the belt as he usually did. When he nodded that he was ready, the three of them headed for the door.

"You men keep quiet if you want to live through the next two minutes," Bat warned, ticking his gaze toward El Diablo. "You try anything, my quiet friend here will come back from the dead again and haunt you for the rest of your short, miserable lives."

El Diablo shot the men a wicked grin and slipped out the door, followed by Jonah and Bat. Across the way, the sheriff and his other deputies were still trying to break up the fight, or at least to separate the combatants long enough to shoot the Indian. One of the deputies had already suffered an encounter with a horse trough, and in the moonlight El Diablo could tell that he was dripping wet from the waist up.

Bat touched Jonah's arm and led him around to the back of the jail, where the horses waited. The three mounted hurriedly, then nudged their mounts out into the street, leading the two empty horses along. When they reached the street, they exploded from the alley, bearing right down on the sheriff and his men.

The deputies scattered and Jonah took advantage of the sheriff's greater courage to plant a boot right between the man's eyes. With a screech, the sheriff dropped his shotgun and fell to his knees. Scalphunter and Johnny Thunder leapt onto their mounts. El Diablo's whip lashed out, knocking a deputy's revolver from his hand, then four of them, El Diablo, Jonah Hex, Scalphunter, and Bat Lash, set out for the short end of the street and the wide, dark desert beyond. Behind them, Johnny rode in circles around the deputies, keeping them off-balance. For good measure he kicked the sheriff again and fired two rounds into the dirt in front of his deputies. Then he fired another through the plate glass of the sheriff's office window and rode off in the other direction, howling and screaming like a madman.

"Get after him, boys!" the sheriff cried. "Don't let that bastard get away!"

They were too late, though. By the time the half-drunk deputies had untied their horses, Johnny Thunder was out of town in the other direction, riding hell for leather toward Mesa City. The four new acquaintances, meanwhile, had topped the nearest rise and, after pausing just long enough to witness Johnny's escape, resumed their fast pace into the wilderness. Beyond the town's limits, the fort loomed sleepily, its soldiers apparently ignorant of what had taken place in the town.

El Diablo knew that none of the four had a particular destination in mind. They needed to be out of town, and they needed to figure out what their next step would be. Whatever the reason they had found themselves here—and he agreed that it was likely not by chance—they would discover it in due course.

"Who was that feller?" Jonah asked as they rode.

"Calls himself Johnny Thunder," Bat answered. "Don't know him from Adam, but he's a mite handy to have around in a pinch."

"That's certain," Jonah replied. "Wouldn't have minded gettin' a little better acquainted."

"Some other time," Scalphunter suggested. "We need to put some distance between ourselves and the town of Willson."

El Diablo held his tongue, as he usually did, and rode. To the east, the sun had started to glimmer at the tops of the mountains. The sky above was rosy, even though there were hardly any clouds to catch its light. El Diablo remembered the old seaman's saying: "Red sky at night, sailor's delight. Red sky at morning, sailors take warning."

He didn't know what a reddish sunrise portended when there seemed no reason for the color.

But if it had to do with them, he was glad they were well away from town and had brought Jonah out with them. Any force powerful and urgent enough to summon the four of them would not be easily dealt with, and likely they would need all the guns they could pull together.

CHAPTER TWENTY-TWO

As frightening as it was to do things like skulk around in warehouse crime scenes and the like, Lois Lane preferred it to the kind of research she spent the next day doing. Clark hadn't come home that night, and she had spoken to him once on the phone, then made apologies for him at the *Planet* the next morning, saying that he was home in bed with a high fever. Clark had a reputation as being vaguely sickly, so no one was surprised by this.

After some catch-up paperwork and a quick read of a feature story that had been through the hands of a copy-editor and an editor, Lois got back to work on her investigation into the origins and fate of the container people. Instead of putting herself in danger of arrest or bodily harm, though, today she would only be risking her sanity. Using the *Planet*'s resources and those available on the Internet, she worked on tracking the ownership of the vessel the container came over on—a freighter with Dominican registry, called the *Marie Claire*—and the origin of the container itself.

The work took hours, typing on keyboards and peering at listings and bills of lading and certificates of ownership. At times she had to have another window open on the computer screen so she could use a dictionary function to translate documents from Spanish, Russian, and Kaziri. At other times she had to sip caffeinated tea just to stay alert, rising from the computer and stretching to work the kinks out.

It was painstaking and dreadfully dull labor. She kept feeling like she was getting close to the end of it, but then discovered another layer of bureaucracy that needed to be penetrated before she could close in on the truth.

Every now and then she took a break, tried calling Clark on his cell phone. All she got was voice mail, so she left messages. A couple of times during the day, she thought the world kind of flickered around her, like a fluorescent lightbulb trying to come to life, but then it stopped and she wasn't sure if it had ever happened or if her eyes were just freaking out from staring at the computer screen all day.

Finally, as the shadows outside grew longer, she believed she had the answers she needed. The container had indeed been filled and sealed in Kaziristan, on the Caspian Sea. From there it crossed Azerbaijan, Armenia, and Turkey by rail and was loaded onto the *Marie Claire* in the Mediterranean port city of Alanya.

Fifteen days later it had turned up in Metropolis. When no one claimed it—and when the smell began to leak out—the authorities had finally opened it inside the warehouse. Tapping a connection at the Special Crimes Unit,

Lois arranged to get a couple of the crime scene photos e-mailed to her. She quickly wished she hadn't, but knew she had to see what it had looked like when they'd opened the doors.

Almost indescribably awful, as it turned out. Some of the people—the last ones to die, she guessed—had been pressed up against the doors, the nails on their fingers worn off from trying to claw their way out. Some had resorted to cannibalism to try to stay alive, only to succumb to the heat and the lack of drinking water. Some, having died of thirst or hyperthermia, had withered, their skin turning almost as black as if they had burned to death.

The shipper had been a company called Regis Exports. She had tracked it as far as she could from here, only to find that it was a dummy corporation with an address in the Cayman Islands that was almost certainly a post office box or something similar. The U.S. recipient was supposed to be yet another company with the equally generic name of Phoenix Enterprises. All Lois could find out about them was that they rented an office suite in Queensland Park, which had never been furnished. They had a telephone with voice mail, but she couldn't determine if a phone had actually been installed in the suite. The owner of Phoenix Enterprises was, according to incorporation paperwork, a Metropolis man named Ivan Kashegian. It could have been a Kaziri name, but then again, since she couldn't find any further information on Mr. Kashegian, and since the address he wrote down on the paperwork was a Suicide Slum address that didn't actually exist, it could as easily have been an imaginary name.

Or at least, that was what she thought until she finally got out of the office, just after six. She tried Clark's cell again, to no avail, then headed over to Queensland Park to see the Phoenix Enterprises office for herself. The building was nine stories of chunky gray stone. On the ground floor, a comic book store called Paulz Komix and a shoe repair shop flanked a glass door that led into a small, marble-tiled lobby. According to a signboard inside, Phoenix Enterprises was on the fourth floor. The elevator was out of order, so she hiked up the four floors. By the time she got there she had discovered that the air-conditioning was also out of order. The fourth-floor hallway was sweltering and smelled like mildew. A thin green carpet covered the floor, but it was worn away in spots. Black mold fuzzed the walls here and there.

Nice place, she thought. *If I ever go freelance . . .*

Suite 409 had a plain wooden door with brass-colored numbers nailed to it, and no further identification. Lois knocked. No answer, of course. She tried the phone number she had come up with. It rang three times, then voice mail picked up. "Phoenix Enterprises," a man's voice said. "Leave a message."

With her ear pressed against the door, Lois hadn't heard anything from inside, so she guessed that either the phone was not really here, or its ringer was turned off. She knocked again, tried the knob just in case. No one came to the door, and she couldn't open it.

She started for the stairs again, having learned no more than she'd known before, but she stopped outside the door to Suite 412. A small enamel sign on this door said CAR-LEY & FLEISHER, INC. She knocked.

"Hang on!" a man's voice called from inside. Lois waited almost a minute, then the door opened. The man who greeted her must have weighed more than three hundred pounds. His hair was graying and wild, shoulder length, and he had a beard that wouldn't have been out of place on an outlaw biker. He wore a cheap white dress shirt that had mostly come untucked, a red-and-black-striped necktie that seemed far too small for his bulk, black suit pants, also cheap, and loafers that seemed to have given up under the strain of his weight. "Yeah?"

"My name is Lois Lane," she said. "I'm a reporter for the *Daily Planet,* and I was looking for Mr. Kashegian, or anyone involved with Phoenix Enterprises."

"With who?" Fleisher or Carley or whoever this was spoke loudly, as if Lois was still on the other side of the door. Given the ripe aroma wafting from his office, she wished she were.

"Suite 409," she said, pointing. "Do you know them?"

"Hang on," the man said. He turned toward the inner office. She couldn't see much beyond his bulk, but what she could see hinted at budget office furniture and no real attempt at decoration. "Russ!" the man shouted. "You know the people in 409?"

A negative reply was bellowed from within.

"Sorry," the man said. "We don't know 'em. You ask the building manager?"

"Is there a manager on the premises?" Lois asked.

"Downstairs, basement, number five," the man said. "If they had to go in there to fumigate—we had cockroaches in the building, you believe that? Big suckers. I think they killed all the mice, though. Anyway, it would've been Mikey down there who let 'em in. He's got a passkey to all the suites."

"Thank you," Lois said, eager to get away.

The man started to shut the door, but then he tugged it

open again. "I like your books," he said. "The mysteries you write? I like mysteries by female authors. Sue Grafton, Kathy Reichs, J. Carson Black, like that. Just wanted to tell you."

He closed the door firmly, as if embarrassed by his praise. Lois was a little embarrassed herself, having been so anxious to get away from him only to learn that he was a fan. Not the kind she'd invite to dinner, maybe. But she worked hard on her novels, and it was gratifying to know that people were willing to shell out their hard-earned dollars—or at least make a trip to the library—to read them.

Feeling a little ashamed of her reaction to the guy, who had not only been a fan but had tried to be helpful, she went back down the stairs, this time bypassing the ground floor and shoving open the heavy fire door on the basement level.

The basement was lit only by a line of bare bulbs connected by exposed wiring, screwed into ceiling-mounted sockets. It smelled like heavy machinery—grease and steam and steel. Much of the space was simply screened off by chain-link fencing, behind which tall shapes hulked silently in the dark. About halfway down the length of the basement was a door with a metal 5 nailed to it.

Lois knocked on it. She could hear music inside, loud heavy metal. A minute later the door swung open, and a short, scrawny guy in a smudged, oil-stained red T-shirt and jeans with the knees blown out looked at her. His feet were bare, his toenails overgrown and black with grime. Her first thought was, *I hope he's not a fan, too.*

"Help you?" he asked, his voice just shy of a shout.

"If you're Mikey. I'm trying to find some information on the tenants in Suite 409," Lois said.

"You don't look like a cop."

"I'm not. I'm a reporter."

"What do you want to know?"

"I'd like to talk to Ivan Kashegian," Lois said. "I'd like to know if he ever actually uses this suite, and what kind of business he's in. Do you know him?"

"Come on in," Mikey said, beginning to turn back into the apartment. It was dark inside, with a reddish glow. "I know all our tenants."

"Can we turn the music down?" Lois called after him. She found herself in a room lit by a pole lamp, running from the floor to the low ceiling, with red bulbs screwed into all three sockets. She wasn't sure if he was going for a disco effect, a brothel, or Hell, but she found the effect disconcerting no matter what.

Mikey vanished through an open doorway into an equally dark room. Inside there, he shut the loud rock off altogether, then returned. He fixed her with a strange expression, eyebrows arched, a half grin playing about his lips. His hands were clasped behind his back, almost as if he were shy. "This guy Kashegian done something wrong?"

"I have no idea," Lois said. The near silence was jarring after the throbbing music. "Would he?"

"People are funny," Mikey said. "Guess you never can tell."

"That's certainly true."

He brought his left hand out from behind his back. It held a cordless phone. "I guess we can call him and ask if he wants me to answer any questions."

Lois wasn't ready to let him know she had been snooping around—not until she could see his face. Sometimes a person's first reaction was the best clue she could get as to his state of mind. "No, that's not necessary," she said. "I'd like to see him in person, but it doesn't have to be right now."

"Sorry," Mikey said. "But I think it is necessary." His right hand emerged, and it held a big handgun, semiautomatic, she thought. It was blue-black in the red light and looked sinister. He pointed it at her chest and twitched the barrel toward a low cloth-upholstered chair. "Sit."

"Just be careful with that thing," she said. "I haven't done anything to you, I'm just looking for some information."

"We'll let Ivan judge that," Mikey said.

This would be a good time for Superman to show up, Lois thought.

But she hadn't talked to him in almost twenty-four hours, didn't even know if he was still on Earth.

Superman would be nice, she decided. *But it kind of looks like you're on your own here.*

CHAPTER **TWENTY-THREE**

October 1349

A bitterly cold wind swept the streets of London, blowing out the fog but leaving ice crystals behind. The chill didn't bother Superman. The Phantom Stranger seemed immune to it as well, but Jason Blood shivered and rubbed his hands up and down his arms and stamped his feet on the icy cobblestones. "I need a heavier coat," he complained. "Or central heat or something."

"Central heat is unlikely," the Stranger said. "We could perhaps go inside someplace." He pointed toward a pub with an ornate sign reading PIG AND GARTER.

"Not to be ungrateful," Jason replied. "But I don't think I'd go into a place with a name like that under any circumstances. And given that we're in England during the time when the Black Death killed a third of its population, I'm not exactly looking for chances to mingle with the locals."

"A reasonable argument," the Stranger said.

"We could all use some period garb, though," Superman pointed out. "Anyone who sees us in our outfits is sure to raise some questions."

"As a temporary measure I can cast a glamour," the Stranger offered. "With the plague present in such a virulent form, as Jason points out, I doubt we would want to borrow someone else's clothing or put on anything purchased from a shop."

The others agreed to his idea. They had come here because the Black Death was the first option on the list they had come up with of history's worst mass deaths. This one seemed like a long shot because it didn't appear to have been caused by man, but they still decided it bore investigating.

Unfortunately, as they had discovered when they sat down to discuss the possibilities, the list was a long one. When they narrowed it down to mass killings at the hands of people, it got worse, because the bulk of those had happened in the twentieth century, many during Superman's lifetime. The Stranger and Jason Blood had lives that had spanned the centuries, so they didn't count, but Superman was a child of the past century. He didn't like to look at the statistics in black-and-white: 30 million dead in China, mostly during Mao's reign, 20 million in the USSR, 11 million in Germany, 10 million in Japan. Lesser numbers were still staggering: more than a million in Rwanda, in Nigeria, in the Sudan, in Afghanistan, Pakistan, Indonesia. And still the world turned, and still people died every day at the hands of others, or from preventable disease, hunger, poverty. *Shouldn't I have been able to prevent some of this slaughter?* he wondered. *What could I have done that I didn't do?*

He knew there was much that he *had* done—that most of his successes would never make the history books or the statistical analyses. How could one put a number on the lives saved, over and over, by defeating one threat or another? Super-villains, alien invasion, even the recent troubles with the OMACS. This current situation was another one like that—if Superman and his allies were successful, they would have saved Earth's entire population, and they were the only ones, with a tiny handful of exceptions, who would ever know it.

Nonetheless, the failures wore on him.

The Stranger spoke a couple of words and wagged his fingers. "Now anyone looking at us will see us in appropriate dress," he said. "And our accents and language will seem correct as well."

"That's well and good," Jason said. "But it doesn't do much for the cold."

"Give it a moment," the Stranger assured him. "I worked in something that should help with that."

"If it doesn't kick in fast, you can add me to the dead wagons," Jason said.

"I'm sure you'll be fine," Superman assured him. They'd been on the street for fifteen minutes and hadn't seen a soul, not even coming or going from the pub. The street was narrow, thick-beamed buildings crowding it on both sides, the wind whistling between them like a mourner's cry. He could hear people inside some of them, and the sounds were awful—people dying, shivering and weeping from the pain, others afraid to go out of their homes because they hadn't caught it yet and didn't want to.

The metaphorical ball, Superman knew, was in the Stranger's court. Superman and Jason were mainly here as muscle, in case they found the men they sought. But it would be the Stranger who located them, if they were here.

"Anything?" Jason asked after a few more minutes had passed.

"They have been here," the Stranger reported. "I don't know that they are now. I do not believe so. But they have been, and not so long ago."

"Can you tell where?" Superman asked. "I could look . . ."

"The traces are faint," the Stranger answered. "As if they had passed this way without staying long."

"But they might be up to something?" Jason asked.

"Always a possibility," the Stranger said.

The wind died suddenly, leaving a silence in its wake. At the same time Superman smelled a sharp, bitter smell that reminded him of both almonds and of Janna from Club Mysterium. "Stranger," he said.

"Yes," the Stranger said. "Something . . . stay alert."

"Too cold to be anything but," Jason said. "Even with your spell, Stranger."

With the wind gone, a fog materialized at the end of the block. Too quickly to be natural, Superman thought. The hairs on the back of his neck stood up—not just from nerves, but because something like an electrical charge traveled toward them down the block, just ahead of the fog. He braced himself, noticed that the Stranger and Jason had, too.

"Y'think Etrigan would be a good idea?" Jason asked.

"Let's wait and see," Superman suggested. The fog drew closer, as if carried along on the back of a charging animal. Superman spread his legs, tense and ready for anything.

Except what came with the fog.

Her color was predominantly gray, allowing her to blend in with the cold, clammy mass, but mixed in with the gray were a pearly off-white, a pale peach, a yellowish green. She looked like an English girl, maybe nine or ten years old, except that she ran toward them without moving her legs, her mouth dropping open as she neared them. When she was within a dozen feet, she stopped short. With a gagging sound, a thick, meaty tentacle burst from that open mouth, then two more, one from each eye socket.

The girl's flesh ripped like dry tissue, tearing apart down the middle of her face, her neck, her abdomen. Then a new tear opened up across her waist. She split into three sections, each reaching, grasping tentacle dragging more of itself behind, shredding what remained of their girl-shaped shell. The creatures that confronted them now each stood about six feet high, with two tentacles a couple of feet longer than that. Colored like the "girl" who had carried them, their heads were big and round, with saucer-sized eyes and what Superman could only assume was a mouth, or mouth and nose combined, which consisted of several loose flaps of skin that seemed to conceal an opening much like a tent with a many-layered doorway. Thick, stubby legs propelled them forward. Each one bellowed as it approached, sounding like off-key trumpets played by unskilled beginners.

"Time to slip into something more comfortable!" Jason shouted, backing away from the creatures. "Yarva! Etrigan! Daemonicus!"

As Jason Blood vanished and Etrigan emerged, Superman thought Jason had made the right choice. Hard as he was to control, in this sort of situation Etrigan would be far more helpful than Jason.

"Let me try something!" the Stranger shouted. He threw both his hands into the air and blasted the tentacled creatures with a golden light. It washed over them without apparent effect.

The Stranger shot Superman a frustrated glance. "I guess we do it my way," Superman said. He had to move quickly, as Etrigan was already in motion, lunging toward the oncoming beasts. Long practice enabled him to switch between powers as fast as thought, and he aimed heat vision at the attacking monsters.

The attempt was no more successful than the Phantom Stranger's had been, and the creatures were too close to try anything else. Etrigan engaged one, his clawed hands tearing at it even as its tentacles writhed around his neck and right leg.

Fearing the worst—that since his heat vision hadn't worked, these were beasts powered by magic—Superman dashed to meet his, sidestepping a grasping tentacle and throwing a powerful right jab. His fist slammed into the thing's head, right between those huge eyes. The head gave, rubbery under his hand, as if there were no skull inside. Big eye flaps blinked once, so the creature had felt the blow, but it hadn't slowed the thing.

It wrapped its suckered tentacles around his ribs and began to squeeze. From the center of each sucker, a sharp barb emerged. Propelled by magic, the barbs pierced Superman's flesh. Sudden intense pain from each wound told Superman that they weren't simply hooked knife blades, but that the beast injected some sort of poison through them. A glance over at the Stranger and Etrigan revealed that they had suffered similar attacks.

Superman kept up his barrage against the thing, punching it over and over. The tenor of its bellowing changed, and it expelled bursts of putrid breath, fluttering the skin flaps over its mouth.

This isn't working, he thought, desperation forcing him to seek something that would. The monster's grip threatened to collapse his ribs, and the poison it shot into his body burned.

Etrigan screeched in pain, almost completely animalistic now, without even enough conscious thought to speak in his annoying rhymes. The Phantom Stranger fought back, his ever-present hat having been knocked from his head, his face a rictus of agony.

As with the version of Etrigan he'd had to battle back in Camelot, Superman's powers couldn't do much against these creatures directly. But that didn't mean he couldn't use them. Giving up trying to batter the thing into submission, he switched tactics, working instead on peeling the tentacles off him. He gripped the end of one and worked the first few barbed suckers free, feeling his flesh rip with every one. The other tentacle continued to squeeze, so he bent his legs and pushed, forcing himself to one side and dragging the beast along. Step by step, he hauled the thing over to the nearest building and then muscled it against the sharp corner. There he pressed its back against the stones while he kept working at the one tentacle he had started to strip off.

The thing wailed in fury. Superman pushed harder, trying to crush it against the rock wall. At the same time, he managed to peel a two-foot length of tentacle off himself.

The barbed hooks still extended from the suckers, trying to find new purchase. Superman twisted the fleshy arm, turning the barbs toward the creature itself, and then with a sudden motion raked them across one of its huge open eyes.

Green acidic blood spurted from the wound, sizzling against Superman's skin but not harming him. The monster bucked beneath him, and its other tentacle released. Free of its grip, Superman took flight instantly, grabbing the tips of both tentacles as he went. In midair, it couldn't reach out toward him and dangled helplessly below. He flew about half a mile into the air and across the city's rooftops, stopping only when he could hover above the Thames. There he hurled the beast down, watched it slam against the dark water and sink beneath the surface.

One down.

He streaked back to the road where the others still fought. "This is gonna hurt!" he shouted as he approached. Without slowing, he reached out with both hands and grabbed the two remaining creatures. The speed of his passing tore them off the Stranger and Etrigan, and he deposited them in the same manner as the first.

By the time he returned, the Stranger had already banished Etrigan and returned Jason. Superman landed beside them. His costume was torn and bloody, but Jason and the Stranger both appeared to be unhurt.

"I understand we owe you some thanks," Jason said with a grin.

"They were tough opponents," Superman said. "I assume they were sent by our three friends?"

"They carried the stink of Mordru," the Stranger reported. He picked up his hat, dusted it off with a gloved hand, and replaced it on his head. "I can only assume he left them as a kind of booby trap for us, should we seek them here."

"But how could they know we'd come right here, at this time?" Jason asked.

"I suspect the trap was not so specific," the Stranger said. "Likely they suspected that we would come to this general era, and the creatures would have manifested themselves anywhere and anywhen that we showed up."

"Which means they knew we'd reason out the sacrifice angle," Superman pointed out. "And we'd come looking at mass deaths."

"So it would appear," the Stranger said.

"Which means anyplace else we go, we might run into more of their little gifts," Jason added.

"We should expect to," the Stranger said.

"I know we've been a little busy," Superman said, "but have you been able to determine whether this is the time we're looking for? Any sign of magical activity?"

"Plenty of magic," the Stranger replied. "But not by the men we seek. They have been here, but they are not now, and this is not the event we need."

A wave of disappointment washed over Superman. He knew it was unrealistic, but he wanted this whole thing to be over. He wanted to get back to his own life, back to protecting the citizens of Metropolis, working at the *Planet,* seeing his wife. Although he hadn't known of this threat for very long, he felt as if it had been hanging over him for all the centuries of its existence.

Probably, he guessed, he still carried around some of the uncertainty of the other Clark. His level of confidence was lower than it should have been.

He knew he could deal with Savage, Faust, and Mordru. Intellectually, at least. He had faced down greater threats, alone and with allies. He could take these three.

But where it counted, in his gut, he wasn't so sure. Three magicians, against whose powers his own were meaningless. He had never encountered such a challenge.

In his gut, he was glad the Phantom Stranger and Jason Blood stood at his shoulders.

CHAPTER **TWENTY-FOUR**

May 1872

Jonah would have been happy never to go near Willson again as long as he lived, but he had one further obligation before he could ride away with his new acquaintances. He agreed with their assessment that they had been drawn together for some purpose, but he had promised Josie Bates that he would take her back to Texas.

He left the others in a secure spot, near the top of a rocky slope from which they could see a pursuing posse or an Apache raiding party for miles, and rode back to town. When he got there the morning sun, strangely pinkish, was high in the sky. He circled around the town, coming at it from the south, a direction neither they nor Johnny Thunder had ridden off in. He stopped a quarter mile away and looped General's reins around a thick, thorny mesquite. From there he ran toward the hotel's back staircase, crouched to offer as low a profile as possible. Tall yucca stalks erupting from spiky balls offered

cover, as did green patches of greasewood and the ubiqui-
tous mesquite.

A short while later he had reached the exterior staircase unobserved. These stairs were mostly used by working girls, so they wouldn't traipse through the saloon and
the company of drunks, gamblers, gunfighters, and other
polite society. Jonah raced up them, pausing outside the
door just long enough to peek in and make sure the hallway was empty.

Since it was, he went inside and rushed to the door of
Josie's room. The knob was locked, so he rapped urgently.

"Who's there?" she called.

"Open up, it's me!"

"Jonah?"

"Hush!"

She rattled the door as if trying to alert the whole hotel
of his presence. What seemed like twenty minutes later,
she yanked it open, and Jonah pushed his way in.

"Where have you been?" she asked. Her pretty face
was puffy, her eyes bloodshot. "They said you were ar-
rested, and then you ran away. I thought I was stuck here
forever."

"Good to hear you didn't worry none about me, but
just your own self," Jonah said. "But I told you I'd get you
home, and I will. There's just gonna be a small delay."

She chewed nervously on her thumb. "How long?"

"Couldn't say. Few days, maybe a week. You can stay
here, enjoy the scenery. Or if you wanted I'm sure you
could talk some other *hombre* into takin' you home."

"I want *you* to," Josie said.

"That's good, because I got to go that way anyhow, and

I could use the money. I'm afraid you'll have to wait a spell, though."

Josie's eyes glistened, and she moved to Jonah, pressing her body against his. "Couldn't we go right now?" she asked. "There can't be anything more important than that, is there? You know I'll do whatever it takes to get home." The way her gaze bored into his left no doubt as to her meaning.

It would have been dishonest to say it wasn't a tempting offer. He really didn't know Bat and the others. They were only speculating that there was some grand purpose behind their meeting, but none of them knew that for sure. And Josie, vulnerable and needy as she was, presented an attractive picture. Tempting as a two-dollar slicker in a monsoon, but if Bat, Scalphunter, and El Diablo were right, then he had more pressing business elsewhere. Besides, they had taken the trouble to bust him out of the hoosegow, which was more than Josie had done. "You'll appreciate it more if you have to wait on it some," he said. "If you have to work at it a little, too, mebbe."

She sniffled, but it was an act, and Jonah could see through it. She wanted what she wanted, that was all there was to it. When he turned her down, she backed away, spun on her heel, and lowered her chin toward her chest.

"Do me a favor," he said. "Until I get back, keep your eyes and ears open. You hear anything about a posse or a bounty on me, anything like that, let me know when you see me again. I'll need to know just how careful I have to be around these parts."

"If I'm here when you get back," she sniffled.

"You'll be here." He went back to her door, opened it a

crack, peered out. The hallway was still clear. "I'll see you soon," he said as he let himself out.

He made it back to General without being seen, and a couple of hours later he had reached the base of the hill on which he had left the others. Shielding his eyes against the brilliant, pink sun, he looked up the slope but couldn't see them, even though he knew where they were. Hidden by the rocks and desert plants, he figured. He gave General a nudge and the horse nickered, then started picking his way up the hill, stepping carefully on loose soil and stones, avoiding the slashing yucca leaves and the thorns of cholla and prickly pear and ocotillo.

As he neared the summit, he experienced a familiar tickle at the back of his neck. He had been wrong about it once or twice before, but with as many enemies as Jonah had made over the years, it didn't do to ignore it. Someone, unless he was mistaken again, was sighting down the barrel of a firearm at him.

He remembered the first time the sensation had saved his life. It had been during the War for Southern Independence. He'd been assigned to the Confederate Fourth Cavalry, a special unit created by General Lee himself. Most Confederate forces were composed of people from the same geographic region, but the men of the Fourth Cavalry had been chosen because they had something special to offer. In Jonah's case it had been his marksmanship skills and the fact that he had never shown fear in the face of battle. He had—completely accidentally—led the men of the Fourth into an ambush, and by that time he'd lost his faith in the cause of the Confederacy anyway. The few survivors blamed him for the deaths of their comrades, and he had spent the rest of the war trying not to be killed by either side.

But earlier, during the Battle of Antietam, he had been ordered to carry a message to Jeb Stuart, whose troops held the northernmost flank of the Confederate position. To get there, Jonah had had to loop around the rear of the rebel forces and cut through one of the cornfields that surrounded Antietam Creek. He'd been walking his horse through the tall stalks when he'd felt that same tickle sensation. Guessing what it meant at once, he hurled himself to the dirt just as a minié ball sailed over his head. He returned fire with one of his familiar Colt Dragoon copies, not having laid his hands yet on enough money to purchase the ivory-handled beauties he would later favor. The weapons did their job, cutting the Union soldier down where he stood. The ruckus alerted four more bluecoats who had accompanied the first one, but Jonah spotted them through the cornstalks before they saw him. When it was over there were five dead Northerners and one Texan who swore always to pay attention to his instincts.

He assumed it was his *compadres* eyeing him down a barrel, and didn't blame them a bit. They didn't know him any better than he knew them. There was nothing to say he wouldn't have gone back to town and returned with a posse, in exchange for his own freedom. For that matter, Jonah Hex could have been captured and some other man might be riding toward their position wearing his coat and hat. To alleviate that worry, he took off the hat so they could see his damaged face better, and waved it in the air. "It's me, Jonah!" he called.

"Keep on comin'" a voice answered. Bat's. Jonah didn't make friends easily, and didn't expect to become lasting friends with Bat or the others either. He didn't much like people, but that was because he'd known so many of them. Anyway, friendships didn't seem to fit into the kind of life that had built itself around him, seemingly without intent on his part. He hunted wanted men for the bounty on their heads, and that tended to be a solitary sort of occupation that didn't leave a lot of time for sharing chuck around a campfire.

Or for tending to a marriage and the life of a farmer. If he had been better at that last, he might still sleep with Mei Ling at night, might get to watch his boy Jason grow into manhood. But he'd never been able to make a go of farming, and every time he strapped on his Colts to earn some pay, Mei Ling objected. Finally, she had given him an ultimatum and made good on it. As far as he knew, Jason would grow up in China with Mei Ling's relatives looking after him.

So he didn't have much use for friends. But he respected the way Bat carried himself in a fight. And Bat and the others could have easily left him in that jail for the rest of his life with no skin off their own noses. No, he didn't think the two would become lifelong pards, but there were certainly worse men he could ride with for a time.

He kept General's nose headed up the hill, and soon Bat, El Diablo, and Scalphunter separated themselves from the rocks. They had weapons in their hands, but carried casually, not pointed at Jonah any longer. "You get your business taken care of?" Bat asked.

"All set," Jonah replied.

"Then we'd best keep ridin'," Bat said.

"Makes sense to me," Jonah said. "I didn't see as there

was much effort bein' put into findin' us, but it won't hurt to put some more distance between us and town. Thing is, any of you got any idea where we ought to ride to? I mean, if'n we were all drawn together for some reason, seems like that reason ain't sittin' here jawin'. But I don't know where it is we should be."

"Perhaps we'll happen upon it," El Diablo suggested. "As we happened upon each other in the saloon."

"And mebbe the Apache'll happen upon us while we're talkin' about it," Bat said.

"Not all Apache are as evil as you seem to think," El Diablo countered. "If it weren't for an Apache friend, I would not be here now."

"Mebbe not all," Bat said, rubbing a hand through his thick hair. "But enough of 'em are that I'd like to stay alert just the same. I value my hair too much to drop my guard." He glanced at Scalphunter. "No offense."

"None taken," Scalphunter said. "I understand that some white men fail to see the power of taking scalps. It is not your fault; you were just raised poorly."

"Can't argue with that, in my case," Jonah said. His father had sold him to an Apache chief, as a slave, in order to raise a stake on which to go prospecting in California. He'd been treated like a slave, until the day he had saved the old chief from a rogue puma. After that, his treatment had changed, and he had become a kind of second son to the old man—earning the undying enmity of the chief's real son, Noh-Tante. The bad blood between them had finally come to a boil when Noh-Tante forced a final show-down that ended with Jonah killing him. For his troubles, the tribe branded Jonah with the "mark of the demon," scarring his face forever. "But I can't imagine even if I was brought up better I'd be interested in separatin' a man from his locks."

"Have you tried it?"

"Can't say I have."

"When you do, tell me if you change your mind."

Jonah shook his head, amused in spite of himself at the Kiowa's certainty that he *would* try it, sooner or later. He had never known any such inclination, and didn't imagine that it would come over him sudden-like.

"I don't claim that the Apache are nature's innocents," El Diablo clarified. As he spoke, he circled his black horse, inspecting its hooves, legs, flanks, mouth. "Certainly they commit more than their share of what we might call atrocities. But if you look at things from their point of view, they've been living on this land for hundreds of years, if not thousands. Certainly well before the first Europeans arrived here."

"And those would've been your folks," Jonah pointed out.

"Spaniards, yes," El Diablo admitted. "There is some dispute about who precisely was first, but the first major European force to journey through this area would have been that of Coronado, on his expedition in search of the seven cities of Cibola. Since then, the incursion into Apache territory has never ceased. The rush to California's gold fields, back in '49, made it worse. They must feel like an occupied people, under a slow, steady invasion. I think that under similar circumstances, any of us might be driven to fight back in any way we could."

"Reckon there's some truth to that," Jonah said.

"Whatever their reasons, I still'd rather not be caught here by 'em," Bat observed. He climbed onto his mount's saddle. El Diablo and Scalphunter followed suit, and Jonah had not dismounted. "I say we keep goin' in the direction we were headed, away from Willson, and see what we see." He glanced at the sun, blazing overhead but still with that strange pink tinge. "Don't like that," he added. "Looks like blood got into it."

Nobody had a response for that, so they started down the far side of the ridge. At the bottom lay a grassy valley, which they cut across at an easy trot. The air was hot and dry—blood on the sun or not, it still heated the day right up. But the valley floor was smooth and even, the grass haunch high on the horses and golden, the spiny chollas easy enough to avoid, and the four men rode in genial silence, the way Jonah liked it.

On the far side of the valley, to the west—the direction Jonah had just come from—hulked another low range of mountains. As the pink sun dipped behind it, streaking the sky with the colors of freshly butchered meat and sliced melon, the face Jonah and the others could see slid into purple shadow. There looked to be three possible passes across this range, and the men debated which to choose. But when the sun finally vanished behind the peaks, one of the possibilities stood out from the others. A greenish glow emanated from a canyon at the base of the mountains that seemed to lead toward one of the passes. The light reminded Jonah of fireflies caught in a glass jar.

"You ever seen anything like that?" he asked his companions, nodding toward the display.

The others had noticed it, too. "It looks like powerful magic," Scalphunter said. "Bad magic."

"It is surpassingly strange," El Diablo commented.

"You're a master of understatement, Diablo," Bat said.

"That there's one of the oddest sights I ever laid eyes on, and I laid eyes on a few."

The four men turned their horses, in an unspoken and possibly unconscious simultaneous motion, toward the lights. Since they were proceeding on the possibly faulty assumption that forces greater than themselves had assembled them for some purpose, then riding toward what looked to be a physical manifestation of powerful forces was probably a reasonable plan.

Either that, or they were riding into a trap. Or a massacre.

Jonah supposed they'd find out which it was soon enough.

CHAPTER TWENTY-FIVE

Mordru wondered, not for the first time, why he was playing second fiddle to Savage. Or was it third wheel to Savage and Faust? Either way, the arrangement made him uncomfortable. They had agreed to be equal partners from the beginning, an equilateral triangle, but metaphors made his head hurt. He, alone of the trio, had the powers of a veritable god, and he believed that Vandal Savage and Felix Faust should bow in obeisance every time he entered their presence. Yes, the whole thing had been Savage's idea, but without the abilities of the Dark Lord Mordru it would never have come to fruition.

Still, here he was, on the very cusp of that which he had sought for so long. Or close enough, at any rate. Total domination of the Earth would have been more like it, but then again, total domination would be an all-consuming task, leaving him little time to enjoy what he had wrought. By dividing the Earth into thirds, he would have the pleasure of exercising his will over massive numbers of people.

They were not much more significant to him than cattle to a rancher with vast holdings—perhaps that, he thought, was even too grandiose for them. Maybe people were like the individual blades of grass on which the cattle grazed throughout the day. Cattle, after all, had specific financial value to the rancher, and Mordru's experience ruling the alternate, temporary Earth had demonstrated to him that there were very few individual people who were worth anything at all.

He had installed figurehead rulers in the various nations he controlled, but those people knew their power was illusory and that their titles and lives could be snatched away at Mordru's slightest whim. He would do the same on the real Earth, or his third of it. He found it amusing that the general populace cursed their apparent rulers, never knowing who truly called the tune to which they danced. Every now and then he let rumors drift into the population, taking pleasure in the fact that people sometimes whispered his name in fearful tones. Their terror added to his aura of godlike mystery.

He, Faust, and Savage had returned to Earth—what had once been, and would again be, the one and only true Earth—for the penultimate stage of their long ritual. They had set up a temporary, if less than suitable, camp in a remote desert canyon, because it was where their mystical nine-pointed star had finally ended up, and because it was a fitting location for the final sacrifice that would finalize their efforts. The camp looked, from the outside, like one of the adobe structures the local Indians had built in the vicinity for a thousand years. Inside, of course, it was far more comfortable than those had been, although still not as luxurious as Mordru preferred. But they wouldn't have to stay long, so he raised no objections.

They had tracked the progress of their mystical star, the symbol of their partnership and the magical talisman that made the whole project work. Once in the hands of the papacy, it had remained in the Vatican for a number of years, part of a secret, rarely discussed collection of magical artifacts. A new pope, wanting to rid the Holy See of what he considered tools of Satan, had ordered the collection destroyed if possible, and if not then dispersed throughout the world.

There was, of course, no destroying the demon-forged star. It made its way into the hands of Hernan Cortés, who carried it with him to Mexico City in 1519. By 1541, it had been handed off to Francisco Vázquez de Coronado, described as a good-luck charm. Coronado wanted nothing to do with it, but left it in the care of one of the five friars accompanying his expedition, a man called Fray Juan Avìla, who had been in Mexico for ten years and was ready to go anywhere—even the uncharted wilderness to the north—for a change of scenery.

Fray Avìla, a lean man with sunken cheekbones, deep-set eyes and a hooked beak of a nose, didn't trust the star any more than Coronado had. But he knew better than to refuse the governor's demand. He tucked the thing into a leather bag carried by one of the expedition's many mules and walked alongside the beast. Every now and then, mostly at night when they had stopped to rest in some sheltered spot, out of the desert heat and the wind, he took the star out of the bag and handled it. Only occasionally, for the first few weeks, but then more and more as the days went on. Soon, he was slipping a hand inside the bag even as they walked, caressing the star.

The expedition consisted of 225 mounted soldiers, 60 foot soldiers, more than 1,000 Indian servants, guides, and scouts, and of course the five friars, including Fray Marcos de Niza, who had made the trip to the legendary seven cities once before, and himself. Fray Avìla told no one of his growing preoccupation with the star. He wanted to keep his connection with the object to himself, afraid that if he revealed it, others would want their own turns with the thing. The star gave him the strength to keep walking in spite of the elements and dangers they faced. It imparted the wisdom necessary to know who among their party could be trusted—a surprisingly paltry handful, that grew smaller as the expedition progressed— and to know what he needed to do to protect himself against enemies. God Himself spoke to him through the star.

Nineteen days into the journey, God warned Avìla that the others had become aware of his secret. Hands trembling, sweating in spite of a cool breeze, Avìla walked close to the mule, reaching inside the bag often as if to reassure himself that it was still there. Stiff, spiky grass slashed at his ankles. His stomach growled from hunger. It had been days since they'd seen a river or spring, and water was short. He cast his gaze in every direction, and everywhere he saw suspicious, distrustful eyes staring back at him. Each of the soldiers, he knew, only waited for the word to be given, perhaps by Coronado himself. They would draw their weapons, dispatch Avìla, and take the star for themselves.

Gradually, throughout the afternoon, he slowed his pace

and that of the mule. Others passed without comment, or with only a word or two spoken. Soon, he was near the back of the long procession, where he wanted to be. He waited his chance, anxiety growing within him but tempered by a certainty that he was doing God's bidding.

Finally, the opportunity presented itself. They had narrowed to a single line, walking an ancient Indian path along the edge of a deep, rocky canyon. Avìla swallowed dryly, wishing he could spare another tug from a water-skin the mule carried. The moment approached. Ahead, the line of men curved to the left, and for a moment those ahead were out of sight. He slowed even more, making a wider gap between himself and the soldier immediately in front of him. Then, after that soldier vanished from his view, he sped up. When he knew that those behind couldn't see him, he flung open the bag, yanked out the star, and hurled himself over the side.

Fray Avìla slid down a long, rock-strewn slope. His legs and arms and hands were cut by slashing stones, his gray robe shredded, his face battered by rocks that flew into him as he descended. He had no idea what might wait below, but God had led the way so far, and He would continue to keep his servant safe.

Above, he could hear commotion, shouts of feigned concern. A search party was hastily composed and sent after him. But the searchers picked their way cautiously down the slope where Avìla had skidded. He had a good head start. At the canyon's bottom was a narrow patch of bare earth, but in the distance, near the canyon's wall, a thick mass of green indicated tall trees and water.

Star clutched tightly in his fists, Avìla ran toward the trees.

They were farther away than he had first thought. But any tracks he left on the hard-packed soil were faint, and he was thirsty, so he kept going. The whole time he was watched by five Apache warriors who had stopped to quench their thirst.

They knew, of course, of the size of the expedition in the hills above, and had kept their distance from it. But one man, alone and unarmed, carrying a strange object— this aroused their curiosity. And they needed some way to protest the vast party cutting across their land. They waited in the shadows of the big cottonwoods until Fray Avìla hurled himself into the pond created by a spring that dripped water down the hard rock canyon wall, and then struck. Capturing Avìla, they carried him back to their village so all could enjoy the sport they had in mind.

The next seven hours—until he lost consciousness— were far from pleasant for Fray Juan Avìla.

During that time, the expedition's search party found the grove of trees hard against the canyon's wall. The expedition found a route to the canyon floor. Waterskins were filled at the spring, horses and cattle and mules drank their fill.

No one knew what had become of Fray Avìla, although hoofprints in the soft earth beneath the trees suggested his fate. But the star he had carried, which he had dropped beside the roots of one of the cottonwoods, had been covered by leaves and dust, then the droppings of the cattle, and the expedition went on without it.

There it stayed. The canyon became part of Mexico, and then with the Gadsden Purchase of 1853, part of the United States, in the territory of Arizona. The little spring continued to flow, the cottonwoods grew taller and thicker.

The canyon, far from civilization and deep in Apache country, was seldom visited.

It was here that the three sorcerers built their base. They found the star, dug it from the ground, cleaned it off, and set it in a place of honor inside the adobe building.

The time had come to put it to use again. And the Apache village that had been erected inside the canyon would be just the thing for a final blood sacrifice, Mordru knew, symbolizing the millions of Indians who had already died and those deaths yet to come.

CHAPTER **TWENTY-SIX**

Worse, far worse, than mass death from "natural" causes were the man-made genocides that littered the pages of history. Genghis Khan was one of the worst perpetrators, responsible for the murder of hundreds of thousands, possibly millions, at Nishapur and Bokhara and Samarkand, and on and on. Since Vandal Savage claimed to have been the Mongol leader, Superman, the Phantom Stranger, and Jason Blood took a close look at those massacres.

But although they were horrific in their cruelty and staggering in number, they could find no magical component, no ritual associated with those mass murders. The Mongol leaders, even those who succeeded Genghis Khan, killed in huge quantities, seemingly because they wanted to establish empires and wanted any city on which they set their sights to bow before them rather than dare to fight back. Having heard reports of thirty thousand dead in one place, fifty thousand in another—30 million, by some estimates—many of their later targets did just that.

The next stop was China, in 1644, where Emperor Chang Hsien-chung, upon conquering Szechwan Province, ordered the deaths of all the scholars, then the merchants, the women, the public officials, finally commanding his own soldiers to kill each other. The three heroes arrived outside Chengtu in April, 1644. A steady rain fell, flooding the fields surrounding the city. The Stranger's glamour ensured that anyone observing them would see three harmless Chinese peasants.

But the first being to see them wasn't a person at all. Once again, their quarry had anticipated their arrival and left a surprise behind. In keeping with the local mythology, this one was a dragon, fifty feet long and nearly as tall, purple-scaled, with eyes that glittered like gold, long horns of pure white, and a three-tined tail that swished from side to side with lethal intensity. Superman heard some of the nearby workers scream at the sight of the dragon and run to the relative safety of their homes. Then the beast attacked, loosing a blast of flaming breath at them, and he had to focus on the problem at hand.

Between his superstrength and -speed, the Stranger's mystical powers, and Etrigan's ruthless muscularity, they defeated it handily.

A short hop into the future, to 1648, and over to Bohemia. The Thirty Years War had begun in 1618, finally coming to a close in 1648. During that time the population of Bohemia had dwindled by more than 3 million. Estimates put the total loss of life at more than 11 million, counting all those killed in combat and through associated disease, poverty, and famine.

Here they encountered a small army of vampires, a

hundred strong. They defeated the bloodsuckers in short order, but the battle was gruesome and unpleasant.

Back to China, moving forward in time to 1686, when the Triad Rebellion was defeated in the province of Kwangtung and almost seven hundred thousand people lost their lives in the space of a month. Here the gift left by Savage, Faust, and Mordru was a giant, sixty feet tall, able to hurl entire houses at them.

When they had bested the giant and made ready to move on, Jason Blood shook his head sadly. "Do they really expect these things to stop us?" he asked. "Or do they think we'll just be so depressed, drifting from mass death to mass death, that we'll give up and let one of them put us out of our misery?"

"Impossible to say," the Stranger answered. "So far, I doubt they have realistically believed that any of the creatures left in our path could destroy us. They know our capabilities well enough for that. More likely, they are trying to slow us down."

"And maybe there's an element of what Jason said in it," Superman added. "They don't think we'll give up, but they're trying to wear us down, to dispirit us. Maybe even to make us lower our guards by giving us foes that we can beat without too much trouble. Ultimately, they assume, we'll catch up to them, and if they can throw enough psychological barriers in our way before that, then they'll have an edge."

"I agree," the Stranger said. "I obviously take a long view of human history, but even the worst disasters and genocides have been leavened, over my many years, by scientific discoveries and artistic advancements, the beneficent policies of true statesmen and women, and so on.

The development of classical music, then jazz, then rock and roll, for instance, can alleviate the pain of many millions of deaths. But facing these mass killings one after another wears upon my spirit, as I'm sure it does on yours. The ambushes left by those we seek only add to the despair that grows in my soul."

"If it's getting to you that bad, Stranger, maybe we should take a break from it," Jason suggested.

"We cannot," the Stranger countered. "We dare not. Even as we continue our search, the merging of the worlds grows closer and closer. We cannot afford to delay in the least."

Superman swallowed hard. He had been leaning toward Jason's point of view—a quick trip home, maybe a few hours with Lois, would do him a world of good. But the Stranger's point was a good one. By traveling through time, it was possible that they could return to their Earth slightly before they had left, losing no time even though they allowed themselves a break.

But it was also possible that the merge would be completed while they rested, and that once merged, the worlds could not be separated again. If they missed their one window of opportunity because it was simply too hard, too sad, to go on, then they would have lost it all.

"It is hard," he said at last. "And depressing. But everyone gets depressed sometimes, right? If we let ourselves dwell on that, then we might give our enemies the edge they seek. Better to acknowledge the sensation and keep working, knowing that only progress can keep the ultimate darkness at bay."

"Your words are wise ones, Superman," the Stranger said. "And I concur. We forge onward. Agreed, Blood?"

Jason shrugged. "It's not like things can get worse," he said.

They shifted through time and space again, visiting some of the most tragic events of human history. The African slave trade claimed more than 50 million lives. The Great Indian Famine of 1710 took 20 million lives. Lesser events, like the 1665 Great Plague in London, killed sixty-eight thousand, and the Dutch massacre of the Chinese in Batavia in 1740, claimed more than seventy thousand. Eventually Superman came to see the creatures that met them at every stop as welcome relief from the reality of so many lost lives. He could lose himself, for a minute or for ten, in battle with something that could be fought.

Sitting on rocks on a bloody plain, the site of yet another genocidal massacre, the three discussed their next stop. "The American West," the Stranger suggested.

"The Indian wars?" Jason asked.

"That, and the spread of disease. Not just in North America, either. Similar conditions existed in Central and South America. Some estimate the number of deaths of the indigenous populations of the Americas, caused by the advent of Europeans, to be in the neighborhood of 85 or 90 million."

Superman shook his head. "Incredible," he said. "You know I think of myself as an American. Maybe that should be Kryptonian-American, but still. Like every other American schoolkid, I learned about the smallpox-infected blankets, the destruction of the bison herds that were the staple of existence for the Plains Indians, and of course those comparatively few killed by American soldiers during that time. But I never thought the numbers were so staggering."

"Simply an estimate," the Stranger said. "But an educated one. The number is certainly no less than 50 million, possibly as many as 100 million. Somewhere between is the likeliest figure."

"I feel as American as you do," Jason said. "I didn't end up there by accident of birth or even the whim of a rocketship, but chose to live in the United States. And I spent many of the years in which that massacre was taking place there, without ever being conscious of just how awful it was."

"Most people cannot comprehend such numbers," the Stranger said. "Their minds simply will not grasp them. We three, however, cannot afford to turn away from the truth, however horrific. We must face it head-on, if we are to succeed."

"Agreed," Superman said. "Let's go, then. Pick a time and place and let's test the waters."

They went first to Indian Territory, in January of the year 1839. It was the end point of the so-called Trail of Tears, Jason knew. The United States government had made a treaty in 1835 with a minority faction of the Cherokee people—without consulting the majority—requiring that the Cherokee give up their lands in Georgia and move to land set aside in Indian Territory—which would become Oklahoma in later years. Other tribes had already been removed—the Ottawa, Shawnee, Potawawtomi, Sac, Fox, Miami, Kickapoo, and the tribes called the "Five Civilized Tribes," who had blended their ways with those of the Whites most completely: the Choctaw, Chicasaw, Creek, Seminoles. Finally, only the fifth of those tribes, the Cherokee, remained. They fought the removal all the way to the Supreme Court. Jason remembered editorials and speeches decrying the relocation—it had been something of a *cause célèbre* among intellectuals of the day. But in the end, President Van Buren had ordered the treaty carried out, at gunpoint if necessary. The long march to new lands across the Mississippi, the harsh weather and exposure to elements, resulted in the deaths of about a quarter of the tribe, around four thousand people.

An icy wind was blowing across the bare plain when they arrived, kicking up puffs of snow that had fallen a day or two before. Pale wispy clouds scudded through a pewter sky. Jason knew that the Cherokee who survived brought to the West the very civilizing influences the white Georgians who wanted their land insisted they could never learn—schools, printing presses, substantial homes and churches—and the less civil institution of slavery. But those things, he saw, were yet to come. The Cherokee people had arrived over two years, but the bulk of them, those who had refused the order and been forced to walk the one thousand two hundred miles from Georgia, had only just reached their new homeland. They were weakened by disease and hard travel, dispirited by their exodus. Accustomed to solid houses of brick and timber, here they lived in tents, using what few trees dotted the horizon to build fires to ward off January's chill.

His memory of these events had been from a distance, because he hadn't been here on the scene when it really happened. It had been dinner party talk in Gotham, nothing more. Nothing real. Looking across the barren plain toward the wind-whipped shelters, it couldn't have been more real.

"Is this the place?" he asked quietly.

The Stranger stood almost trancelike, hands loose at his sides. He was sniffing out magic, it seemed, the way a hunting dog might catch the scent of rabbits or quail. "Not here," he said after a few moments. "Not now. But we're very close."

"There's no trap here, no ambush," Superman pointed out.

"Perhaps because they know that if we've made it this far, we'll get the rest of the way. There will be at our next stop, you can count on that." He took in a deep breath, blew it out. "In fact, I would wager that whatever challenges face us at our next destination, they will be the worst we have faced yet."

CHAPTER **TWENTY-SEVEN**

May 1872

Scalphunter glanced at his companions, snuggled into their bedrolls in the little clearing between mesquite and greasewoods. They hadn't dared risk a fire because of whatever unknown force caused the eerie green light in the canyon, as well as the possible presence of Apache warriors. Scalphunter resented their frequent portrayals of Apache as devils on Earth, sadists who lived only for the chance to bring harm to others. He had no illusions about Apache customs, but the Apache and Kiowa peoples had allied themselves from time to time, particularly against the steady encroachment of the whites, so he felt obliged to offer defenses now and again. He knew the others didn't lump all Indians into the same hated group, and they trusted him as much as they did each other.

Of course, he had been born white, and they all knew that. But he had left that life behind as a boy and never looked back. Where it counted, in his heart and head, he was Kiowa, just as much as if his parents had been. He was Ke-Woh-No-Tay, and Brian Savage was simply a memory, as if from an especially vivid dream.

They had taken shifts staying awake. Scalphunter had the last one, and the sky was beginning to gray in the east, although still with a pinkish cast. Wishing he had coffee, he swished some water around in his mouth and spat it onto the thirsty earth. "Hey," he said, to no one in particular. "Sun's up."

Jonah Hex turned in his bedroll, grunting something unintelligible and shoving a Colt out, barrel pointed toward Scalphunter. "It's just me," Scalphunter said. "Easy."

"Sorry," Jonah offered. "Don't much like bein' woke up, is all."

Bat sat upright, chuckling at Jonah's response. El Diablo seemed to skin out of his bedroll in one smooth motion—he was stretched out inside it, then he was standing tall, and Scalphunter never spotted the transition.

"This outfit got a chuck wagon?" Bat asked.

"No such luck," Jonah said, rubbing his eyes. He climbed out of the bedroll, a bit creaky in the joints, it seemed. "I got some jerky in my saddlebags, I think, if you didn't bring anything."

"Just joshin'," Bat said. "I got some of my own, and mebbe some huckydummy to go with it. Cup of Arbuckle's'd wash it down right nice."

"No fires," Scalphunter reminded them. "Anyway, we should roll out quick."

"He's right," El Diablo added. "We don't know what those lights might portend, but I think the sooner we investigate, the better. Who knows if the source might also be moving on today?"

There had always been something strange about El

Diablo, Scalphunter thought. Something not quite human. Bat and Jonah, white men to their cores, stared at him as if it was insane to contemplate taking action without breakfast. Scalphunter had ridden for days without food, sometimes fighting or hunting along the way. But the white men were soft, wedded to their comforts.

"Sounds good," Jonah said, surprising Scalphunter.

"Makes sense to me," Bat put in. Both men stooped to roll up their bedding, and Scalphunter followed suit.

A short while later they approached the mouth of the canyon. All of them, Scalphunter included, had eaten a little something from their war bags or saddlebags on the way, chasing the dried foods with water from canteens. The sun was at their backs as they neared the mouth, throwing shadows far out in front of them. The reddish ball of the sun would most likely blind anyone looking toward the east, and if an observer saw the riders at all, it would not be with much detail.

Along the way, they discussed a plan, but ultimately, since none of them knew what might lurk inside the canyon, they discarded the idea of planning anything. They would ride in, see what they saw, and respond to it as needed.

The canyon was typical of the area. Steep sides flanked it, mostly rocky with outcroppings of mesquite, cholla, and ocotillo, and spreading away from the middle like the wings of a bird in flight. The floor was narrow, barely more than the length of a dozen horses standing end to end. Dry grass carpeted some of the floor, spotted with a few taller plants and marred by sections of bare earth. About twice as far in as the canyon was wide, at this point, it curved to the left and vanished behind its own walls. A rider passing by might think it ended at that point, unless he looked closely.

Jonah Hex gave a casual shrug, but Scalphunter noticed that he loosened his rifle in its saddle scabbard, ready for anything. The others did the same. Four abreast, they rode into the canyon, sun chasing them, shadows preceding.

The first thing Scalphunter noticed was that the temperature inside it dropped significantly, even though he could feel the same sun against his back. "Cold in here," he said.

"Yes," El Diablo confirmed. "Unnaturally so."

"Anyone knows unnatural . . ." Jonah began, but he didn't finish the thought.

Bat shivered involuntarily. "Strange, that's for sure," he said. "Mebbe the sun just ain't warmed the ground in here yet."

"Could be," Scalphunter admitted. *Not likely, though,* he thought. He didn't bother to say it, knowing that it had already occurred to everyone else. The Kiowa had stories about oddly cold places—that they indicated the locations of restless dead, those killed not in battle but through other violent means. Deaths that hid their souls from the view of the Great Spirit. These stories were never told to the Eastern scholars or journalists who occasionally came looking for tales of the savages with which to amuse the whites, but were preserved for telling inside teepees after the night's meal was finished and the fire died down, after whatever stories and songs might have been shared in public.

He shivered, this time not from the cold. He didn't like this canyon, and they had just barely entered it.

* * *

Bat could see by the tension of the other men's bodies that they were no fonder of this canyon than he was. Jonah's face was hard to read, mangled as it was. El Diablo's was set in its perpetual, disinterested condition. The mask he wore probably helped to create that impression, but his mouth rarely seemed to smile or frown, nor did what could be seen of his eyes. If he hadn't taken his hat off to sleep the last few nights, Bat would have doubted that he actually had a forehead. And Ke-Woh-No-Tay, or Scalphunter, seemed to have perfected that Indian trait of never letting his emotions show on his face. *Hate to sit across from him at the poker table.*

But each of his companions was almost preternaturally alert, sitting straight in their saddles. Their heads were still but their eyes in constant motion, checking each bush, each spindly spray of ocotillo, each rock big enough to hide a scorpion. He swore he could almost see their ears twitching like their horses' did, picking out each rustle from the breeze whispering through cactus thorns, the sound of a lizard's feet scraping a stone, the distant cries of a hawk riding the wind.

Better stop payin' attention to them and start watchin' out for myself, he thought. *Wouldn't do to be caught flatfooted if somethin' did happen.*

None of the things he saw or heard or smelled—the dust of the trail, the dry spice of the desert before summer's rains freed the miasma of scents kept locked inside it—were out of the ordinary for a place like this. Which didn't explain why it all seemed so wrong. The biting chill in the air. The silence in between the lizards and birds and breezes. The clarity of the light, as if the air inside the canyon was thinner than it ought to be.

A fat drop of sweat rolled down the back of his neck, tickling like the fingertip of a ghost.

He lowered his right hand to his .44 Smith & Wesson Army revolver. Didn't draw it, just felt its grip against his palm and was comforted by the sensation. Slightly.

"Snake," El Diablo said suddenly. His voice was quiet, and for a second Bat wasn't sure what he'd said.

"Snake?" he repeated.

"Snakes," Scalphunter clarified. He pointed ahead of them, about halfway between them and the bend in the canyon.

The grass there rustled, writhed as if it was alive.

If that was a snake—or snakes—then they were some damn big ones.

Then the first few broke into an open patch of dirt, and Bat saw that they weren't big at all—no bigger than your garden-variety sidewinder, anyway. It was just that there were several of them.

Not several. Many.

"That's a lot of snakeskin," Jonah said. He sounded almost amused.

They kept coming. Bat didn't even bother trying to count—his horse was too busy shying and rearing and whinnying in near panic—but he tried to estimate, giving up when he got past a hundred, and there seemed no end in sight. There were rattlers, of course, by the score, and now that they had revealed themselves they set their tails in motion, kicking up a ruckus that had become almost deafening in the space of a minute. Bat recognized other snakes—coachwhips, gopher snakes, hognose, hooknose,

and longnose. They came in every color combination—
pinks and sands and black stripes and bright red, pale blue
and sea green. Their advance was like a flash flood, flowing toward the riders, filling the canyon's floor.

The horses protested, unwilling to take another step. It
was everything Bat could do to keep Faro from turning
and running away. For a few moments there he thought
his horse had the right idea.

"This is not natural," Scalphunter said. "These snakes
would never hunt together."

"Natural or not, they'll be on us in a minute," Jonah
pointed out. "Anyone got any ideas?"

"High ground?" Bat offered. He nodded toward a
nearby slope that was steep but not impossible for the
horses. "Mebbe climb that cliff there."

"I have another thought," El Diablo said. As usual, his
voice was soft and calm. Rather than elaborate, he nudged
his big stallion right toward them. The horse's nostrils
flared, eyes widening in near panic, but he did what his
rider demanded of him. The others watched as the man in
black rode into the flood of serpents, his cloak fluttering
behind him. He drew a revolver and fired at the snakes as
he went, but his bullets missed or the creatures dodged his
shots.

A few seconds later, he reined the stallion to a stop.
The horse considered, then obeyed. He stood there calmly
as the snakes slithered around him, ankle deep.

"They ain't even real!" Jonah said, barking out a laugh.
"They're just in our heads!"

He was right, Bat realized. Had to be right. El Diablo's
horse, however well trained, would not simply stand still in
a sea of snakeflesh. Besides, with the snakes that thick, El

Diablo's bullets could not have missed every target, but Bat had not seen any snakes show evidence of having been hit.

Jonah spurred his mount forward, and Scalphunter followed. Bat brought up the rear. His cayuse nickered anxiously as they approached the snakes, but relaxed when he realized that although he could see, hear and smell the serpents, he couldn't feel them.

"Somebody's playin' us," Bat said.

"That's certain," Jonah agreed. "Now we know it, though, let's keep pushin' into this canyon and see what they're tryin' t'keep us away from."

"Yes," El Diablo said, turning his black steed. He reared back and pointed up-canyon. "Onward we ride." He started in that direction, and the others followed, laughing at their own terror of the nonexistent serpents. In what seemed like mere seconds, they had passed through the writhing mass, and as if needing to be believed in to exist, when Bat glanced behind them there was no indication that the snakes had ever been there.

He cranked his head this way and that, working the tension-caused kinks out of his neck as he rode. The air was still uncommonly cold, and the other things that had bothered him before still existed, but the more distance he put between himself and the spot where he'd seen the snakes, the quicker the fear drained away.

So when the flying things dropped toward them from the rocky cliffs on either side, leathery wings beating like drums, he wasn't ready.

"Above!" Scalphunter shouted.

"More mirages?" Jonah wondered.

Scalphunter raised his long gun and squeezed off a shot. A bullet rocketed into the air and slammed into one of the flying things' chests. Black blood spurted from it and the thing shrieked, a high-pitched, piercing sound. The rest of them began to bellow and rage as if in response.

They looked like men, for the most part, but they had wings like bats, and their skin was black as bats, the color of darkest midnight, like no black man Bat had ever seen. Not a one of them had any hair, their bald heads tapering to crests, yellow eyes fairly glowing in contrast to their dark skins. Their open mouths showed sharp yellow teeth; and yellow claws, like old bone daggers, tipped their fingers and toes. They were naked and without identifiable gender, although their faces and wedge-shaped heads appeared masculine.

The one Scalphunter had shot plummeted to the ground, landing with a heavy thud. The others, wailing their shrill cries, dropped toward the men like a whirlwind. The flaps of their wings kicked up dust that stung Bat's eyes, nearly blinding him. The smell, as the flying men came closer, reminded him of the time in Natchez when he'd accidentally fallen through rotten floorboards into a den of rats. The furry, filthy beasts had scurried and squealed, and he'd smelled the stink of them every time he closed his eyes for a week. The stench of these flying men was like that, only worse, as if they had putrid breath in addition to the rodent smell.

Bat drew his Smith & Wesson and began firing without aiming, counting on the sheer number of the men filling the sky to catch the lead he threw. Gouts of blood spattered, hot and thick, onto his upturned face. It stank and burned, and he tried to wipe it with his free hand as it landed, clutching his frantic cayuse with his legs so it didn't ride right out from under him.

The other men were shooting, too, the bitter smell of gunpowder mercifully diluting the stink of the winged men. More of the flying men fell, but those who avoided the bullets continued to fly lower. They stooped like hunting birds of prey as they neared, talons out. Bat shot at one that swooped close to him, but he missed and the thing snagged his hat, sending it flying into the dirt. He fired again. This time his slug hit one, but another dived in behind him, its sharp claws slicing through his vest and shirt, raking his flesh. The wounds burned as if liquid fire had been poured under his skin, and he screamed.

"You okay, Lash?" Jonah called out.

Bat didn't answer right away. Two more of the flying men were fluttering around his head, and he was waving his revolver in the air, trying to swat them away. Talons ripped the skin on the back of his hands. He jerked his trigger, and one of the beasts took a bullet square in the face, spinning backward with a spray of dark blood and dropping to the ground. The other one flapped a few more times, hands grabbing at Bat. Another shot boomed. The flying man jerked away as if tugged by a string. Bat glanced over at Scalphunter, who held his rifle in his hands, a thread of smoke wisping up from the barrel.

"Thanks!" Bat called.

Jonah and El Diablo both shot more of them from the air, then it was over. The winged men were all down, either dead or badly wounded. Bat had lost blood, and it looked as if everyone else had been similarly scratched or gouged, but they all remained mounted and mostly unhurt.

"We got lucky," Bat said. He wished he had iodine or something to pour into those scratches. At least his hat hadn't blown too far away.

"Luck, hell," Jonah said. "They just weren't no good. They had weapons, or the brains to shove boulders down on us, we'd all be done for."

"What were they?" Scalphunter asked. His tone indicated that he didn't think anyone would be able to answer, but he had to ask anyway.

"Demons," El Diablo speculated. "Or harpies, perhaps. Maybe nothing we have a word for. Nothing natural."

"Believe you're right about that," Bat said. "So far, ain't nothin' natural about this canyon. And we ain't even found whatever was makin' the green lights yet."

"Perhaps we won't," Scalphunter said.

The Kiowa had gone ahead of the others a short distance. Bat rode forward a few paces to see what he was looking at. When he stopped beside Scalphunter, the man nodded toward a thick growth in front of him. Mesquite, mostly, with thorns an inch or more in length. It grew more closely together than any mesquite Bat had ever seen, with scarcely any light showing between branches and gnarled trunks. Where there might have been spaces, cactus had grown up, filling them in.

The patch of abnormal growth continued all the way to where the canyon twisted to the left.

"We ain't gettin' through that," Bat observed. "Not on horses, leastways, and probably not afoot either."

The others had joined them. "What if we go over it?" Jonah suggested.

"Plan on cuttin' yourself some of them wings and learnin' to fly?"

"We could mebbe work our way along the canyon walls," Jonah said, ignoring the jibe. "On foot, anyhow. Then come down on the far side."

"We have no idea how far it stretches," El Diablo pointed out. "Or if there is a 'far side.'"

"That's so," Jonah admitted.

"I have one other question," El Diablo said. "Did any of you notice this growth before we fought those flying things?"

"Didn't notice it," Bat said. "What's your point?"

"Simply that I don't believe it was there before," El Diablo answered. "I think it . . . grew, if that is the right word . . . while we were fighting, or just after we vanquished them. I believe what we are seeing is one defense after another."

"Meanin', we get through this, there'll just be somethin' else waitin' for us on the other side," Jonah said, picking up the thread. "Somethin' worse."

"Exactly."

"What, then?" Bat asked. He hated the idea of coming this far only to be turned back by a bunch of overgrown thorn trees. "We give up? What if the reason we're all here is back there in that canyon?"

"I ain't sayin' give up," Jonah corrected. "I'm sayin' maybe we regroup, try to figger out a better way in. Might be we could climb the canyon walls and go down from the top. Or see we can't find a back way in."

Bat shrugged, then nodded. Frustrated. "We're so close," he said. "Leastways, I think we are, but I reckon we don't really know." He shook his scratched fist, caked with drying blood, at the mesquite. "I don't know what your game is, whoever you are! But we'll make you sorry you ever messed with the four of us!"

CHAPTER TWENTY-EIGHT

The town looked almost like a movie set, except that movie sets tended to be cleaner and better painted. The buildings were a mixture of adobe and wood framed. Some of them had been vividly painted, but others had already been scoured by wind and rain to a kind of sandy brown or gray color.

The main street was dirt, rutted by wagon wheels and strewn with horse dung. That, and the horses that had deposited it, provided the most pungent odors. Sweat and tobacco, smoked and spat, offered counterpoints. At midday, people were out in force. Men mostly wore jeans with suspenders and long-sleeved collarless shirts and big hats. Several wore United States Army uniforms. Women wore dresses with layers of petticoats beneath them. The proper ones allowed their skirts to drag in the mud as they walked, knowing that they could be washed but unwilling to expose their ankles to the men around. Less proper ones lifted their skirts above the ankle—sometimes considerably above. The men seemed to know which were likely to do that, and if they were in small groups or alone, instead of with the more proper women, they responded with whistles and hoots.

The Phantom Stranger had, through his glamour, supplied Superman with a short buckskin jacket that had ragged, uneven fringe across the chest, back, and down the sleeves. Beneath the jacket was a faded red shirt, in which tears had been sewn up with yellow thread. His jeans were blue, and they were worn over black boots with pointed toes and tall heels. A brown hat completed the look.

Jason Blood's outfit was similar, except that his deerskin jacket was almost yellow and his shirt a richer red, and his hat was white. The Stranger's look was barely changed. His standard blue trench coat had become a patched greatcoat, and his blue suit was cut in a more old-West fashion. The turtleneck was gone, replaced by a shirt with a tab collar. The gold medallion was hidden somewhere. Superman noticed that even with his super-vision, he still couldn't make out the Stranger's eyes.

The three of them had materialized behind a livery stable, then walked around to the main street. If anyone noticed that they were strangers in town, it would be assumed that they had just dropped their horses off at the stable.

"This is the place," the Stranger muttered, as they watched the traffic on the street. Men and women in buckboard wagons, supplies loaded in the back for their nearby ranches. Others on horseback, weaving around the ones on foot. Some just sitting on the boardwalk, shaded by an overhang, chairs tilted back against the wall and booted feet on the faded boards. "If not here, then some-place nearby."

"If you say so," Jason said. Superman agreed. It was the Stranger who could sniff out magic, if anyone could. He and Jason Blood were hired guns in the Stranger's range war. Except it wasn't just cattle versus sheep at stake.

"Look at the sun," Superman said, nodding toward the pink ball in the sky. "Not quite red, but it looks like it's on the way."

"Which confirms that we've come to the right time," the Stranger said. "Do you feel the effects?"

"I'm okay," Superman replied. "Maybe weaker than usual, but not totally powerless. What's our next step? We look around for Faust, Savage, and Mordru?"

The Stranger was about to answer when another voice cut him off. "Howdy, gents," it said. Superman turned to see a sheriff, rotund but with a flinty glare, standing behind them, having just emerged from the door of a dry goods store. Purpling around his eyes and the bridge of his nose indicated recent bruising. He smoothed his mustache as he regarded them. "You all are strangers here, ain't you?"

"Yes, Sheriff, we are," Superman said. "Just passing through, really. Nice town."

"I like it," the sheriff replied. "I like it when it's quiet, if you get my meanin'. I see none of you boys is armed."

"Should we be?" the Stranger asked. "I thought this was a peaceable town."

"You thought right," the sheriff said. "Where you headed?"

"Not altogether sure about that," the Stranger replied.

"We're looking for some men. When we find them we'll know where we're going."

"You lookin' for Jonah Hex and his owlhoot partners, you're gonna have to look elsewhere. They busted out of my jail and ain't been seen since. I oughta run 'em down, but way I figger it, gone is just as good."

"No, that's not them," the Stranger said. "Fact is, I don't think the men we're looking for came anywhere near here."

"Well, I'm glad to hear you're no friends of theirs," the sheriff said, unconsciously gripping the bridge of his nose, where the bruising was. "You keep your noses clean while you're here in Willson."

"We plan on doing just that," Jason assured him. "Don't worry, we'll be no trouble at all."

The sheriff wandered away, hitching up his pants as he did. Superman and his two companions turned toward each other. "Jonah Hex," Superman said. "He's a good man, under that rough exterior."

"He's entered the realm of legend," the Stranger said. "But that was when he was at the height of his abilities and his fame. He was a bounty hunter, but somehow couldn't seem to resist getting involved in conflicts that paid him nothing whatsoever. Justice was more of an idea than a reality in a lot of these Western towns, and Hex found himself, more often than not, taking the side of the powerless against the powerful."

"You think he's part of all this?" Jason asked. "The reason we're here?"

"It's certainly possible," the Stranger said.

"It would be almost too much of a coincidence if he weren't," Superman added.

"He won't remember having met any of us before," the Stranger cautioned. "It won't have happened for him yet. And in order to keep from altering the timeline too much, we'll have to wipe his memory of meeting us now."

"That's what I was thinking," Jason said.

"I guess we'd better find him," Superman suggested. "Maybe he can lead us to the sorcerers."

"We could ask the sheriff which way he went," Jason suggested. "But that might be impolitic."

"And unnecessary," Superman said. He was here as the muscle, but he brought other attributes to the table as well. Looking around to make sure no one watched them, he took the Stranger and Jason Blood in his arms and rocketed into the clear blue sky. He couldn't go as fast as under a yellow sun, but the sun was not yet red enough to hold him back much. Within seconds, the town had shrunk to the size of a child's toy, with the secondary toy of the adobe fort nearby, surrounded by open desert. From this height he could see for hundreds of miles in every direction, without even using his X-ray vision. He turned slowly, still clutching his companions, scanning the ground. He saw Indians and ranchers, coyotes and javelinas, cattle and cacti.

Finally, he saw an unconventional grouping of four men, on horseback, near the mouth of a deep canyon. He was surprised to discover that he recognized all four.

"Got them," he announced. "It's Hex, Bat Lash, Scalphunter, and El Diablo. Hold on."

That last was mostly for effect, as he had no intention of dropping them. Angling toward the four riders, he flew fast but not at superspeed, not wanting to buffet his passengers too much. He brought them down for a gentle landing, below a bluff about a quarter mile from the mounted foursome. "I didn't want to scare them," he said. "We should probably approach them in a more conventional fashion."

"If they're too easily scared, they're not the men we need," the Stranger said. "But I understand your reasoning."

"You really think we need reinforcements?" Jason asked.

"If those four are the men Superman says, then I believe we're all here for the same reason," the Stranger replied.

"I didn't think they met each other this early in their lives," Superman said.

"Bat Lash and Scalphunter are old comrades, but the others are new to them. History did not record this meeting, because they had no long-lasting memory of it," the Stranger pointed out. "Since we cannot allow them to."

Superman glanced at his clothing, half-expecting it to have been tattered by the flight, as ordinary clothes would have been. In reality, however, he was wearing his uniform, and the rest was just the product of the Stranger's magic, so it wasn't even disheveled. "Should you magic us up some horses?" he asked.

"That should not be necessary." The Stranger started walking toward where the riders had been. Superman and Jason Blood followed, Superman wondering how the Stranger planned to introduce them.

The Phantom Stranger didn't feel things the way other people did—the way he vaguely remembered feeling them, though so far in the past that he couldn't recall who he had been then, or what, if anything, had happened to change him. Most men, hiking through this desert in a full suit and greatcoat, would have been hot, sweating, risking over-exertion. Not him. He felt as cool as he had in Jason Blood's air-conditioned apartment. The heat didn't disturb him. The thorns and stickers of the desert foliage didn't pierce his garments. Rattlesnakes dived back into their holes rather than risk running into him.

It was true that he didn't know how Jonah Hex and whoever rode with him would react to their sudden appearance, on foot in the middle of the desert and apparently none the worse for it. He knew many, many things, having experienced most of human history firsthand, and one of the things he had learned most thoroughly was the fact that people could always surprise him. They could be predicted only to a certain extent. They could be manipulated, and if that became necessary, he would resort to it. In the end, though, there was no telling how people might respond to any given situation.

He didn't see that they had any options, though. He had thought that he and Jason Blood were the only ones aware of the coming crisis and working to forestall it. But another thing he had learned over the aeons was that forces greater than he had plans and schemes of their own. He thought of them as the forces of Order, although he could not remember who, if anyone, had taught him that. He sided with Order against Chaos, its natural enemy. It was entirely possible that Order had summoned Jonah and the others to this place, just as it had brought him, Superman and Jason.

Possible, too, that they had been brought here by the other side. Maybe they were posted specifically to keep out would-be meddlers. If that turned out to be the case, they'd regret having taken that side—even if Superman was weakened by the reddening sun.

The time had come to find out. They walked quietly— the Stranger mystically dampening the sounds their boots would have made on the desert floor—and presently they could hear the low voices of the men. He glanced at his companions, an unspoken question. Receiving nods in reply, he shoved aside a thorny mesquite limb and stepped into the open, at the top of a slight rise. The horsemen were still mounted, at the foot of the slope. They all spun around, weapons drawn, as he, Superman, and Jason came into view.

"Rest easy, gentlemen," the Stranger said. "I believe we are all on the same side here." Wishful thinking had its place, after all. "If I could make some introductions . . ." He ignored the looks of disbelief on the faces of the Westerners and launched right in. "Jonah Hex, Bat Lash, El Diablo, and Ke-Woh-No-Tay, also known as Scalphunter. My friends here are Clark and Jason."

"Pleased to meet you," Superman said.

"Same," Jason added. "Your reputations precede you."

Jonah Hex snorted a laugh. The sun that had browned his face and neck had no impact on his scar tissue, its surface as pink, smooth, and free of whiskers as a baby's skin. "And yet you come up on us without iron in your fists?"

"Like the man said," Superman answered, "we think we're all on the same side."

"I didn't know there was sides," Bat Lash said. He rocked back in his saddle, a friendly, casual grin on his face.

"There generally are," Superman said. "You men encountered something strange inside that canyon, right? Something malevolent."

The Stranger suppressed a smile. Superman had been using his superhearing, then, listening in on the men as they approached.

"Yes," El Diablo said. Behind his mask, his dark eyes flashed with intelligence and curiosity. "You speak the truth. We did, at that."

"We have a hunch that some men we're looking for might be responsible," Superman explained. "They're bad men. Extremely bad. I can't stress that enough."

"Men have called me bad, too," Scalphunter said. "I find that it all depends on where you sit."

"Often true," the Stranger said. "But not in this case. What these men have in mind is harmful to all of you, and everyone you've ever known. You have noticed the sun?"

"Been turnin' reddish these last couple days," Jonah said. He regarded the three strangers thoughtfully.

"These men we're after did that," the Stranger said. "And that's just the beginning, the least of what they're up to."

"So you three're out to stop them?" Bat asked.

"That's right," Jason replied, picking up the thread. "And if you've got a grudge against them, you might want to throw in with us."

Bat touched the back of his hand with the other, then let it drop back to the horn of his saddle. The Stranger could see fresh cuts on it. "We might could owe them a favor or two I wouldn't mind payin' back."

"But as for trusting the three of you . . ." El Diablo

began. "How do we know you gentlemen are what you say? You could as easily be these bad men you speak of."

"We're asking for your trust," the Stranger said. "That's the best we can offer. If you are the men I believe you are, then you carry within you a powerful sense of right and wrong. You must decide for yourselves, each of you, if you are willing to join us or not. If not, then I hope you will go about your affairs and let us go about ours. We will accomplish the task set before us, I assure you. It would be easier with your help, as you know the area, the landscape, better than we. And if it comes to a fight— which we believe it will—the more hands, the better."

"You're askin' us to trust you," Jonah said, "but you ain't told us much. First names for those two, no name at all for yourself. You walk up out of the desert with no horses. You're not carryin' weapons, but you say you're spoilin' for a fight. I don't see no canteens, but you don't look thirsty. I've seen some right strange folks in my time, but you three just might be the strangest."

The Phantom Stranger started to answer, but Superman interrupted. The Stranger allowed the Kryptonian to go on. "You're right," Superman said. "There's a reason we haven't been very forthcoming. It's likely you won't believe a word of what we would tell you. I wouldn't ask you to put your lives on the line without knowing what you'd be fighting for, and I'm sure my friends wouldn't either. But you might want to get down off those horses— this could take a while."

The men exchanged looks, then did as Superman had suggested. The Stranger's first inclination had been to psychically encourage them to join in. Superman's approach, however, was no doubt more practical. If it worked, the men would support their cause of their own free will, and they would be better allies for it. If they chose not to—or turned and ran away—then he, Superman, and Jason would continue on their own, as they had begun.

The endgame approached. The Stranger would rather go into it with these men, whom history had judged and found heroic.

Against Vandal Savage, Felix Faust, and the Dark Lord Mordru, they could use all the heroes they could get.

CHAPTER TWENTY-NINE

Superman didn't know the Phantom Stranger all that well—he doubted anyone did—but he suspected that he had more faith in his fellow humans than the Stranger. While he was certain the Stranger could magically "persuade" the Westerners to pitch in, Superman preferred to let them make up their own minds.

If they made the wrong decision, then the Stranger could work his whammy.

"Go ahead and drop the glamour, Phantom Stranger," he said. "Let's show them who we really are."

With the slightest hint of a shrug, the Stranger nodded. At once, the period dress vanished and Superman stood there in his standard blue and red costume. Jason now wore a white shirt and dark blue dress pants, while the Phantom Stranger appeared in his typical dark suit, cloak and hat, complete with white turtleneck, gloves and gold medallion.

Jonah Hex and the others were so stunned, Superman nearly burst out laughing.

"This is who we are," Superman said. "Forget those fake names he told you. I'm called Superman. He really is Jason Blood, but he shares his being with a powerful demon called Etrigan. And tall, dark, and handsome there is the Phantom Stranger. We come from more than a hundred years in this Earth's future, and if we can't accomplish what we came here to do, this Earth won't have a future."

Jonah, Bat, El Diablo, and Scalphunter exchanged looks. Superman half expected one of more of them to start shooting, just because it was the only rational response to such an absurd claim.

Instead, Bat Lash broke into an amused chuckle. "Well, hell," he said, "Why didn't y'all say so in the first place?"

"Then you'll help us?" Jason asked.

"He didn't say that. But we'll listen," Jonah promised. "Way you're dressed, mister . . . Superman . . . you hadn't've had a pretty good yarn to spin, we'd already be on our way."

Everybody took seats on large rocks or cleared thorns away from patches of bare earth, and Superman launched into an explanation. He began with the memories—fading, but not gone yet—of the alternate Clark and his horror at seeing Lois's death. He segued from that into fearing for the life of the other, real Lois and everyone else on Earth. He explained as well as he could how the success of the sorcerers would mean that Earth's history would change as of this point in time.

"As I understand you," El Diablo said, "we would die?"

"That's right," the Stranger replied. "And so would your loved ones. You'd never have any descendants. There might be versions of some of today's people on the new Earth, just as there was a version of Lois Lane and of Superman's alter ego. But they will not be the same people, and they'll live in virtual slavery, subject to the whims of these three sorcerers."

"I've tried slavery," Jonah said. "Didn't much take to it."

"I'll have no descendants," El Diablo put in. "But that doesn't mean I like the idea of letting evil men rule the world."

"We still have no way of knowing if these tales they tell are the truth," Scalphunter pointed out. "These men may be the evil magicians they speak of. Even if not, why should we believe that they have the powers of strength and immortality they claim?"

"I suppose a brief demonstration wouldn't be out of line," Superman agreed.

"Brief being the key word," the Phantom Stranger added. "We have important tasks awaiting us, and time is of critical importance."

"I'll make my part quick," Superman said. He sprang to his feet, offered a smile to the four men he hoped to convince, and flew.

Or hovered, more precisely. Just a few inches off the ground, at first, then a foot. Jonah and Bat gaped, while El Diablo and Scalphunter only betrayed surprise in their eyes and a slight tensing of shoulders and arms.

Once he knew that all eyes were focused on him, he took off. Straight into the air for about a hundred feet. There he stopped and did a slow pirouette before launching into a display of aerial acrobatics—spins, twists, a superspeed dive toward the ground, pulling out of it at the last possible split second, then back into the sky for a couple of loops. As a finale, he did another dive, this time not pulling out. He hit the dirt and kept going, tunneling under the people on the surface. Less than a minute later he popped out on the other side of them, with an enormous boulder held over his head for good measure. He carried the boulder into the air, then slowly lowered his feet back into contact with the ground. Making sure no people or animals were in harm's way, he tossed the boulder as easily as if it were a softball, swung one mighty fist into it, shattering it into millions of pieces, and with a blast of superbreath, blew the fragments into the open desert.

Demonstration complete, he turned back to the others. "That's some of what I can do."

The four men sat in silence for a moment, looking at him with disbelief. Slowly, it registered on their faces that they really had seen what they thought they had.

"It's all true, gentlemen," Jason Blood said. "You don't want to see an example of my power, if you can help it, because the demon sharing this space with me isn't the most pleasant fellow, or easily reined in once he's loose. And I have a feeling the Phantom Stranger isn't much for showing off. But trust me, if you can—everything Superman said is true. We're all in trouble unless we can find these guys and shut them down."

"If the alternative is to have you fellers as enemies," Bat said, "then you can count me in."

"As long as you did nothing to interfere, we would not think of you as opponents," the Stranger assured them. "But we would appreciate your help if it's freely offered."

"You can bet on it," Bat said. "Leastways far as I'm concerned."

"I'm in," Jonah seconded.

"And me," El Diablo said.

Scalphunter simply nodded his affirmation.

"Tell us," Jason said. "What happened to you in that canyon?"

"What didn't?" Bat said with a grin. "We saw weird green lights in there last night. Tried to go in this mornin' to check 'em out, and it seemed like somebody or t'other surely didn't want us pokin' our snouts into their business."

"First we were attacked by snakes," El Diablo explained. "Except they were only imaginary snakes, not real ones. We went beyond those, and were attacked again, this time by real creatures, but like something from nightmares. Winged men, with skin as black as coal and talons like huge eagles."

Bat shoved a finger through a rip in his vest. "They'd owe me a new wardrobe if'n we hadn't've killed 'em all. Anyhow, I didn't see as they had any pockets or coin purses."

"Finally, we encountered an impenetrable jungle of mesquite and cactus," El Diablo continued. "One which had not been there just moments before. We turned back then, determined to reconsider our approach."

"Do you have any idea what's back there?" the Stranger asked.

"None at all," Jonah said. "This's unfamiliar country to all of us."

Superman tried to peer through the canyon walls with his X-ray vision, but he found it blocked to him, as if the walls were made of lead. "I can't see through," he said. "I think they've got it magically shielded."

"More ways than one," Bat agreed.

"Mebbe we could go in from the air," Jonah suggested. "If you think you can carry all of us."

"We'll have to build a platform or some other device," Superman said. "There are a few too many of you to fit you under my arms. But the weight won't be a problem."

"I can take care of that," the Stranger offered. "Is everyone ready?"

Leaving their horses tethered to the scrawny, tangled mesquite trees, all the men stepped into a basket that the Stranger materialized from nowhere. Superman caught the lines attached to its four corners and lifted it into the air. He flew over the canyon walls, the makeshift gondola just clearing the tops of the trees. Jonah directed his progress to the point where the canyon hooked to the left, beyond which he said he and the others had not been able to see.

As they cleared that barrier, Superman could see what had been blocked from his super-vision before. The sight chilled him to the bone.

The canyon widened considerably at that point. Less than a mile from the bend, a spring seeped down the western wall and formed a pond around which massive trees had grown. Not far from the pond—any water source in this arid land was better than none—an Indian village had been built. Apache, he guessed. There were a few teepees and dozens of three-sided wickiups made of local plant material: mesquite branches and the wands of ocotillo and yucca stalks, built around communal fire pits.

But there were no people in the village. Instead, they

were a quarter mile farther up the canyon, penned inside a corral like livestock. The corral's fences were made of glowing blue light, like neon but without the physical tubes. There was barely room for them all; more than a hundred people, Superman estimated. Women, children, men, of every age. Some sat on the ground, if they had room, while the others stood. No one leaned on the fences—Superman was pretty sure that some had tried, as he saw burned shirts and arms on several of them, where the mystical bars had scorched them.

Beyond the corral stood a small adobe building, looking out of place.

"Why are they all fenced in?" Bat wondered.

"I have an idea," the Stranger offered, "that they're being kept for a specific purpose."

"What purpose you reckon?" Bat asked.

"Sacrifice," Jason answered. "Ritual magic doesn't always require blood sacrifice, but it does tend to focus the sorcerer's mind. In the case of these three, we know they've been using sacrifice on an enormous scale—unprecedented, really. But for the final step, they need another big one, and I'm betting those people are it."

"I believe that is the band of an old friend of mine," El Diablo said. "He was the one who . . . sent me here."

"We must stop this," Scalphunter said.

"That's why we're here," Superman reminded him. "To put a stop to their evil plans."

As he lowered the Stranger's basket to the ground, the Apache in the pen—dark-haired, bronze-skinned, some wearing buckskins or long, colorful broomstick skirts, many with bands tied around their heads—stared at the newcomers with disbelief, even horror. Some shrieked in fear while others remained silent, watching their approach. Superman couldn't understand what they were saying.

Almost as if reading his mind, Scalphunter explained. "They fear us because of our method of travel," he said. "And your manner of dress. They know we are not those who have confined them, but they do not know if we are in league with those others."

"At least we got here before they were killed," Superman said, grateful for that small favor. He set the basket down, at which point it vanished completely, then he landed beside Scalphunter. "Can you explain to them that we're here to help?"

"I do not know if they'll believe me, but I can try," the Kiowa said. He walked to the side of the pen—those standing near that fence drew away from him, unsure of his intentions—and spoke to them in what Superman assumed was Apache.

After a few minutes, he returned to the others. "They say they were imprisoned by three men. From the way they describe them, I believe the men are the sorcerers you seek. They live in that house." He pointed toward the adobe structure Superman had seen from the air.

"Then I guess we need to pay them a visit," Jason said.

"Reckon so," Jonah added. "My trigger finger's already gettin' all twitchy."

"I agree," the Stranger said, his voice unusually tight. "But before we can, I believe we have another problem to contend with."

Superman followed the Stranger's gaze, turning to peer over his own right shoulder. Even as he did, however, he realized that what the Stranger had seen first was becoming more apparent, all around them—crystallizing into semitransparent visibility while he watched.

Indians. Not just Apache—Superman thought he recognized Sioux, Crow, Klamath and Modoc, Mohawk and Montauk, Cheyenne, Shawnee, and Susquehanna. There were many more styles of dress that he could not place, but given that there were thousands—no, he corrected, tens of thousands—of them, it was unsurprising that his fairly limited knowledge of historical Indian costume was tested beyond the breaking point.

Looking closer, he realized something else. Many—perhaps most—of the figures he saw had significant wounds, caused by bullets, knives, spears, clubs, fire. Others showed evidence of the ravages of disease and starvation. Now he heard them, their bare or sandaled or booted feet crunching the detritus of the desert floor, their passage through the spare foliage, the susurrus of all their breaths, inhaling and exhaling. None of them spoke, which in its way was worse than if they all had. The smell of death accompanied them, wafting from the canyon walls and floor like freshly opened graves.

"They look like ghosts," El Diablo said. "The spirits of the Indian dead."

"Something like that," the Stranger agreed. "But I fear they are more than ghosts. They gain more substance by the moment."

"Yep," Jonah added. "One more thing—they look a touch riled about somethin'."

"I have a bad feeling," Superman said, "that what they're *riled* at is us."

CHAPTER THIRTY

Mikey looped a length of thick rope around Lois several times, pinning her into the chair in which he had made her sit. His breath was rank, alcohol-laden, his teeth yellow, glinting with silver. Once the rope had gone around her and the chair a few times, he tied her wrists, then took the ends behind the chair and knotted them. Making sure the knots were tight—too tight, already cutting off the circulation in her arms—he picked up the cordless phone he had brandished before and went into another room. Lois heard his voice muttering softly, but she couldn't make out what he said.

She was furious with herself for walking right into this. Her father, General Sam Lane, would have given her no end of grief if he had seen how ill prepared she had been when she knocked on the building manager's door. She couldn't have known, she believed, that Mikey would be in cahoots with Ivan Kashegian, but she should have been more alert to the possibility anyway.

*Not like Dad would ever be satisfied with anything I
did,* she thought, *so there's no real point beating myself
up over what he'd think.* Even so, she couldn't help judging herself according to the precepts he had drummed into
her as a young girl—as the first of two daughters, to his
eternal chagrin, since he had desperately wanted a boy.
Strategy, he had always insisted, was more important than
strength of numbers. A small force could beat a larger,
better-armed one if it could outthink its opponents. The
worst mistakes in battle were underestimating your
enemy and overestimating yourself.

Sam Lane took a militaristic approach to everything in
life, it seemed, from mowing the lawn to choosing a
movie. He was, of course, a lifelong soldier—most didn't
make general unless they were—so that made a certain
amount of sense, but it had been hard to live with and
even harder to shake off.

It should have occurred to her that Mikey was more
than he seemed. Any building manager who paid attention would have known that there were irregularities with
Phoenix Enterprises. Before approaching him about that
tenant, she should have made sure she had a clear escape
route. She should have thought through the potential
complications of that line of questioning before embark-
ing on it.

Lois tried to struggle against the ropes, but all she did
was chafe her upper arms. Even though Mikey had pulled
a gun on her, and hurt her by tying her so tightly, she
didn't think he seemed like a truly dangerous man. She
had encountered more than her fair share of killers and
sadists over the years, and thought she could spot them
when she ran into them.

But if he turned her over to Ivan Kashegian, and if—this was a stretch, but not one she could afford to ignore—Kashegian really was responsible for the deaths of the eighty people in the shipping container—then all bets were off. If he believed that she had connected the dots, he could easily decide that one more dead body was a much smaller problem than having eighty murders pinned on him.

On the plus side, meeting Kashegian had been her original goal. Not tied to a chair, however, and not with him holding all the cards. If there were to be a graceful exit from this situation—short of Clark's intervention—it would have to be accomplished before Kashegian got here.

Mikey remained on the phone in the other room, though. For all she knew, he could have been talking to a lover, not to Kashegian at all. The conversation had continued for some time, the tones low and intimate. If it was Kashegian on the phone, and he was here in Metropolis, he might arrive at any moment.

She needed to make some kind of move, and she needed to do it fast.

And it had to be dramatic enough to get him off that damn phone.

The chair was low, so her center of gravity was, too. And it was heavy. Hours in the gym had to have more impact than just keeping her belly flat and her legs toned, though. She pressed her feet flat against the floor, then pushed up off her toes. The front legs of the chair lifted a little. She rocked it back down, did it again. The third time, she shoved with everything she had, trying to buck sideways at the same time.

It worked. The chair tipped backward, then rolled, and she and it both came down hard, with a loud bang. She was able to keep her head from hitting the floor, although on impact she bit her cheek so hard she tasted blood.

Mikey dashed into the room. Carrying the gun, she noted, but not the phone. "What the hell was that?"

Lois craned her neck to look up at the man. "It's no surprise you're not married," she said. "When you invite a lady over you're supposed to pay attention to her."

"I'm a little busy here," Mikey said.

"Then you have to expect me to try to get away. It's only reasonable. Wouldn't you do the same?"

"Yeah, I guess so."

"Is Kashegian on his way over?"

Mikey grinned, showing gold. "In person? He's sending someone to pick you up. How important do you think you are?"

"I like to think very," Lois replied. Her neck was already getting sore. "You want to straighten me up again?"

"I think I like you this way."

She was glad she wasn't wearing a skirt, at least, but she really didn't want to pull a muscle in her neck or shoulders. "Maybe you do," she said. "But will Kashegian want damaged goods?"

Mikey considered that for a moment. "Nah, probably not." He walked around behind the chair, stooped, and hoisted her back to an upright position. "Keep it that way, 'cause I ain't pickin' you up again."

"Stick around, then," Lois urged him. "No telling what trouble I might get into if I'm bored enough."

He shrugged and flipped a wall switch. An overhead light came on—a plain white light, for a change. Then he crossed to the pole light and turned off the red bulbs there. "I like a little atmosphere when I'm listening to music."

"So I gathered," she said. The overhead light illuminated more of the front room of his apartment. She was almost sorry he'd turned it on. The gray carpet, on which her head had been resting just moments before, looked like it had never been vacuumed or cleaned in any way. She could make out crumbs of food, insect parts, bits of paper, plastic, metal, and other kinds of trash strewn all over it. Mikey plopped down onto an old couch that had a threadbare blanket thrown over it, as if to hide the hideous gold, brown, and orange upholstery peeking through. He folded his hands over his gut—weapon still clutched in his right—and regarded her with a bemused expression. Between them was a low wooden coffee table piled high with magazines—a fairly equal mix of automotive, nudie, and cooking, it seemed. The cooking ones surprised her, but then she was supposed to be working on not stereotyping people, she recalled. An old TV in one corner balanced a VCR and a DVD player. "Nice place."

He caught the sarcasm. "You don't have to like it. You ain't stayin' long anyhow."

"Do you know when my ride will get here?"

"They'll get here when they get here," Mikey answered.

"Worked for Kashegian long?"

"Who says I work for him?"

She glanced at the ropes binding her to the chair. "You'd do this kind of thing on a volunteer basis? I thought you looked smarter than that. If you're going to risk a felony rap, you should at least get paid for it."

"Who says I'm risking a felony rap?"

"Kidnapping. Imprisonment. Assault. Battery. I'm no

prosecuting attorney, but I have a feeling the law frowns on this sort of thing."

Mikey shook his head. "No, I mean who says you'll ever make it to court to testify against me? Soon as our visitors show up, you go away, and I never see you again. You were never here."

"You're forgetting something," Lois said. "I'm kind of a major asset to the *Daily Planet*. They like to know where I'm going when I'm away from the office. You might also have heard that I'm friends with a guy named Superman, who also tends to keep tabs on me."

"I hear stuff," Mikey affirmed. "Doesn't mean I let it worry me, you know? I sleep pretty good at night without a lot of worries messing up my head."

"You're a pretty together guy, I guess," Lois said. "Most people get worked up about the idea of spending years in federal penitentiaries. Must be nice to be so centered."

Mikey smiled. "Guess I'm just mellow. Easygoing."

"That's the way to be," Lois said. "I meet a lot of important people. Politicians, celebrities, athletes, that kind of thing. You might be surprised how many of them are stressed-out all the time. Always fretting about their poll numbers, their Q ratings, breaking the next record, or having someone break their last one. It's kind of nice to meet a guy who knows how to take it easy. You probably don't take a cell phone or a BlackBerry on vacation, either."

"Don't have a cell phone or whatever that berry thing is," Mikey said. "Haven't taken a vacation, either. I've worked at this building for nineteen years."

"Without a break?" Lois tried to sound surprised and impressed at the same time. "That's hard work."

"I'm good at it," Mikey said. "I can fix almost any kind of plumbing or electrical problem. I know what the tenants need and how to get it. And I provide special services for some of them."

"Like Phoenix Enterprises."

Mikey didn't respond.

"The thing is," Lois continued, "you should be well compensated for this kind of special service. I mean, you do something like this—breaking any number of laws, potentially bringing the wrath of Superman and the *Daily Planet* down on your head—you ought to be able to take a week in the south of France on the bonus you get. You don't think Kashegian's got cash-flow problems, do you? Because I can assure you, he's loaded."

"He takes care of me."

"What, a fruitcake at the holidays? Maybe a few bucks slipped into the rent envelope now and then? I don't mean to be judgmental, but look at this place, Mikey. When's the last time you bought a new piece of furniture? You should be able to afford a cell phone if you want one. Kashegian can afford it, and if you don't demand what you're worth, he's never going to really respect you."

"If you're trying to turn me against him, it won't work," Mikey said. "He's been a tenant for a long time. We have an understanding."

"Yeah, I bet. He understands that you jump when he says to, and he understands that he can take advantage of you anytime he likes. Without having to worry about you demanding anything in return."

"If I need something—"

"If you need something, you can go to him and beg for it? And if he gives it to you, he makes you think he's doing you a special favor, and you're indebted to him for it? That how it works, Mikey?" She was bluffing, since she had no clue what the relationship between Mikey and Ivan Kashegian was really like. But his responses told her she was on the right track, so she kept pressing, pressing. Maybe it wouldn't do any good. Maybe it would make him angry enough to slap her around before Kashegian's goons came to pick her up. She didn't know how he would react to the prodding.

At this point, she figured her best options were to try to provoke him, or try to seduce him. And she was afraid the latter might prove successful.

"It's a give-and-take kind of thing," Mikey said after a moment. There was a defensive edge to his voice. "We do each other favors, help each other out."

"Somehow I bet you do more helping than he does," Lois guessed. "Just based on the fact that he's a wealthy, powerful man, and you're . . . umm, not."

"I do okay," he argued. "Sure, I don't have a lot of money. But I never wonder where my next meal is comin' from or nothin' like that. I got a roof over my head"—he glanced up toward the ceiling and chuckled—"a whole building, in fact. I don't need a lot of stuff. I mean, it's not like I even like fancy clothes or that stuff. T-shirts, Dickies, a six of Soder Cola and one of Bud in the fridge and some frozen dinners in the icebox and I'm golden, you know?"

"But what happens if you need a new TV?" Lois asked. "Or a new refrigerator, or if you get really sick and can't work? Do you have anything put away for that? Or is Kashegian laughing at you from his penthouse, knowing he's got everything he could ever need and more, while you're down here in the basement hoping he'll come through with a couple of dollars so you can buy that extra six-pack on your birthday?"

His smile was gone altogether now. Lois decided not to let up. She knew that in his NCO days, Sam Lane had prided himself on his ability to break a man's spirit in six weeks or less.

She was trying to do it in six minutes.

Wouldn't the old man be proud of you now, Lois?

"Don't get me wrong, Mikey. I don't like you or anything. Right this minute I can think of very few people I like less, what with you tying me up, holding a gun on me, and everything. Worse, I don't respect you, and that's entirely your fault. You won't stand up to Kashegian, won't demand any kind of equity in your relationship, and that means you've made yourself into his doormat. I know you don't care what I think, but I feel like I should let you know anyway. How it looks to an outsider. I have to say, it looks bad for you."

"Like you said, lady, I don't care what you think."

"There's no reason for you to. For your own sake, though, you need to think about these things. Kashegian's using you. You think when a doormat gets too encrusted with mud he sends it out to be dry-cleaned? Of course not. He throws it away like a used tissue. He'll do the same with you when he feels like you've outlived your usefulness. Or when you know too much—when you know something that might get him in serious trouble."

She paused for breath, and for impact. He watched her, seemingly rapt. Maybe just impressed by the auctioneer-like speed at which she could yammer when she needed to. "For instance, suppose you were the last person to see a well-known *Daily Planet* reporter alive, before delivering her into the hands of Kashegian's thugs. Either her body would turn up, or she'd be officially missing. In either case, an investigation would be launched. Since it was known that she had come to this building, the investigation would begin here. The people upstairs who sent me to you would be questioned. You'd be a focus of the search.

"How long do you think you'd stay alive? Kashegian would have you killed before my corpse was even cold. He'd have to."

Mikey gnawed on his lower lip. The gun dangled, almost forgotten, in his right hand. His left was clenched, softly pummeling his thigh. Lois could tell that she had gotten through to him. The next few minutes would tell if it was enough.

"There's only one way for you to survive this, Mikey. You put yourself in this position—you made yourself expendable, and now that's the way it's got to be. If you want to get through this, you have to have something that Kashegian wants. A bargaining chip."

He blinked a couple of times, as if she had shined a light into his eyes, and stopped hitting himself on the leg. "But . . . what do I have like that?"

Lois couldn't quite believe how stupid Mikey really was. No wonder he had set himself up to be used and cast aside by a dirtbag like Kashegian.

"You have me."

"But they're coming for you."

"They're not here yet. You know Kashegian wants me.

You know that you and I together could put him out of business, lock him away, and you'd be safe. All you have to do is hide me somewhere. Then you could either negotiate a deal with him or with the authorities. For once, you'd be the one in the catbird seat."

"The what?"

"Never mind. I think you get the point. But if you're going to save yourself, we've got to get busy."

"Yeah," Mikey said. He jerked to his feet. "Yeah. I've got an empty suite upstairs. They'd never find us there without searching the whole building."

"Untie me, then, and let's get going," Lois urged. "There's no time to waste."

Mikey crossed to the chair, went behind it and started loosening the knots. As the ropes dropped away, Lois's arms began to tingle, the blood flowing unrestricted through them again. "I've still got the gun, lady, so don't try anything," he muttered.

"I can barely move," she assured him. "You don't need to worry about me." When the ropes had fallen to the floor, she forced herself out of the chair on unsteady legs.

Aiming the gun at her, he went to the door and opened it. "We'll take the elevator up to seven," he said. "There's an empty office there, with a private bathroom. We'll be okay there."

"Elevator's out of order," she said. She didn't add the sobriquet "Einstein," although she thought it.

"The stairs, whatever." He backed out of the door, beckoning her with the gun. "Come on," he said. "We don't have much time."

She followed him into the dark hallway. She had barely

closed the door behind her, at Mikey's insistence, when she heard another voice. Male, deep, with an eastern European accent. "Fascinating conversation, Mikey," it said. "I don't think we heard all of it, but we heard enough. Mr. Kashegian will be very interested in what you and Ms. Lane had to say. Especially you. Now put the weapon on the floor, and back away from it slowly."

CHAPTER THIRTY-ONE

May 1872

"Why are they mad at us?" Jason asked no one in particular. "We're not the ones who made ritual use of their genocide."

"True," the Stranger replied. "But by doing so, our sorcerous opponents have established a tie with all those deaths, a connection that they can use for their own ends, however nefarious."

"So even though they took advantage of the slaughter of hundreds of thousands, maybe millions, now they can take advantage of the spirits of those same people?"

"So it would appear."

"Mebbe we should jaw about it later and figger out what to do about it now," Jonah Hex suggested. "They'll be on us directly."

Superman agreed. The Indians had taken on further solidity. As they did, their wounds seemed to come to life as well, oozing blood and other bodily fluids. They completely surrounded the small group of men and the much larger group of Apaches in the corral. Their numbers filled the canyon floor, and they flowed down the rocky slopes like water during a monsoon. They still didn't speak or let out the war cries that they might have in life—the magic that had returned them to Earth seemed to have denied them that ability—but the noise of their approach echoed like thunder in the canyon.

Superman rushed to the Stranger's shoulder. "I want to try something," he said. "But before I do—they really are dead, right?"

"Without doubt," the Stranger said. "I don't know what kind of spell was used to bring them back, so I don't know if they can feel pain, although I expect not. They might act like they do, but that will be illusion, not reality."

"Let's hope you're right," Superman said. He flew a few feet off the ground, just high enough to make sure no one got in his path, and aimed his heat vision at the nearest rank of dead Indian warriors. Twin beams, red as lasers, emanated from his eyes. When they struck the Indians, he heard the sizzle of roasting flesh, smelled the too-familiar stench. The warriors dropped their weapons and fell to the ground, writhing with what looked like authentic agony, their mouths working soundlessly. "You're sure about this, Stranger?"

"As sure as I can be," he answered. "And it seems to be working."

From his vantage point, Superman wasn't so sure. The Indians struck by the beams were falling, some cut in half, others just injured. But even on the ground, they kept coming, crawling or wriggling toward those who yet lived.

Worse, parts of some—a severed arm here, clutching a

tomahawk, there a torso with a rifle in its hands—continued to thump forward, as if to finish the battle.

Changing tacks, Superman sucked in a great breath, supercooled it, and blew it out, enveloping one section of the attacking force in a frosty cloud. Desert plants iced over, unfortunate casualties of the effort. The dead Indians froze in place, rimed with ice. *This just might do it,* Superman thought.

Before he could congratulate himself, however, they began breaking through their icy coating. In some cases, limbs snapped, dropping to the desert floor to join the ones his heat vision had seared off. Still, the Indians came on like deranged snowmen, almost on top of the living.

Disappointed, Superman lowered himself to the ground. "It's not working," he said. "I don't know if there is a way to stop them."

"We've been right patient while you tried, Superman!" Bat called. "Think we'll have a go at it our own way!" He and his comrades started firing their weapons at the Indians. Bullets hit, tearing flesh and shattering bone, sending sprays of blood into the air like miniature fountains.

Against the racket the Indians made, the guns sounded like popcorn popping, and were about as effective.

Through the din, Superman heard screams. He spun around to face the mystical corral. The people penned inside wailed with fright. Some had already fallen, and the rest huddled together in the corral's center.

"The fences are closing in!" Scalphunter shouted. "When they touch, they burn! If it continues, they will surely all die!"

Jason Blood grabbed Superman's arm. "I didn't want to release Etrigan here," he said. "But we're fighting on too many fronts, and if the murder of those Apache is the final step in the ritual, it has to be stopped no matter what!"

"What can Etrigan do against that power field?" Superman asked.

"Maybe nothing," Jason said. "But maybe I can hold off the army of the dead while you and the Stranger do something. The guns those cowboys are shooting aren't doing much."

"I guess it's worth a try," Superman said. "At this point, almost anything is."

Jason nodded, then closed his eyes, turning his attention inward. "Gone, gone, the form of man," he intoned. "Rise the demon Etrigan!"

Superman watched the four men who had never seen the demon's transformation. Jonah and Bat watched with openmouthed amazement. As usual, Scalphunter and El Diablo were more circumspect.

Etrigan barely spared the four a glance. He faced the oncoming Indian army and lowered himself onto his fingertips like a racer ready to bolt. "They all smell dead, if disquieted," he rhymed. "They form a huge host, of soldiers they've most, but my thoughts they've engrossed, and I long to taste ghost!"

So saying, he tore into the dead army, loosing a long, loud snarl as he did.

"He will hold them off as best he can," the Stranger said. "I have arranged it so that their guns will not run out of bullets, but you and I had best do something about those imprisoned in that corral before it's too late."

"You have any ideas?"

"I have already tried to dismantle the power fence," the

Stranger admitted. "But I can do nothing to undo the spell that created it."

"Which leaves me?"

"So it would seem."

"I'll take a crack at it," Superman said. He flew into the air, figuring that if he moved at superspeed, he could swoop down into the pen and remove the threatened Apache two at a time.

On his first approach, though, he couldn't get within ten feet of the people. An invisible barrier crackled with blue energy, mimicking the "fence," when he tried. The energy burst knocked him back. He tried once more, faster, hoping to speed through it before it stopped him. Again, the barrier held. The charge seemed stronger this time, hurling him fifty feet through the air before he could catch himself.

He stole a glance at the demon, who continued working his way through the ranks of the dead, shredding them or blasting them with flame as he went. The men with guns continued shooting, aiming at the Indians' heads. Their efforts were mostly in vain—even headless, the supernatural beings continued their determined march.

Meanwhile, the power barriers were closing in on the Apache, leaving them nowhere to go. It wouldn't be long before each passing second killed everyone on the edges of the group.

I'm not going to let that happen, Superman thought.

As he had when demonstrating his powers, less than an hour before, he flew a short distance into the air, then turned and powered downward in an open space. Instead of simply digging a tunnel for himself, however, this time he needed a bigger one. At superspeed, his hands turned into spades, he excavated a shaft with an eight-foot diameter through packed earth and solid rock, searing the walls smooth with heat vision as he went. He came up in the center of the corral. The sorcerers who had magicked it up had not bothered to protect its underside. With gestures, Superman encouraged the Apache to move into the tunnel at a steady pace, not panicking so that they trampled one another, but a couple at a time. They hurried through the shaft, coming out in relative safety on the other side.

As long as something could be done about the army of the dead, who still closed in on all sides. Now some of the Apache, though unarmed, took a stand against the dead, swinging sticks, hurling stones, using whatever weapons were at hand to fight them back. The dead kept coming, lashing out with their own weapons, clawing and pounding with fists. They were everywhere now, swarming the massed heroes and the rescued Apache.

"Can't you do anything?" Superman asked the Stranger, who stood with his legs spread for balance, fists clenched, concentration immobilizing his face.

Superman punched the dead men, one after another, trying to knock them far enough away that they wouldn't be a threat. He had thought about scooping them up and flying them out of the area, but unless he took them off the planet, there was no guarantee that they wouldn't attack whoever they came across. At any rate, there were so many that even at superspeed he could barely make a dent in them. And with so many mortals around, he couldn't risk more extreme measures that might slow them down. Etrigan did what he could against the army of the dead, blasting his Hellfire at some and tearing apart others, but every walking dead man he dismembered continued the attack as random pieces.

"I have been trying," the Stranger said. "But it seems our enemies have built solid defenses into their spells."

"That's what I was afraid of," Superman said. "Maybe what we need is to shift our focus—work on taking out Savage, Mordru, and Faust instead."

"Working on it," the Stranger replied, distracted. Superman could see that he was putting intense mental effort into something and figured he was just getting in the way.

"I'm going to try something else," Superman said. He took a running step and launched into flight, fast and low to the ground. In the air, he inscribed a circle around the defenders, leaving a couple of rows of the dead so that he didn't accidentally run into any innocents. At high speed, he flew around and around, gradually enlarging his circle, slamming into the walking dead as he went. They fell like bowling pins before his attack, knocked into pieces or just pulverized into dust.

The Apache and the other men saw what he was doing and a shout of excitement went up, in two languages. Superman kept widening the circle, plowing through the dead men. Their parts tried to carry on the assault, but they were more easily beaten back or destroyed by the defenders. The smells of desiccated flesh and rotting marrow were ghastly; only the speed at which he flew kept Superman from choking on them.

"Superman!"

It was the Phantom Stranger, summoning him. Superman stopped what he was doing—he had cleared a ring around them of a little more than a quarter mile—and returned to the Stranger's side. The Stranger had also called Etrigan, who had reluctantly given up his blood sport.

"What is it?"

"I've determined that they are inside that house," the Stranger said, pointing toward the out-of-place adobe structure. "They direct the army from there. We'll never finally defeat it unless we engage them."

"Sounds like it's time for a showdown, then."

"Count me in," Etrigan said. "I want to win, to vanquish the enemy outside and in!"

"The house is surrounded by mystical shields," the Stranger cautioned. "We'll have to throw everything we've got at it, just to get through those. And then we'll still have to face our most dangerous foes."

"Sounds about right," Superman said. "That's the kind of thing we do, isn't it? Do you have a plan?"

"I do," the Stranger said. He beckoned them nearer. "If you like them desperate and last-ditch. Listen . . ."

CHAPTER THIRTY-TWO

Bat's revolver was getting hot to the touch. He hadn't had to reload it in some time, but considering he was using it to shoot long-dead Indians into pieces too small to continue to do any damage, that seemed like the least of his concerns.

The smell of hot gunpowder burning his nostrils was a relief compared to the slaughterhouse stench of the dead warriors. He feared he'd have that stink seared into him for life, since so many of them had scratched and punched him with fingers or fists that seemed as dry as parchment, but bony and leather-tough. Superman had become a whirlwind, flying through the lines of the Indians and demolishing them. Bat, Jonah, and Scalphunter fired nonstop, while El Diablo squeezed his trigger with one hand while working his whip with the other.

Together, they had reduced the number of attackers, from nearly infinite all the way down to simply overwhelming. Any part as big as a disembodied arm could still do some damage, he had learned—one had thrown a knife at him, nicking his hip, and another had grabbed on to his ankle while he was busy wrestling with two whole men, then climbed up above his boot where it had dug its fingers painfully into his upper calf. When he found a moment he shot it off, but the ache stayed behind.

With their numbers drastically reduced, Superman had flown back over to the Phantom Stranger. Bat wondered idly what they were discussing, but he couldn't spare too much attention because a dead Pawnee charged him with a war spear, about four or five feet long with a chiseled stone tip. He fired a slug into the Pawnee's chest, blowing out a chunk of withered flesh and old bone, but the brave kept coming. Bat fired again. This time his bullet smashed into the Indian's forehead and blew a big chunk of skull out the back. The impact staggered the dead man. The Pawnee warrior dropped to his knees, then pitched backward.

Bat noticed that Jonah had been attacked by four at once. Bat shot one of them, then ran to his companion's side. Reversing his revolver in his hand, he used it as a club to batter away the one he had shot, who still hung on tenaciously. "You havin' any fun?" Bat asked.

"Had more," Jonah replied. "That saloon brawl, night we met, was a durn sight more entertainin' than this. Not that there ain't somethin' endearin' about fightin' a bunch of Indians been dead longer'n we been alive, mind you."

"That's about how I felt about it," Bat said. "Leastways in the beginnin'. I don't mind sayin' my trigger finger's gettin' a mite weary now, though I 'preciate the fact I ain't had to pay for any of these bullets past the first five or six."

"It is a blessin'," Jonah agreed. He fired a few more rounds into the skull of the one Indian still hanging on to him, and that one fell away. "But if we had a few less of these fellers to plug, then I wouldn't mind usin' my own ammunition."

Bat tried to calculate how many of the walking dead men remained. "There's less than there was," he said. "A lot less."

"But how much of that is 'cause that Superman *hombre* knocked 'em down?" Jonah asked. "He seems to've found somethin' else to do now."

Jonah was right, Bat observed, wiping stinging sweat from his eyes. Superman and the Phantom Stranger and the big yellow beast that Jason Blood had turned into seemed to have given up the fight and turned their attention to the little adobe house that squatted up-canyon, away from the action. The trio moved with obvious determination, as if they had decided there was something more important over there. Many of the Apache who had been imprisoned had been able to take weapons away from the dead men, so the defenders weren't as outnumbered as they had been. "Reckon we can spare 'em," Bat said. "But I hope they know what they're doin'."

"I get the feelin' they generally do," Jonah said.

Scalphunter had worked his way near enough to join the conversation. He swung his rifle like a war club, knocking a dead Arapaho warrior's head flying. "I believe they are wise men," Scalphunter said. "Especially Phantom Stranger. He seems to understand many different worlds."

"Important part is he understands *this* one," Bat said, not as sure as the Kiowa about their new allies. Bad enough that El Diablo wouldn't tell them his real name—neither would Phantom Stranger or Superman, and the big yellow monkey hadn't even told them *what* he was, much less who. If he hadn't been fighting on their side, with his fiery breath and powerful claws, Bat would have taken him for something that should be killed outright for the good of humanity. "I'd hate for them to be walkin' away from this fight without a durn good reason."

"Trust in that one," Scalphunter said flatly.

"I hope you're right, Ke-Woh-No-Tay," Bat said. "You're not, we got us a heap o' trouble." He fired some more shots at the next batch of dead braves swarming them. "My Colts're like to melt 'fore we get finished here."

The Phantom Stranger had reported that the adobe house was well defended by the combined magics of the three sorcerers who had taken refuge inside. From their stronghold, they controlled the advance of the dead Indian warriors, and until Superman had freed the captive Apache, they had also manipulated the power fence that closed in on them, killing whoever it touched. The adobe looked solid, with thick walls and narrow window slots. It seemed to have been made of native earth from the immediate vicinity, but Superman assumed that was an illusion intentionally cast by those who had magicked it into existence.

Getting inside would be no Smallville Fourth of July picnic.

"All-out," the Stranger had said. "That's our only hope."

After a quick conference, Superman, Etrigan, and the Stranger agreed on an approach. Superman flew over the building, examining it with X-ray vision and confirming that the mystical barriers blocked that as well as physical access. By the time he landed on its north side, Etrigan and the Stranger had already begun to approach it, the demon taking the east side and the Stranger the south.

NOW!

The unspoken word reverberated in Superman's head, thanks to the Stranger's psychic projection. Etrigan heard it, too. Simultaneously the three began to assault the house. The Stranger hurled balls of concentrated magical power, golden and glowing, at its walls. Etrigan released a long, loud breath of fire, roaring like a flamethrower on steroids. Superman bored into his wall with heat vision. The invisible shield around the structure began to glow red under his attack, but the red spread and faded to pink, dispersed by the protective barrier before it could penetrate.

They kept up the assault for a full three minutes, even though Superman could see that it was futile. After that time, he heard the Stranger's voice in his head again. *It isn't working,* the Stranger projected. *We need another approach.*

"How about old-fashioned muscle?" Superman suggested aloud.

Unlikely, but feel free to give it a try, was the response.

Since it seemed to have more potential than continuing a failed attempt, Superman took the Stranger's words as encouragement. He flew a quick mile away from the house, then turned and barreled toward it at full speed.

Running into the defensive barrier around the corral had hurt. Slamming into the one around the house felt much like standing under a red sun and letting Doomsday use him for a punching bag. Unconscious for at least a few seconds, Superman flopped facedown into the dirt. When he came to, he could hear Etrigan roaring his anger at the building his flames couldn't penetrate.

Superman rubbed dirt from his eyes. His head throbbed. The red sun analogy had been too close to home—the pink sun overhead robbed him of at least a portion of his powers, and the sorcerers' magical defenses did the rest. He had put almost everything he had left into that flying attack, and all he had accomplished was very nearly injuring himself.

Not far away, the battle against the ancient dead raged on. Superman walked—not trusting himself to fly for the moment—to where he could see Etrigan. The demon's flames had had no greater effect than Superman's attempts had.

"Any luck there, Stranger?" he asked, in a normal conversational tone.

Not a bit, the Stranger replied mentally. *But we must not give up.*

The same conclusion had already dawned on Superman. He was stronger than Etrigan, more physically powerful than the Phantom Stranger. If Earth had ever known a more potent champion, he was unaware of it.

Now Earth itself hung in the balance. However much he ached from the battering he had just taken, he had to keep going, could not rest until he had succeeded or died.

And I've died once, he thought. *Don't want to go through that again.*

He took a few deep breaths, steeling himself for what was to come. Shook his head to clear it. Shook his hands out.

Walked up to the building. He could almost touch it— his fingers came within an inch, less, before some unseen membrane blocked them.

Not much to break through. Less than an inch.

Magic.

He tried pushing through the earth to see if he could lift it from below, shake the wizards out. Unlike the corral, though, here the protection completely surrounded the edifice, even from beneath.

Superman balled his right hand into a fist, cocked his hand back, shoulder swaying with it, then hurling it forward, swiveling at the hip, putting his weight into it. His fist drove into the membrane. The sensation was much like biting down on a 50-million-watt live wire.

He shook it off. Threw a left. Another right.

And again, and again, and again.

Blows that could level mountains. Could change the Earth's orbit, if that was the intended effect.

At first, the only effect was the feeling that he was electrocuting himself over and over. He kept it up. After a while, the membrane seemed to take on a physical manifestation. Although still invisible, he could see minute cracks in it where his blows weakened it.

Encouraged, he kept slugging.

The Phantom Stranger and Etrigan came to stand beside him, watching. They might have said something, but he didn't hear. The thunder of his punches against the defensive shield was all he heard. He kept battering it, over and over.

He became aware of a golden glow on the membrane. He risked a glance to his left and saw the Stranger, arms outstretched, the glow beginning at his fingertips and infusing the whole of the barrier. "Keep going, Superman," the Stranger said. "It's working."

Their combined efforts bore fruit. The Stranger insinuated his magic into the infinitesimal fractures caused by

Superman's punishing fists. The gold color spiderwebbed through the cracks, expanding like the breaking of thin ice under the weight of a foot.

Superman kept hitting it. The Stranger focused his magic into the webbed cracks. A smell like ozone, sharp and electric, but oddly tinged with the tang of fresh apples, wafted from the membrane.

And then it was gone. Just that sudden. There but weakening one second, vanished the next.

"You're in, you're through, you omnipotent two!' Etrigan shouted.

"So it would seem," the Stranger agreed. "Shall we step inside?"

"Allow me," Superman said. The door was around the corner, facing south. Too much trouble to walk. He pushed his mighty fingers through the dried adobe bricks, facing away from each other, and ripped open the wall as if it was paper. "Anyone home?" he called.

"I am so sorry," Vandal Savage's voice came back. "You seem to have just missed us."

Superman bulled through what remained of the wall. The Stranger and Etrigan came in his wake. Inside he found a large room, sparsely furnished, with only a few large, rough chairs and a raw oak table.

Standing behind the table were the three magicians: Savage, Mordru, and Felix Faust. Different heights and builds, but they all had dark hair and scowling faces, eyes flashing with hatred at the intruders, and they all favored dark blues and purples. Superman had a sense of three brothers, maybe triplets, although not identical, who had been caught at something unsavory. Vandal Savage held an odd, nine-pointed star in his hands.

"Missed you?" Superman asked. "It doesn't seem that way."

"Appearances, I'm sure you've heard," Faust began, "can be deceiving. In this case they certainly are."

"I command you to halt!" the Stranger shouted, understanding Faust's meaning before Superman did.

His command came too late. Superman dived at the sorcerers, plowing right through the table in the process. Even as he started to move, the three began to fade from view. He snatched for them, but caught only the strange metal star, which burned his hands so intensely that he dropped it on the floor.

Then they were gone completely, and he stood on the other side of the room, alone.

"Too late, again," the Stranger said. Frustration lent a sorrowful tone to his voice.

"And yet . . . what's this?" Etrigan asked. He picked up the star Superman hadn't been able to hold on to. Superman scanned the star with his X-ray vision and microscopic vision, but could determine nothing unusual about it except the shape. It had been made of three triangles welded together by incredible heat. "Some unknown threat? Were they remiss? Or is this some oubliette, a parting kiss?"

The Stranger held out a gloved hand. "Let me hold it, Etrigan," he said. The demon hesitated, as if unwilling to part with it. He turned his face toward the floor, looked up at the Stranger, and offered the star like a shy child parting with a favorite toy.

The Stranger took the star, wrapped both of his hands around its sides. He might have closed his eyes, but Superman couldn't be sure. A moment later, he hurled it to the ground as if it had bitten him.

"That's it!" he said. "The object through which they focused their will, their power. That's what started this entire process going, and they've used it again, recently, to initiate the final step."

"And they just left it behind?" Superman asked. "Does that mean they don't need it anymore? That we're too late?"

"They did not leave it, Superman. You *took* it from them, but you would never have been able to if you were not the product of both Earths, merged into one being. I hoped not to have to admit it, because I was playing the odds, but I suspected that the two of you together would be able to counter some of the magic our enemies have performed. As for its being too late, it is never too late to try," the Stranger replied. "I have no idea if it will help, but we should destroy that . . . that abomination, now. Then we must follow those three, wherever or whenever they've gone."

Destroy a simple welded metal star? Superman thought. *Thing's hot, but how long would I have to touch it?* He stepped forward, bent to pick the thing up. "It'd be my pleasure."

He touched it. The heat was gone. Just cold iron now. He closed his hand around it.

And his mind went slipsliding through space-time.

Vandar Adg leaned on his knuckles, staring in superstitious wonder and terror at a meteor that had struck the earth near his camp the night before. It still steamed in the crater, half-embedded. Adg approached slowly, finally reaching out a fingertip, barely grazing the hot, pock-marked surface—

—eyes opened, and the Dark Lord Mordru beheld himself in a rippling pond. Never born, never to die, always the same age and with incredible skills. All the fish in the pond floated on the surface, their glassy eyes never again to see anything. And the Dark Lord tasted death, and he liked it—

—the jungle closed in around the ancient city of Kor, trees growing together in dense, broad-leafed stands that shielded the ground from the sun's rays. The cries of birds and monkeys, the chitter of insects, the pad of human feet, all had gone still, because the Flame of Life had been touched by Felix Faust, some of it stolen and the remainder polluted, and as Faust crept back into the trees, the coals he had lifted held close to his breast in a leather pouch, he laughed because after this a darkness that would never be lifted would engulf Kor—

—and the images came faster: Camelot, knights on horseback, their once-shining armor stained and dented, rusting, corrupted by contact with the demons of Morgaine's armies—

—an age of fear sweeps across Europe, the shrill wailing of a witch tied to a stake as the fire licks her legs, a scholar copies a book by candlelight behind shuttered windows, hard men with thick arms and deep chests haul another corpse from the torture chamber to a pit grave behind a church—

—palace intrigue, as slender hands drip poison from a glass vial into a golden cup encrusted with rubies, and the slender hands place the cup onto a tray and hand it to a serving wench, who will in turn hand it to the adolescent

sister of the girl—barely fifteen herself—to whom the
first hands belong—

—Indian slaves in Latin America locked inside a thick-
walled mud structure, two hundred of them in a space
made for thirty, as punishment because one of them
barked out the name of an ancient god after a log slipped
and crushed his leg, while working on a new, luxurious
house for a priest—

—through it all, the faces of Vandal Savage, Mordru,
and Felix Faust, grinning at the suffering of others, laughing mirthlessly at pain and misfortune—

—through it all, blood and smoke scenting the air . . .
blood and smoke and the acrid tang of terror—

—through it all, a sun that once rose yellow in the east
turning ever more red, like a spot of blood seeping
through a blue shirt—

Superman dropped the star. Depression had flooded
over him. "I can't," he said, his voice cracking. "I can't
break it. I can't even hold it."

He had never felt so useless, so out of his depth, in his
life.

CHAPTER THIRTY-THREE

This was not at all what she'd had in mind.

Lois had figured that getting out of Mikey's apartment would give her more opportunities to distract him. Failing that, at some point he'd go to the bathroom, or get hungry and want to return to his own place, and she could work on an escape then.

She had not counted on climbing over the side of the frying pan, only to land right in the ever-loving proverbial fire.

Mikey moved to comply with the newcomer's demand. He unlocked his knees, lowering into a crouch, his gun held loosely in his hand. Lois hated to see him do it. Giving up his weapon would only lead to one result—the murder of both Mikey and Lois. As long as he remained armed, they had a chance, however slim.

His back was to Lois. If she could do anything to save the situation, it had to be now, while Kashegian's goons were focused on Mikey, eyes riveted to that gun. She couldn't really see them in the shadowed hall, but she knew they would be peering through the gloom at that hunk of metal, unwilling to relax until Mikey had put it down and kicked it away. Their fingers would be taut on their triggers, breath held, waiting to see what Mikey did.

The nearest of the two thugs was about two feet in front of Mikey. She could just see the blued steel of his SIG Sauer in his fist, illuminated by the bulb over Mikey's door. His bulk stood in the dark spot between that and the next bulb back. The other man was behind them both, farther back in the hall, away from the staircase door.

The space between Mikey's door and the chain-link fence was less than three feet. Not much space to try anything.

But no more time to think about it. Mikey's hand had almost reached the floor. He was off-balance, leaning forward to lay the weapon down gently.

Putting both hands on his backside, Lois shoved with all of her strength.

Mikey careened forward, losing his balance and splaying toward the nearer of the two gunmen. The man shouted a curse and fired wildly. His bullet *spanged* off the concrete ceiling and rocketed down the hall. The thunder of the shot echoed, deafening in the enclosed space.

Knowing it would come, Lois ducked the shot at the same time that she pushed Mikey. He had released the gun as he fell, his scrabbling hand sliding it back toward her. She snatched it off the floor and threw herself against the chain link, trying to will her body to melt, Plastic Man–style, through the spaces. Another shot roared, the muzzle flash lighting the area behind her. This shot went wild, too, and she saw why—the first bullet had lodged in the second thug's upper chest. He staggered in and out of the circles of light cast by the ceiling-mounted bulbs, one hand clutching his jacket, where blood showed between his fingers, and the other still holding his weapon. His finger spasmed and another shot rang out, slamming into the belongings stored behind the chain-link fence.

"Sergei!" the first goon shouted. Lois hated to do it, but she knew that his distraction would only last another second or two. As he stared in horror at what his first shot had done to his companion, she leveled Mikey's gun toward his knee and squeezed the trigger.

This shot seemed even louder, although her ears still rang from the first ones. The muzzle blast was hot on her hand and face, the bright flash blinding in the dark hallway. The gun kicked viciously; trying to hold it still sent a jolt of pain shooting through her elbow and shoulder.

But the bullet struck home, tearing flesh and shattering bone. The man cried out and pitched forward into the light, agony marking his face. Mikey moved faster than Lois expected, snatching the gun from his hand.

"Drop it, Mikey," Lois ordered.

His back was to her. He froze, so she stepped forward, pressing the weapon she held into his back. "I mean it," she said.

He nodded and held the gun out to his left. Lois took it from his fingers and tucked it into the waist of her pants.

One more weapon unaccounted for, and she had turned her back to it. She knew that was a bad idea, but with guns on both sides, she hadn't had much choice. Now she shoved Mikey away with her left hand and swiveled, gun level, finger on the trigger.

The second thug—Sergei, she remembered—had slid

to the floor. His weapon rested against his thigh, forgotten. He held both hands to his wound, as if he could keep his very life essence from leaking out. His head tilted back against the wall, mouth hanging open.

He would not last until an ambulance came, she was sure. The other guy would be fine, although he might need a pin or two in his knee to hold his leg together. Unfortunate, but given that he had meant to be part of her execution squad, not tragic.

"Let's call an ambulance, Mikey," Lois said. "And the police."

"Oh . . . okay," he stammered. "Just don't shoot me, lady."

"Do as I say, and we won't have any problems," she told him. "And while we're waiting for them to get here, you can tell me all you know about Kashegian and his operation. You'll go to jail, but if you cooperate, you can probably get protective custody, someplace where Kashegian's creeps can't get to you."

He opened his apartment door, switched on a light, crossed to the phone. "The number's 911," she reminded him. "Dial it."

He did. A few moments later, he sat down on his ugly couch. His face was blank. He was in shock, Lois believed. The EMTs could check him out when they arrived. She leaned against the wall, beside the door. Her turn to hold the gun on him for a while.

"There was a shipping container full of dead bodies," she said. "Kashegian's shipment. It came here from Kaziristan. I want to know the story behind it."

"He does . . . doesn't tell me about stuff like that,"

Mikey said. His eyes looked like shards of broken window glass, without expression.

"You'll have to do better than that."

"He brings in . . . prostitutes," Mikey said. "Wives. For American clients."

"Which is it?" Lois asked. "Prostitutes, or wives?"

"Huh?"

"What are they?"

"Both," Mikey said. He turned his blank face toward her, like a sunflower reaching for light. "Either. The only difference is whether they get paid every night or every month, he told me."

"There were men in the container, too—not just women."

"Guards. Escorts. To keep them out of trouble until they get here. They're men who want to sneak into the country, and he lets them ride for free if they'll keep an eye on the women."

"And they voluntarily allow themselves to be sealed up in these metal coffins?"

"I asked him about that once, too," Mikey said. "I'll never forget what he said. 'Compared to what they're running from, it's like paradise, that box.' That's what he told me. It's like paradise."

"There's only one similarity I can see," Lois said.

"What's that?"

"Once you're in paradise, there's no getting out. Paradise is forever."

CHAPTER THIRTY-FOUR

May 1872

"Thanks for your help, Jonah," Superman said. He shook the scarred man's hand, looked into his blue eyes. "We couldn't have done it without you."

"Don't know as that's true," Jonah answered. "Three of you look to be mighty capable *hombres*."

"We are," Superman agreed. "But without you men holding off the spirit warriors, we never would have been able to concentrate on the house." The last of the dead Indians had vanished when the sorcerers left.

"I'm glad we were able to help," Jonah said. "Shootin' them ghosts was a right good time. And I wouldn't've passed up the chance to watch you in action. That ain't somethin' I'll soon forget."

"Actually, you will." The Phantom Stranger had explained to the four why they had to be made to forget everything they had seen. The men had all agreed, without argument.

Superman went to the next man in line, the man known

as Scalphunter. "Ke-Woh-No-Tay," Superman said, clasping his hand, "I appreciate everything you've done."

"A pleasure," the Kiowa said.

"Let me say, also, that I understand—probably better than you'd believe—what it's like to be two different people," Superman added. "I know you're struggling with being Ke-Woh-No-Tay and also Brian Savage, and those two aspects of you must seem constantly at war. But I can also tell you that if you embrace both sides of yourself, instead of trying to deny or fight one or the other, you'll be happier and at peace."

"I will not ask how you have this knowledge, but I thank you for the insight."

El Diablo grinned at Superman as he offered a black-gloved hand. "Does the same apply to me?" he asked.

"I believe it does," Superman said. "I'm sure your situation is different, but the duality is similar. It's hard enough in life being one person—or so I've heard. Trying to balance two can be a challenge. But from what I've seen, you're up to it."

"He's up to most anything, you ask me," Bat said with a broad smile. "Never seen a man move like he does."

"I'm not sure I have either, Bat," Superman agreed, shaking Bat's proffered hand. "You think you can replace that vest?"

Bat turned and showed him where the tears had been. No sign of them now. "Don't need to," he said. "The Stranger fixed it right up."

"So he did. I guess he's good for something after all."

"Looks like he's waitin' on you to finish up here," Bat pointed out. The Stranger and Jason had already said their good-byes. Superman, still trying to come up with a way to destroy the nine-pointed star, had come last. He followed Bat's gaze and saw the Stranger and Jason, standing together. He realized that a few days before, a week maybe, that sight would have surprised and worried him. Now it seemed natural, as if they had always been partners.

And he with them.

He bade farewell to his new comrades, knowing that they would see him again, albeit without remembering this occasion. Those other times had already happened, for him, so this could well be the last time he would be with them. They were brave men, with high spirits and good hearts, and he was glad for whatever time he'd been able to spend with them.

He joined the Stranger and Jason. "Time to go?"

"Beyond time," the Stranger said.

"And they won't remember any of this?"

"They already don't."

Superman glanced back at the four men, but they were already fading from view.

They would forget. He never would, he swore. No matter what happened from here, he would hold their courage and selflessness within him for the rest of his life.

"Weird. You can't snap it, Blue?"

Superman shook his head in response to Dr. Occult's question. "I can't even hold it for any length of time."

The iron star rested on Jason Blood's dining table, with a sheet of newspaper—not the *Daily Planet,* Superman had been relieved to see—underneath it to protect the table's surface. Dr. Occult and Zatanna had been summoned as soon as Superman, the Phantom Stranger, and Jason returned from 1872.

"Etrigan tried to melt it with his fiery breath," Jason said. He sat casually in an easy chair, legs extended and crossed at the ankles. "But he is bound to it, having been part of its creation, and he can't destroy it or affect it in any other way."

"We even thought that I could carry it in a container of some kind and fly it into the sun," Superman added. "But the sun was turning red, so I wasn't sure I could even survive the trip. And for all we knew, that might be exactly where they wanted it, to hurry the process along somehow."

"It's been getting redder here, too," Zatanna said. She cocked her head toward the window, where dawn had broken and a rosy ball rose up out of the Atlantic.

"The merge is well under way now," the Phantom Stranger declared.

"But you think if we can break that star we can put the kibosh on the whole process?" Dr. Occult asked.

"It might help," the Stranger replied.

"Can't hurt, anyway," Jason said.

Superman crossed to the window, looked out at the red sun rising and down on the early-morning traffic jamming the intersection of O'Neil and Adams. Somewhere out there, Bruce Wayne was probably calling it a night, retreating to hang his cape and cowl in the Batcave or whatever it was he did at the break of day.

A bird fluttered to a landing on the redbrick window ledge in front of him. At first, his vision and thoughts focused far away, Superman paid it little notice. When it pecked on the glass with its slender beak, he looked at it.

Just a small brown bird with a darker head. Nothing out of the ordinary.

"Get away from the window, Kal-El!" the Stranger shouted.

Superman obeyed without questioning. The Phantom Stranger could see things he couldn't, and urgency tinged his voice. Superman had just taken two steps back when the bird burst through the glass. It landed on the floor, prompting surprised exclamations from everyone except the Stranger. Scarcely had it touched down when its color changed to a bright, glowing magenta. The bird's shape changed as well, becoming less birdlike and more ovoid, almost as if it reverted to its former egg self. But as it morphed, it also began to spin. "Look out!" the Stranger cautioned. "It is not what it seemed to be."

"That much is clear," Zatanna said. "But what might it be?"

As the shape spun ever faster, it threw off tiny shards of color, minute dots of magenta light that scattered throughout the big room. They disappeared as soon as they landed.

"No clue," Jason said. "But it better not get wet paint on my artifacts."

"That's not paint," Dr. Occult said. "But I don't know what—ow!"

The shards had grown larger, although the spinning egg didn't seem to have changed in size. One of them had struck Dr. Occult in the hand. More hit him then, and everyone else in the room. Superman experienced them as faint impacts, but it was obvious that the others were stung by them. Jason and Zatanna both held out their hands to shield their faces, and Dr. Occult snatched his fedora off a rack, using it for the same purpose.

"Damn," Dr. Occult said. "Whatever they are, they hurt."

"Anyone got any ideas on how to get rid of this?" Jason asked.

Before any suggestions were offered, the shards grew larger still. They chipped wood furniture, shattered glass in a cabinet. Superman inserted himself between the egg and Zatanna and Jason, who both had bruises already forming on their faces.

The magenta egg spun faster, making a whirring sound.

"It's going to blow," the Stranger announced. "Brace yourselves!"

"Niatnoc eht tsalb!" Zatanna chanted. Instantly, a golden aura encircled the egg. Just in time, Superman noted. The egg exploded with what looked like the force of a neutron bomb. The aura created by Zatanna's spell swelled, bulging at the sides, but kept the explosion confined. For a nanosecond, it appeared that the blast had been powerful enough—probably enhanced by the containment field—to create a miniature black hole, which sucked the flame and whatever molecular debris still remained of the egg into itself. Then the golden aura was empty. Its job done, it dissipated quickly.

All that was left behind was a faint smoky smell, as of a long-cooled fireplace from which the ashes had not been cleaned.

"Thanks, Zatanna," Jason said. "That would have been rough on my apartment."

"And the rest of Gotham City," Dr. Occult added. "Not to mention atomizing us."

"Do we know where it came from?" Zatanna asked.

"It carried the stench of Felix Faust," the Phantom

Stranger said. "I believe it's a kind of welcome-home present from our quarry."

"Maybe we should have set up headquarters inside my Fortress of Solitude," Superman said, "instead of coming back here."

"Perhaps," the Stranger replied. "But they already knew of this place. Would you have them become aware of your Fortress, too?"

"It's safely in interdimensional space," Superman said. "But I get your point. Maybe it's only safe there because villains like those three don't know it's there. If they can track our movements . . ."

"Precisely," the Stranger said. "We are as safe here as anywhere, I believe. Which is to say, not very. The sooner we deal with them, the better."

"Here's a thought," Dr. Occult said. "If these mugs attacked you here, after what you already told us about the old West and everything—does that mean they're running scared?"

Superman caught on immediately. "Meaning that even though the sun outside is turning red, and the merge seems to be taking full effect, it can still be stopped. Because if it couldn't, they would have had no reason to attack us again."

"That's a good point," Jason said, turning away from examining the damage done to some of his collection of demonic artifacts. "There's got to be a way to undo what they've done, or they'd simply wait for the merge to be completed and all of us to vanish along with our Earth."

"I agree," the Stranger said. "Which makes the destruction of this star all the more crucial. Since we believe it to be the item through which their efforts were focused, if we can destroy it, it's possible that we can undo any magic it facilitated."

"But how?" Jason said. "We're still stuck on that one."

Dr. Occult's appearance shifted, as quickly as a smile might turn into a frown, and suddenly Rose stood there instead of Richard. She held the Symbol of the Seven in her hand, a small stone disc with white V shapes cut into red—or a red cross on a field of white, Superman realized. The talisman represented the power of the mystical Seven who had raised Richard Occult and Rose Psychic from infancy and trained them in the magical arts. "I might have an idea about that," Rose said. She passed the disc over the shattered window, and the glass became whole again. As she described her plan, she did the same with Jason's other damaged items.

Watching her heal them, listening to the measured tones of her voice, Superman began to think that maybe her idea had a chance.

It was as good as any others that had been offered. And they had to try something.

He glanced through the restored window at the red sun outside. They had to do something, and it had to be now.

CHAPTER THIRTY-FIVE

The Phantom Stranger thought of Order the way some people thought of God, as a powerful force for good throughout the universe, but one that required worldly allies to implement its goals.

He worked tirelessly on behalf of Order, but he needed help sometimes, too. He was glad that he had recruited these compatriots to battle for the cause. Each had his or her strengths, complementing his own. Each took the struggle seriously, and once committed, seemed willing to follow through on that commitment wherever it would lead. None of them shied away from danger or discomfort.

The same went for Jonah Hex, Bat Lash, Ke-Woh-No-Tay, and El Diablo as well. The Stranger knew a moment's sorrow that those four would never know the full measure of what they had accomplished. He had left them with what small gift he could: the understanding that they had been part of something bigger than themselves. None of them would recall the details, but they would all know it had been important, and that they had succeeded with their part.

Now it became important to succeed with the bigger part. The Stranger regarded his comrades as, once again, they joined hands around Jason Blood's table. In the center of the table they had left the nine-pointed star, reminding everyone of what was at stake.

"I'll take the lead this time," he said when everyone was settled. "As ever, empty your minds and take in my words, visualize them. Let the decency in your hearts color your thoughts and your will. Let your purity of motive open your hearts and the essential goodness of the world flow through you."

He paused. All he heard was measured breathing from the others at the table. Superman and Jason had closed their eyes. Rose's fluttered. Only Zatanna's remained opened but unfocused.

"We call upon Order for assistance," he said, continuing in the same even, steady tones. "To aid Order, we need Order's aid. What we ask is too big a task for us to accomplish ourselves, even as powerful as we are. We call upon Order and the forces of righteousness that inhabit every being on this Earth. We seek to utilize their power in concert with our own."

He tried to picture the result he was after, but he wasn't even sure what form it would take. He knew that this failure of imagination jeopardized the whole effort. He could not let it, though. He forced thoughts of failure from his mind, worked at visualizing the effects of the spell instead of the specifics of the spell itself.

He pictured red light, slowly darkening to black.

There was nothing in the light. No shapes, no shadows. Simply light and absence. The red turning deeper red, through scarlet and crimson and vermilion, graying. Black. Finally, ultimately, black.

As he did, he felt something previously unknown in his long aeons of experience, as if his own being had opened somehow and limitless reserves of strength flowed through him. The hands of Rose Psychic and Superman, which he held, fairly hummed with energy.

He remained quiet, visualizing the darkness over and over. As he did, he noticed that the quality of light streaming in through the apartment's windows was changing. Though it was barely eight in the morning, dusk appeared to be coming on.

It was working!

Within minutes, the sky had turned black as night. Starless. Around the city, lights flickered on. The Stranger heard shouts of dismay, of terror. He had anticipated that, but knew it was a small price to pay. A few minutes of darkness, to prevent an eternity of it.

He released hands, and the others did the same.

"Did the trick," Superman said.

"It's pitch-black out there," Rose observed.

"We've shielded the Earth from the rays of the red sun," the Stranger said. "We need to work quickly now—the world needs sunshine, and we cannot deny it for long without ill effect."

"I feel stronger already," Superman announced.

"As we hoped," the Stranger said. By blocking the red sun, they negated its effects on the Man of Steel. Not as good as exposing him to the rays of a yellow sun, but they didn't have one of those handy.

And never would again, if they couldn't reverse the sorcerers' magic.

"Do you feel strong enough to take another crack at the star?" Jason asked.

"That's kind of why I'm here, right?" Superman picked up the star. Held it in his hands. The last time he had tried that, the Stranger remembered, he had almost slipped into some kind of coma. This time, his expression remained calm, almost serene.

The muscles in Superman's shoulders and neck bunched up, then his arms. Although his face gave only the slightest indication of any effort, his knuckles went white against the iron he held.

Throughout the room, breaths were held. Every gaze rested on Superman now. The rest had done what they could. Earth's future, quite literally, was in his strong hands.

Hands born on Krypton . . .

It was sometimes reported that Earth was Superman's adopted planet. Those who phrased it that way had it backward, though. He had come into consciousness on Earth, unaware of his Kryptonian heritage. It wasn't until late in his adolescence that his adoptive parents, the Kents, had decided to reveal to him what they had been able to piece together of his origin on another planet. Earth had adopted him, and he had eventually adopted Earth. He thought of himself more as an Earthling with a Kryptonian background, not a Kryptonian who had decided to settle on Earth.

As he put pressure on the iron star, he was terribly aware that all of Earth's tomorrows might hang in the balance. Somehow it seemed right to him that Earth's champion, in what might be its darkest hour, its final moments—would be someone not born here.

He might have been born elsewhere, but he would not give up. He would not abandon the Earth he loved or its people. He forced every thought from his mind except the images of Lois, his ma and pa, Jimmy, Perry, Lana. They paraded through his consciousness, a procession of those who had made life on this planet not only pleasant but absolutely fulfilling.

He squeezed the iron harder. It started to give under the pressure, its rigid lines compressing at the edges, wrinkles forming in the once-solid metal. The muscles in his arms bulged and rippled as he forced the two sides he gripped toward each other, bending the iron out of its previous shape. Once it started to give, it bent easily, the enchantment seemingly broken.

With an exhalation, a grunt, he pressed the two sides together, then yanked in the other direction. The star fell apart in his hands, the welds broken. Instead of a whole, he held six separate pieces of cold, dead iron. Those in the room with him reacted with shouts of joy and triumph.

With his hand flat, he held the pieces still and focused his heat vision on them, careful to melt the iron without scorching his own flesh. Years of using his heat vision to shave had taught him precision aim, and his own limits. He melted the pieces, which pooled on his palm, then he superheated and melted the pools into vapor. When he was done, there was nothing left of the star whatsoever.

He clapped his hands together, looked at the Phantom Stranger. "Time to bring back the sun?"

"I believe we should, yes." The Stranger took his seat

at the table, holding out his hands. The others followed suit, and the Stranger once again began to intone a spell. Five minutes later, the darkness outside grayed, lightening. The day's second dawn.

Only this time, the sun that shone down did so from a higher position in the sky.

And it was yellow.

"Yellow?" Vandal Savage slammed his meaty fist on the table, causing the plates and glasses scattered over its surface to jump. Wine sloshed from his glass onto the polished birchwood. "How can this be? I planned for every eventuality!"

"Obviously you didn't," Mordru countered. He wore an angry scowl and twisted the stem of his own wineglass between his narrow fingers, as if trying to unscrew it from its base. "Or we would be celebrating our victory now. Instead, the world we put so much effort and time into has just winked out of existence, and the original Earth—the one you promised us we would own—has a yellow sun once again."

Felix Faust stood in the doorway, hands clasped behind his back. He had been monitoring the several crystals on which the progress of the convergence had been projected, and had come into the dining room, moments before, to report what he had seen. Vandal thought Faust cringed a little at the rage exhibited by himself and Mordru, as if afraid that at any moment they might start unleashing bolts of destructive energy at one another.

If he persists in blaming me, we just might.

"There must be some way to reverse what they've done," Faust offered. "To set things right again."

"There is only one way," Vandal said. His fists remained clenched, but he rested them on top of the table instead of banging them again, trying to project calm. "We started the process at Camelot, and it has unfolded until now. We could repeat it."

"And wait another two thousand years," Mordru pointed out.

"At least we could reasonably expect Superman to be dead by then," Faust added.

"But not the Phantom Stranger," Vandal said. "Or Etrigan. And who knows who might be born, in the interim, to block us? For that matter, now that he knows we've done it once, the Phantom Stranger might already be taking steps to ensure that it won't work again."

"We are defeated," Mordru said. He looked glum. His lower lip quivered, and for the first time, Vandal thought, he showed some of his incredible age. "We have won and lost many battles over the aeons, but always I thought we would win the war."

"If you're going to weep," Vandal warned him, "don't do it in my presence."

Mordru shot him a ferocious glare. "Weeping is not my way," he said. "Revenge is."

Vandal tensed. He started turning over defensive spells in his mind, ready to block whatever the Dark Lord might attempt. "Against me?"

Faust took another step backward, through the doorway.

As if mere walls would shield him, if it came to battle here.

"Against those who thwarted us, of course," Mordru said. "They are the ones who must pay most dearly. When that is done, if anything remains to be settled between us, we can take care of it."

"And what form would you have this revenge take?"

For once, Mordru smiled. "Violent, painful death seems the only appropriate measure to me."

Vandal Savage returned his grin. From the doorway, even Faust shared it. "I knew there was a reason we three worked so well together for so long."

CHAPTER THIRTY-SIX

Superman flew straight up into the sky, high over Gotham's brooding skyscrapers, exulting in the bath of yellow rays that washed over him. His strength was back in full. And the sense of well-being was not just physical, but mental as well. Emotional. He had finally shed the trace memories of that other Clark, the one who had lost his Lois. He didn't know if it was simply because his physical condition had improved, boosting his spirits, or if somehow the elimination of the false Earth from the time stream meant that the other Clark had never existed, and could therefore have no hold on him. He didn't especially care what the reason was. He had been unsettled, uncomfortable in his own skin, lacking in confidence.

No more. He was *Superman*. There were things he couldn't do, but a very, very long list of things he could.

Near the edge of Earth's atmosphere, he turned back. There were good-byes to be said to Zatanna and Dr. Occult, the Phantom Stranger and Jason Blood. Before he left, Jason and Etrigan's minds had to be wiped of the memory that he was Clark Kent, just in case. He had left them all behind for a quick hop into the sky, but he needed to get back before they assumed he was just an ill-mannered oaf and took off.

He was just reaching the tops of the skyscrapers when the lightning hit him.

The bolt was blue, not white, and it struck with cold energy instead of the heat he would have expected. It crashed into him with dizzying intensity, knocking him several blocks off course. He spun through the sky until he could catch and orient himself.

When he had, he looked for whoever had attacked him.

It didn't take long.

They floated, or seemed to, on top of a cloud. It was no natural cloud, but as pink as cotton candy, as if a rosy sunset cast light on it from below. Vandal Savage, Felix Faust, and Mordru, looking much as they had back in 1872 Arizona. Except this time they weren't running away. Instead, Faust worked a mass of blue glittering light in his hands, stretching what looked like another lightning bolt from a ball of it. White flame danced around Mordru's upraised fingertips. And Savage held up a scepter topped by a crystal sphere, inside which unknown energies flickered.

"I thought I'd seen the last of you three for a while," Superman said, hovering a short distance away from them.

"You mean you wish you had," Savage replied.

"Well, of course I wish I had. I wish you'd never shown your faces in the first place."

"We could say the same of you, meddler," Mordru retorted.

"I bet. Sorry about your little scheme, by the way, but it didn't fit with my own long-term goals."

Superman could see Savage steaming. "Little scheme?" As his face reddened toward eggplant, the energy inside the crystal sphere seemed to darken in response.

"That's right. And by the way? You're not welcome here. I'd take off if I were you."

"Clearly, you are *not* us," Mordru said. "Instead, you seem to be a person who doesn't know when he is outclassed and outnumbered."

"Enough idle talk!" Savage screamed. He flung his arm forward, pointing the scepter at Superman. A bolt of green fire lanced from the ball. Superman dodged it, but the fire flew on, exploding against the upper floors of a building.

"Careful!" Superman shouted, streaking toward the building. "The people in there have nothing to do with our dispute."

"And you think I care?" Savage returned.

"Erotser gnidliub!" Zatanna's voice cried. In response to her command, the building magically restored itself to the state it had been before Savage's blast.

Superman stole a glance around and saw that the Phantom Stranger, Etrigan, Zatanna, and Dr. Occult had taken to the nearby rooftops. "I tried to warn you," he said to the trio of sorcerers. "Now you've made everybody angry."

"Do you honestly believe we weren't *trying* to draw you all out?" Mordru asked.

"If this is to be battle, let it begin!" the Stranger said.

"Agreed!" Savage answered. He let loose another bolt of green flame from his staff. Dr. Occult blocked this one with the Mystic Symbol of the Seven. As if that had set off a chain reaction, the skies over Gotham City were suddenly ablaze with mystical combat.

The artificial cloud rocked and swayed with the force of the trio hurling one magical blast after another. Superman dodged those he could; others struck him with impacts ranging from featherlight to debilitating.

While the blasts pummeled him, the Stranger, Zatanna, and Dr. Occult did their best to limit damage to the nearby structures. Etrigan climbed as high as he could, King-Konging his way up the rooftops, trying to get near enough to blow the cloud-craft from the sky with his Hellbreath.

Catching a momentary breather between attacks, Superman released a superbreath at the cloud, trying to blow it into the upper atmosphere, where the wizards' attacks wouldn't threaten innocent life. A mystical barrier deflected the exhalation back at him, and he was faced with the unpleasant task of trying to maintain a steady position against the force of his own power. He guessed that Etrigan's flames weren't reaching the cloudship for the same reason.

Change of tack, then. He ducked and dodged and weaved his way through an array of mystical bolts and sped straight toward the cloud, his right fist out and ready for impact. When he reached the edges of the cloudstuff he felt a chill, as if it really were made of ice crystals. But this ice contained a deeper cold—that of the grave. The chill of pure evil, lacking all human warmth.

Superman shivered but kept going. Up, through the pinkish cloud matter. The farther he drove through it, the worse the cold got. Intense pain, like a million tiny daggers rending his flesh, tore through him. Different defenses, then, than they had used at the adobe. Potent ones just the same.

The daggers turned into barbed anchors. Weight dragged at him, as if he had picked up thousands of ocean liners. Metamorphosing into humanoid shapes, the thousands he pulled through the sky pummeled him with blows. The punishment sapped his strength, so newly returned to him. He punched back. His fists swished through empty air in most cases, only occasionally getting the satisfaction of firm contact. Since that seemed less than effective, he poured on more speed, and eventually the anchors tore painfully from his skin.

He flew on. The cloud had not seemed that big from the outside, but he was lost in it. He should have been in a straight line for whatever platform held the sorcerers. Should have smashed into it by now. All he could see in any direction was cloud stuff, pink, damp, and fluffy. Disorienting. Any direction could have been up, any down. He might have accidentally blundered through a dimensional trapdoor hidden inside the cloud, and entered a limitless universe containing nothing else. Even the sounds of the combat, the screams of Gotham's citizens, the steady, deep rumble of Batman's voice joining the fray, which he had heard just before entering the cloud, were muffled out of existence.

He beamed his heat vision, trying to evaporate the cloud matter. Tried to see through it with X-ray vision. Neither worked.

Keep flying, he told himself. *You'll get through it or you'll find them, one or the other.*

But he didn't, and worry began to set in despite his attempts to keep it at bay. Who knew which direction he flew? Or what he might run into, lost in this enchanted fog? He remembered the sensation of being lost in Hell, the terror at the idea that he might be trapped there for eternity, through no fault of his own.

As concern deepened into despair, a white light cut through the cloud. Superman flew toward it, realizing as it grew more distinct that it was the Phantom Stranger— only huge, seemingly floating in space. He held up a gigantic gloved hand, digits curled toward the palm except for the index finger, which pointed up and slightly to Superman's left. Superman remembered the Phantom Stranger guiding Clark through Hell's Stygian darkness, and he took heart at this apparition. "Keep going, Kal-El," the Stranger's voice boomed, although the image's mouth had not moved. "You're almost there."

It's a trap, Superman started to tell himself. But he followed the Stranger's direction anyway, unable to convince himself.

And a moment later, the cloudstuff thinned. He could see blue sky through it, and directly ahead, something solid that blocked his view. Pouring on the speed, he flew into the solid thing, through it. A platform, made of some substance he couldn't name, but it shattered like plastic before his power.

Vandal Savage, Mordru, and Felix Faust cried out, spinning and tumbling through the air. Savage tried to fire a blast from his staff, but it went wild. Superman caught the sorcerer by the necklace of medallions around his neck. "Release me!" Savage commanded.

"Sure about that?" They were nearly a mile above the city and climbing.

"Think you that I have need of your paltry power to save myself?"

"I don't know, Savage. It's a long drop."

Faust and Mordru had already stabilized a section of the platform. They were hardly out of trouble yet, however, as Etrigan had leapt onto it. His huge teeth were clamped onto Faust's left arm, worrying at it like a dog with a rawhide chew toy. Faust tried to bat him off with his fists, but Etrigan was having none of it. His Hellbreath steamed, and Superman could smell Faust's sleeve smoldering. Mordru had problems of his own to contend with, as Dr. Occult had used his talisman to loop tendrils around Mordru's arms and legs, holding him fast.

Superman lowered Vandal Savage to the remains of the platform, arriving there at the same time as the Phantom Stranger. The cloudstuff had dissipated, and now the broken surface was just a hunk of material floating in the air. Below, police had cordoned off the street, but Zatanna and Dr. Occult had managed to keep the buildings whole, and nothing dangerous had fallen. Superman spotted Batman crouched in an empty window, watching in case he needed to step in.

"What are we going to do with you?" Superman asked, when the three sorcerers were reunited.

"There's nothing that you can do to us," Savage replied, defiant even in certain defeat. "Except fear us."

"Hardly likely," Superman said.

Etrigan released Faust's arm, and the wizard rubbed it gingerly, eyeing the demon as if he might attack again at any second.

"I have an idea about that," the Stranger said.

"I'm listening."

"The time stream they created still exists. In a very limited way. The version of Earth they created there is gone, and I doubt they would be very comfortable or happy there."

"Sounds good to me," Superman said.

"You . . . you don't dare—"

Superman tapped Savage lightly on the chin—a finger flick, really. He had long since learned to control the strength with which he punched people, knowing that he could easily knock a human being's head off with a miscalculation. The blow was enough to snap Savage's head backward, silencing him. He glared at Superman from beneath his bushy brow. "Try that again, human, and—"

Superman aimed another finger at the mage's chin, and Savage clamped his mouth shut.

The Phantom Stranger raised both his hands and gestured at the three sorcerers. Once again, they shimmered and started to fade from view. "That's you doing that, right, Stranger?" Dr. Occult asked.

"Yes," the Stranger confirmed. "I bound them to me so that they could not escape of their own volition, then sent them, as one, into the time stream they are themselves responsible for creating. Since they are connected to its origins, it was a simple enough matter."

By the time he finished speaking, the three had vanished altogether.

"What'll happen to them, being sent into a time stream that's disappearing?" Superman asked.

The Stranger shared one of his rare smiles. "I couldn't say. And there is, of course, no guarantee that they won't be able to free themselves, as powerful as they are. But for however long they stay, I imagine it will be a most unpleasant experience."

"It couldn't happen," Superman said, returning the Phantom Stranger's grin, "to three more deserving people."

EPILOGUE

Clark opened the *Planet* to reveal Lois's story on human smuggling, from the banner headline to the text that ran both above and below the fold. Ivan Kashegian and Phoenix Enterprises had been charged by the district attorney, and Lois implicated both by name in her piece.

"This is terrific, Lois," he said, scanning it at superspeed. "Great work. Nicely written, too."

Lois carried a mug of steaming coffee into the dining room. Early-morning light flooded in through the large windows. She looked beautiful in it, he noticed. But then, she had looked beautiful in the near-total darkness of their bedroom the night before, too. All it took was a glance into her bottomless brown eyes to remind him how in love he was. Or the line of her firm jaw, or the way her dark hair draped forward when she bent over the keyboard, or any of a thousand other things about her, physical and not.

Like the concern and empathy with which she wrote

about the women and men who had lost their lives inside a shipping container.

"Thanks, Clark," she said. She sipped from the mug. "I'm just glad," she added, setting the mug down on the dining table, "that I was able to get the story. I mean, I'm all for respecting national borders, but to me they're secondary to respecting the rights and dignity of human beings." She flashed a smile. Clark ignored the newspaper now, just staring at her, entranced. "And nonhuman beings, too."

"We're definitely a minority," Clark said. "I wouldn't say persecuted or oppressed, but a minority just the same."

"It's a big world," Lois said. "Plenty of room for the occasional Kryptonian, as well as everyone else. The trouble isn't space, it's other people—governments that don't let their people live in freedom, that line their own pockets while their citizens starve. If everyone would co-operate, or work in the best interests of their populations instead of just themselves, there'd be plenty of room and resources for everybody. Until that happens, though, people are going to look elsewhere for a better life. That's when people like Kashegian can take advantage of them."

"It's hard enough to start over," Clark said. "When I carried the memories of that other world's Clark around in me—" He broke off, a trace of that Clark's sorrow over the loss of his wife emerging in his consciousness, unbidden and unwanted. He swallowed back a sudden lump in his throat, blinked away tears that threatened to fall. "Let's just say I felt out of place in this world," he continued when he was able. "Once I found out I was Superman, it was like I was an alien here."

"And you haven't felt that way in a long time," Lois observed.

"Not since I first learned about my powers and my past," Clark said. "As far as I'm concerned, I belong on Earth, nowhere else. So the whole stranger in a strange land sensation was odd. Unpleasant, even."

"I'm glad it's over, then."

"So am I. I appreciate Earth's willingness to accept me, and others who come here to find new lives. Glad there's no border patrol at the outer edge of the atmosphere turning away infants. And glad, too, that my Kryptonian parents didn't have to pay someone to smuggle me here."

"I'm happy about that, too," Lois said. She pushed the coffee mug aside and rose out of her chair, leaning on the table, palms against the open *Daily Planet*. She pressed her lips against Clark's and held them there for a long time. Her eyes were open, alert, locked on his.

When she broke the kiss, she sat down again. "I think most people are happy you're here, Clark. Whether they think about it or not. You contribute a lot, and Earth is a better place for your presence."

He tapped the newspaper spread in front of him. "And for yours."

She laughed, a sound like the bells of heaven chiming. "I don't know about that."

"No superstrength," Clark said. "No silly costume. Using nothing but words, you can make people think and feel, spur them to action. That, Lois, is power. Power used for good.

"And that," he added after a pause, "is the best kind there is."

ABOUT THE AUTHOR

Jeff Mariotte has written more than thirty novels, including the original horror epic *The Slab*, and the Stoker Award nominated teen horror series *Witch Season*, as well as books set in the universes of *Buffy the Vampire Slayer*, *Angel*, *Las Vegas*, *Conan*, *30 Days of Night*, *Charmed*, *Star Trek* and *Andromeda*, and a novelization of the movie *Boogeyman*. He is also the author of more comic books than he has time to count, including the original Western series *Desperadoes*, some of which have been nominated for Stoker and International Horror Guild awards. With his wife, Maryelizabeth Hart, and partner Terry Gilman, he co-owns Mysterious Galaxy, a bookstore specializing in science fiction, fantasy, mystery, and horror. He lives on the Flying M Ranch in the American Southwest with his family and pets in a home filled with books, music, toys, and other examples of American pop culture. More information than you would ever want to know about him is at www.jeffmariotte.com.

LAST SONS

ISBN: 0-446-61656-7

By Alan Grant

SUPERMAN. MARTIAN MANHUNTER. LOBO.

Interplanetary bounty hunter Lobo is a notorious maverick. Happily wreaking havoc as he brings in his prey, he cares little who his clients or targets are—even when his latest quarry is J'onn J'onnzz, Martian Manhunter of the Justice League of America. Suddenly Lobo finds himself confronting . . . Superman. Cogs in the machinations of a powerful artificial life-form, these three aliens, the sole survivors of the planets Krypton, Mars, and Czarnia, have only one thing in common—they are the last of their kind . . .

LAST SONS

Available wherever books are sold.

INHERITANCE

ISBN: 0-446-61657-5

By Devin Grayson

**BATMAN. AQUAMAN. GREEN ARROW.
NIGHTWING. ARSENAL. TEMPEST.**

A gunshot shatters the Gotham night as Slade Wilson, the superhuman killer-for-hire Deathstroke, fails to assassinate the young son of a visiting Quarac dignitary. Now three legendary crime fighters, Batman, Green Arrow, and Aquaman—and the three young heroes who had once been their loyal sidekicks—join forces to stop Slade and those who hired him. But as the hunt stretches across continents, opening lost memories and old wounds, it turns into a desperate race against time: for Deathstroke is but one player in a plot to destroy all of Gotham . . .

HELLTOWN

ISBN: 0-446-61658-3

By Dennis O'Neil

BATMAN. LADY SHIVA. RICHARD DRAGON. THE QUESTION.

There are a lot of unanswered questions about Vic Sage, the Question: how he spent—or misspent—his youth; and how he came to be a journalist in the country's worst city. This story will solve these mysteries, retell and embellish some tales already told, and tell a new tale of how Vic, with a bit of help, brought some measure of serenity to a truly dreadful place. From his first meeting with Lady Shiva, where he was almost killed. To training with Richard Dragon, the best martial artist in the world (except perhaps for Lady Shiva and Batgirl). And how Batman, while threatening his life, also saved him, this story will finally provide answers about the Question. Who he is and what he did.

Available wherever books are sold.